2394

Mirrors of the Past

p.roscoe

2394
MIRRORS OF THE PAST

iUniverse books may be ordered through booksellers or by contacting:

iUniverse
1663 Liberty Drive
Bloomington, IN 47403
www.iuniverse.com
1-800-Authors (1-800-288-4677)

Because of the dynamic nature of the Internet, any web addresses or links contained in this book may have changed since publication and may no longer be valid. The views expressed in this work are solely those of the author and do not necessarily reflect the views of the publisher, and the publisher hereby disclaims any responsibility for them.

Any people depicted in stock imagery provided by Thinkstock are models, and such images are being used for illustrative purposes only. Certain stock imagery © Thinkstock.

ISBN: 978-1-5320-0367-7 (sc)
ISBN: 978-1-5320-0368-4 (hc)
ISBN: 978-1-5320-0366-0 (e)

Library of Congress Control Number: 2016913187

Print information available on the last page.

iUniverse rev. date: 11/08/2016

Prologue

Often, a constant breeze blows in the flat deserts of their world, creating small sandstorms that virtually mask the presence of all who travel there.

Over this lifetime, Resha and Swallow have become accustomed to walking and sitting on the naked earth. The two women are covered from head to toe with a fine coat of rosy dust after traveling on foot to their destination. They had picked a spot outside their village under a solitary tree where the desert collided with the foothills to meet for their talks. Before sitting in the shade of this solitary giant they pause to beat some of the dust off themselves. The younger one, Swallow, and the older one, Resha, then sit across from each other on their desert's sandy soil.

On the trek to their meeting spot, the dust of their world's deserts has filled the subtle lines of the ageless older woman's face, leaving observers with an image of an eerie klain (lime green) mask covered with faint rosy lines etched by fate and time. Gazing at Resha, Swallow shifts her focus to soften her vision, and for a brief moment, Resha's face blurs into a verdant green landscape traversed by bloody rivers and creeks. In passing, Swallow mentions to Resha how striking she looks with that rose-colored dust accentuating the indistinct lines that now trace her features. The blush that rises to Resha's skin is barely noticeable as she ardently tries to ignore Swallow's compliment and readies herself for her tale.

Although Swallow appears to be in her midtwenties, almost three quarters of a century has passed since she has left that decade behind. She wears her flaxen hair pulled back in one long french braid that runs down the center of her back and ends at her waist; its color is a striking contrast against her smooth pale lime-green skin. Resha's hair is a similar length, but she wears her dark amethyst-colored locks in two narrow face-framing braids pulled back and stylishly woven together with the rest of her hair into a single long plait. It's her usual custom to wear her mane draped over her right shoulder.

Swallow is pretty and willowy; however, her frame is well muscled and taut, as the bodies of most of the young are. There are still traces of timeless beauty in the mature woman's face. Like most of the older ones, she is lean, slight of frame and has no extra padding.

It is the year of our Goddess 159 a.d. It would have been the year of our Lord 2394 A.D. had the calendar not changed two years after the disaster happened.

Over the younger woman's shoulders, their world's three cerulean suns form a triangle that brightly shines in the midday sky. During the day, the suns' combined heat leaves little available moisture in the air, and the faint, ghostly white silhouette of their nightly crimson moon is imprisoned in the center of this trine. In the daytime, the moon is paled by her blazing azure guards.

Since the disaster, their world's moon is held hostage by man-made suns that encircle her and never allow her to fully set. However, each night after the suns go down, the moon rises alone from the west once more and transforms the nearly pitch black night's sky into a crimson and dark cobalt blue spectacle with her neighboring numerous suitors—a field of brightly shining emerald-green stars. Every night, these stars attend to their spectacular red mistress, and it appears each is trying to gain her favor against the deep cobalt-blue night sky. She is at home in darkness, her brilliant blood red splendor surpassing the suns in all their combined daily glory.

In the century following the disaster the remains of their world slowly crumbled into decay. So the terrain of Resha and Swallow's present world is now mostly flat. Since the beginning of civilization, their world's natural ancient features have been slowly eroded away and replaced by humans' so called improvements. This progress reached its pinnacle around the year 2200, but the humans couldn't seem to control themselves. Their world's suppressed fear and the exploding numbers of its population drove the peoples' expansion well beyond the limits of what the surrounding living planet could tolerate. By the time Resha was born, things had been critically out of balance in the natural world for a long time. She opened her eyes to sprawling cities and walked her first steps in things called shoes, on rigid, unforgiving deteriorating pavement.

Over this last century, her naked feet have now grown accustomed to the powdery soils of her new world. This planet she has now grown old on; however, the world Resha was born into still haunts her distant dreams and faint childhood memories.

Visible to the north is one of the few randomly placed, newly developed semi natural breaks in their world's flat terrain. This vista is striking and consists of two new features. One is a grouping of dark coffee-colored hills that the wicked winds created after the disaster. These merciless storms produced by the changes in the atmosphere, blew and eroded away all the progress civilization had painstakingly made in the previous centuries. Now undulating and surging up from their flat desert's surface, these stands of hills are few and far between. In the distance past, as the population of their world multiplied, men had done away with most of the natural features to make room for the new dwellings needed to shelter the burgeoning populace. In the years following the disaster, as their world fought back to regain its rightful existence, many of the cities were destroyed. Since then, time, wind, and weather have dismantled all but a few of the cities that survived the initial catastrophe, blowing them away and leaving few recognizable remnants aside from these new hills. Those in control since that time have valiantly tried to reconstruct some of their world's original features by adding pulverized stone to rusty steel and covering the remaining bones of their world's largest groups of abandoned, decayed structures. The hills that resulted from this artificial reconstruction now intermittently rise and fall amid their world's recently evolved flat rosy deserts.

Next to this particular set of hills, stands the newest addition to their landscape: a large collection of translucent, steep, crystal rock towers that miraculously started to grow at the beginning of this past century. Each of the mature crystal towers is a different brilliant, striking color. This particular grouping of crystals forms a transition between one of the deserts and the adjacent coffee-colored hills and is visible to the north of the tree Resha has chosen for her story site. Besides the areas occupied by the newly grown towers and hills the majority of the remainder of their planet is now covered only by vast ruddy deserts.

Almost a century ago, clusters of these multicolored crystal towers suddenly began rising like forests of colossal trees in pockets on the edges of some of the rosy deserts. These kaleidoscopic forests of crystals now extend up into the heavens and invade their world's newest creations: the recently formed nocturnal clouds of their skies. In their brutal new world, as the three suns begin to set, these clouds form and gather around the crystal towers like guardians of the night. There is no rain in their world, but in the cooling darkness, the moisture from these clouds condenses on the higher planes of the crystal obelisks' faces and, drop by drop, makes its way to the ground just before dawn, starts to heat the morning air.

These colored crystal spires also somewhat filter the harsh daylight and cut the intense, scorching rays of the trio of suns. Shortly after these mammoth towers stopped growing, smaller flowerlike clusters of clear crystals sprouted up randomly on a number of the multicolored full grown structures. Now, when the suns rise, their rays hit these clear little gem flowers and randomly cast prisms out in all directions. It's not unusual to see pockets of rainbows in the sky and on the ground surrounding the towers, where the clear crystal flowers have now set seed and blossomed.

The massive, vibrant crystal towers are somewhat opaque at their bases, so they cast shadows, which result in dappled shaded areas surrounding each tower. In these semi shaded areas, most of the struggling plants of their hostile, evolving world have begun to grow. These plants started to appear about a hundred years ago and began sprouting up slowly at first about ten years after the skies were newly seeded with clouds. In this last decade, a moss like vegetation has appeared and is beginning to develop in patches on the branches of some stands of shrubbery. In the more deeply shaded areas, a few patches of moss have even spread to the ground beneath.

Since the newly formed clouds have been providing more and more water over the past few years, the plants have been widening out from the base of each crystal tower and a small number of them have recently started to invade the harsh sunlit regions. The plants evolving in full sunlight are significantly different from those found in the shaded areas. They are developing to survive in fierce light and heat and have transformed to grow under the unforgiving rays of their world's three brutal suns. Thus, their stature is scrubbier and they consist of a dense, thorny, woody thicket. To aide in conservation of water these plants also possess small, brittle, waxy green leaves.

Because of all the radical changes their world has witnessed since the disaster occurred, only a few of the ancient large, solitary trees are still alive from the Before Time. Resha and Swallow have decided to meet in a shady spot under one of these trees for the telling of Resha's tale. Most of the remaining primordial giant trees are singularly scattered and alone throughout their world. Even before the disaster, these towering elders were endangered. Toward the end of the Before Time, there wasn't enough space to support these colossal giants in the humans' rapidly overpopulating world, so one by one, they were killed and transformed into more useful items. Areas covered by vast forests of trees rising into the skies in the ancient past gave way over centuries to high-rises used to house the ever-mounting numbers of the peoples' mushrooming population. Most of the few trees that had survived were located in the remote areas where the elite had built their compounds and where, in the century before the end of the Before Time, the trees had room to grow.

In the time leading up to the disaster, these giants served a dual purpose in the elite's fortresses. Since they towered above many of the surrounding natural features, they became a part of the surveillance systems, and they also provided greatly needed shade for the outdoor recreation areas of these strongholds. The elite sequestered themselves away and dwelled in these sanctuaries for many scores of years leading up to the disaster.

After the end of the Before Time, many of the trees protected by the elite's now-decaying compounds perished in the harsh, unyielding climate changes of the last century and a half. In the year or two after the final demise of the planet's old climate, most of these lumbering giants had died when the sun waned and the cold invaded. The few ancient, towering trees that managed to survive the changes since the disaster are now the sole survivors of their kind.

Although these ancient relics still provide and set new seed each season, few seedlings have managed to endure and grow in the unforgiving climate changes of this last century—at least not until now. Having enough water to grow has been the seedlings main challenge since the disaster. Little does their world know that part of these two women's destinies is tied to the survival and new resurgence of these massive trees.

During the last century of the Before Time, prior to the disaster their world was viciously overcrowded. Overpopulated cities covered nearly every available space on the planet. As the planet became more and more crowded, the people overflowed from the land masses and moved onto great 'home' ships anchored on their vast seas, eventually occupying these vessels as permanent dwellings.

Then, after the disaster and the deaths of almost all of the world's inhabitants, the landscape and tenor of their world changed.

Shortly before the disaster, the sun began to die, and the temperatures plummeted, abandoning the surviving life-forms and leaving them alone on a planet struggling to survive. During the year leading up to the disaster all living things had to endure and survive eleven months of unrelenting cold. In that time, many of the inhabitants who were not able to relocate to warmer climates perished. Few living things could escape the radical climate change, and many were unable to survive. After the man-made suns were ignited, the temperature at first began to rise out of control and until the suns were stabilized over the next several decades this had caused the vast seas to slowly evaporate and disappear,.

Over the last century, any remnants of their ancient home ships and magnificent, immense cities have been rendered unrecognizable and eroded away by time and their new merciless climate.

Almost a century before the disaster happened, in order to attempt to control the exponentially escalating population of the world, the elite ruling class, prescribed drugs to everyone, especially those of childbearing age. In addition to attempting to limit the rapidly increasing number of people, the drugs were administered to manage or reduce certain undesirable behaviors. The first objective of these drugs, of course, was to control the number of births by acting as birth control and dampening the common person's sex drive. The drugs also contained a blend of sedative-like medications used to suppress aggressive behavior to 'help maintain some semblance of order'. These 'therapies' were designed to take away the people's will, with the objective of leaving them easier to be manipulated and controlled by the ruling class.

The medication had been modified many times over the past three centuries but the drug regiment stayed intact even after the elite controllers had died. Before the last of the elite had perished they had passed on the role of being the controllers to their loyal companions, protectors and caretakers, the androids. Of course, part of the androids newly assumed tasks as the new controllers was the routine administration of the medications. In some fashion the drug regime had been maintained up until very recently. However, after the massive population reduction following the disaster, the prescription's focus had shifted to encouraging birth instead of inhibiting it. Yet, all during this time the goal of breaking and controlling the peoples' will had never wavered.

In the year 2391, about three years ago, the number of times the androids visited the people began to slowly ebb and so the drugs were not administered as consistently. During this past year, for the first time since Resha was born, the frequency of these drugs almost completely halted.

In the years directly following the disaster, their world's few survivors wandered aimlessly. Most had been severely psychologically altered by the effects of the drugs they were forced to regularly consume. The medications, along with the shock of all the deaths, and the many drastic changes their bodies and their world had experienced left the survivors stunned, feeling lost and without direction. At that time the drugs were then again manipulated to help the people better evolve to adapt to the changes happening to their planet. After the heat of suns began to regulate and the final catastrophic drop in the population had stabilized, those left alive became nomads (normads in New Speak). Their planet had changed so drastically that they had difficulty adjusting to the emptiness of their new world and had felt vulnerable staying rooted in one place for too long.

Shortly after that, in an attempt to establish a new order, the Book of Ways had been compiled and written. After spending years tracking down the lost souls of their world the androids in charge had felt that the surviving people needed a task and a set path to fill their aimless lives so they had complied 'The Book' based on the jumbled pieces of all their world's ancient religions. At that time, this book had been considered a goddess send, for it provided a direction for them to follow and a strict new path for the people who had survived the disaster. The new controllers gave this guiding manuscript to the survivors of their ruined planet by instituting a cult like gathering and instructing the people through short fables as to the proper ways to proceed in their new lives. It was a feeble attempt to bring a new direction and meaning to their lives but the people had clung onto it for in the beginning, it was the only stabilizing force in their lives.

Years passed, and as the population grew, more and more of the younger ones were indoctrinated in the teachings of the Book of Ways. Since the integration of this text into the normads' lives and the start of the silence more than a century ago, individual thinking and discussion had been held in check by the drugs that were routinely given to the surviving population. Creative thought was also discouraged to the point of being almost forbidden.

After the Book of Ways was firmly established as the 'one correct path', the people followed its rules blindly. Their allegiance to this path was enhanced since the people had little individual will of their own because of the drugs. After the path was set to encourage order and cooperation, the controllers, who by that time were solely the androids, eventually started building small villages for the survivors to occupy and populate. These villages began cropping up in random places across their barren, sparse, new world. The androids eventually rounded up all the remaining people and encouraged them to make their homes in these little villages. The rural communities were strategically placed far enough apart to prohibit easy contact between the inhabitants. No one truly knows why, but some speculate that the controllers did so to prevent the spread of diseases among the fragile remaining population. In the beginning, one clan occupied each new village. These new villagers were loosely related by 'blood ties', which encouraged a feeling of family among those occupying the settlements. The idea was to engender new bonds of trust in each clan and promote a spirit of cooperation with the aim of starting a new population.

Since the seasons were eradicated by the disaster, the people are moved from village to village on a preset schedule determined exclusively by the Book of Ways. It is said that things were structured this way also to promote and secure the ties within each family. The people vacate their old villages and then march and colonize new ones approximately every ten years. Still, compared to the Before Time, their world is now barren, almost void of human inhabitance.

About a year ago, shortly after the androids stopped coming around, Resha met Katina. Her stories made Resha remember that she was one of the few left who learned how to speak and think as a child, so she began her journey back to what she remembered as normalcy. She started this symbolic voyage by teaching herself to talk again and then began to speak to the others of her clan. Resha's new conversations inspired those around her who knew of the Before Time to also start to speak, and a new language started to emerge and develop. She soon discovered that the younger ones who had never learned to talk were eager to learn, and their desire for knowledge soon surpassed most of the older ones who had survived. After the dialogue began, a few of the younger ones actively sought out teachers to instruct them. New words soon took the place of the words that Resha couldn't summon up in their old forms from her memory. This budding innovative language is now called 'New Speak'.

After the Book of Ways was introduced, the people spent so much time following its directives that they almost lost their creative capabilities. The prescribed drugs had depressed their spirits and prevented most from realizing, developing, or voicing their feelings and thoughts during the last century or so.

Resha was one of the first to start speaking again. Even today, more than a year later, she is still unaccustomed to thinking and talking after so many decades of silence. Fortunately, Resha does not give up easily, and she has been progressively recovering her mind and voice since her discussions with Katina a year ago.

A short while back, Swallow came to Resha, asking about how the people became who they are. Above all Swallow wants Resha's perspective because Resha is the oldest woman in her clan. In an attempt to minimize unwanted attention, Resha and Swallow have decided to meet outside of their village to talk in privacy. For their first scheduled meeting, the two women have arranged a get-together about three miles (or two kilanss in New Speak) outside the borders of their village.

And so the old world ends and a new one rises, trying not to re-create its own past.

— 1 —

THE REUNION

As Resha clears her throat to begin her story, Swallow leans back on her elbows and nestles in, getting more comfortable. It's midmorning, and a rare gentle breeze of arid air is blowing across Swallow's face, dancing with a loose strand of her finan (flaxen) hair. Watching Resha's mouth move carefully pronouncing the words, Swallow secretly smiles to herself, fascinated by the sounds echoing in her ears.

In all of Swallow's ninety-two years, she has not heard anyone speak more than a few words at a time. She can barely contain her excitement as she eagerly anticipates Resha's coming story. Before Resha begins her tale, she tilts her head and gazes into Swallow eyes inquiring. "I look at you, and you remind me of myself when I was your age. Are we closely related? You know, are any of your genes direct descendants of mine?"

The light flickering through the stirring leaves of the ancient tree harboring their meeting place illuminates the momentary confusion dancing on the younger woman's face. "Yes, my genes are from your great, great, great, second cousin on my mother's side but I thought you knew that."

"Ah yes, you're right. I remember now. I believe you told me this before, when I mentioned to you that we might be related somehow.

Forgive me, for I'm still a bit fuzzy because of the effect of the drugs. After all I've been on them much longer than you have. Now back to my story.

"Let me start with my awakening at the beginning of this last year, the year of our Lady 161 a.d. meaning 'after disaster,' or the year of our Lord 2393 A.D., as it was known in my youth. At the end of this past year, it had seemed to me like a good time to die. I had spent a bit over one hundred and sixty-seven years as a member of this family, and I was one of the few left who was born in the Before Time.

"I decided last year that it was a good year to die because I was tired, and the week before I made that decision, I had lost my last baby tooth. This seemed like a sign to me somehow, although I hadn't used that tooth for a very long time, since all my teeth had been lost during the disaster and had to be synthetically re-grown last century. At that time, I was given a new lease on life. These new teeth, which I called my baby teeth, were designed to replace themselves as they wore out. The new ones that grew to replace my other baby teeth had long since taken over but this last survivor refused to give way till last year.

"I haven't seen many radical changes in human behavior during my time on this planet, but in the passing of the last one hundred years, things seem to have grown increasingly more stagnant, and I was growing tired of all this nonsense. That fact alone almost supported my belief in the words of the prophets from the year 2070, who foretold of the end and the great losses to come.

"That is, of course, if I remember the stories that passed on their teachings correctly. Unfortunately, I can't be sure of this, since slightly more than a century and a half after their words were spoken, the silence descended on our world, and most of the human knowledge has been forgotten or distorted since that time. I believe the profits' teachings were especially vulnerable because their words were not written down and shortly after they surfaced spreading their word, they were killed for heresy. As there were many rapid changes during that time especially after our technology failed and there was no written record of their teachings, they were soon forgotten by most. This fact alone leaves me questioning my own memories because I have no written proof of this foretelling and from 2263 on, our people have blindly followed the Book of Ways which denies their teachings.

"In the beginning about two centuries before I was born, the incidents that led up to the disaster and all the rapid changes of the early Before Time, seemed good and new. There was much excitement about their new equality and freedom because of their budding and rapidly growing technology. This brought a mix of anticipation and fear in some, as change always did. Yet most of our ancestors adapted very quickly. It seemed almost too quickly.

"Back then, the throwaway society had spread into every corner of the world and quickly became the new fashion. In the two centuries preceding the disaster, the money and power this new technology bestowed on many, became the solitary focus of the elite in their world. Early on, and because of this singular focus on money, greed set in. Back then when the new technology was first developed, only a few abused the power it bestowed on them and as it became the norm, many enjoyed its conveniences. However, few fully recognized the responsibilities the use of this new technology conveyed on us all. Most profited from it, but as always, some used its tools to exploit others and amass great wealth."

Quietly, Resha looks down into the dirt for a few moments, as if to gather her thoughts, and then she raises her gaze back to Swallow, pausing until Swallow's eyes meet her own before continuing. A look of wonder crosses Swallow's face as Resha resumes her story.

"That's when the elite first came to power, and this is why I must tell you my story. I want to pass on my knowledge to you so that someone knows about our past. Just in case something happens to me. I feel it's time for me to speak of the tales of yore. Knowing them may be our only chance of avoiding some of the same mistaken paths our ancestors traveled down. Maybe if enough people know the truth, we can do things differently."

Suddenly saddened by the thought that Resha might die, Swallow severs her locked gaze with Resha and looks down at her hands tightly laced together in her lap. Then to distract herself from her feelings, she sits up and grasps a stick lying on the ground next to her. As she crosses her legs in front of her, she begins drawing lines in the soil between her and Resha, absentmindedly practicing some of the letters she has already learned to scribe.

"Ma'ama, what do you want of me?" Swallow says.

"Swallow, all I ask of you, is that you listen and remember as best as you can." Resha momentarily places her hand on top of Swallow's holding the stick, and then, as if Swallow's hand's aflame, she quickly removes it.

Swallow hesitates, before looking up to return Resha's gaze smiling. The connection she feels with this woman is uncanny and almost takes her breath away. Leaning back to stretch for a moment, Resha lies in the warm rosy dust, letting it caress her supple body. This tranquil movement distracts Swallow from her writing, and out of the corner of her eye, she watches every gesture of Resha's well-muscled frame, sighing to herself. After stretching in the dirt, Resha sits up again and makes a feeble attempt to dust herself off as Swallow returns the stick to its resting place on the ground beside her.

"Last year, I felt as if I had done all I was supposed to do in my life, at least thrice over, and I had no desire to face it all a fourth time through. That year, a new cycle had begun. The androids again herded our clan together—and others like us who were once city dwellers—to return us to what was left of the old ghettos where we had been born. In the half century directly after the disaster, this migration was considered critical so that the ancestors of the city dwellers would conceive the new members of their families in their rightful birthplaces.

"The Book of Ways tells us we must always travel back to the place of our family's birth, at least once every cycle, usually at the beginning of a birthing time. However, since most of the cities had all but disappeared about a century ago, and now their remnants are almost gone this tradition has lost favor in some of the young ones. And so I chose like many others do now, not to make that journey.

"I have not returned to the city since the end of the cycle before last, over thirty six years ago. During that last time, those in our clan who chose not to go to the cities were relocated early to our new village. The birthing time and changing villages usually don't coincide so it was just happenstance that it all occurred this way."

Resha pauses again to formulate her thoughts wondering about things she is not yet prepared to share with Swallow. She's not trying to be withholding, but Resha's not sure if Swallow is ready to hear all of her inner thoughts, quite yet. If she reveals too much too soon, the truth might be extremely harsh for Swallow to know. Therefore, until she's relayed what she has witnessed these past centuries, she will need to be cautious about speaking of her speculations and suspicions. After all, they are only her beliefs; she has no tangible proof to confirm her thoughts and therefore doesn't want to burden Swallow.

Besides, at my age, I've begun to wonder if this traveling to the cities even has a purpose or if it's just another needless task for us all to survive. If we make it through the journey, it means we are worthy, and if not, too bad. It seems the Book of Ways may have been written by taskmasters just to keep us busy and provide a purpose. After all, when we are busy following the Book of Ways, it does make it easier for us to be controlled.

"Maybe I was just feeling this way—about dying, I mean—because in preparation for our trek to our new village, the shots had started once again. At the last two physicals before the birthing time, the hormone supplements were also given. Before that time, I hadn't been heavily medicated for the past few years. This might have left me being extra sensitive to the drugs' effects."

I still wonder why they are not more secretive about giving us these supplements. After all, since what we eat and drink is so tightly controlled, they could easily slip them into our food without our even knowing it. I also wonder why there is such a big fuss around the giving of these shots and all the preparations for the new births, since this happens every cycle.

Then I remember my age and that I have been through this many times before. I realize there are those for whom this is their first time. *These young ones are still learning the process of the Book of Ways.* Upon remembering this, I chuckle to myself as I recognize how trivial most of us have become and how convinced we are, that the Book of Ways is the only way.

After pausing to smile at Swallow, Resha once more begins relaying her tale. "The Book of Ways tells us that we are now given shots called hormones to enable the maximum number of births for our clan, but I question why they are then wasting these shots on me and others like me.

"Having to get these shots only makes me ill-tempered and cranky, and I wonder if they affect others this way also. Maybe it's something in the shots, or maybe it is just because my body has long since been used up for birthing. Besides I have always found mating with men barbaric, and nowadays I deliberately avoid the mating day when it comes. The day preceding and two days after this ceremonial day, those not wishing to take part in the mating festival with the men leave the village with the young. During this last cycle, it seemed that many, many more young women chose to accompany my group on our trek, than in times before.

"Since now the males can be impregnated and carry the young of other males, this does not seem to seriously affect the number of births. Maybe it's just time for the men to share in the wonders of birth. I know you don't remember the birthing practice of the Before Time, but their old mating ritual is very unlike our present practices."

Resha pauses for a few moments, contemplating. *Anyway, at my age, I now suspect that our population is being controlled and that each clan is only allowed to give rise to a certain number of offspring each cycle. So let the men take their turn at being the ones who bear the responsibility of suckling this next generation.*

"At the biyearly exams, our people are given other shots besides the hormones. I have recently begun to question if the controllers put something in all of our shots that's supposed to make us forget ever having received these inoculations before. If they are using drugs to make us all forget and remain compliant, it seems as if they may be losing their grip on me, or maybe the controllers finally feel that I'm no longer a threat at my age and have lessened my dosage. Who knows?

"For many years now, my memories of what has been done to us have stayed with me, and now with the drugs finally wearing off, I have begun to recall quite a bit of my past. As the frequency of shots has dwindled over the past few years, all sorts of memories have started to come back to me."

Swallow touches Resha's arm to get her attention before she speaks. "Resha, are you all right? This part seems to be disturbing to you."

"I'm all right, my dear. It's just been so long, and I'm impatient to get it all out. Since my mind is still clouded by the drugs, it's sometimes difficult for me to remember. Also, since I'm one of only a few people left who have even known anything of the Before Time and most have known only the Book of Ways, you must understand that these are solely my thoughts and not give them too much credence. I know there is no one in our clan of one hundred and eighty-nine who is even near my age, and it seemed until now, with your queries, none of the younger ones perceived that they may have a choice, never mind questioning 'the Ways'.

"Since we have little contact with the other clans except through chance meetings when we exchange villages or occasionally during our birthing gathering, my chances of encountering other old ones who might validate my memories of the Before Time have been limited, so I'm anxious that I might forget important information that I feel I must tell you. After all, in the past, the only chances I have had to encounter and talk to any my age about these things has been we migrate to a new village, which is roughly every ten ials—or years, as they used to be called—as decried in the Book of Ways."

"Ma'ama, would you mind if we walk a bit while we talk? I promised myself I'd hike into the low hills to the north today to explore."

"That would be fine, Swallow." Getting on her feet first, Resha offers a hand to Swallow.

When Swallow is up, the young woman puts her arm around Resha's shoulders as a guide for her to set a comfortable pace for them both. They walk in silence together for a few steps before Resha speaks again.

"I have had but one other opening for such a conversation in this last cycle of thirty-five years. This has limited my talks with anyone around my age who remembers the Before Time. Over the past century and a half, it has been especially difficult since talking has been frowned upon, and sharing ideas has been almost nonexistent. That's why I was so surprised for you, such a youngster, to ask of such things."

Swallow smiles as if to encourage Resha to continue, but having been trained to hold her tongue, she utters nothing.

"You know, talking like this does aid me in recalling my past. The only other I have discussed some of this with is Rada. Well, her given name was Rada. Her friends just called her Katina. Do you know that since the end of the Before Time, to change your name like that is considered just short of sacrilege? After all, to deny your given name, the one assigned to you at your orientation into the Ways, was unheard of in my younger days."

Resha clears her throat and then continues. "My chance meeting with Katina was only a year ago, and in all my years, I've never met anyone else, who so openly defied the Ways."

Thinking about Katina, Resha briefly stops, turning to look back at the spreading branches of their shade tree standing behind them in the distance. Both women stand for a moment and look at that one lone tree. Swallow, sensing Resha's isolation, puts her arm

...ng her and then joins her gazing ...distance.

...llow's profile. *She looks very striking,* ...*ave made a good choice in passing on* ...*may just work out yet.* "You know, ...left in our world." Resha says as her ...e parched air. Almost in a whisper, ...ling during my childhood studies ...here used to be thousands of great ...called forests." Resha sighs. "Even ...my lifetime, somehow, there is an ...of them."

...ches mask two of their world's three ...s now visible. Although it is not the color of the sun Resha knew in her youth, it carries with it a flash of old memories she'd nearly forgotten until now. *Just more things for me to pass on.*

"So where should I really start my story?" Resha looks down and then back at Swallow, searching her eyes for understanding. She senses the clear warm aqua-blue of Swallow's eyes reaching inside her. *Maybe a good place to start here would be with Katina and my first lucid recollections and remembrances of the Before Time.*

Swallow, trapped by Resha's isolation, is unsure how to respond but finally asks, "Would you mind if we continue our walk as you relay to me your time with Katina?"

Turning toward the direction of the hills, Resha looks away from their tree. She hesitates, nodding as she takes her first step, leaving their tree behind, which physically signifies the beginning of their long figurative journey together into the past. Swallow follows the older woman's lead as they head toward the coffee-colored hills to the north, and Resha begins her tale.

> *'The telling of false tales can rattle the*
> *brain as well as swell the tongue.'*

— 2 —

Lifting the Fog

"In the beginning listening to Katina, at best, was confusing to me. She simply noted my confusion and responded by saying that she remembered all, even the Before Time. Back then, I recoiled slightly from that quiet statement, for to expose others to such sacrilege was, to me considered abusive. Yet my curiosity prevented me from withdrawing completely. Like a wildcat, fearful yet tamed by hunger, I knew I had to discover more.

"From the moment Katina opened her mouth her words began to stir the pot of my own recollections. She brought to mind images that shed light on the closed-up old attic of my memory. These images aided my memories crippled keeper in cleaning away the cobwebs that had held my thoughts captive in their ancient, rusting cage for the past century and a half. In the beginning, clearly remembering seemed an impossible task to accomplish. At first, only mixed bits and pieces would stay in my drug soaked mind as I fought their effects that were eroding away all my crisp recollections.

"Before my encounter with Katina, when I did remember, I only tried to recall the good things from my past. Like what it felt like to be young and beautiful—many had said I was, you know—and the exceptional moments of my earlier life.

"In my youth, there was much overcrowding and little time to one's self. Because of the overpopulation, peace and silence were unknown in my world. Too many people and too much conflict left no room for tranquility. I can distinctly recall the first time I ever heard silence. It was when I was thirty-eight, after the second great die-off had taken its toll."

Stopping for a moment, Resha looks at Swallow, who is staring down at their footprints in the sand. Moments later, Swallow drops her arm from Resha's shoulders and lifts her head gazing directly into Resha's eyes. The look on Swallow's face is that of a trusted companion, not a youngster or apprentice. Standing there Resha first glimpses the real Swallow and she seems wise beyond her years. Unconsciously responding to this perception Resha subtly raise her left eyebrow in silent admiration. "Well, I suppose you don't really hear silence, but just the same—you know what I mean. Of course, my not knowing silence must be difficult for you to imagine, since you grew up with silence all around you and it's all you have ever known."

Swallow's only response is a wisp of a smile.

"Well anyway, back to Rada—I mean Katina, of course."

As the two women turn they slowly continue their walk, Swallow shifts her arm to around Resha's waist. This time, the two women are in sync stepping forward together.

"As I listened to Katina a year ago, it seemed to me that she appeared to have full recollection of the past, and since my clan wasn't due to report to our new home for five days, I used my influence to stay and camp with Katina's group for three of those five days.

"I was drawn to Katina like a mistreated pup that, over time and repeated abuse, grows to be completely loyal to its abusive owner. Although Katina was by no means really abusive to me, at that time, I felt as if she might be causing me great harm. However, despite these disturbing warning feelings, I continued to come to her gatherings for those three nights, eventually sharing my stories and eagerly listening to hers.

"Each night, as we all sat around the dwindling fire, Katina talked quietly, repeating the same things over and over to those of us compelled by our own curiosity or boredom to listen. Looking at the sea of faces surrounding me, I slowly realized only a few showed even the slightest signs of understanding Katina's tale, and none seemed to comprehend to the extent that I did. Most in the group were young and just thought of Katina's stories as an entertaining way to pass time. The older ones present seemed to be drowning in a collective sea, lost in their own confusion, pain, and silence of their pasts. Sitting there, it seemed that the abuse and trauma of the last century had dulled even the sharpest of their senses. My awareness and memories of my past allowed me to understand, and my own comprehension of the past was what drove me finally to respond to Katina's words.

"By the end of the second night I could no longer keep quiet so I looked at Katina and plainly whispered, 'Yes, I do remember the Before Time.' At first, Katina seemed to pay no heed to me and continued on; clearly, she hadn't heard me or possibly, she hadn't grasped the meaning of my words, so I repeated myself, louder this time, saying, 'Yes, I do remember the Before Time.'

"Katina stopped talking suddenly staring at me as if a haunted phantom had mysteriously appeared. I could've sworn that fear mixed with confusion was dancing across her face. Then I clearly witnessed a cog in her mind slip into place as she met my gaze and smiled. The deafening silence between us seemed almost smothering as I stared back into her clear blue eyes and I swear that I witnessed a flame of pure pain and recognition before her delight stamped out that feeling and the blaze of suppressed pain hiding behind it. In response, I simply returned her smile.

"It was clear to me, that it had been a long time since she had experience pure joy, which her earlier expression clearly revealed. A tear welled up in her right eye as Katina reached out for me to take her hand. I, spellbound, got up and moved to sit closer to her. At first, I attempted to sit next to her, until she put up her hand to stop me. 'No, you must sit across from me so that I may read your eyes, your face,' she said. 'I must know if I'm losing you or my place so that I can alter my story so that you may understand.'"

Resha stops talking turning towards Swallow and ponders what she's saying while peering directly into Swallow's clear aqua-blue eyes. With one foot in the past, she realizes, *Her eyes remind me somewhat of Katina's, only Swallow's have a suggestion of green, are a touch more expressive, and are less clouded over by these past two centuries of pain and horror.*

Innocence can be a good thing; it lets the soul soar and leaves those surrounding the innocent blessed by its saintly glow. Oh, to regain my innocence once more and to be blind again to all the pain of the past centuries.

"You see, I had realized by then that although Katina considered herself their teacher, none of her students, up until that meeting, could really understand and grasp her stories. It had taken a reflection of herself, which she saw in me to truly reach her. If the others had thought anything of her at all, she was but an impetuous old woman who entertained them and helped to pass the time. Exasperatingly, Katina had just kept repeating the same words each night with the slimmest hope that she would eventually touch at least one of them or by rare chance find someone like me who could remember and exchange stories." For a moment, Swallow and Resha stare at each other in silence. Then Swallow breaks the mood by grinning and the sparkle in her eyes captivates Resha and nearly takes her breath away. "Please continue," Swallow says.

Clearing her throat Resha begins once more. "That third night, Katina and I got little sleep. After the others bedded down around the red-hot coals of the fire, we talked on into the night until dawn. We spoke of forbidden things, like herbs, how rare they had become toward the end of the Before Time. And how they had almost disappeared after the disaster happened. We both agreed that they were probably still around, but with the scarcity of the controllers, the extinction of the elite, and the immense changes to the planet, where they had been hidden along with the well kept secrets of their origins and uses, most likely would not be discovered soon, if ever." Suddenly, Resha shakes her head and grows silent for a few moments.

At this point in the story Swallow's staring towards the hill in the distance.

Looking at her Resha recalls a touching image of Katina and to redirect the potent feelings this image has evoked she looks down and shakes her head, saying,"And after all, if they were forgotten by all others and will not be discovered by us, those who remember, who will even question and seek them out? Who else will even be interested in where these herbs are hidden and their uses, if not us?"

"Katina and I also briefly talked of observing the many unnatural changes since the end of the Before Time and recalled the promises unfulfilled by those who were in political power back then. As the crimson moon crept across the deep cobalt night sky toward home, we talked of the elite's broken promises of the beginnings of a new world. There were promises of new freedoms back then, just before it fell apart, but the elite were unable to relax and were still trying to control everything. Shortly prior to the end of the Before Time, when the guarantees made by the elite failed to materialize, they retreated into their fortresses and went into hiding to protect themselves from the devastation that their greed eventually had caused. As a last ditch effort to right their wrongs in the decades leading up to the disaster, they built and sent out androids to interact with, take control of, and manage the common people. Over time, the common people had nicknamed the elite along with their androids, the controllers.

"Katina and I both recalled the uprising of those androids and the gradual extinction of the elite because of, or maybe in spite of, those same androids. I think by that time, maybe even the androids realized that the system that had been created over the centuries by the elite was unbalanced and would not sustain itself.

"Shortly after that discussion with Katina, our talk dropped off into silence, and in that calm, one of the fellows sleeping around the fire stirred and uttered the words *purple potatoes* in his sleep. Mildly startled by this strange statement, Katina and I looked at each other in astonishment and began giggling like children. Once our laughter started to escape, we couldn't seem to contain it, so we stretched out our glee to enjoy it to the fullest. Our half-hushed merriment softly echoed so eerily in the sleeping camp that the hair on the back of my neck stood up. But to hear and share in laughter again after it being absent for so long had felt so good, that Katina and I shared as much mirth as possible on into that early morning. After our outburst of laughter, we intertwined comical stories from our own past memories into our serious discussions of what we had witnessed, which made the painful memories easier to bear.

"Following the waning of our first attack of glee, we next discussed, in sadness, the repetitiveness of our artificially prolonged lives for the past one hundred years in the care of these same androids. Death wasn't an option for us; we weren't allowed to die, for in the end, the elite had instructed their androids to preserve at all costs the humans who had survived.

"These unimaginative androids, who lacked emotion and feeling, could only do as they were told. We couldn't blame them for their insensitivity, for they were only reflections of those who had created them, and they mirrored the thoughtlessness and lack of caring for the rest of humanity that they had seen in their creators.

"Just then, as if to break this depressing spell, Katina and I shook our heads and laughed again. It was a bitter laugh this time, because in looking back, we were both fully aware of the foolhardiness of the elite and their creations, the androids, especially since we now knew from our own experience the damage that had come from the elite's folly and greedy quest focused solely on gaining wealth and power.

"Katina and I then paused in silence, tightly bound together by our shared thoughts and emotions. It was no wonder there was no new laughter. In that instant, we both wordlessly realized that in order to laugh, one had to be taught to play and view things with irony. But who could teach laughter to the humans now surrounding us, when everything was so sterile and tightly controlled by these humorless nonhuman controllers? In the end, we couldn't blame the androids, for they were created by humans who bordered on being nonhuman themselves. The truest expression of this was the androids' inability to connect and empathize with those they directed and cared for. They were so much like the elite in all aspects that the common person who they had been programmed to be concerned about wasn't even aware when the last of the elite died quietly of an unknown illness under the care of those they had created.

"Anyhow, I wander from my story. My dear girl, you look a bit bothered. Is there something you would like to ask me?"

"No, not quite yet, Ma'ama. Maybe later." A flicker of what Swallow perceives as anger fleetingly crosses Resha's face and causes Swallow to hesitate. "I hope you do not mind me calling you that. It seems fitting to me, and I enjoy the sweet taste it brings to my mouth."

"No, my dear, I don't mind. It is just hard for me to hear, because I have had no real family of my own. Most of my life, I have been drugged, and I have wandered alone in the dark for so long that it feels as if I've almost lost track of all time. You see, I still feel young, as if you are not only my surrogate offspring but also my partner and friend. Okay. On then."

In response, Swallow half smiles, not knowing what to say but clearly touched by Resha's statement, she links arms with her as they continue on their trek.

"As I was saying, Katina and I slept very little that night, and when the others arose the next morning under the violet light of the rising sun, we smiled to greet them at the ashen coals of our dwindling campfire. Soon after they woke, one young woman with closely cropped mauve colored hair rose and stirred the dying coals to new flames. Breakfast was cooked, and Katina and I were offered a meager share. Not having much of an appetite that morning, Katina pulled me aside to tell me how much she had enjoyed meeting someone who could remember the Before Time. One of the others who, as Katina would says, 'at least possessed half a brain' called

Katina's name, trying to gain her favor and get her to rejoin the group. She, in turn, pulled me farther away. At that point, I shook my head and thanked her for her time, the kind comments, and the stories we had shared. I then asked if our paths might cross in the future. The light in her eyes slowly ebbed and dwindled as she looked down and shook her head in doubt.

"I would like to say yes or that at least there is a chance, but to my recollection, in all my years of storytelling, besides the eyes of my own clan members, I have not ever seen eyes in a familiar face reflecting my campfire more than once.'

"Sadness sat heavy on my heart as I half-smiled in return and said, 'Well, I guess there's always hope.' At that time, I didn't want to fully unshackle and release the small glimmer of promise of a future reunion that attempted to set seed in my heart and mind.

"'Yes, there is always hope,' she echoed flatly as the radiance departed from her face. 'Anyway, we still have our memories. I will take mine to my grave before I forget you, and I promise I will always keep hope alive of a future reunion.'

"I gently took her hand before I told her, 'And I will vow to do the same,' although silently, I had to admit to myself that I wasn't overly optimistic about keeping this vow, for by this time in my life, I knew the chances were against me seeing Katina again. We then clasped hands as we briefly and awkwardly hugged to finish our good-byes. I walked away without turning back so that Katina would not see her pain reflected in my eyes.

"After rejoining my clan that morning, we began preparations for leaving camp and heading to our new home. We set out as the last of the three suns had barely cleared the horizon.

"After four days of uneventful travel, we entered our new village. Upon arriving there, I was struck by something vaguely familiar about this new place. When we consulted the village's record of families and I discovered it was Katina's old village, I was only mildly surprised by this finding. It was almost as if, for me, the scent of Katina still lingered in the air to refresh my newly seeded memories of our talks. This made me wonder if there might be a chance that Katina might've left something behind that I might find and keep as a tangible reminder of what we had shared, so I paid close attention as we cleaned the huts and common areas.

"I was disappointed when we found nothing, although I just knew if I was diligent and waited, I would eventually discover something to hold as a keepsake to use to rekindle my time with Katina. Finding a memento that could also help solidify and encourage my new recollections of the Before Time and the stories Katina and I had shared was important to me."

By that time, Resha and Swallow were approaching the edge of the foothills and Resha slowed to pause. "May I have a little water, my dear?"

Silently, Swallow removes the waterskin from her pack handing it to Resha.

After drinking, Resha hands the skin back and says, "I think I'll head back to our village to allow you your leisure to explore the hills on your own. We can meet again next week, and I will continue my story, if that is all right with you."

Swallow nods her approval restraping the skin to her pack. She then waits and watches Resha swiftly retrace their footsteps till she is almost out of site. While watching Resha leave, Swallow ponders her fondness for this woman, wondering where it will lead. Then she turns slowly and starts her ascent into the low-lying hills, thinking of nothing but her footsteps in the soft, chocolaty dirt, caressing her feet with its warmth and discoloring her skin.

'My true trodden path is chosen and not marked by faint footsteps from my past.'

3

ALONE AGAIN

After leaving Swallow, Resha travels at a comfortable pace, and soon her village is in sight. Arriving on its outskirts about an hour before her evening meal she notices the skies are starting to gray and darken. Looking to the west, she sees an indigo blush where the first two of their world's three suns has already set. Minutes later with the second sun dipping below the horizon, she relaxes for a moment to gazes at the last sun, hanging in the sky and watches it as it dips below the horizon. Standing there she observes a burgundy flash appear in the silent evening as the last sun barely kisses the rosy ground, swiftly following in the pursuit of its comrades.

Soon it will be dark.

During this time of early evening most of their pale ghostly moon falls just below the horizon, where it takes on a crimson hue as it begins to rise again into the deep cobalt-blue night sky. Resha knows that afterward, the apparitions of the moon's neighboring emerald-green stars will rise to haunt the surrounding night sky. The first crest of the rising moon is barely peeking above the horizon as she sets foot in her village.

Resha heads directly for her hut immediately aware that she dearly misses Swallow's shielding presence. This newfound feeling surprises her. As she crosses the threshold of her hut, she becomes a bit more secure, but for some reason, she still feels uneasy, restless, and not her usual tranquil self. Pacing the open floor plan of her living room she is suddenly driven to stop to study its unchanged appearance.

Although her home is not large, it normally feels roomy. This night, it does not. She looks around again, as if to ferret out the cause of her mood. Nothing in particular catches her eye.

I don't understand why I'm so uneasy. Nothing has changed.

The only furnishings in her front room are a bench next to the fire pit and a small chair in the corner. Furniture is sparse in her world, and her hut's arrangement is typical of most dwellings in her village.

Lately the gray synthetic wood-like material that is used to build their furnishings has been particularly scarce and hard to get so she has come to appreciate it. In the past, their furniture had always been made and left behind by the controllers. Now with the androids coming around less frequently new furnishings were harder to come by, and her clan has learned to make do with what they already have.

Pausing to look up at the night sky through the large open skylight in her ceiling, Resha finds she's still restless. She shakes her head and walks into her bedroom. Even though this room is small, in the past year, she has never felt cramped by her sleeping quarters. It's meager and barely large enough to hold her bed and night table but to her it's always felt cozy. Her hut's sparse furnishings and view of the early evening sky through her skylight have always added to her home's illusion of spaciousness, which has made her feel at ease, but for some reason tonight is different.

Why am I so tense? Nothing has changed and there is no reason for my edginess, except that I have now aligned myself more strongly with Swallow. Maybe it's just the readjustment of my boundaries with the rest of my clan that's bothering me.

Still, for the first time since living in this village, she feels almost helpless and ensnared by her surroundings. She tries her best to compose herself, but tonight the razor-sharp edge of her nerves will not be blunted.

Coaching herself in a whisper, she says, "It's less than an hour till dinner. Just cool yourself down and relax, Resha."

In the past she has used this self-talk as a meditation when strong emotions were trying to gain unwanted control over her. Tonight her soft voice echoes into the emptiness of her living room and is nearly swallowed up by her solitude. When her words return to her, the sound of her own voice seems like that of a stranger. This false perception only increases her edginess. Unfortunately, distortion has her firmly in its grip. *The voice in my head is too full of emotion to be my usual soft, serene voice.*

"Well, maybe I should go for another walk just to kill time. Or even though it is not my turn to help prepare our meal, maybe I will go pitch in."

This second option seems like the best choice for her because she then will be around others in her clan, which might soften her edgy mood. Heading in the direction of the main eating area, Resha hopes that company and a meal will quiet her nerves. *Maybe after I fill the empty cavern in my stomach, I will at least be able to sleep somewhat peacefully this night.*

> *'The meeting of two minds may sometimes bind two hearts, but the meeting of two hearts always binds two minds.'*

4

SWALLOW'S TREK

After Resha departs, Swallow heads directly into the hills with the warm, chocolaty earth coddling her naked feet. The dark dirt beneath her is soft and powdery and feels different from the rosy, sandy dust that she and Resha had been sitting on under their favorite shade tree for most of the day.

She stops abruptly, placing her pack on the ground and bends down to picks up a handful of this dirt in order to inspect it more closely. It's deep brown, but the color is not what makes this dirt feel different. As she examines it more closely, she can see and feel that it's softer to the touch, finer, and its particles cling to the skin on her hand, unlike the sandy soil beneath their tree. Swallow, curiously, flings a handful of dirt into the air. As it falls to the earth, it leaves a wisp of a chocolaty trace lingering in front of her until the gentle breeze cooling her skin carries it away. *Yes, this is very unlike the desert soil I sat in earlier today.*

Before her talks with Resha, Swallow never considered such things as dirt. If she noticed the soil at all, it was only because it felt good under her feet. She picks up a second handful and inspects it even more closely. At first glance, the dirt appears to be a uniform powdery chocolate brown, but as she looks closer, she can see that it's made up of many different elements.

She remembers the word Resha had used to refer to these pieces of soil when Swallow offhandedly called attention to the dirt on Resha's face during their morning story session. Looking more closely at soil in her hand, she can see that some of the grains in her hand are almost black, while others are white and shiny. Some reflect the light and a small number of the dirt flecks are difficult to see, almost transparent. Looking closer still, she also notices that some are similar in color to the surrounding crystal towers.

I wonder where this dirt comes from. Maybe the crystal towers are related to the dirt like I'm related to Resha.

She dumps the handful and brushes her hand against her pants to remove any remaining traces of the soil. All sorts of wonders are opening up to her in this new world as the effects of the drugs she has been on for most of her life start to abate.

Feeling the urge to move on, she picks up her pack heading up the first hill, eager to see what's on the other side. Arriving at the top, she can make out the silhouettes of many similar hills fading off into the distance. They go on for much farther than she anticipated. Swallow focuses on one hilltop a few crests away that's much higher than the surrounding hills and quickly starts toward it. Hoping that at its pinnacle, she will be able to see much more beyond these present hills.

She picks up her pace and soon reaches the base of the highest hill, noticing as she starts her trek upward that the suns are slowly descending in the sky.

After this, I will need to turn back, or I'll not eat tonight.

Her stomach groans in protest at the first fleeting thought of missing dinner. In no time, she reaches the foot of the summit and proceeds to climb to the top with ease. There is just enough light left to clearly see beyond the hills. Gazing out at the terrain beyond, she discovers that it flattens out again into another rosy plane dotted with brilliantly colored crystal towers and little else. This scene holds little interest for her, as it seems to fade endlessly into the horizon.

Just more of what I have already seen before.

She then systematically rotates around, attempting to scan the entire surrounding landscape in one glance. In the direction opposite of where she has been facing, she can see her village far in the distance. Beyond that and farther off to the right, she can just make out what is left of the remainder of several crumbling structures. There are a number of central structures still towering above the rest of the surrounding ruins which catch her eye. From this vantage point to her, it all seems like an indistinct mass of debris.

I wonder what that looks like up close. The suns are swiftly sinking; I guess I had better start back.

Swallow turns and promptly retraces her footsteps down the hillside, heading in the direction of her village.

If I hurry, I still might make it back in time to get some dinner.

> *'I followed the dust in the wind only to discover my own footsteps being covered by the sand.'*

5

NEW HOME

Although Resha hasn't seen much of Swallow during the past week, except for their brief encounters at meals, she is comforted by knowing Swallow's dwelling in the next hut. Intentionally keeping her distance from Swallow this week to allow herself room to explore the feelings she experienced at their parting last week, Resha is baffled by this new feeling of dependence. Being shaken by this feeling she is taking this week to regain some composure and control over herself. After all, what if Swallow's mind-set isn't the same? What if she decides to stop their meetings? Resha feels it would not be wise to become too attached too quickly, just in case.

The week following their last story session passes quickly. Now, feeling more comfortable in her own skin again, this morning Resha wakes at sunrise and gets out of bed. Despite regaining her composure, she's eagerly looking forward to today's chat with Swallow. After dressing, she sits down on her bed, waiting for Swallow to come get her.

Resha's mind is still drifting in and out of the fog caused by the mandatory series of shots her clan had received almost a year ago, right before the move to their new village. She recalls that this past move seemed a bit off to her, so she strains to recall her clan's earlier relocations. She's able to remember that before past moves, her clan received at least five different series of shots spread out over a year's time. Comparing the details of these older relocations to this last move, she recalls. *Funny... this last year, we only received our prescribed shots once.* Wondering what is going on, she considers the past few years, and remembers that her clan has only received their mandatory drugs once or twice a year, which is also unusual. Speculating why they didn't receive any shots this past year before the series given in preparation for their move, she falters, questioning her capacity to clearly recall the past.

Could I have forgotten about receiving the shots? Or maybe the androids just neglected to administer them? She tries to clear her mind of the drug-imposed confusion, and it finally dawns on her that during this last move, something else radically changed.

Struggling against the seemingly impenetrable black mist blocking her memories, she fights to understand why this last move felt so different from her past moves. While she wrestles to hold on to the drifting images in her mind, Resha tries desperately to clearly recall the details of earlier migrations. Finally, the shadows in her head start to fade and dissolve, and she distinctly remembers a scene from a previous move ten years earlier. During that move, at least two dozen androids were present, preparing the people, administering the shots, and closely directing her people's transfer. She recalls that in the past, when her people migrated, the androids acted together like a well-oiled machine, and it took little time to relocate Resha's clan and settle them in their new village.

Now, searching the memories of several past moves, she's finally able to remember. In these images, she sees the androids supervising and directing her people's resettlements from beginning to end. In fact, many times, the androids remained a bit longer after the settlement of a new village to help the people adjust. Often, the controllers actually lent a hand with the larger, more complicated tasks, such as converting a few storage huts to living quarters or organizing and collecting new supplies, if such needs arose.

During this last move, however, only two androids directed Resha's clan. They gave her people their inoculations and shortly thereafter disappeared. Her people had much less direction and were left unsupervised for most of the actual move.

I wonder what's going on.

Resha would have realized these differences earlier had she not been drugged. With her head somewhat clearing now, she speculates about why things changed so much during the last ten years. Now recalling that she has not seen much of the androids during the past few years, she again wonders why they're not around so much.

I will need to mention this change to Swallow.

Moments later, Swallow shows up right on schedule outside Resha's hut, and her knock interrupts Resha's thoughts.

"Who is it?" Resha asks certain it's Swallow. "I'm in the bedroom. Just come back here."

Swallow walks in and briefly pauses in the front room. "It's just me. Are you ready?" She always enjoys entering Resha's hut and hates to leave once she's there. It feels like home to her. Making her realize how much she misses living with another.

Heading toward the bedroom, Swallow meanders through Resha's living room, admiring the countless touches of color Resha has used to decorate. Since many of these shades reflect their world's surrounding landscape it makes her feel as if she's outdoors and more at home. This feeling of being home is one of Swallow's favorite things about entering Resha's hut. Most of the accents are rosy and green like the colors of their desert floor and the sparse plants of their world. Within weeks of their first meeting, Resha taught Swallow how to dye fabrics. Swallow loves the effect but thinks the process is too much trouble for her to bother. Besides, not decorating her hut gives her an excuse to always come to Resha's, which she dearly loves to do.

Gazing through the bedroom doorway, Swallow notices a new addition: a bed covering made of a color that reminds her of the pictures of the sky in the Before Time that she recently saw in a book

Resha lent her. After seeing this bed covering, she's sure this is her new favorite color, pausing to adore the look of it, even though she doesn't know its name.

While standing in the doorway to Resha's bedroom, a warm smile spreads across Swallow's face. "What is that color, Resha?" she says, pointing at the bed. "I haven't seen something that shade before."

Resha looks down smiling at her bedcover. "It's called sky blue; the color is similar to your eyes."

Swallow shyly looks at the floor. "It's very pretty." She quickly changes the subject. "How would one make a dye of that color?"

Running her hands across the bedspread Resha says, "I don't know. The only thing I've seen in our world that's similar is one of the crystal towers. I suppose if someone could grind a small piece of it finely enough, one could then make a dye from its powder.

"I found this covering on my last trip to our food storage bunker, tucked away in a corner, hidden under some things I had to move to get to the bookshelves. It didn't look like it had been disturbed recently, so it must've been stowed there for several decades at least. It appears to be stuffed with something that gives it added thickness and warmth. It's entirely possible it might've been secreted away by one of the elite as far back as a century ago."

Resha gets up from the bed and heads toward the door brushings past Swallow standing in the doorway. Following her into the front room, Swallow's drawn in by Resha and is soon standing at her side. As they head outside together, Swallow slips her arm into Resha's and says, "I'm looking forward to today's tale. If I remember correctly, today you will tell me of what happened after your meeting with Katina."

Resha nods, and a few moments later, the two women leave their village, heading in the direction of the shelter of their ancient shade tree.

It's dawn, and the three suns appear sapphire as they rise above the horizon with their combined light reflecting off the crystalline sands of the rosy desert floor. This illusion casts an indigo shadow over the whole scene.

In the early morning half-light, Resha heads toward the dim outline of their tree, the only distinct shape visible on the horizon. As soon as they're out of earshot of the village, she starts her tale.

"After my discussions with Katina, my senses perceived a new world, one bright with possibilities, so even though I was still in a drugged state, I began to wonder about our lives now compared to the Before Time. So directly after parting with Katina and arriving at our new village, I ended up secluding myself in my hut for many days to reflect on the changes that had occurred since the Before Time's end.

"Five days passed quickly before I emerged from my self-imposed seclusion and still I continued to question many of the habits of our current lives. My talks with Katina had awakened my curiosity and after gaining a bit of clarity, I found new questions coming to my mind about the ways and meanings of our existence. During these early days in our new village, as I was still under the influence of the drugs, queries drifted in and out of my hazy mind. For example, why did we usually find the storage huts fully stocked with food and raw materials whenever we occupied a new village? And why, over the years, we had been trained to find our new monthly supplies located in bunkers usually about six and a half miles from each new village?"

"I'm sorry to interrupt, Resha, but I don't understand the terms *miles* and *years*. What do these words mean?"

"No worries, Swallow. It's I who should apologize. I sometimes forget. Those are old terms from my childhood. My memory is especially bad after receiving the mandatory shots, and sometimes I get confused and go back to the words from my youth. Please let me explain.

"*Years* is an old term for our new word *ials*. Some words were improved after the disaster to show that certain things had changed and to help usher in the new era. After our old sun had died and the cycle of our moon had been altered by the addition of our three new suns, the length of a year changed slightly, so we called this new cycle an ial instead of a year to mark this change.

"The second word, *mile*, is a measure of distance akin to our word *kilanss*. A kilanss is roughly one and a half miles. However, that term was changed years before the disaster even occurred. I was very young, so I don't remember exactly when it was changed or why, but during that period, those in power decided it was time for our world to have a single global system of measurement to minimize conflict. In the century before this one, our world worked toward a unification of cultures and economies. During my childhood, our world leaders tried to bring together our systems of measurement as a movement to define the coming new era of a unified worldwide economy. They felt that establishing new terms to replace the old could easily demarcate the changes and in time, make the new changes easier to accept.

"The word *kilanss* was chosen to replace my land's term for miles. As I said, I was very young when this happened, but I had already learned my measurements, so sometimes I slip and use the word *miles* instead of *kilanss*. I'm sorry if my misspeaking has caused you confusion. I will try to be more careful in the future."

"No worries. I was just wondering and now that I know what these words mean, it doesn't matter if you use them in our future discussions, for I will understand."

"Okay. Where did I leave off then?"

"I believe we were talking about our supplies and how they got to the bunkers, ma'ama."

"Yes, that's right. As I said, I was just beginning to settle into our new village after our move, but my head was still in a fog because of the drugs. At that time, so many questions flowed in and out of my brain. Who replenished our supplies? Where did they come from? Then, as I reflected on how we had survived the devastation, a flood of fresh new questions rose in my mind like the tides of the oceans I had known in the Before Time."

Swallow sheepishly raises her right eyebrow in confusion, reaching toward Resha to stop her once again. "Resha, what are tides and oceans?"

"Again, sorry. That's right. You don't know the oceans, for they were gone before you were born. Please let me briefly explain. A long, long time before the disaster happened, about three quarters of our world was covered in water. At that time, the land was in the form of what we then called continents, which were surrounded by this water. Vast bodies of water were located in between the continents. The largest of these bodies of water, were called oceans."

Raising both eyebrows, Swallow says almost imperceptibly, "I can't imagine that much water. What happened to it all?"

"Please let me explain a few things before I get into that. Anyway, back then, the tides controlled the movement of the water in the oceans. These tides were directed somehow by the moon and its cycles. This interdependence was a complex matter that I must admit I don't fully understand myself, but at that time our moon used to go through different phases. During these changes, she would appear differently in each night's sky on a monthly cycle. Sometimes she would look like a full shining globe, like our present day's moon; at other times, she appeared as half a globe; and during a new moon, she was invisible in the sky. I know this is a strange concept, but let me continue with today's story. We can talk more about these differences at a future date if you wish, once I have more fully researched the changes that occurred and understand them better myself.

"Also, at that time, it was necessary for all living things to ingest a great deal of water to live. Drinking too much water from the oceans could make a person sick, because ocean water contained a substance called salt.

"Over that century's time, because of pollution and our increasing population, water soon became our world's most treasured commodity. In order for us all to have enough to survive, we began to take the salt out of the oceans so that we could drink their water.

This, of course, had devastating long-term effects because of the enormously increasing population of humans. The most noticeable effect was that after a number of decades of consuming the water from our oceans, we were affecting the oceans' reserves. Over time, the oceans began to shrink in size. Then, after the disaster, the placement of the three new suns, and decades of the suns' intensified heat, the increase in temperature took the final toll on the water supplies. Due to a miscalculation the new suns had a synergistic effect on each other. So when they were first ignited the heat was unbearable and much more intense then the scientist had planned. These higher temperatures eventually had devastating effects on the oceans, which began drying up all together. Of course, the decrease in water in the oceans then affected many of the major food sources, which for centuries the oceans had provided.

"Since this all happened before we could produce synthetic food, our food sources then had to shift, and we became dependent more and more on using only the foods we produced on land. With overpopulation continuing to increase, the land available to produce food was also diminishing. Ultimately, we found ways to grow food artificially, but this artificial food lacked certain nutrients that were present in naturally grown food so over time these substitutes were less healthy for us humans.

"This reduction in food sources began to affect the wellbeing of the population and had many unforeseen and uncontrollable side effects. In an effort to combat some of these problems, supplements were developed to minimize the most harmful side effects. However, supplements were expensive, and in the beginning, most of the common people couldn't afford them. When those in power back then realized the devastating health effects and the potential threat of future food shortages, they developed a program to provide supplements to the masses. At that point, consuming pills to maintain health became our way of life. In the end, the reduction in healthy food sources and decreasing quantity of food caused those with power and money to start hoarding. When the masses finally started to go hungry, many fights broke out, and people began to kill each other just to get enough food to survive.

"The ultimate outcome of this all was massive starvation, and at that time many died because of this hoarding and the fighting it caused. Since overpopulation had become our world's greatest problem by then, those in power did little to curb or control the outbreaks of violence. They justified not taking any immediate action by saying that the fighting was just a natural population check and implied it wasn't their fault or responsibility. However, a few of the more vocal rebels began to question what was really going on and the underlying causes for all the ills of their time. Unfortunately, it was already too late, for the few small seeds of distrust that had previously been sown and left to fester, were now growing. Eventually, the populace realized how those in power were manipulating events to keep the people off balance and gain even more influence.

"A few years later, after a sufficient numbers of people had starved to death or died because of the suspected intentional spurred conflicts, the elite caught wind of the grumblings of criticism from the populace that were starting to surface. These complaints accused them of manipulating the fighting responsible for all the death. It was said they were using the unrest to their advantage to keep the people at bay. To squelch these rumors; the elite swooped in and started the development and production of synthetic foods. Regrettably, by then, the distrust had already spread, and most people assumed this action was just an attempt by the elite to appear to be saving the day by developing a new synthetic food source and supplying it to the starving masses.

"In no time, a rumor circulated that synthetic food had been developed decades earlier but hadn't been implemented and had been kept hidden from the starving masses to help curb the growing population. Ultimately, the elite had moved too late; at that time the masses' distrust of those in power had grown beyond repair. This distrust, in the long run created a breach in communication that led to devastating future repercussions.

"Then, some decades later, when the elite informed the people that their sun was cooling, so much distrust had been bred from past lies that the people didn't believe what the elite and their scientists were reporting. By that time Rebel groups had amassed enough power to hinder the development and installation of a new artificial sun that those in power were insisting was necessary for their planet's survival.

"Even though the people's suspicions of that particular endeavor were unwarranted, it turned out there was still a valid underlying reason for the people's distrust of those in control. Little did they know just how valid their growing distrust was.

"Years later it came out that rampant experimentation with cold and hot fusion by the elite's scientists over the previous seventy-five years had been directly responsible for their waning sun. After discovering this, the rebels started sabotaging nearly every scientific effort made by those in power. This prevailing standoff between the rebels and the elite delayed the initial installation of the one new artificial sun for decades. Finally, the elite's scientists managed to place a single artificial sun somehow tied to the orbit of their moon to supplement their dying sun. They figured they would ignite it, if or when it was needed.

"The scientists then took on the task of trying to revive their cooling natural sun. These new experiments had additional devastating effects on our sun, which I don't fully understand, except that these new actions caused the natural sun to decay at a faster rate than before.

"With the sun now cooling at a faster rate, additional testing predicted that one new artificial sun would not be enough. When they realized that all the efforts made till then would not be enough, fear in the scientific community began to grow and spread. Feeling that their world was doomed unless they took extreme action drove some of the scientists to be even more reckless than before.

Meanwhile, they continued to try to correct the damage they had inflicted on the existing sun. These new series of experiments started to stabilize their crippled sun, but additional measures were needed quickly to avoid an ice age.

"This near scientific frenzy and the turmoil cause by this new discovery left no time for the final testing stages. Now with their sun too weak to provide enough warmth for the survival of the humans on the planet, the scientists installed two more suns to compensate for the decrease in temperature of their old sun. Since it took time to implement and place the additional two suns, nearly a year passed before all three artificial suns were ready to ignite. After ten months of wicked ice and snow, the scientists knew the people couldn't survive another year of this. With that they decided to ignite the three new suns in orbit before their old sun became useless. If it wasn't done quickly the scientific infrastructure and population of their planet would be irrevocably damaged. In three months' time, they placed the two new suns in orbit, and just in time, they ignited all three in the shadow of their disabled old natural sun. The three new suns began to blaze in a trine as the old sun passed away in the backdrop. The earth warmed once again and the snow and ice began to melt.

"Unfortunately, an unforeseen synergistic effect was created by the ignition of the three new suns and their dying sun, which created a temporary period of devastating heat that rained down on the planet. These unbearably hot temperatures eventually took its toll on what was left of the remaining oceans, as they began to evaporate and dry up that next decade. The heat and other changes caused by the new suns also destroyed the little cloud cover our ancestors' world still had. This caused a drought to ensue. If I'm correct, this period of devastating heat ended a little over fifty years before your birth."

Swallow takes Resha's hand. "I hadn't realized how different the Before Time was. It must have been very difficult for those who survived the changes."

"It was, and I think that was part of the reason we were drugged—to make us forget and stop fighting. But please let me return to today's story. I will provide more facts about the disaster and the drugs another time, once I research and understand better what really happened.

"Before my talks with Katina a year ago, I had no thoughts about the whys and wheres of our daily lives. I just accepted all things that happened to me and around me. Before then, I never pondered where our supplies came from. They were always just there, so there was no need to inquire about their origin. All that we needed was supplied.

"But after our talks, I began to wake up, and it seemed that the drugs were finally beginning to loosen their hold on me just a bit. My head was starting to clear, so all sorts of things began to provoke odd, fleeting inquiries in my mind. I began to wonder where our supplies came from and who brought them to the underground bunkers. For that matter, where did the bunkers come from? So many questions ebbed and flowed and drifted mistily in and out of my dazed, drug-soaked mind last year that I couldn't keep track of them all. Then, just when I needed help with my recall, I remembered that before computers, we would scribe things on a material called paper to aid our recollection."

"Like the paper you have given me for my lessons in learning to scribe?" Swallow asks.

In her mind, it seems a strain to think of such things, but her curiosity and her close ties to Resha had opened a door she wasn't aware of before. Not knowing which direction to pursue with all these new visions roiling in her head and not wanting to interrupt Resha's story again for too long, she silently waits for Resha to continue.

"Yes, Swallow, and I also remembered I had seen things in the bunkers we used to call books, which were used before computers to relay information. In the century before I was born, these books had almost been completely replaced by electronic tablets, computers, and phones. But I had been raised on books, because when I was a girl, my mother and father had a fondness for the old ways so the collected many and even had what we used to call a library, a room full of books for their reading pleasure. They respected the old ways, so they schooled me in both old and new.

"As a young child, I can remember spending days lost in that room. The texture of the paper in these books fascinated me, and as I grew older, my parents' love for books became infectious. At age four, when I began to read, I would often go to the library and read the classics with one or both of my parents. They would do most of the reading but I was eager to listen and they let me take brief turns reading aloud to them as the hours of the day quickly disappeared.

"One day, when I was about five, my mother showed me her special collection, which she kept in a smaller hidden, locked room off the main library. She explained to me that her great-great-grandmother had decided to keep a paper history of events when she was about twenty years old. Her great-grandmother and then her female descendants carried on this tradition ever since creating new paper documentation was outlawed around the year 2100. By that time, keeping a paper history was considered breaking the law and akin to treason, so her great-grandmother built this special, secret room for hiding their collections in order to protect herself and her family. Because she loved books so much and because she had started writing her history before using paper had become illegal, she couldn't seem to stop herself from continuing with this act of treason.

"Looking back now, I wonder if she might've also foreseen the way things were headed, and this was her way of trying to preserve some of our written knowledge. Who knows? In the end, it really didn't matter, though. When everything crashed during the information wars and when the production of electricity dwindled because of our waning sun, we were finally forced to leave the city and all our possessions, including our treasured books, behind. My family lost all our written history with that move. Then, when the widespread production of electrical power completely failed about ten years after the disaster, our electronic technology eventually became useless.

"Since we had almost forgotten before the disaster how to communicate without this technology, and now it was gone, new conflicts arose. As people with power began to hoard all things of value and take advantage of those less powerful, fighting and looting began again. Finally, people resorted to only using physical clashes to settle all their differences. Soon larger skirmishes broke out and spread. This fighting killed many more over the next few decades, so our numbers again declined. I can't remember when the newest drug regime to control our fighting was initiated, but it must have been shortly after all this occurred.

"During this time, other things transpired that I can't recall clearly because of all the confusion, or I was too young to fully understand at the time, but I do remember that all the death and the loss of all we had known, and depended upon only increased the isolation of those who had survived. This isolation and all the preceding events over the last century caused a major disconnection between the people.

"In the last hundred years of the Before Time, we relied so heavily on electronics to convey all our information that we almost forgot how to talk, and then it was suddenly gone. Because of this loss, virtually all communication halted, and the remaining few humans who survived the disaster became disoriented and totally detached from one another.

"In the end, the few who survived the final stages of the devastation were lost, and the shock of all the dying, along with the failure of the link we had depended upon for so long to maintain our relationships, left us uprooted. Those few of us who survived after the full effects of the disaster took its toll just wandered aimlessly for many years to follow."

"Resha, I have another question to ask. I want to understand. You have talked of the disaster many times, and you have said it's also spoken of many times in the Book of Ways, but still, I do not understand fully what happened. You speak of how crowded things were in the Before Time and how little space there was because of this overcrowding, but what happened to all the people? What thing caused so many deaths at the end of the Before Time, and why did all the people die so suddenly in such large numbers?"

"Well, Swallow, that's a good question, but it wasn't really all that sudden. Would you mind waiting a few weeks' time for the answer? The reasons for the end of the Before Time were complicated, and I was just a child, so I didn't understand much of what occurred. Also, since it was so long ago and we were drugged, it is difficult for me to recall. Many of the tech records were lost or are now useless, so I don't have easy access to the information you are requesting, and it may take me awhile to find these things out.

"In order to do the telling of that story justice, I will require more time to prepare. I also need to take another trip to our bunker for research materials. I think I remember a journal there that may help fill in some of the gaps in my memory and explain some of the events I couldn't understand when I was younger. I must go get that book and read it to prepare my story."

Swallow raises her eyebrows and nods. "Fair enough. I can wait, but I will be looking forward to the telling of that tale. Do you need help in researching what happened? I would be happy to help with your studies."

Resha smiles and clears her throat. "I don't know if you can help me, Swallow. It also requires reading some of the older books, and I don't know if you have mastered your reading skills well enough to aid my investigations or if you might just hold me up by helping. Besides, recently, with the drugs wearing off, I have become more curious myself about reading and scribing again. This interest has driven me to try to reteach myself how to scribe and read properly. I must know how to do that better in order to do my research, and it will also aid me in teaching you and the others who may wish to learn these new skills.

"As you know, recently, my curiosity prompted me during one of my trips to the bunker to collect some paper, pens, pencils, and a few books to bring back to my hut, so I can study and use them. I also require these tools to organize my thoughts better about the disaster and the end of the Before Time.

"These books I have chosen, along with the journal I spoke of earlier, may be of particular help for me to fill in some of the holes that are now present in my knowledge and memory. While I'm researching, I can jot some of my notes in the margins of pages of the books I use, which may aid in your understanding of reading. Since the drugs are now wearing off, I hope to be able to have the focus to complete this task soon.

"If you like, I will bring a few of these books and my notes with me for you to see during the session when I tell the story of the disaster. Some of these may aid you with your lessons in learning to scribe and read by yourself, along with providing some helpful information to me.

"Of particular use to you might be an old book that we used to call a dictionary, which I discovered in the main bunker. I'm reluctant to loan it to anyone yet, because I need it in relearning to read. It is indispensible to me because I must look up the meanings of many words that I don't know in my research."

"I would like that. It would be nice to have a book to look up the meanings of words new to me," Swallow responds curiously. "Learning to read and scribe takes a lot of work because I find it is hard to stay focused for too long. I find myself falling asleep when reading and scribing, and when I try to start over again after I have rested, I lose my place and have trouble picking it up again."

"Don't give up. That may be partly because of the shots we were given before the move. I still don't know what was in them, but I have noticed over the years that I'm much less clear for a long while after they are given. Last time, it took many months before I was clear enough to even realize what I needed to do. If you continue to try, you may find it easier to focus after a little more time has passed." Resha shifts her position on the ground to get more comfortable.

Swallow pouts, nodding. "You mean the shots may be making it hard for me to think. Oh, I always wondered what those shots were for. Okay then, for now, I will just do the best I can to understand."

"Yes, I would encourage you to just keep trying, for that is what I have always done." Since she and Swallow skipped the teatime meal, Resha is getting hungry and tries to wrap up this part of her tale, because she wants to finish it in time for them to get to their evening meal.

"Now, back to this part of my tale then. Almost a year ago, with all these questions about our lives churning in my mind, I began to wonder about our villages and how they had been arranged. I was curious why each of these villages had fifty to a hundred mud huts, which typically each housed one to four people, with about twenty extra huts remaining for storage.

"Who had built our villages? In these villages, the huts were gathered around three larger structures: a central dorm, a meeting hall, and a kitchen and dining area where we all ate. Even back then, this design seemed a bit outdated to me. It was peculiar that the meeting hall was rarely used, for the few times we gathered, most preferred to meet outdoors, but such a hall was still found in each village. At that time, I wondered why all the villages were so similar and why they had been constructed in such a fashion."

Swallow gazes at their village in the distance over Resha's shoulders, allowing Resha's voice to lull her into an escape from all the loss and destruction she has heard about so far in today's tale. In the distance, their village now appears to her to be only a number of small bumps on their world's flat horizon. Even though she knows her hut is one of the closest to their story spot, she cannot make out any distinct marking that might give it away. Fearing that her ears and her lapse of attention might've betrayed her, she realizes she has lost a small part of the telling of Resha's story. However, she doesn't want Resha to know this, so she says nothing as she silently tunes back in to Resha's tale.

Shortly after this, Resha, sensing Swallow's distraction, breaks from her story. "Swallow, I'm parched, and I think this may be a good place to end my story today. We can pick up from here next week," Resha says, starting to get up.

In response, Swallow rises, picking up her pack. "Yes, Resha, that's fine with me. Also, this might give me time to try to scribe part of this tale to aid in remembering it while it is still fresh in my mind. If I finish it, I can bring it next week for you to see, if you like."

Raising her left eyebrow in silence, Resha notes that for most of today, Swallow has called her Resha instead of calling her ma'ama. "That sounds like a good idea to me."

> 'As time loops upon itself, it finds itself desperately
> trying not to get caught in its own well-worn path.'

6

REFLECTIONS

Since most of the people are still fighting the effects of the drugs, they are oblivious to how repetitious their lives have become. In truth, much of the villagers' present lives consist of doing the same things over and over again. Most are so busy fighting the mind-numbing and body-deadening effects of their prescribed drugs that they don't notice anything else. Everything's done for them, and all their needs are provided for, which only compounds their problems, because there is nothing driving them to try to go further.

Sometimes an individual may decide to attempt a project, but because they are so dazed and unclear, they find it difficult to focus and complete any tasks they set out to do, and inevitably, a mild frustration sets in before they can finish. Over time, this frustration breeds complacency and an acceptance of the limitations of their daily lives. This reality has left many of Resha's village's inhabitants doing things in an inefficient manner, so none can seem to make headway in breaking free of the aftermath of their prescribed drugs.

After the passing of six months the effects of the drugs begin to wear off and Resha starts to remember what she was like without them. Since, for some reason unbeknownst to her, she escaped being drugged as a child, and still has clear memories of that time. These lucid childhood memories give her a distinct advantage in recovering from the numbing effects of the treatments because she has an old frame of reference the others in her village don't. This makes it easier for her to see past the actions of the drugs and attempt to break free. To help her accomplish this task, she now spends much of her time alone, poring over a few books she sequestered from the bunker on her last trip for supplies.

At some point on that trip, she found a dictionary, which is of particular interest to her. The intense, focused research on the subject of the disaster she has recently started, soon makes her realize she has forgotten the meanings of many of the words she knew as a child. The complicated task of reconstructing the language of their world is challenging because of the drug-imposed silence that began in the late twenty-first century and lasted till this past year. She immediately realizes that because of the silence, there will not be many like her with coherent memories of before the disaster to guide their people's journey back to civilization. Given this, she knows she needs outside help to teach the others, and the dictionary has been like a gift sent from the goddess to guide her own self instructed lessons. Since bringing the book back from the bunker, she has set aside time each day to relearn her old language and traditions. Each morning after rising Resha starts every day by randomly picking and memorizing a handful of words from her newly found treasure, the dictionary.

On this day, like previous mornings, she closes her eyes and runs her hands across its immense pages arbitrarily stopping to discover new words. Today her fingers first land on the word *squabble*. When she was a child, the word meant to argue, to dispute something. She smiles to herself, realizing that in the world they have been living in this past century, there is no need for this word. It is no wonder she forgot it. There have been no arguments or discussions, only a blind, drugged state that has lasted for nearly two centuries, leaving her people with no free will to even consider such things.

Realizing how limited her vocabulary has become a deep sense of loss for the richness of her childhood, invades. She decides to try to recapture that richness and resurrect it, hoping to rebuild some of the culture she remembers from her earlier days and share it with others.

She has begun this task with an old Webster's dictionary, the 111th edition, recognizing that this book must have been an exclusive special-order printing, since by this time, it wouldn't have been published in book form. Noting the printing date she realizes that paper books had been banned decades earlier. Since this dictionary is printed on paper, it's tied to an earlier time, one she remembers with joy. The strong memories of the treasured reading sessions with her parents provide the strength for her to explore further. This causes her to reflect on and long to share with others the good parts of her early world.

Although these memories bring her joy, she understands the past cannot provide all the answers her people will need to move forward. She knows instinctively it would be a grave mistake to sculpt their future by attempting to re-create the past she knew when she was young. Bits of what went before will be useful in their new world, but this alone cannot help them move forward and create a new world of wonder and beauty for their future lives.

She vows not to lose sight of their past, their present, or the new future they will be creating. Holding the massive book fondly in her lap, she instinctively comprehends that this dictionary can't contain all of the current world's truths and lies. They also will need to create new words in her lifetime.

In fact, some of the new speak words developed recently are already more commonly used than the older terms in this dictionary. So now whenever Resha discovers one of these newly created words she writes the new speak version of a word in the margin next to the original word. By doing this she is crafting, as best as she's able, a more comprehensive record of their newly evolving language.

Today, as she runs her fingers down a chance page, they trip over the new word *cosa*, handwritten in the margin next to *amethyst*. Flipping through until she encounters another word jotted in the margin, she randomly bumps into the new word, *finan*, penciled in next to *flaxen*. Thinking back, she figures there might be fifty or so new words that she has already placed in the margins, and she knows that these efforts are just the beginning.

She also understands that to teach others, she herself needs to recognize what happened so that she may answer the questions that others might ask. Realizing that her knowledge is limited, she's aware that there will be no way she can answer all the questions that are ahead and teaching this new language to others will be easier if she has a written book for all to refer to. After she's finished adding the modifications to this old dictionary it might become one of her peoples' new reference books.

In fact, things have changed so radically from the past she remembers that she knows in reality, they will all be teaching, relearning, and creating their new world together. This proves to be humbling thought for someone of her years and experience.

Much of the old language might not even apply to their new world so she understands that after all her efforts and teachings, their language will always be evolving. Therefore, after she is finished what their new language eventually becomes might be radically different from what this dictionary presently holds as truth.

Still, she must start somewhere, and though it's anybody's guess where all this will lead, this well-worn dictionary seems like as good a place as any to start. Besides, because a large sum of their past knowledge was lost when their technology failed, this book is, at least to her, an integral part of what she knows of her people's past.

She decides that she will start from here and do the best she can to study to broaden her knowledge so she is able to teach those who wish to learn to read and scribe. In fact, she has already discovered something new herself. She has remembered that when she was a child, they used to refer to scribing as writing.

Finding that her conversations with Swallow are aiding her in reconstructing their language only enriches her meetings with Swallow and makes their talks even more precious.

*'The trick of learning from the past
can be tricky, but it's not impossible.'*

7

A Dreamscape

Most of Resha's clan members don't venture out of their village often. They seem to be content with doing their daily chores and filling their days with mindless tasks. After all, it's what they have grown accustom to doing. Eat, sleep, rest and work has been the only things most have known their entire life.

Up until the time Resha started to remember the innocent days of her youth and how to think, she had been much the same as the others but after she had met Katina, things started to change.

Beginning her discussion with Swallow this past month had been the first major deviation from her old tedious pattern. Since then her new world had blossomed. She became increasingly aware of the little things in her life and more importantly, Resha started to remember and to expand her logical thinking. She steadily grew tired of her old approach to life and was no longer happy solely with 'The Ways'. As the intensity of her frustration increases she desperately searches for something more meaningful to do in her life.

That next morning Resha wakes before sunrise, roles over in her bed and being too restless to immediately go back to sleep she lies there wondering.

'Before my talks with Swallow my chores were enough to occupy my entire day. Like the others I had been mindlessly content with

47

just filling my time but now, with Swallow's inspiration as my guide I've been given new hope of a better more useful life.

These days I finish my chores in a short space of time. I give them enough attention to do them justice but not enough time to get lost in them. I spend most of my free time discovering new things to make me feel more useful.'

It's early and Resha gazes out the window where in a few hours her world's suns will rise. She knows she's still tired and if she gets up now she will feel the effect later this day so Resha closes her eyes again and drifts off into sleep soon reentering her dream of The Before Time.

> *I was four years old and holding hands with my mother in our old city. We had come out of the alleyway onto 34th Ave. and were instantly immersed in a sea of people so she took my hand as we walked the two blocks to the music store, her errand for that day. She was saying how she needed sheet music to learn how to play the new piccolo that her brother Ted had given her for her birthday.*

In a half-awake state, I realized at that moment that our present world has completely forgotten about music. It was important to many people in my youth, including my mother, but now it was gone.

Still trapped in this semi-awake dream state, my adult mind keeps distracting my child's mind from enjoying and fully experiencing her dream. The adult in me recalls that recently, I read about how music had developed before I was born. 'During the centuries before me, many people had spent their lives being musicians—that was the word. In fact, upon looking back, I think that may have been my uncle's calling, for he loved music with a passion. What had happened to that world? Along with the loss of everything else, what had become of music and playing instruments?'

In this dream, I was just a child, and at that tender age, I didn't have many answers to these questions now rumbling around in my adult head. They seemed to only spark more questions for me in my innocent youth so I strained to remember that trip to the music store, and the result was that I semiconsciously slipped back into sleep and reentered the same dream, but this time, seeing this world only through my innocent child's eyes, it was crisper, almost overpowering.

> *Music was so important that in the two blocks we had to walk to the music store, we passed three people on the street who were just playing for pleasure and spare change.*

The part of my adult mind still lingering outside the dream focused and paid closer attention to every detail.

> *These street musicians seemed different from my uncle somehow. They seemed to wear their poverty like medallions of joy. Most were lean from lack of food, but their hunger for their music seemed to provide a kind of sustenance for their bodies like no morsels of food could. The power of playing music lent them energy from a nebulous, untouchable, and invisible source.*

Again my adult mind took control interrupting my child's dream. 'This naive child in my dream clearly didn't fully understand the power that seemed to possess the musicians she passed along her way. In fact, their driving forces may have completely eluded the younger me and hidden till now somewhere in my subconscious, till having this dream. Now, being grown and older, I can finally grasp these concepts, and since I seem to be reliving some of my memories through my dreams, my mind can pay extra close witness through those innocent childhood eyes of mine.'

Switching back to the child in the dream once more, I began to experience it through my child's eyes again.

My mother stopped on a corner to listen to a young girl dressed in rags playing a violin. She had her eyes closed as she swayed in time to the sweet lullaby she happened to be playing when we passed. Her long blonde hair was pulled back into a tight ponytail that she wore over her left shoulder. Although her clothes were ragged and soiled, her face and hands were scrubbed spotless.

She had placed an open violin case at her feet, in which those passing by rewarded her talent with some spare coinage. There wasn't a lot of money in the case, but many who lived on the streets or in the abandoned ruins of the poorer quarters of the city had to make do with what they could get.

I looked around at the gathering crowd surrounding her. Most seemed lost in the melody she was playing. Even at that age, I could tell that some were possessed by her music. They had their eyes closed and were swaying in time to her song. Others seemed to momentarily be cast into states of near ecstasy as they listened, wide-eyed and staring. As we all watched her, the harsh world around us faded into the distance and took second place to our new reality: the delight of this young girl's music.

The violinist was only nine or ten years old, so her mother stood guard a few feet behind her. I remember wondering if she was guarding the money or the girl. I know my mother was very cautious with me whenever the two of us traveled without my father in the city together, so even at that age, I was aware of some unknown threat and the perceived need for protection.

We stopped and took our place among a handful of admirers. Her violin looked very old, but it had been well kept. My mother bent down and whispered something to me expressing her feelings about how beautifully this young woman played, but the sound of the violinist's music had captured my ears, so I cannot recall if I even listened to my mother's exact words. She said something akin to how she too still liked to play the old instruments, unlike many of the privileged, who had long ago succumbed to the ease of preprogrammed and artificially composed music or, worse, those who only listened passively and didn't attempt to play themselves.

Again the adult in me interjected. 'Even back then, it seemed that the old instruments were falling out of favor.'

I looked up and asked my mother why others didn't play and why we were not being taught to play instruments in school.

"Good, quality instruments are no longer being made in any quantity, so they are very expensive. If one wants to own an instrument, he or she needs to have it commissioned or make it him- or herself. Since most don't have the skills to craft such a thing or the money to pay for it, we all do the best we can. Besides, it's very difficult to get the good quality natural materials required to make such an instrument, so it seems the art of crafting instruments is also dying.

Anyway, nowadays most are content with just listening to machine-composed music," she said. "In my opinion, it seems inactive listening is becoming the norm because learning to play takes time and patience. These are two luxuries that most, except the wealthy, in our world no longer have.

I thought that composing music might be dying with my generation, but this young girl gives us all hope." She paused for a moment to look at the young girl sweetly playing and momentarily closed her eyes to get lost in the music once again. A few moments passed and she sighed opening her eyes once more to gaze down at me. "Also, the funds for the schools must be used for more important things, like computers and such. Moreover, there is much negative judgment in our world, and people are not encouraged to do things they are not good at, so most don't even try to learn unfamiliar things."

As her words touched little my ears, a wave of sadness invaded and began to slowly engulf me while I stood there, enraptured in the music. My mind drifted away as I listened to this young girl's song, playing in the background and it seemed to me her music echoed back the same sadness that I felt slowly creeping into my heart.

My mother then said, "The violin this young woman is playing has probably been passed down to her through the elders in her family. I'd venture to say that it looks more than hundreds of years old."

Now fully captured by my four year old mind and body an omnipotent voice boomed over head 'At that age, I had been too young to fully understand, so I nodded and smiled to hide my confusion. Back then I had been too innocent to know where to begin with asking questions about such things.'

> *Shortly thereafter, the young girl finished her tune, and my mother placed a few coins in the case at the girl's feet. Her mother nodded appreciation as <u>my</u> mother's thankful eyes, met hers. My mother then took my hand, and we left, passing other musicians along the way. We walked in silence for the remaining block to the music store but didn't stop again.*

I awoke from this dream suddenly and sat up in my bed. *Today I feel much the same as I did back then as if I'm finally waking up after more than a century and a half of being drugged and remembering how I was in my youth. It seems that I'm as out of place in this time as I was in my childhood.*

This dream made me wonder if there might be any musical instruments remaining in our world. *If there are, over time, maybe I might be able to search them out. Most likely, if they are still around, they are in the cities, somewhere in storage. Or maybe I might find one or two simple instruments secreted away somewhere in our village's supply bunkers. If I'm lucky it might be possible to uncover them and maybe even learn how to play.*

This idea delighted me. *Sometime in the near future, I need to make a trip to the ruins of the nearest city so I can look for an instrument or two. If they are still around, most will likely be found in the larger bunkers under the cities. That's if they have not all been destroyed by time or the chaos during the end of the Before Time.*

Resha uncovered herself and swung her legs over the side of the bed. Sitting there she remembered that as a child, she had heard faint rumors that the elite had excavated large bunkers off some of the vacant underground transportation tunnels that, at that time, still ran under most cities. These tunnels had all been abandoned and closed a century before the disaster occurred. They had been discarded because it had been decreed that there was no longer a need for them since there were no jobs to commute to any longer. Also, by that point in time, there was no public money available to keep the municipal transportation running, so the elite took over the tunnels and eventually closed off all access to these underground areas.

Resha recalled that toward the end of the Before Time, the elite's fears of an uprising had overtaken their sanity, and some of them ultimately took shelter underground. Over the last few decades of the Before Time, rumors circulated that a small group of the elite had collected anything of value and stored everything they had in secret underground bunkers.

Maybe their fears had been justified, but no one will ever truly know for sure, because no one is left now to tell their side of the story.

Resha finally gets out of bed to a glorious sunrise speculating. *It's possible I might even find an instrument stored in one of the smaller bunkers outside some of the villages, but in all my past explorations of these bunkers, I've never seen one.*

This newly proposed quest gives my next planned trek to our village's bunker a new dual objective, but it also drives my restlessness even deeper inside me. I feel as if I will burst as my old memories mingle with my clearing mind and our new multifaceted world is jumbled together with my past experiences.

> *'Sweet memories circling down a drain may*
> *next lead to a new brightly colored future.'*

8

THE NEXT MEETING

Because she's engrossed in her studies, the next week passes swiftly for Swallow, and before she knows it, her next meeting with Resha has arrived. This morning, shortly before sunrise, Swallow and Resha planned to meet in front of Resha's hut for their usual walk to their meeting place. However, on this day, Resha rises especially early, and as she's waiting to leave, energy begins to grow inside her. She's not used to feeling so energized so she becomes increasingly more uncomfortable while waiting for Swallow and finally decides to go for a walk in order to calm herself down.

Swallow, on the other hand, is feeling particularly relaxed and lingers in bed a bit longer than is typical for her, half dreaming of the day to come. When she does rise, she finds herself mildly invigorated, but the feeling of being wrapped in her warm blanket lingers, and she languishes in this sensation, which delays her departure. When she's finally ready to go, she looks out the window first and immediately spots Resha hurrying through the group of huts nearest them, heading away from her and toward the central dining area.

At first, Swallow thinks of running after her, but the sensation in her body has left her moving as if in slow motion. She hasn't felt this way for a long time. Thinking back, she realizes that the last time she felt this secure was two years before her mother was taken ill, almost five years ago. The memories that flood her mind after this thought, are edged with a soft melancholy, but she's in too good of a mood to let them invade fully and take over. As if standing outside of herself, she acknowledges her sadness and then lets it go, wanting this day to be a particularly enjoyable one. She's been looking forward to seeing Resha all week, and she still is, but something in her approach to Resha has changed. This new shift delights her, and she wants to enjoy this novel sensation a bit longer before she faces the day, so she stops herself and decides to wait for Resha's knock at her door.

Resha, on the other hand, is trying to burn off some of her energy, not wanting to disturb Swallow too early. On her way to the dining area, she runs into a small group of early risers gathering in line for their morning meal.

"Resha, where are you headed?" Steedy asks. Steedy's a tall, lanky youngster with a mop of blond hair that's rapidly approaching his waist.

Resha says, "Just for a walk, Steedy." She's mildly surprised that one of the youngsters is the one to approach her.

"Come join us for morning meal," he says, and a few others chime in.

"Thanks, but I have to meet someone. Maybe another day." Resha starts past the group, but Krey jumps out in front of her, grabbing her arm.

"Come on, Resha. Join us," he insists.

Gently removing Krey's hand from her arm, Resha responds politely, "No, thanks," as she brushes past him heading off in the opposite direction. Suspecting that Krey won't be satisfied by her polite rebuff, over her shoulder she says "I've already eaten," and quickens her pace back toward her hut. Krey attempts to chase after her, but is stopped by a surge of new breakfast goers now blocking his path.

As her hut comes into view Resha slows her pace and smiles. When she's about thirty paces closer, she spots Swallow coming out of her hut and waves.

A broad grin spreads across Swallow's face at seeing Resha, and she returns the wave with a slight nod.

Resha hurries forward, and when she's nearly at Swallow's side, she says, "You look relaxed and happy this morning." Upon seeing Swallow, the tone of her voice has mellowed, and so has her mood. It's as if the ease Swallow's feeling this morning is infectious and Resha soon finds herself caught up in the same disposition. "Are you ready?"

Swallow again smiles silently and nods, refusing to respond otherwise.

Still mildly invigorated, Resha returns Swallow's grin. "Cat got your tongue?"

Swallow's puzzled by this saying and is almost pushed to ask for an explanation, but instead she takes Resha's hand and holds her ground, refusing to utter one single word.

Resha holds on as Swallow pulls her away from the village and toward their favorite meeting spot. Shortly thereafter, the two women linger on the outskirts of their village trying to get their bearings. In minutes, the first light of the earliest sun rising will be visible, highlighting their tree. They slow their pace as they walk blindly into the desert and leave behind the silence of their mostly sleeping village. It still too dark for the two women to see clearly where they should be heading so they stroll towards where they think their old familiar friend is. More than three-quarters of the way there, they stop to watch the first of the three suns clear the horizon and briefly stand silhouetted by a halo of blue light. Resha turns her back to Swallow in order to get a better view of the sunrise. After a brief hesitation Swallow moves closer and nuzzles up to Resha's back supporting her chin with one hand by placing her elbow on Resha's shoulder. There's finally more than enough light for them to see a clear image of their tree, and they correct their course slightly to head directly toward it.

As they near the rim of shade surrounding their tree, the last of the three suns clears the horizon, and the air is already getting warm.

"Today will be a hot one," Swallow says, and she gives thanks when at last they enter the sheltering shade of their tree.

Sitting down first, Resha shields her eyes from the suns looking up at Swallow. "You brought a bigger pack this week."

"Yes, I figured since this was becoming a regular meeting, I would pack us a lunch. However, I didn't get the chance to scribe last week's story, for it was much more difficult to focus than I thought it would be."

"That's okay. As I said last week, the drugs the controllers had given us before our move still have not quite loosened their hold on us yet. Things may be clearer for you as time passes, and it may be easier for you to concentrate after the drugs wear off. When you have started scribing your stories, you may bring them to share, if you wish.

"Besides, my research about the disaster has been slow going, so I must apologize, for I'm also not prepared, and not sure when I will be so I will be delayed a bit longer. In fact, I'm not sure when it will all come together so all I can promise is that when I'm ready, I will tell you. I'm telling you this now, just in case that segment of the story is delayed somewhat or my tale seems rather jumbled. I'm having a bit of difficulty because it's a complicated story. Many complex technical and scientific causes led up to the disaster, and the records I have found so far are sketchy at best."

Swallow sits down next to Resha, placing her pack on the ground behind her. Lying down, she rests her head upon the pack letting her statue reflect her mood. "No worries. Although I'm eager to understand the Before Time and its end, I know you are doing the best you can, so I will be patient and wait." She gives Resha a brilliant smile and settles in for today's tale. As Resha starts talking, the lulling sound of her soothing tones influences Swallow, so she closes her eyes and she discovers that this has an added benefit, for it enables her to better envision today's tale. With her eyes closed, Swallow also finds she's able to concentrate more keenly on the sensations her own body is experiencing and is thankful for the feeling of the cool morning earth on her back. She knows the heat is already threatening to stifle them so she treasures this coolness, realizing that it will be only but a pleasant memory in an hour or two.

"Today I will start with the crystal towers and how they came to be. They first appeared on our world about a hundred years ago. Watching them grow back then, it seemed to me they developed at an amazingly fast rate. But of course, since then, I have also witnessed other such miraculous wonders.

"Near as I can figure, this all happened about a decade and a half before you were born. One morning, like all the rest at that time, I awoke and got up. While arranging the covers on my bed, I noticed an orange speck in the distance, just above the horizon. I was sure that it hadn't been there the day before, and I had never seen anything like it. At first, I looked away, thinking it must be only a mirage, but its tint was so unusual that for the next hour, as I did my chores, my eyes kept returning to it, as if they couldn't escape it. Because its shape and size were barely visible from my hut, I rubbed my eyes looking once more and it was unmistakably there, lying on the floor of our then-flat rosy desert. An hour later I looked again still not sure if my eyes were playing tricks on me. Was I just imagining it? Peering closer to make sure it was real I then left my hut in an attempt to try to get someone else to confirm my sighting. It was still early, so many of the villagers hadn't risen yet. As I walked toward the dining area, I ran into Jossie and stopped her, touching her arm to get her attention. Pointing to the orange speck on the horizon to show her what I'd discovered, I said, 'Look.' She briefly gazed halfheartedly in the direction I pointed and shook her head. 'Resha, you're always imagining things and making a big deal out of every little thing.'

'No, I'm not. I just want you to look at something over there,' I said, pointing at the orange speck.

Pulling away, Jossie returned to her task at hand. 'Resha, I don't have time for such nonsense.'

"Disappointed, I wandered around to the other side of the dining hall, I was beside myself, trying to get anyone to look, but they were all in a haze, and I couldn't seem to drag their attention toward my new discovery, no matter what I did. The effects of the drugs we were all on at that time, seemed to leave them completely unconcerned about anything besides what was directly in front of them, so questioning if the speck was genuine or not didn't concern them. Frustrated by their lack of interest, I was forced to confirm my own siting.

"My curiosity later that day finally drove me to leave the village, walking in the direction of the orange spot. There were no clouds to buffer our three suns' heat back then, so my trek to my new discovery was brutally hot and almost unbearable."

Not believing what she has just heard and seemingly unable to control herself, Swallow opens her eyes, sits up, to remark, "There were no clouds?"

"No, the clouds started to appear about a year after the crystal towers finished growing. Near as I can figure, that was about fourteen years before you were born, over a century ago, but I'm getting ahead of myself. The appearance of the clouds is a story for another day."

"Sorry for butting in. I just can't imagine our world with no clouds to cool our nights. The heat must have been unbearable."

"It was. Over the next fifty years or so after the disaster, many people died from heat exhaustion and exposure. In the decades that followed, those of us left were somehow artificially changed by the controllers to allow us to adapt to the heat and withstand a wider temperature range. It took some time, but as you can see, they eventually succeeded."

Swallow settles back in, resuming her position, and closes her eyes once more, barely missing seeing Resha hold up her arm and smile at the klain color of her skin. *In the Before Time, our skin used to be the same color as the controllers',* Resha thinks. Then she continues her story. At that time we were only able to spend short periods of time outside in the sun, so my trek to my new discovery was quite a feat. But I will explain all that in the story of the clouds. Now, back to today's tale of the crystal towers.

"That day as I left the village, the dazzling glare of the sun reflected off our deserts' crystalline sands forced me to keep my eyes on the ground so I only raised them periodically and for brief intervals to allow me to keep on course heading toward the orange speck on the horizon. In an attempt to protect my skin from the rays of our merciless suns, I had wrapped my body in clothing and placed an extra shawl over my head to block the constantly blowing sand. The sweat from my body soaked into my heavy clothing. I was thankful for the constant breeze which helped me stay cool by evaporating the moisture. As I neared the speck, I could see it was a rock. Venturing to look around, I shielded my eyes with one hand. It was only then that I noticed a couple smaller similarly conspicuously colored rocks placed at measured distances surrounding the orange one. Back then, the orange one was the largest but looking at them today you'd never guess that. That first day, I counted only three. Each one was a remarkable, amazing color.

"As I got closer, I stopped at each of them to inspect these strange rocks more carefully, and I could see that the three rocks were dense. Their colors were opaque, so no light was able to shine through them. There was something about them—their structure maybe—that reminded me of the rocks I had collected in my youth, which we used to call crystals.

"I recalled my prize possession at age five: my father's collection of crystals, which he had passed down to me on my fourth birthday. Over that next year of my childhood, I had added only a few new specimens to those he had originally given me. I hadn't seen a crystal since we left my collection, along with most of our belongings, behind in the care of the city during the exodus from our homes shortly before the disaster occurred. Yet I still remember them.

"The specimens in my collection, however, differed from these new rocks. Many of the various colored rocks in that early collection were almost transparent, and I could actually see through most of them. However, these new rocks were not but something about them still haunted my memories and reminded me of my childhood rock collection. Maybe it was just my nostalgia for the past, but I couldn't shake the feeling that they were related somehow.

"You must understand how shocking these new colorful discoveries were to me back then. Prior to the end of the Before Time, many years before the disaster happened, most of the colorful things in our world had been taken away and hidden by the elite. Those few vibrant things that remained had been stashed away or destroyed in the chaos of our world during the unavoidable strife and fighting leading up to the impending disaster.

"From that time on, till the growing of these new crystals, the palette of the surviving world had been very limited. Only a few of the natural colors had survived the drastic changes caused by our overpopulation. By the time the disaster occurred, our spectrum had become but a ghostly shadow of its former array. Then, after the disaster, with the increase in our dependence on using drugs to cope, colors, like most other things, grew to be unimportant, or they were forgotten as our world's shrunken palette was accepted as the new norm. In addition, during that time, we had forgotten, destroyed, or lost the ability to make different shades of color. These two things had left our world devoid of most colors, and since the people back then had no memory of the former wide array of colors, these hues, weren't missed by many.

"So, a century ago, when I happened upon these new rocks growing in the desert, their shades seemed a striking contrast to the then present colors of my world. They were so amazing, so pretty, that I was struck by these new shades and wondered where they had come from. Since I had collected crystals in my youth, I decided to take a small one back home with me to keep in my hut as a trinket.

"Walking back and forth between these three brightly colored crystals, my feet were burning from the heat of the sand beneath them. The harsh temperature was almost unbearable, but, even with the heat searing my feet, I was driven to stop in front of the smallest crystal to try to pick up. I was attracted to it first, because it was the same color as my hair: amethyst, you might call it cosa. As I hesitated, in front of it I found myself dreading the thought of kneeling down in the blistering hot sands. In order to shield my lower legs and feet, I removed the extra shawl from around my head placing it on the sand in front of me. The crystal was only about a hand's width across and two fingers high, but as I tried to lift it, it resisted and wouldn't budge. In desperation, bewildered by the fact that I couldn't even move it, I stood and tried kicking it, only hurting my foot in the bargain. It was so small, but it seemed much too heavy for me to move, so I figured it might be bigger than I had first suspected. Since I couldn't dislodge it, I was suspicious that it was anchored somehow and that the rest of it must be buried in the sand.

"Kneeling down once more, I began to dig around the crystal's base, hoping to unearth enough of it to get it free. The more I dug, the deeper it seemed to go. On this first visit to the crystals, they had all been about the same width but the cosa one was definitely the smallest of the three.

"The scorching sand was thwarting my efforts, burning my knees, toes, and hands as it fought against my every attempt to unearth my find. I feverishly worked to deepen the hole, only to have the surrounding hot sand refill it faster than I was able to dig. When I finally widened the hole enough so that I could reach a depth of two feet, I tried again to wiggle the rock free. Still, it would not move. Standing up, I sighed and watched as the sand slowly started to seep back into the hole I had struggled so hard to burrow. Frustrated, I stood up, kicking the remaining sand back into place.

"I picked up my shawl and went to next-largest rock, which was a jade color. It was only a bit larger than the cosa one, so again, I simply tried to pick it up. To my dismay, I found that I couldn't move this one either. I tried to dig the jade rock free, and for a second time, my efforts were thwarted so I returned to the crystal that had started this quest: the orange one. It was the largest of the three, and I had no better luck unearthing that one. I figured that maybe if I returned with my feet protected and something that we called a tool, I might be able to break at least a small piece off of one of these crystals. Still kneeling next to the orange rock, I refilled the hole I had dug at its base.

"After I was done I rolled over sitting on my shawl to inspect my knees and toes. They were nearly scorched from the hot sand. Tired, frustrated and not quite ready to leave yet, I sat on my shawl beside the orange crystal and slowly moved my hand over it, admiring its structure. The sun was relentless back then, so its rays made the crystal almost too hot to touch. I had to remove my hand every few seconds to prevent myself from getting burned. After a few minutes, I could take no more of the sweltering temperatures and finally decided to leave. My toes in particular felt as if they were beginning to blister. So I gave up and sprinted back to my village to try to avoid damaging my feet further. I planned to come back with some tools to retrieve a piece of one of these jewels a few days later. Recalling that I had seen a few tools stored in one of the smaller sheds next to our food storage bunker, I tried to remember if they might be useful.

"As I neared my village I left the scorching sand of the open desert behind and was relieved to place my feet on the cooler hard packed soil of the path leading to my hut. Arriving at my hut I entered and sat down to inspect my burns more closely. Reddened and sore, my feet were not as badly blistered as I had first thought. Sitting on the chair next to my hearth, I administered an adequate coating of salve and began to plan to get the tools I needed to go back and try to break the smallest rock free.

"Swallow, just to be clear, tools are things used to aid us in completing a task, like the hammer I showed you how to use last week."

"Yes, I pictured you using something like that to break one of the crystals free, but I'm puzzled. I don't remember you having any crystals in your hut."

Smiling, Resha raises her hand to still Swallow's further potential queries. "Just wait. Please let me finish my story. So, I awoke late that next morning, and while lying in bed to give my feet a little time to recuperate, I planned my trip to the bunker to get the tools I would need. When I got up later that day, I discovered that the salve had done its work well. I would need a day or two to fully heal, but at least I could get up and walk short distances without too much discomfort. Thinking the trek to get the tools would take me much less time than our usual trips to replenish our village's monthly food stores, I planned to make the trek three day from now. However, I found out that the assumption I had made about how long the trek was going to take would only prove to be mistaken.

"I got up early the morning of the day before the planned trip and swiftly completed my chores for the next two days. The rest of that day dragged by as the anticipation of my trip grew.

"The morning of the trip I got up a little later than usual and took my time leaving the village, heading down the well-trodden earthen path to the bunker. Even though it was a long walk, I thought I had plenty of time, so I wasn't feeling rushed. I figured I'd be back well before tea meal so I slowed to enjoy the walk, stopping along the way when something caught my eye or interest. Since I left so late that day, it was a little past midday before I had the bunker in sight.

"As I drew near the compound, I could see three men from my village rummaging through the food storage bunker and loading up the village's carts with supplies. I snuck up and ducked behind an adjacent toolshed to hide. Peering at these men, I briefly wondered why I hadn't been asked to go help get our food, for it was usually my regular job. I watched as the largest fellow ducked back into the bunker for additional supplies, and just as the question left my head, I overheard the smaller of the two fellows still outside, say, 'Too bad we couldn't find Resha the other day to ask her to come with us. She's always fun to take along, because she knows the most about many of the strange things that are here in the bunker, and I like to question her about what she knows.' The other fellow helping outside seemed focused on getting the work done and refused to answer. While following the silent man back into the bunker, the smaller, talkative one said begrudgingly, 'Even if you think she is not telling the whole truth, her stories are still entertaining.' After that last statement, this poor fellow finally gave up and joined the other working in silence.

"Apparently, they had planned this trip on the day I was exploring my newfound treasures. Back then, I simply thought, *Oh well, no great loss to me. I can come here anytime.* Still, I felt uneasy about being discovered taking the tools, for I didn't want to have to explain why I needed them, so I stayed hidden and quietly snuck into the toolshed to look around. Immediately I noticed a large group of tools in the far corner and spied a long pry bar and a large hammer with a head that tapered to a point, so I grabbed those two and quietly moved them next to the door.

"While shifting through the group of tools to get the two I needed, I noticed a few dozen small planks of synthetic wood stored behind the group. About half of them were a little larger than the size of my feet, so I grabbed a small satchel from a shelf near the door and loaded it with six of these foot-long planks, hoping to fashion these planks into some type of protective footwear. After finishing this chore, I put the satchel by the front door.

"I again checked on the men. They were still in the process of gathering the supplies and loading their carts, so I decided it would be best for me to stay hidden and wait till the food gathers left to return home.

"Removing a small book I had stashed in my belt earlier that morning, I sat down in the shed among the clutter to try to read to pass the time while I waited. Sighing and resigning myself to being patient till it was safe enough to leave I struggled to comprehend what I was seeing on the page in my drugged haze and soon became frustrated, ending up mostly looking at the pictures till I lost interest. Eventually, I closed my eyes and fell asleep. Several hours passed before I opened them again, and by then, I found it was approaching early evening. Checking on the men once more, I could see that they were finally finishing up and almost ready to head back home."

At that moment, Resha seems to lose focus for a few minutes as her story tumbles her back into her past, and her memories overtake her.

I wonder what's taking them so long, I shook my head thinking. I hadn't expected to spend the whole day on this task. Had I known it would take them so much time, I might've tried to sneak out earlier. Getting up to check on the men one last time, I looked out the window and watched the suns' light dimming. *Good,* I thought. *He's shutting the door and finally heading for his cart.*

"By that time, one of their two carts was overflowing, so two of the men each picked up one of its handles as the third grabbed the less loaded cart. Then they all headed off, pulling their carts in the direction of the village.

"As soon as these fellows were out of sight, I placed the satchel filled with boards over my shoulder, picking up the two tools I had put aside and left the shed, slowly following the cart tracks back toward the village. I took my time so I would get too close and be seen.

"As I neared my hut, the suns had set but our moon hadn't quite risen so I was able to sneak into the village under the cover of darkness. My habit of picking my home on the edge of our settlements aided me in not being seen while getting to my hut. After quietly entering my dwelling and shutting the door I realized. *Hey I'm good at all this sneaking around.* It had turned out to be easier than I had thought it would be. *Now, where can I hide these for safekeeping?* I held up the hammer and looked at it while thinking. I carried the tools into my bedroom and stashed them under my bed. *This is as good of a place as any.*

"I spent the next two days preparing for my second trek out into the brutal desert climate. I ended up wasting one of those days just attempting to design footwear that would allow me to maneuver yet would provide some protection for my feet. During my first attempt at designing this footwear, I wrapped two boards in cloth and tried to secure one to each foot with clothing, but this made my footwear too cumbersome and left me having to stop and adjust the cloth, as the boards shifted every few steps. Next, I tried strapping the bare boards to my naked feet. This method proved to be more uncomfortable and damaging to my feet than yesterday's hot sand had ever been.

"The next morning, I continued to try to craft suitable footwear using the boards, but being unsuccessful, I ultimately abandoned the idea, deciding that maybe the best thing to do would be to get up very early and complete my trip as quickly as possible. Besides, the first trip had done no real permanent damage, and I felt that my feet might even adapt to the heat after repeated exposures. At the end of the day I placed two of the boards along with some extra clothing I figured I could use to kneel on, in my pack and put my pack by the front door in preparation of tomorrow's journey

"The rest of that second day went swiftly. In the morning, I got up before the sunrise and headed out to retrieve my cherished crystal with my pack on my back and my newfound tools in hand. I soon discovered after entering the desert, that before dawn, the sand was much less hot. I thought. *It might be smart to plan my future trips during the night or in the morning to spare my feet.*

"Approaching the crystals as the second sun began to rise, I noticed right away that things looked radically different. The crystals looked considerably larger. Wondering if I might be mistaken or in the wrong place, I looked around and then quickened my pace, racing toward the group. As I drew closer, I realized I hadn't imagined the change in size; the three rocks were indeed much larger. 'Nope, this is the right place,' I muttered to myself, 'but these crystals are at least ten times larger than they were five days ago. I don't understand what's going on. Maybe I'd better set up a schedule to check these rocks at least once a week to track their progress.'

"Not knowing what to do next, I looked around more carefully, and soon spied two additional crystals, one red and one blue, now budding about five kilanss behind the original grouping of three. Then, looking out to the desert beyond the neighboring hills, I spotted at least a half dozen more of them barely breaking ground. They seemed to be sprouting up and growing everywhere. I thought, *if they're growing, they might be alive.* Halting in front of the orange crystal the one that had started this adventure, I dropped my pack and tools kneeling down next to it. I carefully removed away some of the sand at its base. About a foot and a half down, I discovered a root like structure extending in all directions, which had been absent on my last trip. *Yep, it's growing. I don't know if I feel right breaking off a piece of some living thing. Maybe I will wait on this.* I wondered. That day, I headed home devoid of my prize with the pack on my back and only the tools I had brought with me in my hand.

"True to my word, I came back just before sunrise the following week, and I wasn't surprised that the crystals were larger still. Upon inspecting more of the surrounding desert on my third trip, I counted a dozen or so others sprouting up. *So now there are about seventeen total.* Shaking my head, I wondered where they were coming from.

"One morning about a month and a half later, while doing my weekly scheduled check on the rapidly multiplying number of crystals, I saw a group of controllers—androids—approach by air. They looked almost identical to the people of the Before Time but were somewhat larger. What really gave them away from my vantage point was their flesh-colored skin and the fact that they were flying under their own power without the aid of a machine. That was why I was certain even from so far away that they were controllers."

Swallow breaks into Resha's story once again. "In the Before Time, were people able to fly with the help of machines?"

Resha laughs. "Yes, in the past, there were many ways that machines helped us." She pauses to let this sink in. "Now can I continue?"

"No, I have another question. So our skin wasn't always this color, was it?" Swallow says.

Resha half smiling, confirms Swallow's query with a nod but refuses to comment further.

A moment later, Swallow looks at Resha sheepishly and says, "I know—that's a story for another day, right?"

Resha's smile breaks into a grin as she nods once more, trying desperately not to laugh out loud. Swallow's growing comfort in interrupting her amuses her. She pauses for a few moments again, waiting to see if Swallow has yet another question, but Swallow says nothing more so she continues her story.

"Back then, I was fascinated by the sight of the androids flying, for in all my then nearly seventy years, I hadn't seen the controllers out in the open more than a handful of times, and never had I seen them airborne.

"Fearing being caught, I crouched down behind the lime-green—klain—crystal I had been examining. It was as wide as my full height and half as tall as me in size but still scarcely large enough to completely conceal my presence.

"As I knelt there watching, five controllers flew in from the north and passed almost directly above me on their way to a spot far beyond my hiding place. They landed a good distance away, but they were still clearly visible in the sun-drenched open desert.

"By the time they touched down, it was late morning and starting to get hot, so to try to stay hidden and out of the sun as much as possible, I decided to move to a better location. This was a risky move on my part, because the controllers' vision had been cued to detect any movement, no matter how small. I think since they were originally designed for combat, they were particularly sensitive to picking up quick gestures. While keeping a careful eye on the controllers working in the distance, I very slowly crouched down, till I was laying face down in the sand. The clothes I had picked to wear that day coincidentally matched the color of our desert sands. I slid under an overlying shelf jutting out from the crystal by my side. The ledge was only about a foot above the ground, but underneath it was a small spot of shade cast by the crystal's overlying ledge. I hoped that by harboring myself there, I would be a bit more protected from the fierce midday suns' rays and, thus, more comfortable.

"Peeking around the front of the rock, I still had a clear view, even though the group was far away. Concerned they might soon take flight again, I carefully rolled under the shelf as far as I could, trying not to press my body against the main part of the crystal, fearing it would grow warmer as the minutes of the day passed. Then I readjusted my position to enable myself to look around the front of the crystal to continue spying on the controllers. I kept hoping my rosy clothes might blend nicely into the desert floor, and since my skin nearly matched the crystal's color, I hoped that fact would provide me additional camouflage.

"They were taking their time inspecting a large area of the open desert looking for the perfect spot. At last, they found what they were looking for, a short distance from where they had originally landed. When they were satisfied with their location, the controllers pointed a long finan metal rod at the ground. From where I was lying, they appeared to be drilling with an eerie black light into the sand. A few hours passed, and upon finishing their hole, they dropped a few small pieces of something into it, leaving it open.

"During the drilling, the controllers were so focused on their task that I went completely unnoticed. But now that they were finished, and because I was still a little fearful of being caught, I held my breath as they lifted their heads to survey the surrounding desert. Fortunately, I had concealed myself well and wasn't noticed. After they completed this task, they silently rose into the air and appeared to be leaving the same way they had come.

"At that point, I grew more concerned that I might be discovered from the controllers' new vantage point above me. I turned over on my back and pressed one side up against the hot crystal under the shelf, ignoring its searing heat as best as I could. Zigzagging overhead, the controllers seemed to be looking for another spot. As I watched them pass back and forth far above me several times, my fear heightened. During their last pass over my head, the first sun had already started to set, and thankfully the air was starting to cool. They seemed to be assessing the area around me, so I waited until I was doubly sure they would not come back. By sunset, I was almost positive I had evaded being captured, and my fear began to subside. While resting there in the dark, I relaxed and was lulled by the now cooling air surrounding me. Eventually I drifted off to sleep and sometime later, I awoke, as the moon was beginning to rise.

"Watching the moon slowly lift above the horizon, I thought, *I'll be safer exploring that new hole cloaked in the shroud of night.* So I waited a bit longer, planning to check out their drilling site after the moon was full in the night's sky.

"After a short passing of time, under the light of the risen full crimson moon, I finally felt comfortable emerging from my hiding place. Getting up I walked to the spot where they had finished drilling a few hours earlier. By then, the moon lit the desert floor, making it appear almost burning red. Fortunately, the sand had already started to cool. Upon arriving at the hole, I got on my hands and knees and peered as best as I could into its depths, but all I could make out was a deep shaft emptying into darkness. It was too deep, and its diameter, only about a hand's width across, so it was too narrow to allow our scarlet moon to shed any illumination on what had been done there. Wondering why the hole hadn't refilled itself, I reached in it to feel its sides. To my surprise, they were glazed and slick against my hand.

"At that point, I knew my curiosity about what had been done there would not be satisfied that night, so I headed home under the watchful bloodshot eye of the full moon. Now sitting at her pinnacle in the velvet night sky she was fully raised, her crimson light reflected off the crystalline sands of our desert floor and became my beacon home. After that outing, the heat of our world back then had driven me to grow accustomed to night traveling. My trek home that night was uneventful and so I entered my hut and crawled into the sanctuary of my bed just in time to have a decent night's rest.

"As I drifted off to sleep, I decided I would recheck the hole by the light of day after a few days had passed. I must say in advance that I was only mildly surprised by what I discovered upon my return visit there.

"Three days later, two hours before dawn, prior to anyone else waking, I left my village, heading in the direction of the crystals. That particular morning I used the light of the moon to locate the klain crystal and follow it to the general area of the mounting number of rocks.

"By the time I arrived in the area, the first sun was rising and this allowed me to identify and walk directly to the klain one. As I approached my beacon crystal, the one that had been my shelter three days earlier, I noticed right away that it had almost doubled in height and girth. It would be easy to hide under it now. Then, as I looked off in the distance in the direction of where the new hole was drilled, I could barely make out a mauve rock just peeking above the ground.

"Running toward it, I slowed as I approached, and I could clearly see that it was now about two fingers high and a hand's width in height. I knew from what I had seen three days earlier that its hole had been very deep, and still, the crystal had managed to grow above ground in only a few days' time. This one crystal confirmed my suspicions that the controllers must be planting these rapidly growing rocks. I hiked around that area for a few more hours, exploring and trying to reason out the pattern and method with which these crystals were being grown, but I found no discernible blueprint for their growth.

"On my trek back home, I again stopped to look at my friend the klain crystal. With my thoughts drifting back to the Before Time, I speculated that growing these crystals must have been like what our ancestors had done with the widespread forests of trees I had read about them planting in the early Before Time.

"The klain crystal's rate of growth was astonishing to me. While strolling by it, I ran my hand along its length, only forced to remove it when the heat became too uncomfortable for my hand to tolerate. Upon reaching this crystal's end, I paused and smiled, realizing I would have no trouble hiding beneath it in its present state. Yet something else about it had also changed.

"Upon examining it more closely, I could see that its color appeared less intense and more translucent than I remembered it being on my last visit. This fact was especially evident around its edges. The edges particularly reminded me of the crystals I had collected in my youth. However, the rate at which these crystals had grown, still truly astonished me, for they all were doubling in size unbelievably fast.

"During the next few months, I continued to revisit this site and others like it on a weekly basis to observe the progress of these growing monoliths. Many other sites like the first one started appearing, randomly dotting the surrounding desert's vistas, during the second month of my inspections. But only once more during all my visits to any of the crystals did I again witness the controllers planting more of what I then called seeds. Yet the results of their work were undeniable because crystals were cropping up all around me.

"Over the next five months, I noticed other vibrantly colored rocks arising in many of the flat areas surrounding our village and beyond. I eventually discovered that each new individual crystal was spaced at what seemed like a preset distance apart from the others. There were budding outcroppings visible on many of the distant horizons, and they all appeared to be growing skyward. It looked like the controllers were growing these crystal structures in many of the flat deserts created during the devastation after the disaster.

"At the end of six months' time, it appeared to me as if the group of three crystals I had first discovered had stopped growing. On one morning, I stood in the shade beneath my original orange discovery and let my eyes slowly crawl up its side. At about twenty meters off the ground, I saw a glint of light and could see that it was reflecting off a small clear crystal sphere that I hadn't noticed before that time. I began looking more carefully at the rest of the orange tower and discovered many of these small clear crystals budding somewhat randomly all over its surface. They were just starting to sprout up, and most were only about the size of my littlest fingertip, so it was no wonder I had missed them in the past.

"I next turned toward an amethyst tower to my right and discovered these clear crystal spheres also growing there. After noticing on that tower one single bud closer to the ground than any of the others I had seen on the surrounding towers, I went over to examine it more closely. It was about a meter over my head, so I climbed up on a jagged shelf, stepping up onto a small ledge about a meter above the ground, to get a better look.

"The multisided crystal bud was now at eye level. I could see that it had many facets, like the pictures of the eyes of an insect I had once seen in a book as a child. The central bud was surrounded by what looked like petals extending out from its base. It was like a small clear crystal flower, and they were blooming and growing in random spots all over these towers. Glancing around at the other towers surrounding these three original ones, I spotted no others. At that time, they only appeared to be growing on the three original crystals. I wondered at first if there might be something unusual about these three rocks that allowed these clear crystals to grow.

"I would discover a short time later that this was the second stage of the growth of the crystal towers and that these little gem flowers appeared after the towers reached their full height and maturity.

"When the towers finally finished growing, they were massive in size, almost a kilnass—one and a half miles—wide at the base. They grew with a shocking swiftness up into the skies and almost out of sight. When fully grown, their outer edges were translucent, and their colors grew more intense and opaque as the suns' light moving inward became unable to penetrate it. Because of their uneven density, odd coloration, and varying shapes at maturity, each of these monoliths provided a shaded, cooler area on the surrounding desert floor.

"Observing the growth of the crystal towers was the first time I became aware that some of the changes the planet was undergoing were being managed by the controllers, and I wondered what might be coming next. I was puzzled by why these crystals were being grown in such a fashion."

Resha pauses and then says, "Hmm, I think this seems like a good place to stop. How about we break a bit for lunch? Then I can start another tale after we eat."

> *'Sometimes precious pretty-colored little stones,*
> *if left unbothered, may grow into mountains'.*

9

LUNCH AND THE CHANCE ENCOUNTER

Sitting up and smiling, Swallow says, "Good thing. I was getting hungry and hoped we would share lunch together."

Returning Swallow's grin, Resha says, "What did you bring for us?"

"Just some of the leftovers from last night's meal," Swallow says, handing Resha a piece of their world's bread, called an apancake. The two women share their meal in silence and after eating, Swallow lies down on her side using her pack as a pillow. After yawning twice, she promptly closes her eyes and falls asleep.

Gazing down at Swallow, Resha shakes her head to dispel the tenderness invading as she's drawn to brush a wisp of hair from Swallow's face. *She looks so peaceful. I'll let her be.*

Feeling restless, Resha gets up to stretch her legs. She heads in the direction of the foothills where she left Swallow after their first talk. Upon reaching the border of the hills, Resha looks around and muses that Swallow's curiosity must be rubbing off on her, as without a thought, she's ended up at the base of the same hills Swallow previously hiked.

Walking into the foothills, Resha pauses to look back to where she knows Swallow lies sleeping. With a longing growing inside her, she searches the landscape for some object that might distract her from being trapped by this sensation. Noticing that she's not far from a group of crystal outcroppings similar to the ones she has been talking about in her story, she stares at them and wonders if they are the mysterious objects that might free her from facing her feelings.

Hearing a rustling from the bushes ahead she turns her gaze towards the path leading to the hills in the distance, just in time to see something furry dart across. She focuses on the little creature and, watches as a small animal she hadn't notice before hiding near some brush, runs for the cover of the nearest hill. She desires to follow it but hesitates, knowing that she will need to get back to Swallow and her afternoon tale soon.

As a vague feeling grabs a hold of her, she turns her back on the creature at the perfect time to see Swallow rise, stretch, and look around for her. Waving, Resha turns her back to the creature and tentatively heads back toward Swallow.

Stopping next to Swallow, Resha looks down and says, "I hated to wake you, so I took the time to stretch my legs. Are you ready for the next part of my story now?"

A soft, sigh escapes Swallow as she sits up crossing her legs. "Sorry. I didn't mean to fall asleep on you. It wasn't you or your story. Last night, I had a hard time sleeping."

Reseating herself in the dirt a bit too close to Swallow, who's now guiltily looking down at the rosy ground beneath her, Resha says, "It's okay; you seemed so peaceful that I hated to disturb you." Resha reassuringly puts her hand on Swallow's left knee. "It really is all right, Swallow."

A vague, unfamiliar sensation tries to break the surface of Resha's normally calm demeanor. As she clumsily removes her hand from Swallow's leg she tries to stuff this disturbing feeling back down inside herself and looks anywhere but at Swallow. However, the feeling keeps rising in her chest, insisting on settling in her heart. Moments later after stealing a glance at Swallow, Resha directs her eyes towards the sand, not wanting to be caught staring at her friend. Searching the grains of sand for anything to distract herself from her unwanted feelings, as casually as possible, she feigns getting comfortable and slides a bit farther out of Swallow's reach. To regain her composure, she shifts her focus to removing a grain of sand from the corner of her right eye as she begins the next part of her story.

'Nature's tears mark a new beginning, but the scars of her past still haunt her broken heart.'

10

That Day's Second Tale

"Since I ended this morning's tale with the crystal towers, I'll start this afternoon with a new tale. Before you woke, I was watching a small animal run into the hills, and if you'd like, I can tell you a bit more about our old world's animals and what I know about them."

A fleeting smile barely crosses Swallow's lips, as she blinks and nods in agreement. "Okay."

"The numbers and variety of species of animals were declining in our world for many, many years prior to the end of the Before Time. I will start with what I was taught in my youth and finish up today's story with the latest return of animals recently into our lives."

Broadening her smile into a grin, Swallow's thankful that Resha is not insulted by her falling asleep earlier. "That would be great."

"This story begins many, many years before I was born. When I was a little girl, I learned from my studies that a variety of different animals previously shared our world with the humans. Controlled and uncontrolled mass extinctions over two centuries caused the decline and extermination of many species long before 2230. I remember reading that this had happened mainly because humanity disregarded the importance of animals in our lives. I guess we didn't want to accept responsibility for the weighty burden of how our own increasing numbers were affecting the world around us.

"Overpopulation and overcrowding bred in us a compelling justification for our own irresponsible behavior and actions toward all other species. I think because of our history of using drugs to buffer us from the world around us we had become insensitive to how much we needed them. Since most humans were naturally egocentric, it became easier for us to ignore the needs of all of the other living things we shared our world with. Back then, we humans felt that we were so busy trying to survive that we lost perspective about what survival really was. As competition increase it drove up the living wage and most had to work harder and longer just to keep up. Many were working so hard just to survive that they didn't have time or energy to be sensitive to the needs of living creatures around us.

"Then, with the advancement of synthetic foods, animals' worth in our world's eyes diminished even further. For most, animals soon became just additional mouths to feed, so in most people's minds, they seemed, at best, trivial. This widespread mind-set meant that it wasn't alarming to most humans when a great number of species almost entirely disappeared over a relatively short span of time. In fact, most people were so consumed by their own daily lives that many didn't even notice what was going on around them. By the time I was born, most animals that had survived our callous disregard and ignorance for millennia had been relegated to zoos and wildlife preserves, where they were allowed to live out the remainder of their days.

"As time passed, the sheer number of animals continued to decline further. Some of the surviving species were considered competitors, and those groups were closely monitored for their usefulness and viability. However, if these predators posed any threat to humans, their numbers were culled, or they were done away with. When a species only had a few members left, their kind's chance of survival was carefully reviewed by those controlling the cloning banks. If it was determined that the species was doomed, its last few members were sacrificed, and their genes became permanent members of the gene-cloning bank.

"This bank was officially established many years before I was born. I was told it was created about a decade prior to the occurrence of the single greatest animal annihilation of our history, which happened around 2178."

Interrupting, Swallow says, "Resha, what's cloning? You have mentioned the term before in passing, but I'm a bit unclear about its meaning."

"The way I understand it, Swallow, it's a process of taking very small pieces of a living thing, called genes, and growing them into a near duplicate of the original creature. This process was perfected in the mid-twenty-second century by making the clones viable, meaning that scientists at that time had developed a way for the animals to mate with other clones of their species or type and produce living offspring."

Solemnly, Swallow quietly nods, signifying her understanding, and allows Resha to continue uninterrupted.

"So even though many of the species had long since become extinct, they still held honored places in the gene pool by taking up a tiny amount of space in miniature frozen test tubes in the vaults at one of the cloning banks.

"I think the elite anticipated what was coming, but back then, they believed they could accomplish anything. This led them to think that sooner or later they would be able to fix the harm that had been done to the living creatures around us, so they didn't give the deaths of hundreds of trillions of animals a second thought. Some of the elite who finally recognized the definitive damage resulting from their greedy behavior created the cloning banks. We learned during our childhood lessons that the privileged did this with the hope of repairing some of the harm that our world's greedy ways had caused. Of course the elite didn't recognize that the greed in our world primarily stemmed from their own behavior. They thought, as most humans with supercharged egos do, that they could manage the situation, and in their own minds, they had everything under control.

"Even now, I still choose to believe that the elite's original intentions behind the creation of the cloning banks were good and that they did this to preserve as many species as possible, but who knows? I guess many of the elite were still grasping for answers to the problems stemming from the devastating pollution and the overpopulation of the humans on our world. I remember being taught as a child that one of the most popular solutions for our problems that was proposed by the elite, had been to leave our world behind and start over someplace new.

"Only a century or so earlier, when outer space exploration was flourishing, humans dreamed of relocating to the stars. As time went by and the population grew, we realize that this solution however attractive was impractical and as pollution and the lack of natural resources became the primary dilemma that demanded our attention, our efforts, resources and focus on finding a new home wavered. In the decades that followed, the funds for the space program were severely cut back as other needs became more critical and demanded our attention. Even in my childhood, some of the wealthy still invested their time and money in the search for a new planet to relocate to, holding on to their fantasy of moving to another suitable planet somewhere in the stars, even when all odds were against this happening. The belief that their class at least would survive was impossible for them to let go of, and they presumed those with enough money would eventually escape.

"After the death of the middle class, the elite still maintained that they were immune to harm, so they believed that if they found a planet that could support our kind, those rich enough could easily relocate. It seemed like a logical next step for them. Their imaginings, of course, included bringing the genes of the extinct animals that had been innocent victims of their greed.

"Like gods, the elite thought they could make atonement to the 'lesser creatures' just by taking their genes along. Once the 'chosen people' relocated and were settled on their new world, they could introduce the animals from their old world as they needed or wanted them. With a smaller human population, those in charge of this new planet would be better able to control the diversity and number of many of the animals they had destroyed on our home planet. This would give the chosen few who were able to relocate a chance to re-create a grander duplicate of our world in a new location. They thought they could craft a new world to their own liking and suited to their needs by instituting better controls over all species' populations.

"Of course, this plan didn't include the rest of us humans, for we would be left behind to survive or perish on the remains of our dying planet, which the elite's unfettered use of technology had helped to unbalance and eventually destroy.

"The leaders never considered that if they found a new world to live on, there might already be other living creatures there that would not welcome the foreign invasion of their home. Ah, people's ego and wishful thinking again.

"Apparently, during the century before all this occurred, this relocation plan was the elite's ultimate solution to overpopulation. It was the answer they thought might work at least for them and their families. By the time the cloning banks were full, these relocation plans were but a fantasy. However, because many whole industries had been developed around the cloning banks and money was to be made as people became dependent upon them for their livelihoods, they became established and entrenched in our society whether needed or not.

"At that time room for animals to live was growing scarcer, and they were viewed as the humans' primary competitors for space, food, and other precious resources. Soon animals outside captivity were a rare find. Fortunately for those dependent on the cloning industry, many of the elite had set up extensive preserves of animals, and other individuals had been harboring exotic pets, which allowed 'the banks' access to a variety of those surviving animals' genes. We were told during that time that at the end of these captive animals' brief lives, their genes were eventually harvested and sequestered for potential future generations' use—whatever that meant.

"During the three decades when the cloning industry was thriving, many new banks were established and quickly filled almost beyond capacity. After that, the species that had survived our blatant ignorance started to perish in great numbers. During one of the last great die-offs, many of the cloning banks' storage space had to be expanded once again to allow room for a vast amount of additional species as the number of remaining animals declined dramatically. It was rationalized back then that because the population of humans was still growing out of control and space was becoming a rare commodity, the animals had to go.

"In the next few decades, those who kept animals as companions started being labeled as selfish and antisocial. Saving the animals, which had begun as a noble cause, soon became shunned. Finally, when the cloning banks were fully stocked with all varieties of species, there was a movement to outlaw keeping any animal as a pet, and eventually, the authorities made it a crime punishable by death. After that law was put into effect, there was a covert movement to confiscate the remaining animals formerly cared for as companions and pets. These surviving pets were slowly seized by the powers that be, and their lives were taken—humanely, of course. These series of eliminations were the final blow to the animals that had survived up until that time. After the animal holocaust, most of the natural world slowly and silently disappeared. By the end of that century, only traces of the formerly surviving animals' shadows remained.

"Not until lately, at the beginning of this past cycle, maybe fifteen years ago, did we again start to bear witness to other species' visits into the proximity of our villages and lives once again. It seems to me that they're presently making a comeback, as over the last decade and a half, their numbers and varieties have been slowly increasing.

"Where did they come from? No one truly knows, but with more and more of them appearing in our midst, it's becoming difficult for us to avoid contact with them. We have no clue why they reappeared. They just started showing up one day. Who knows? Maybe in a twist of fate, the elite's ultimate fantasy of repopulation of the animal species is now being carried out on our own crippled planet.

"Before the animals started to reappear, most of the humans now here had never seen one, and many didn't know or couldn't remember that animals had been here prior to the disaster. So when the animals started to reappear, they were treated as strange curiosities, and many people feared or tried to steer clear of them. Our people didn't know what to do with these odd creatures. We knew only that they were now here and seemed to be thriving in our new sparsely human populated world.

"My own first encounters with wildlife, as they were called in my youth, were almost insignificant. These incidents started in my old village about thirteen years before my talks with Katina. The first interaction I remember was brief and went almost unnoticed, even by me, who notices everything.

"One morning, I awoke to the buzzing of a small creature on the open window ledge next to the head of my bed. You must understand that back then, our world was almost silent. There had been no sounds for more than a century besides the hushed noises of the movements of my fellow villagers. Many scores of years earlier, people had stopped talking, and as a result, our world was gravely silent, as over the last century, they had almost forgotten how to speak.

"Now back to my first encounter. So startled was I at that time by any sound in our empty, quiet world that I immediately got up to see what had disturbed my peace. While staring at the black speck of a creature in front of me, an old phrase crept out of the corners of my mind: *No bigger than a fly.* This phrase echoed in my thoughts. It was a fly. I remembered. Or at least it looked like a fly.

"Many creatures similar to this one had been the first to be eradicated in our old world, because they were considered disease carriers and a threat to human health. The humans at that time had targeted potential vectors for extinction first. In my world, it was easy for humans to blame other species for the decline of human health. We were not truly aware and held accountable until after the animals disappeared, when there was no other kind of living creature left to blame but ourselves. After they were all gone, we finally were forced to face and assume responsibility for our own human frailties, as we no longer could avoid the truth.

"A decade and a half ago, I had grown so accustomed to living without animals that the discovery of this little fly puzzled me. Where did it come from? How had it survived? Then it dawned on me that maybe flies had been cloned and released. Maybe the controllers were dipping into the genes at the cloning banks and experimenting with reintroducing species back into our almost sterile world. Why they had chosen these particular creatures' genes was beyond me, but apparently, they had their reasons.

"After seeing this fly and other similar creatures infrequently over the next year or so, I became increasingly aware of more and more encounters with these and other small beings like them. After about a dozen or so chance meetings with small, strange-looking creatures, I remembered that their group had been called insects. I also recalled that in the Before Time, there had been so many different varieties of insects that it was said they were too numerous to count in one's lifetime. Eventually, they showed up in a variety of different colors, so this new emergence started adding new color combinations back into the stark, barren world of our villages. Personally, I think the most beautiful of the insects are the butterflies. Maybe you've seen pictures of them or perchance were able to see one of them somewhere around. They are the unusual ones with the large colorful wings.

"Like the ones that come to the lights at night? Swallow blurted out.

"Not quite. Those are called moths. They are similar but there are subtle differences and the butterflies are much prettier. Then throughout the next decade, after many insects were established in small numbers, larger animals began to intermittently show up in our lives. These strange creatures bewildered the people around me even more than the insects had. Most of the humans who were not old enough to remember the animals were really taken aback. These creatures were larger and more difficult to dismiss, but at first, these bigger animals kept their distance and seemed to wish us no ill will, so most of us hesitantly welcomed them into the outer edges of our lives.

"In the beginning, these new animals seemed wary of humans, and they would scurry away whenever I approached them, so I personally didn't feel particularly threatened by them in any manner.

"Along with these increasing encounters with our newly introduced old animals, a few of us who knew of the Before Time started to remember the old ways. I began to recall fleeting images of our past and to have dreams about my childhood and the world I had grown to know through books.

"Shortly afterward I remembered that I had read somewhere that before synthetic food was developed, we would raise and eat animals for food. That thought spurred new memories to surface. I vaguely remembered that when I was very young, my parents were still able to buy real meat for the holidays and on special occasions. These recollections brought the taste of nonsynthetic food to mind and made me hunger for old familiar flavors.

"My memories were what finally drove me to start to add natural things to our preprogrammed diet of artificial and imitation roots, dried synthetic meats, and replicated grains. It was around that time that I also began to rebel against the Ways in other small fashions. One of the protocols I rejected was our custom of shunning anything from the new natural world around us. This was how I began to develop my tastes for new things. Slowly, I tried to rediscover the newly recalled flavors from my past and add them back into my life.

"These budding desires drove me to pick moss and other small pieces of vegetation from the brush growing in the shelter of the crystal towers. At first, to make sure they were safe to eat, I would nibble on the new plants. If after consuming them, I had no ill effects, I figured they would be safe for other humans to eat. After that, when it was my chance to prepare our meals, I started secretly adding them to our food for flavor. This was how I started to experiment with supplementing our limited synthetic diet." Resha stops abruptly, seemingly lost in thought.

After a few moments of silence, Swallow asks, "Is that it for today, Resha?"

"Yes, Swallow, I think I'm done for today. Besides, you look tired, so if you'd like, we can pick up from here next week. I just realized toward the end of today's tale that I got a bit off track. So I think I need to backtrack somewhat to tell you about creating our new cloud cover, and then I can talk about the growing of the new vegetation. After I've finished those talks, I can pick up where I left off today. I have to study to prepare for those tales and I need more time than we have left right now, so since that is quite a bit of new material and I need to prepare it, I think it's a good idea to end early."

Resha rises, dusting off her pants, as Swallow says, "Yes, I'm still a bit tired, so continuing with this during our next session sounds like a good idea to me."

'Greed has a way of making the desired,
envisioned future sometimes elude itself.'

11

RESHA'S NEW FIND

Yesterday's talk about her experimentations with their food and her sighting of a small animal during their lunch break convinces Resha, against all reason, early the next morning to follow a set of animal tracks she happens upon on the edge of her village.

Where the hard-packed soil transitions to softer, more forgiving dirt, Resha first spies a set of tracks and begins chasing their trail, heading toward the hills. Looking ahead, she catches her first quick glimpse of a small animal as it disappears into the distant hills. The creature reminds her of a picture of a rabbit she saw in a book as a child. Figuring it might be a tasty treat, she decides to follow it. This decision ends up leading her on a grueling hunt for nearly six kilanss, or nine miles, that day.

Shortly after leaving her village, Resha follows the fresh footprints patiently as the path meanders in and out of the coffee-colored hills for nearly four kilanss. As the trail emerges from the hills and the tracks head off into the flat desert, she takes her first steps into the sand. As she looks down at her footprints, she watches the sand wipe away any recognizable evidence that these footprints are hers. She soon realizes that following the tracks of her quarry in the shifting desert sands will be much more challenging than the trail she has just followed. The impressions left by the animal's paws meander in and out of the hills for the next half kilanss and eventually disappear into a thicket of shrubby brush ahead. At one point, she wonders if she might've lost the trail, allowing her target to escape her.

This thicket seems almost impenetrable. Getting down on her hands and knees to inspect the brush more closely, she discovers a small tunnel barely large enough for her to crawl through. Kneeling there in the sand, she peers through the tunnel that at first glance appears to lead nowhere, and can't decide if she wants to continue her chase. As it's early in the day and she is up for an adventure, she crawls in.

I'll chance the investigation. At least crawling on the sand is easy on my knees.

She takes off her pack and puts it on backward so that it hugs her belly. Then, on all fours, she enters the brush, silently hoping she will not get stuck and have to retrace her path backward as she crawls warily forward for what seems to be three or four more hours. At one point, she has to lie on her back and wiggle forward through a cascade of thorns, trailing her pack behind her, snagged on her right foot. While she's wedged in that narrow section of tunnel, the sharp thorns of the surrounding thicket tear at her tan synthetic gauze shirt and cut deeply into the skin of her upper left arm. While trying to navigate the next patch of thorns, she finds herself crawling on her belly, and her cosa (amethyst) braid gets tangled in an overhanging branch. After pausing briefly to unravel it, for about the next hundred meters, she's forced to maneuver ahead more carefully so that it will not get caught again.

Leaving that section of the tunnel, Resha looks a sight, with streaks of her iridescent blood exuding from her klain skin and bleeding into her cream-colored shirt. As the blood soaks into the cloth, it spreads and creates rainbows on the shirt's left shoulder, running down her sleeve. Continuing to crawl forward as the tunnel meanders in and out of thorns and dense brush almost too thick to pass through, she soon loses all sense of direction. A short distance ahead, when she finds a small space where she can sit up and look around, she's finally able to get her bearings.

Resting there a bit, she takes the time to untangle and rebraid her hair and then shoves it down the back of her shirt to prevent further problems. Then she rolls up the sleeve of her shirt to inspect the cut on her arm. *It's not too bad, and it's a good thing I heal quickly. It's almost stopped bleeding.* After moistening her fingers to clean the dried blood off her arm, she rolls her sleeve back down and finishes attending to her injuries. As she explores her immediate surroundings further, she discovers that she's sitting in a small space barely large enough for her to turn around in, bound on both sides by heavy thorns.

Suddenly feeling cooler than she has been all morning, she glances around realizing that she's sitting in something's shadow. Looking up, she can barely make out the outline of a large periwinkle crystal looming above her a good distance ahead. Noting the direction of the tunnel, she realizes she's heading directly toward one of the crystal towers. Bending down once more to peer through the passageway in front of her, she sees nothing but more twists and turns diving into seemingly impassable brush, so she starts forward slowly.

An hour after she resumes crawling, she catches her first glimpse of the crystal through the undergrowth ahead of her. Because of the denseness of the brush above her, she can no longer see it overhead, but she imagines it towering above her majestically. Sighing to herself, she returns her focus to her quest: the rabbit.

After leaving that section of dense grove, she pauses for a moment and prays that she will at least discover a space large enough for her to maneuver around in. Her upper back has begun to cramp, and she longs to stand to stretch her legs. At last, fleetingly wondering if she's going to be trapped in this brush forever, she speculates about how she's going to get out if the passageway ends. Crawling through that last thorny mess in this direction was bad enough, but at least most of the thorns were pointing away from her. Imagining her return trip through that same way, she begins to dread the idea of going back through those same thorns, which would then be pointing directly at her. Just the thought of that task seems daunting, and she knows that if she must return through that same tunnel, the journey will prove to be much more challenging. She can almost feel the pain imagining herself tearing her skin on the thorns at every twist and turn.

After crawling ahead on her belly another hundred meters or so, she sees that the passageway is widening out so she speeds up her pace, praying that up ahead, she might be able to stretch. At last, she's able to get on her feet, although it's still too cramped for her to stand upright, she manages to move forward hunkered down in a sort of crab-walk manner for another ten meters.

Stopping to get her bearings once more, she hears muffled breathing ahead. If she's correct, her prey might be hidden in a patch of brush slightly to her right and directly in front of her. The animal's still out of sight, but sensing it's hiding somewhere ahead, she holds her breath and waits a minute or two listening for a clue to where her prey might be hiding. At first, the sound of its breathing is slow and barely audible. However, as she begins to slowly move forward again, the breathing grows faster, clearer, and louder. Realizing her prey is closer to her than she previously thought, she wonders what she will do if she actually catches it.

Having nothing but her bare hands to kill it with, she momentarily questions if she's even capable of such an act. All sorts of images swarm in and out of her head as she pictures the possible upcoming confrontation.

Hesitating and, for the first time, questioning what she's doing, she thinks, *After all, did the tracks that lead me here even belong to my rabbit quarry? The tracks looked the same, but in this sandy soil, it's hard to tell, and who knows? Maybe the rabbits of the Before Time don't even resemble this so-called rabbit—if it even is a rabbit.*

As she pictures breaking this animal's neck with her bare hands and witnessing the life draining out from its eyes, fear and disgust rise in her throat, spoiling her yearning for the taste of fresh meat. She briefly considers running away, but her curiosity and the thorns that block her path out, force her to rethink about retreating. Pausing once more to determine if the breathing ahead is even from the rabbit she has been chasing, a new emotion invades. Standing there in the warm sand she realizes that there's just enough room for her to turn around and head back out the way she came, but she's come this far, so she moves forward one step and stops again. Then she remembers the potentially painful retreat she will have to endure, and that thought stops her. Suddenly a bitter previously unrecognized emotion, fear, rises in her chest but after naming it, she will not let that stop her.

Moving forward once more with the taste of this new fear in her mouth, she slows her pace and continues more cautiously. Following the tunnel a few more meters, the path turns to the right and as she move closer she can see a sheer periwinkle rock face through the sparse open spaces in the thicket ahead. As she inches forward another meter, her line of sight completely clears, and she spies a sheer rock wall extending up and out of view directly in front of her. At this point, her sole focus is the crystal wall as she takes a break to examine it through the thicket. She is still quite a distance away, but she can make out a deep crevice retreating into the rock and extending above the desert floor to a height of three meters. Even if she decides to continue, this crystal tower might force an unexpected end to her quest.

Quieting herself so that she can hear the creature's breathing once more, she pauses to get a sense of how far ahead the creature is. As best as she can tell, the animal seems to be moving off farther to her right and away from her. Concerned about cornering a wild animal with its back against the rocks, especially now that she's already fearful, she begins to doubt what kind of animal it is. *For all I know, this creature could have a taste for people.*

Her imagination creates wild images of bizarre animals in her mind's eye. She shakes her head to clear the visions and takes another deep breath, pondering whether she should proceed or give up her quest. She's already come this far, so she decides to chance it in spite of the demons her mind is creating.

Resha starts to move tentatively forward once more, and the creature runs into the path about three meters in front of her and pauses. Finally, she's able to get a good look at it. It's very similar to the pictures of rabbits she saw in her childhood. It's small and furry and doesn't look menacing in the least. Raising an eyebrow, she wonders if she would be able to kill such a cute little thing even if she were able to catch it. It looks young and almost defenseless.

As if reading her thoughts, it suddenly takes off again, rapidly heading into another seemingly impenetrable thicket to her left.

No way can I squeeze in there, and I'm getting tired of chasing this elusive creature, but turning back doesn't seem very appealing either.

Crab-walking forward, she can see that about fifteen meters ahead the path now in front of her appears to open into a small clearing. She also sees that tapered crevice she spied earlier, in the crystal at the far side of the clearing. *It looks like that crevice may widen out into an opening to a narrow cave?*

The sound of breathing becomes fainter as her quarry swiftly moves farther away into a thicket so dense that she knows following will be impossible. Having no choice but to abandon that chase, she questions what she should do next. Resolving to give up her desired rabbit dinner, she sighs. Not wanting to accept that her struggle has been a complete waste of her time, she focuses on the opening in front of her. A sliver of light shining through the transparent crystal wall intrigues her.

At least this quarry can't elude me by heading where it's impossible to follow. And if I enter the clearing, I can at least stand up and stretch.

As she moves ahead again, the path begins to widen, and she's soon at the entrance to the clearing, where she finds herself directly in front of the crevice. Silently standing up after all this time, she stretches and turns to look back at the passageway through which she's come. She knows she's not ready to attempt a trek back that way.

Walking around the outer edge of the clearing to stretch her legs, she discovers, tucked away in some brush, what might be another way out. This path's taller and wider but appears to head in the same direction as the one she used to enter this place. After squeezing though its narrow entrance, she easily walks down this path about fifty paces.

Hmm, maybe I will try this way out. I'm only five feet four, and it would be nice to be able to walk out at least part of the way. If I use this path, I know I can start out walking upright.

Not ready to leave this place quite yet, she turns around heading in the direction of the clearing. On her way there, Resha stops and stretches several times to work out the kinks she's developed on her journey into this place. *Oh, that feels good.* When she's at last standing in the clearing once more, she stops assessing her new aches and pains and halfheartedly thinks, *Maybe it's better if I settle for exploring the cave for a bit. My back's sore, and it would be nice to have a break from crawling for a while. Besides, taking a little time will help me work out my new kinks.*

Smiling, Resha turns to face the entrance to the cave.

'*The elusive hunted prey may guide a merry chase that leads to a different prize.*'

12

The Cavern

After leaving the brush Resha finds herself in a small clearing about fifteen by twelve gliers, facing a sheer periwinkle crystal rock wall with a large crevice. After a moment pause she sticks her head into the fracture to look around. There is just enough light filtering in through the semitransparent rock to dimly light her way.

She pulls her head out of the crevice and walks along the front of the sheer crystal wall peering through the rock from the outside. From inside the crack, it appeared the passageway ended a few meters in, but after examining the crevice through the translucent crystal she can see that a passageway turns sharply to the right and continues on. After tentatively re-entering the fissure, she squeezes through the first narrow channel, successfully arriving at the sharp turn. Inching forward around the first turn with her pack in hand, she can't avoid scraping her back and belly against some sharp rocks protruding from the walls of the slender tunnel. As she moves deeper into the cave, she finds there is still enough daylight filtering in through the crystal rock and entrance to guide her way. In the muted light, she can scarcely see up ahead but she has enough light to tell that the corridor expands, and she's relieved she will be able to walk comfortably through that next section. After rounding the third turn, she enters a large cavern. Here, the last glimmer of the sunlight filtering in through the crystal walls is subdued as it fades away into the darkness.

The vanishing light makes her feel as if she's entering a vast, endless cavern. With her eyes still adjusting to the shadows, Resha can only clearly see about an arm's length in front of her. In the failing light, she cautiously moves forward and soon finds herself peering into a large emptiness as her vision vanishes into a velvety violet darkness. While squinting and straining to see the rest of the cave, she has an eerie sense of some unknown creature's shadows enveloping her, which leaves her feeling more alone than she usually does. As she stands there just within the edge of the darkness, her mind struggles to dispel the hideous monsters she imagines hiding in the gloom. The only sensation that feels real is the touch of the still, warm, dry air coming in through the crevice behind her so she focuses on that.

Slowly creeping ahead into what seems like a large, never-ending cave, Resha can scarcely make out a small pile of long, thin rods on the ground a little farther ahead to the right, against the wall. The top part of the rods fade into the darkness, so from where she's standing, she can't tell what they are. Placing her hand on the wall to use it as a guide she half crawls forward toward the pile till the rods are almost within her grasp. There's something familiar about these rods, but in the dying light, Resha can't quite place them. She drops her pack next to the pile, bends down, and picks up a single rod. Now in her grasp is a cool, dusty handle. Her fingers immediately recognize the feel of a lightweight man-made metalloid material. The familiar weight of the rod in her hand instantly brings to mind the image of an old-style torch she has not seen for centuries. Those torches had been crafted made of thin rods about as long as one and a half of her arms. On top of the rod sat a transparent cylinder, which was hooded by a small, flat disk. As she pulled the rod in her hand into the light, she could see that its design was similar.

These still might be useable.

Running her hand up the shaft toward the cylinder, she discovers a small device on the side of the rod, near the top, just below the cylinder. The mechanism has a button that can be pushed in and then slid upward. This device resembles an igniter switch like those she remembers from the torches of her youth. Upon pressing the button, a spark jumps.

Good. At least I know that still works.

She pushes the button once again and slides it upward one notch. A small flame dances to life in the center of the cylinder. She's mildly surprised it still lights, and as she pushes the button up to the highest position, the flame grows brighter. Now, with this light shining on the nearest wall of the cavern a short distance ahead, she can make out other torches secured to the wall in front of her. Holding the single torch with its ghostly flame, she cautiously moves forward and lights the other torches placed in the wall ahead of her. After setting the seventh torch afire, she can vaguely make out the confines of the cavern. However in this soft light, the cavern's finer details elude her.

I will have to explore things more closely now that I can somewhat see.

With her eyes adjusting to the new light, she feels more confident, so she strides forward and at once spies a narrow cleft on the left wall, exiting this main compartment. This makes her wonder if there might be a network of caves yet to be explored beyond this one. As she sticks her head in and peeks into the cleft, she notices a strange, faint glow coming from deep inside. Intrigued by this glow, this slender passageway captures her attention so she decides to explore it first, postponing checking out the rest of the main cavern till later.

Stepping into the cleft, Resha enters a long, narrow channel that eventually tapers into an even more confined fissure. After squeezing her way through this short, narrow fissure, she follows the faint light down a passageway for a few thousand paces and then can see that the glow's coming through the crystal wall to her left. Searching the surrounding walls for a way behind that wall, she rounds a turn and discovers a crack barely large enough for her to slide in sideways.

Exhaling and then holding her breath, she enters it, still heading in the direction of the glow. The crack continues on for about ten more gliers—meters, before it opens into a small chamber and then dead-ends into what appears to be a sheer, glowing rock face.

She now finds herself standing in a small space about a glier square. Here, a flaking, reflective, finan substance is shinning and completely covering the crystal rock walls surrounding her. Looking more closely, she notices a deep slit, about the width of her arm, running down the center of the rock face. The glowing substance appears to have deeply invaded this slit.

Hmm, so that's what's glowing back here.

Resha moves her torch toward the wall, and the glow brightens, changing color slightly, and now emitting an eerie greenish light. She reaches out her hand and gently touches the glowing substance. At the touch of her hand, the light coming from the flakes suddenly changes color, taking on a reddish hue. This red color seems to intensify whenever she disturbs the flakes with her hand. For some reason, Resha expects them to be hot, but they're the same temperature as their surroundings, and she feels a gentle, pleasant caress that makes her want to smile as the flakes swarm to cover her hand.

They're individuals.

In response to her mild delight, their glow intensifies. After poking at them with her forefinger, she presses firmly inward with both palms against the creatures beneath her hands. Their color shifts to yellow.

This is fascinating. The stronger I prod, the brighter they become and my emotional intent seems to affect their color.

As her disturbance of the initial flakes spreads, inciting their neighbors, she can actually see their brightness amplify and move up the wall. The glow quickly spreads about two gliers on either side and above and below the place where she is pressing her hands. She notices that as their glow moves out from her hands, the intensity of the creatures' radiance lessens as it spreads. After a meter's distance, the light begins to fade into the color and the dim glow she saw before she disturbed them.

She's amazed, for she's never seen or heard of anything like this, even in the Before Time. Withdrawing her hands, she next picks up the torch and holds it up as high as she can. As she touches an area of the flakes with the searing top of the torch's cylinder, a muted, short squeal pierces the air as the heat from the flame causes a small pocket of the creatures to turn black.

Oh no, I think I may have just killed some of them!

As this realization takes hold, she feels a slight queasiness in the pit of her stomach. In the silence that follows, she looks up and sees that beyond the burned part, a dark green glow is spreading up the wall at an even faster rate, and it shines even brighter than before. She shuts off the torch in her hand and carefully places it on the ground, trying to demonstrate that she meant no harm and that her future intentions are good.

As near as she can tell, the creatures cover the back wall and extend inside and throughout the slender crack in front of her. The crack travels deeply into the rock wall, and it appears to have no end, as it rises from the ground upward as far as she can see. Some of the flakes appear to be embedded in the surrounding rock walls.

Maybe there are other slender cracks extending out from this main crack that these flakes have invaded.

As she watches the flakes above her start to fade back to their original color and intensity as the blackened burnt part starts to peel off the wall and fall to the ground. *I'm so sorry.* She thinks raising her hand to gently touch a group of flakes next to her. Their color shifts to a pale blue.

Delighted by her find, Resha gathers a handful and shakes them wildly changing her emotions as she does. The flakes remain silent, but their shimmering light grows stronger and steadies, as the flakes flash and randomly change into a myriad of different colors. It seems as if she may have confused them. She next places this handful of the flakes in the front pouch of her shirt and continues to fill it until the pocket is nearly overflowing.

I may be able to use their glow to light my way and not have to light the torches.

The light from her pocketed shavings spreads and becomes even more intense changing back to near their original color as she calms her mood. When she's finished, the flakes are silent, glowing with a very slight tint of red, so she takes their silence as a sign that she's not harming them and that they're content. Her pouch now extends out well in front of her belly, almost making her look as if she's carrying a glowing midterm infant. After also filling her pack half full with these creatures, she turns, picks up the unlit torch, and retraces her steps out the way she came in.

As long as the light in my pocket lasts, I can use it to guide my way.

Upon reentering the main cavern, Resha begins a more careful exploration of this chamber by surveying each wall closely. Every time the light in her pocket starts to dim, she grabs a handful of flakes, disturbing them, then returns them to their new home. Each time she repeats this she eagerly watches their radiance slowly spread and brighten until it renews its original intensity. The flakes' reactions enchant her, and Resha soon realizes that if she can figure out a way to contain these flakes, they could replace the old torches.

She likes this budding idea, especially after inspecting the walls above the burning torches in the main cavern and noticing that it hasn't taken long for their flames to tarnish the crystal walls. *Maybe if I'm successful, I won't have to burn anything.*

Sniffing the air, she detects the faint smell of burning fuel, and in these close quarters, the smell's quickly becoming unpleasant. She recognizes that if she leaves the torches burning for too long, the fumes might overcome her. After sliding the unlit torch she has been carrying into the back of her belt for safekeeping, she slowly moves along the wall of lit torches and, one by one, puts out their flames. Even by the light of her pouch, she can make out the darkened streaks above where she left the torches burning earlier.

Replacing the torches seems like a wise choice. Maybe by the next trip, I won't even need to light them. These walls are so striking that I don't want to damage them any more than I have to.

As she quenches the last torch, Resha's mind begins to race, creating new designs for her perspective future torches using the light flakes.

When I get back to the village, I'll have to explore the storage sheds and bunker to see if I can devise something to hold these flakes. It'll be nice to replace the old torches with a better light source.

She decides to take a couple of the existing torches back with her and leave them hidden just outside her village, so she places another one in the back of her belt beside the one she already has there. If nothing else, she can use these two as a pattern to fashion her new light sources or possibly use parts of them to craft her new lanterns.

Walking along the wall to her right, Resha soon discovers another crack; however, this one is too narrow for her to enter. Pulling one of the unlit torches from her belt, she hesitantly reignites it, and extends it as deeply into the crack as her arm allows. The fracture appears to open and widen just beyond the reach of her torch's light, which leads her to wonder if it might enter into another even larger room.

She picks up a few small pieces of crystal lying next to her foot and casually tosses one through the crack. This act stirs an old memory of her youth, when her grandfather taught her to measure distances she couldn't see by throwing a stone and counting until she heard it collide with something solid. Recalling her grandfather she can still hear his voice saying. 'This gives a person an idea of how far away the second object is.' She smiles. Her grandfather was always important to her.

Realizing that by using this method, she might be able to compare the size of this new inaccessible cavern to the size of the room she's presently in, she decides to throw a stone as hard as she can into this new cavern, hoping that by comparing the time of that throw to the time it takes a stone to hit the far wall of the cavern she is in, she can estimate the size of this inaccessible chamber.

She hurls another crystal as hard as she can into the darkness of her new find and counts, waiting for her ears to catch a sound. However, she listens for a long time, and no sound echoes back through the darkness. After reaching twenty-five, she silently listens just a bit longer, but still, no sound comes.

Resha picks up a similar-sized crystal and throws it at the opposite wall of the cavern in which she's now standing. She counts to twelve before she hears an echo off the far wall as the crystal bounces to the floor.

Hmm, maybe the first crystal didn't reach its mark or fell short to a soft dirt floor below. Or possibly it collided with a wall that is padded with something. Since this crack is too small for me to pass through, I may never be able to truly find out the size of this new cavern.

She throws a second stone into the darkness of the elusive cavern and waits, but still, no sound echoes back. *I suspect that this hidden cavern is much larger than the one I'm presently in.*

Settled with the knowledge that this information will remain a secret at least for the time being, she withdraws the torch from the crack and extinguishes it, once again. Then Resha shrugs and turns her full attention to exploring the main chamber.

After her eyes have somewhat adjusted to the light given off by the front pouch of her shirt, she no longer needs the walls of the main cavern as a guide. Now feeling more comfortable in maneuvering about, using only the light emitted by her pouch, Resha leaves the safety of her guide walls and walks directly across the main cavern to the far side. Her vision is limited to a few meters in front of her, but there's easily enough light for her to make the journey across. As she approaches the far wall, the light from her pouch gradually illuminates only a small section of it.

The wall's covered with some type of drawings, and they look like they're etched into the rock.

Reaching up over her head to touch the illustration she happens to be standing in front of, she discovers that they are indeed etched into the wall, about a hand's width deep. The collection of drawings extends to the right and left far beyond the distance she can see with her present pouch light.

She steps back and walks along the wall, passing about ten drawings, realizing they appear to be telling a story. Continuing on, she follows the etchings along that wall until they end. When she stops to look at the last etching, she can't tell if it depicts the beginning or the end of the story. She backs up to get a better look, but her light is not bright enough for her to view all the drawings at once and this prevents her from making sense of the story they are telling.

She knows she needs more light, so despite how she feels about the torches, she resigns herself to walking back over to retrieve as many of the old torches as she can carry. After gathering nine, she returns to the wall with the drawings, and one by one, she reluctantly lights the torches and places them into the holes spaced at equal measures within the series of drawings. Eventually, she backs away, trying to take in the meaning of the entire grouping's story. Yet the light is still too dim for her to make out the complete story in detail but there is ample light for her to see just enough to realize they seem to be relaying a story of the past.

She decides to count how many etchings there are and discovers there are seventy drawings total in the series. After finishing the count, she walks back and forth along the drawings a number of times, stopping randomly to pay closer attention to the individual etchings within the collection. Finally settling in front of one drawing, she scrutinizes it in detail, running her hands along its features as well as using her eyes to view it.

Each drawing is about two lengths of my forearm in height and one in width. Yet some vary in style, slightly in size, and also in attention to detail.

Upon this discovery, Resha questions if the same hand has crafted them all. She notices that certain groupings of drawings in the assembly seem similar, while the next few then differ dramatically in style. Wondering if a group of old ones may have gotten together to leave these drawings as a tangible record for someone to find at a later date, she imagines a gathering of elders carving the intricate details into the stone.

Maybe Katina discovered these also.

Puzzled, she wonders. *That can't be. How could they have carved these etchings out of the crystal so cleanly?* She shakes her head and resigns herself to the fact that she presently doesn't have enough information to figure it all out. All she's certain of at this point is the approximate age of the crystal tower she's standing in.

These drawings can't be much older than one hundred years, for all of these towers started to grow only about a century ago.

During the six months it took the towers to reach their full size, these caves would have been inaccessible, so the drawings must have been done after that. This thought leaves her somewhat confused, for it means that nearly one hundred years passed from the end of the Before Time to when these pictures were carved into the rocks. After the disaster, only hand tools remained, and now most of their tools are simple, so she can't understand how these etchings could have been carved. Stepping close to one of these engravings, she again runs her hands over it.

It's so smooth. How could anyone carve this cleanly and this deeply into the crystal walls with so little damage, never mind creating this much detail?

Searching her memories for any stories that might give her insight into how the drawings got here, she can't recall any stories of a group of old ones who could have done this.

Who could've done this then? During that time, there was no one else who would even remember out history, let alone re-create these drawings of it.

Turning her full attention to a drawing located at about the midpoint of the series, she notices a familiar image of an old city in flames. The next etching shows people running from the fires, with androids appearing to chase them. As near as she can make out, this particular group of pictures in the collection is showing the destruction and exodus from the cities.

As she moves in closer, she tries to figure out how this individual rendering possibly could have been constructed. Standing this close creates an illusion that makes her envision these etchings as small windows into her past. The ledge at the bottom of each drawing is about as wide as the width of her hand, which reinforces this window-like image in her mind.

They are more like sculptures intricately carved into the rock than pictures.

This fact also puzzles her. They're precise and elaborately carved, and she knows of nothing in her present world that can achieve this effect. Looking closer still, Resha detects dissimilar subtleties in the brightness and color of the renderings.

It also appears that over time, a layer of dust has collected on the sill at the bottom of each drawing. She moves slowly toward the drawing she thinks might depict the beginning of the series, stops in front of it, dipping the fingers of her right hand into the dust on the bottom ledge of the drawing. Holding up a smudged finger to the light coming from her pouch, she can see that the layer of dust on this fingertip completely obscures the bright klain hue of her skin. Next she moves toward a more brightly colored drawing near the end of the series and uses her left hand to dip into the dust on the bottom of that ledge. Holding up both hands to the light side by side, her suspicions are confirmed. She realizes while peering at her hands that there's a slight klain cast visible on the fingers of her left hand but not her right.

This additional discovery makes her wonder. *There is clearly less dust or color on my left hand than my right. This may mean that there is more dust on the bottom of the first drawing than the last. If this dust has collected over time, the heavier deposit may indicate that these drawings were done many years apart from one another.*

Something inside of Resha is still distracting her—a vacant gnawing in her stomach, is telling her she's hungry. Since she's still deep in the cave, with little to remind her of the outside world, it's possible she's easily lost track of time.

My stomach's so noisy that I know I've missed at least one meal today, possibly even two. Turning toward the entrance of the cave, she can still see some light filtering in. *Probably just one.*

Trusting her stomach's guidance, she decides it's time to head back to the village for something to eat. After snuffing out the remaining torches, she picks up her pack and heads toward the cave's exit.

In a few minutes, she's leaving the darkened cave behind and walking into the sunlight filtering in through the crystal. Its warmth beckons her. Resha pauses near the entrance of the cave to places the two torches in her belt on the ground and opens her pack. Quickly transferring the contents of her glowing pocket into the pack, it's now filled almost to the brim with her new friends. Resha then imagines that she can hear the creatures quietly squealing with excitement, anticipating a trip away from the only home they have ever known. She practically feels their enthusiasm spread from one flake to the next as she gingerly shovels them into her pack with her bare hands. After finishing, she secures its top, puts her pack over her right shoulder, and finally picks up the two torches at her feet before heading outside.

Wanting to get home as quickly as possible, she chooses the new wider way out of the thicket. For a long while, this path parallels her original way in, yet it seems it has never been used before. She's surprised that for most of the trek, she is able to walk out standing upright. By following this path out, she's only ended up crawling under the brush on her belly through three short passageways. Thinking as she crawls into the last narrow passage, leading into the desert. *This new path out was a wise choice.*

All during her trek in, she dreaded finding her way back out, but by taking this new path the journey out was much easier than she imagined. Emerging from the undergrowth just as the first sun dips below the horizon, she rips off a small piece of her torn rainbow stained sleeve to mark this path for future use and then gets to her feet, stepping back to look at the opening so that she'll remember it. From this vantage point, it looks like a blind tunnel that leads nowhere. *No wonder the rabbit chose the other way.* It's almost sunsset so she leaves hurrying on her way.

Heading back to her village, she decides that if she wants to keep the secret of the cave to herself for now, she will need to hide her pack along with the torches on the outskirts of her village somewhere during her travels home.

'Pretty little creatures illuminate
our clouded, dusty past.'

13

RESHA'S DINNER INTERROGATION

The sky's turning a pale, dusky indigo as Resha walks into her village. She's tired and famished after missing the midday meal, and all the way home her stomach has been letting her know it.

Getting back to the village late seems to be becoming a habit of mine.

Her stomach guiding her directly to food, she hesitates and first stops at her hut to change her shirt and clean off some of the dirt.. When she'd ready before leaving she hesitates questioning if she should just skip the meal and go directly to bed. Yet, she knows that if she doesn't eat, she won't sleep well. Hoping against all odds that after eating, she won' t be detained from retreating directly home to bed by having to do the clean up, she sighs leaving her hut heading towards the dinning hall.

Entering Resha realizes just how exhausted and starving she is, but she's in no mood for anything except to be cozily seduced by the rich, earthy aroma of their nightly meal. As she approaches the food line, the scent of imitation root vegetables and synthetic dried meats captures her attention and senses. Resha's so hungry that the angry beast temporarily residing in her belly demands her full attention and causes her to be easily lulled into complacency by the scent of any tasty thing.

Feelings like this are what got me in trouble in the first place. Maybe I shouldn't have chased after that rabbit this morning.

As she gets in line her only desire is to lose herself in the inviting smells of their meager, evening meal. The smell of food greets her almost making her forget how tired she is and she finally comes to her senses and looks around to find the place is still half full. At that moment, her most nagging awareness is that she's dead tired after today's antics, and all she's craving is a hot meal and the comfort of her bed.

The idea of my chores holding me hostage is making me cranky.

As she stands in line, waiting for her turn at the pot, the flavors of dinner embrace her nose and caress her palate, literally forcing her to momentarily close her eyes just to breathe in the aromas more deeply.

With eyes closed and lost in the smells, at first, Resha doesn't think her absence this afternoon has been noticed, but she soon discovers differently. Standing there dreaming of her awaited dinner, Resha feels the person behind her in line, Krey, intentionally jostle her.

Silently resisting responding, she moves slightly forward, trying to ignore his presence, but her actions only make him move in closer.

"Resha, come on. Move forward. We're all hungry, you know. By the way, your presence was missed at tea meal." He asks no questions, because that would be considered meddling, but the tenor and timber of his tone demand an answer.

Resha, not wanting to leave the internal sanctuary she has been secretly creating in her mind refuses to react immediately. Standing there for a few moments, she tries to disregard Krey's prodding, which is tying her emotions in knots and driving them deeper inside her. Unfortunately, she's only able to keep silent for a brief while. Krey's impatience fueled by his hunger finally nudges him to move up closer behind her and pester her once again.

I know Krey well, for he has been one of those interested in my animal teachings and has been following me around these past few weeks. Once he learned to be comfortable talking, he caught on very quickly and kept demanding my sole attention, which was starting to annoy me. What I was doing today was my own affair, and I have no wish to share my doings with him or anyone else as of yet. Expecting he might leave her alone if she doesn't face him, she simply says, "I saw a rabbit this morning." Crossing her fingers, and silently praying he will not respond she focus on dinner. She's hoping he'll let the matter go, but not Krey. When his response assaults her ears, she's only mildly surprised.

"A rabbit? I think you spoke of these creatures this past month. Are you sure it was a rabbit?"

Resha avoids turning, still not wanting to directly face him, for she knows that if she does, he'll assume she's inviting a further lengthy discussion and more unwanted inquiries by him.

Since she's simply trying to enjoy the smell of dinner, she pauses a bit before answering. "I'm not fully sure, for it's been a long time since my last sighting of one, but it looked like a rabbit. Who knows? It might've been some other small creature. It disappeared too quickly into the thicket for me to get a really good look at it." She responds this way because she doesn't want to raise his curiosity and invite further inquiry by appearing to be too withholding.

"Too bad! I would have loved to see one up close."

"Earlier, I thought that it might be nice to catch it and that maybe I could've added it to tonight's meal for its unique flavor. That's what made me miss tea meal."

Her half-true reason for missing tea meal is finally out, and now she's hoping he will leave her alone. Despite Resha's attempts to quell the conversation, it is turning into a full-blown discussion and it's the longest uninvited exchange she has had in quite a while.

"Good thing you were unsuccessful. It might've been carrying a disease of some sort."

Dismayed by Krey's ignorance and somewhat irritated at his closed-mindedness, after a moment's pause, she decides to drop the issue. To escape his prodding even though she's famished, she excuses herself and leaves her place in line. Moving farther away from him to break his assumed hold on her she rejoins the line at its end. She'd rather be hungry a little longer than spoil her dinner by getting into an argument with Krey which appears to be his intention.

After what seems like forever, Resha's finally standing in front of the pot. Since she's last, she picks up the ladle and stirs the stew letting its aromas snake around her nose. Her mouth waters as she takes her portion. Its simple smells rise into her nose, soon making her forget Krey and forcing her to surrender to her senses. Now solely driven by the emptiness in her churning stomach, she closes her eyes to shut out her unwanted surroundings as she yields to the rich, earthen aroma rising from the pot. Focusing on the fragrances enticing her, she ponders and observes. *My annoyance at Krey has left me craving more food than usual, but I don't want to appear to be too greedy, so I'll simply take my regular portion. If I'm still hungry after this plate, I can always return to the pot later, after everyone else has had his or her turn.*

After taking her usual portion her plate is by no means full enough for her stomach's liking but not wanting to attract attention Resha, Resha steps back in line and daydreams of this day's adventures. While lingering there, waiting for the next stop for food, she distracts herself by shifting her attention to reflecting on her chores after dinner. Not able to stand her hunger any longer, she picks up a small piece of meat and pops it into her mouth. *Maybe a better plan if I'm still hungry after eating this is to just munch on the leftovers as I clear the tables. That way, I can get out of here sooner.*

Looking down at her plate, she notices a slight curl on the right side of it. *These synthetic wood plates don't stand up very well to moisture. I must remember to store the ruined ones to dry so we can use them for kindling for the fires to cook our meals. There are always a few at each meal that can't be saved. After that, I'll wipe the still-usable, well-worn plates and stack them in preparation for the morning meal.*

Lost in thought and blindly following the line, Resha soon finds herself absentmindedly standing in front of the apancake pile. She's soon torn from her daydream by their scent attacking her nose. *These apancakes are really just flat bread, but since the disaster, they and anything similar are now called apancakes. I wonder how we came up with that name.*

Again noticing the empty feeling in her stomach, she places three on her plate. This is two more than she generally takes, but there's always some of these left over, and since she's now at the end of the line, she knows they will not be missed.

At last, after sitting down on an out of the way bench, she closes her eyes to savor each bite as the warm food quiets the angry monster that has been filling the hollow of her stomach since early afternoon. After satiating this beast, Resha can finally face the fact, that since she missed tea meal and didn't help prepare dinner, she'll have to stay and clean up after she's finished eating. After consuming every morsel of her meal, she takes her plate toward the kitchen.

Resha's the first to arrive in the cleanup room located off the back of the kitchen. Alone at last, she begins hunting through some of the storage closets to see what might be hidden there. She finds a number of dusty glass jars in a back closet and decides they might be useful for building her new torches, so she puts five aside to take to her quarters after she finishes cleaning up.

On my next trip to the bunker, I can get the pack I left on the outskirts of our village and fill some of these jars with my light creatures.

After putting the jars aside, she comes back to the dining area, where those who have finished eating have stacked their empty plates. Bringing two piles to the cleaning area she begins to scrape the few small crumbs sticking to them, and then wipes them down. After picking up the first plate from the stack to wipe, Resha begins to daydream of the cavern. Before she knows it, she's finished cleaning both stacks. *I'll leave the remaining for the others to clean.* Bone weary, she finally heads off to bed.

> *'To assume anything; especially to assume control only makes an ass of u and me.'*

14

NEXT MEETING: THE BEFORE TIME

A short while after sitting down, Resha begins fidgeting, attempting to get comfortable as she settles in for today's tale.

Resha's unusual wriggling immediately captures Swallow's attention. Wanting to say something but not wanting to appear to be rude, Swallow digs her left hand into the warm sand at her side to distract herself, forcibly restraining a chuckle.

"Let's see. Where did I end last time?" Resha says.

"I believe you finished with meeting Katina, the growing of the crystal towers, and the reappearance of the animals." Now feeling somewhat more comfortable, Swallow makes a request. "I wonder if today we could postpone the clouds and skip ahead to the Before Time and what led up to the disaster. That is, of course, if you are ready. If you start there, then maybe later, when I get back to the village, I can again try to scribe—I mean write—that part."

Looking down, Resha once again shifts her position, trying to settle in. An unknown force soon pulls her eyes to look up at Swallow. Noting a haunt of cryptic humor dancing in Swallow's eyes she tries desperately to ignore it for Resha knows that if she stares for too long into Swallows eyes she'll start laughing. In order to avoid this she quickly looks away. While idly trying to regain her composure she again shifts her position.

In response to Resha's last odd fidgeting, Swallow nearly bursts out laughing.

Suddenly realizing the source of Swallow's covert amusement, Resha smiles and says, "I guess my squirming about looks a bit peculiar to you."

Trying desperately to stifle a chuckle, Swallow answers, "Well, I have to admit that you've been shifting about a bit more than usual. Is something bothering you?"

"No, not really. It's just that I sat down wrong when we first got here, and my foot has fallen asleep. I can't seem to wake it, so I've been moving about to try to get more comfortable."

Unsuccessfully smothering another laugh, Swallow responds, "Oh, I'm sorry. This isn't really amusing, but this is the fifth time you've switched positions, and that's very unlike you. I really should explain why this is so funny to me. When you first started all this squirming about, I had to wonder if you might've sat on something. Immediately after that, a fleeting image came to mind of you getting up and an odd little creature crawling out from under you. I can't seem to get that image out of my head, and that's why I'm having such a hard time not laughing."

Trying to shift the mood to the more serious subject at hand, with muffled merriment still flickering in her eyes, Resha shakes her head, feigning annoyance. Then clearing her throat to assume a more somber tone she begins today's portion of her tale. "Swallow, with the research I have completely this last week, I can at least begin the tale of what led up to the end of the Before Time, if that's what you wish. But to be truthful, I have not finished my research, and I didn't bring the books I promised to give you, with me. However, if you don't mind, I can tell you what I have found out so far, and then when I'm done and fully understand what occurred, I'll complete today's tale and bring those books for you.

Swallow nods signaling Resha to begin. She's not quite ready to speak because she's still fighting to maintain her composure.

Resha purposely keeps her gaze away from Swallow's as she explains. "The end of the Before Time was much more complicated than I ever imagined, but in time, I will do my best to understand so that I can explain. Let me see now. Where should I start? Okay." Unable to avoid the temptation Resha delibertly fidgets one more time just to tease Swallow and test her resolve. This almost spoils the serious mood she has been desperately trying to create.

It takes Swallow all the composure she has left not to crack a smile.

Desperately avoiding Swallow's eyes, for she knows eye contact will only throw them both into a fit of laughter, Resha looks down to begin today's tale. "By the end of the twentieth century, which was nicknamed the information age, many of the elite had amassed great fortunes. Soon afterward, those who had collected these vast amounts of power and wealth began to manipulate and control the money markets of their world. Then, by using their emerging technology in new ways, they were able to accumulate even greater wealth. During this introduction Resha has been unable to keep an edge of lightness out of her voice so she lowers her tone to create a more somber mood before she starts again.

"Back then, they justified their greed by saying that they deserved more than others because they provided jobs for the common person. Unfortunately, they didn't justly recognize and reward the worth of the people they considered common. The existing vast inequality between the wealthy and poor grew wider and as the newborn elite took their "rightful" place and they also began to lose touch with what it was like to not have money or power.

"As the middle class began disappearing during the first decade of the next century, the elite's ignorance bred a growing callousness in the upper class toward the plight of the common person. Soon the ever-increasing disparity between rich and poor created an even greater disadvantage for the poorest of the people. This mounting inequity forced those earning the lowest wages to feel that they needed to work harder and longer hours just to obtain the resources needed to survive in their new ultracompetitive world.

"Many of the wage earners in the poorest families had to take on two or three jobs just to get by. Some ultimately were forced to compromise their health and well-being for the sake of their families, and a negative cycle supporting ill health became established. Unacknowledged fear was still driving the changes in their world and the next mistake was that those who now had the wealth and power were reluctant to halt their efforts to accumulate more wealth and power. The elite's ego didn't allow them to acknowlege the damage they were causing by amassing these dispotionate sums of wealth and power. They were so focused on only making money so with their greed out of control they failed to recognize the harm that was occuring. They next used their power to target and undercut the social programs that were in place to help the disadvantage.

"By the midpoint of the twenty-first century, these changes had caused a new extreme classism to emerge. The government, in an effort to create a new balance, tried to institute social changes to support the disappearing middle class and to establish some additional protections for the lower class, but those with wealth blocked these protections, saying that they would cost the government and ultimately them too much money. Unfortunately, the wealthy had become insensitive to the fact that their money provided an unfair advantage for them and their families in obtaining money and power.

"After eroding away most of the social safeguards during the first three decades of the twenty-first century and shifting the tax structure to unfairly benefit only the wealthy during the last century, the elite held too much power in the government, and the good-intentioned changes were twisted and thwarted every step of the way.

"Still, not all of the elite were bewitched by this ever-expanding insatiable need for more and more money or unaware of the unfair advantage their wealth provided. Regrettably, the greedy methods that had already been integrated into society as the new way to conduct business were shifting the existing social structure and causing it to become more unstable. Over the last half century, the financial safeguards in place to protect the common person had been severely eroded away. During this time, those with the most wealth and financial savvy became more isolated because of this new extreme classism.

"In the newly born elite their isolation caused a fresh wound to split open. Since money and power were the elite's main focus, the fear of not being able to maintain their budding status caused them to feel even more insecure. Focusing solely on money undermined the feelings of satisfaction and satiety for many of the newly rich. Now, as they didn't feel safe, their cycle of obtaining more wealth to feel secure was encouraged and strengthened.

"With the disparity between classes widening, the elite focused even harder on developing new ways to obtain more and more wealth, which then isolated them even further. The common people were caught in the frenzy of their fear of not having enough to survive, while the elite were focusing on thriving beyond all expectations. A new selfish, ruthless business model was established by the most successful of the elite. Then they used their money to spread its practice throughout the world. With their survival supposedly at risk, the next generation blindly accepted the latest business model as the primary way of conducting their affairs without question. Upon doing this, they also unknowingly supported and encouraged this new extreme classism. By that time, the frenzy for money had grown to new heights. With the financial security of the world teetering on the edge of a greatly widening abyss, the rich became richer, and it only became more difficult for the poor to survive.

"A handful of the more socially aware elite became concerned about the plight of the poorer people. Those who were aware of the growing disparity regarding wealth comprehended the instability that was developing from this imbalance of power and resources. This precarious instability concerned them, for they understood that the inordinate greediness of their fellow class members couldn't sustain itself long-term. In retaliation, a few of the more concerned elite attempted to right the injustices and balance the scales. Sadly, in the beginning, too many with wealth and power ignored this imbalance or didn't care, and too few tried to help.

"By the dawn of the mid-twenty-first century, as vast fortunes and resources became concentrated into fewer and fewer hands, the problems only worsened. By the end of the fifth decade of the twenty-first century, the elite possessed the majority of the wealth and available resources. A movement to support those without wealth rose, and they called themselves the ninety-nine percent. Unfortunately, this only increased the elite's isolation and fear. Most of the elite failed to recognize or didn't care that these resources were of limited supply, so by 2063, as the wealth of our world was concentrated into fewer and fewer hands, once again, competition began to rise to new heights. Shortly after that, the common people soon realized their battle to gain financial stability was a futile task.

"In addition, technology and robotics began to replace people and many of jobs that people had been doing in the past were lost as technology blossomed. People were being replaced by machines at an astounding rate. In an effort to stave off discontent, some of the lost jobs were then replaced by lower-paying less rewarding jobs. Money became the sole focus of all, and big business eventually took over, running everything.

"As larger, more ruthless businesses began to dominate, jobs were outsourced to minimize companies' expenditures, and many families were unable to support themselves. Ultimately, the poorest of the poor could no longer adequately take care of their families on the meager wages they were being paid, so they refused to even try to compete and became more and more complacent. The social programs that hadn't been done away with by that time were forced to support a growing number of people, as many of this new ever-expanding lower class refused to injure their bodies or compromise their ethics in order to keep up with the increasing and more ruthless competition. With fewer jobs available to the lower class and wages not keeping up with inflation, many people found they had no recourse but to depend on the government for support. This meager governmental support at least enabled the poorest of the poor to survive without being forced to compromise their health and well-being.

"Over the next two decades, the available money being exploited from the masses by these ruthless business practices began drying up. Fewer and fewer of the common people had the money for the commodities that our society deemed necessary for survival at that time. This shortage of money in the masses eventually caused the competition for sheer survival to escalate as the living conditions for the common person only worsened. More and more people were displaced as housing costs rose, and many of the homeless were forced to move to warmer areas where their survival on the streets was at least possible. However, the fever for money and the power it wielded among the elite only continued to grow and heighten.

"Since the egos of the elite had grown with their wealth and their self-worth had been bolstered and artificially supported by their ability to win any competition in acquiring that wealth at all costs, they felt as if they were doing the right thing. This only reinforced their beliefs that their solution to solve society's problem was the only correct path. They had forgotten how to stop and enjoy what they had. The art of being satisfied with having enough was lost to them. Everyone wanted to be top dog. Since the masses had no money to spare, the elite were finally forced to turn their ruthless quest for money upon each other. Fortunately, after that shift took place, at least the ultracompetitive struggle was confined within the ranks of the elite, but this inevitably caused a brutal battle for control among the most powerful. Unfortunately, the common person was still left fighting an unwinnable battle just to maintain their dignity and health while they tried desperately to survive in this ruthless atmosphere.

"Around the year 2075, a schism started developing within the ranks of the privileged. A small faction of the more socially concerned elite recognized that the disparity between classes might eventually erode away their society's freedoms, which would ultimately cause problems for them and the rest of the world. In addition, the complete ruthlessness of their fellow class members disturbed them. A few decided that they had amassed enough wealth and power and tried to withdraw and ignore the competition still escalating around them. Some even started private social programs to give back. After they were successful in their efforts to withdraw from what was then called the rat race, these socially conscious elite attempted to settle down and live their lives in comfort. However, for many, this would turn out to be a fatal mistake.

"They had never learned to live and survive happily with less, as the common people had been forced to do. Since they had nothing else but their brutal competition and this was escalating the cost of living out of control, they began to lose their status, and this was devastating to them. This trend of 'progress' had become a self generating ruthless machine with no concern for ethics or feelings. The pressures on the elite to then maintain their status drove some of these formerly rebellious individuals back into the arms of the dominant mentality of the upper class, but after reentering that mind-set, they only found themselves disillusioned and isolated even from their own class. To make themselves feel better, some began to compare themselves to those less fortunate than they were. Unfortunately, this way of inflating their own self-worth proved to be hollow and only bred more self-contempt. It appeared that basing one's self-esteem solely on obtaining power and wealth had become a trap for many. Still, some of the former elite continued to rebel and refused to ignore the strife mounting in the masses.

"In the last decade of the twenty-first century, a ravenous, unspoken uneasiness festered among the upper class. Those who rebelled in the upper class feared for their society's long-term stability and this small group of dissenters had become their class's social conscience. Unfortunately these few were forced to carry the whole burden of this apprehension buried deep within the upper class. This defiant group of outcast elites foresaw that if things kept heading in the direction they were going, an uprising of the masses would surely be necessary for their society to regain balance. They suspected that any potential uprising would threaten the elite's security and power and possibly cause their downfall but the real tragedy would come in the numbers of human lives lost during the unnecessary fighting that would be needed to regain balance again. Slowly, the unvoiced, menacing fear of not being superior humans wound itself around the hearts of the whole upper class. In order to combat this fear and try to establish a new balance, the government increased the minimum wage, and thus, the cost of living began to escalate once more. Unfortunately the majority of the elite still felt as if their money could protect them from any uprising of the masses.

"Then as humans marched into the next century, an unrecognized, insidious fear infected all of the elite's ranks. As paranoia grew the elite looked for someone to blame and this blame was directed at the elite who had revolted against the fray and labled by their fellow class members as rebels. Those rebels who maintained their positions and still refused to rejoin the competition to obtain more wealth eventually lost their favored status among their peers. Over a short span of time, their society had become so interconnected and enmeshed that there really was no place for them to escape or hide.

"In an attempt to relieve the strain on the masses, alleviate their growing fear, and align support behind a different approach for their society, this small, rebellious elite faction tried to shift their focus to helping the common folk. Yet the most powerful, who still held the majority of influence, money, and, thus, control, would not let this happen.

"By the turn of the next century, those most dominant in the elite, who still supported a ruthless form of ultra competition, started isolating the rebel group by generating rumors that labeled them as sociopaths, psychopaths, or antipatriotic.

"Eventually, a campaign began to round up most of these rebels and detain them, allegedly for questioning. Then, in order to maintain the status quo, the controlling elite passed laws decreeing that the rebellious former elite in their ranks were criminals. After the majority of the rebels were finally in custody, they were systematically slated to be jailed or placed in institutions for the criminally insane.

"When these so-called criminals were safely shut away around the year 2155, a covert campaign was instituted to have their families ostracized or killed, and the most vicious of the elite seized the belongings of the jailed. With the rebel movement then successfully quashed and with no way for it to rise again or for those rebels to return to their former status, those with the greatest authority and wealth again targeted the wealth and power of those less powerful, and the cycle of quest for power within the upper class began again.

"As you can see Swallow this singular goal of the privileged during the era from 2000 to 2200 was to acquire money and sequester as much power and wealth as possible. By 2250 their greed had become a self sustaining ruthless paradigm. Regrettably once more this made life for the common person even more demanding and in order to create some joy in their difficult lives they turned their focus to their children. As the competition became more cut throat and survival became the commons person's only focus they developed and began desperately holding onto the philosophy 'the more the merrier'. More children created more hope, more joy so as people felt their children were their only hope the population again increased.

"This massive manipulation to gain wealth at all costs was started by only a few men's egos partnered with their unchecked ignorant greed and fear. This drive to amass fortunes by using and abusing the new technology developed in the mid-twentieth century, including computers, also enabled this unchecked greed to grow rapidly and to sustain itself.

"To aid this, a new paradigm arose. Since computer technology was providing a living for a vast number of society's peoples it had now become their new god. Accepting this computer/god belief implied it could do no harm. This implict trust gave those who knew how to manipulate the technology a free reign. As widespread manipulation of information and misinformation spread many innocent were exploited. By the year 2000, the masses were already enslaved by this new technology, as new business practices using computers exploded. Since there was no established precedent as to what was ethical, never mind legal in the use of this new technology, there were few established guidelines regarding how not to exploit these tools to make money. With this 'progress', the accepted business practices at that time developed into a free-for-all as prices escalated to support and maintain this technology's importance in the market. At that time, there was no established legal infrastructure governing the ethical use of this expertise, and as its uses exploded, it soon held a monopoly on what people considered the acceptable business practices and how things needed to be done.

"This new way of doing business had far-reaching repercussions and created an unfair advantage for those who knew how to use the power of this technology, as it spread worldwide like wildfire. Large companies or those with ample money who had the means to hire the best and brightest minds in the computer field were able to manipulate this knowledge and use it however they wanted, so they generally faired best. As competition for the best minds in the computer industry escalated, salaries rose beyond people's wildest dreams. The masses were cajoled and convinced that information held the key to everything and was the real basis of worth in the technology boom. So people became willing to pay outrageous sums of money for the intangible commodity of information. What was worth even more was the ability to spread this information and misinformation without conscience.

"Many individual and small businesses couldn't afford the expense of keeping up with the demands of this new way of doing business as computers use exploded and exponentially developed. Eventually, the use of this technology in business became mandatory, and the costs of doing business escalated, driving up the costs of all products and services in society, upward.

"If the smaller businesses weren't able to invest the money needed to keep up with the rapidly changing technology, they ended up being phased out by the ever-increasing competition for more and better or more precise. With the technology expanding faster than most could maintain, many smaller businesses went under, as the costs of maintaining the technology became prohibitive. At one point peoples' worth was almost solely based on how current their technology was and how they used it. As the illusion that this technology was absolutely needed to compete in today's business market became an assumption, larger businesses gained more and more power. Also as the fear this instability had provoked grew in the common people they were easily sold the idea that they needed to be driven by instantaneous information, whether it was reliable or not. During that frenzied time, no amount of money could be considered enough as the idea of having to keep up with each of the latest developments in this technology was driven deeper into the hearts and minds of the common people, whether it directly benefitted them or not.

"During the second decade of the twenty-first century, what followed was no surprise. An immense wave of small and individual businesses that had been helping to keep the cost of doing business in check went under, and inflation started to rise. 'More and better' became the theme of that time period as micromanagement became the 'best' of the business practices.

"The government couldn't keep up with all the changes in this technology and since its tax structure had been undermined by the self interests of the elite, the regulation of this industry was sorely behind the industry itself.

To complicate matters more, during the last half of the twentieth century and all during the twenty-first century, the laws and power structure that had been in place in earlier times to protect the planet and its people from this type of greed had been slowly and, some say, systematically eroded away.

"During the early twenty-first century, the great fortunes the elite had amassed only supercharged their egos more. Soon they felt they were above the law and immune to any and all of the regulations that had been constructed to protect their society's social structures and the planet's environment. In the last fifty years of the twentieth century, the elite had put additional measures in place to restructure the remaining older laws, especially the tax and environmental laws, which they felt were hindering big business and hurting profits.

"By the end of the twentieth century, in the United States, all the laws that controlled the collection of taxes that supported the government had been rewritten to favor the wealthy. With this change and the concentration of wealth into fewer and fewer hands, the United States' tax basis shrank considerably. Much of the monies previously slated to support the country's infrastructure and pay for social reform all but disappeared.

"After those changes were instituted, the government couldn't afford to compete with big business in hiring those who understood and truly knew how to use the new technology, and because of the driving competition for wealth and the antigovernment sentiments popular during that time, few who excelled in the computer field were willing to work for the meager wages the government was able to pay. Unfortunately, even fewer felt that public service was a noble and worthy way to spend their time.

"By 2015, the focus on money had become paramount, and as such, for a period of time, the egos and ruling status of the new elite was left unchallenged. At that point, many of those who had already amassed great fortunes sought out political positions, which only increased the elite's power in constructing and manipulating the laws further. By then only the rich and powerful had the money and connections to seek public offices. Some of the most egocentric of the rich and powerful seeking public offices, thought they had better answers than the existing political structure and sought 'to right' the methods they perceived as errors being made by the government with a new, progressive way of 'doing business'. Unfortunately, the elite didn't understand or care that the government hadn't been set up to be profitable but to make sure the system was supported and worked for the majority of people, not only for the privileged few.

"As more and more of the elite began to take over the political structure, things became increasingly unstable in favor of money and the bottom line. Money also provided the existing politicians with a way to achieve their goals so that even the elite who were not interested in running for political offices were able to wield an inordinate amount of political power in the form of backdoor influence over the established political figures. This change had a profound impact on the existing way laws were made, and eventually the old intent of the laws no longer mattered as they gave way to a new wave of law making.

"By the midpoint of the twenty-first century, the elite had gained an inordinate amount of control over the government from behind the scenes, and they considered any type of constrictive regulation directed at them or big business's profits as just another hurdle to disregard or overcome. They began spouting rhetoric such as 'Most of the existing regulations are unnecessary and harmful to free enterprise' or 'It's easier to be forgiven than to get permission.' As they started to covertly undermined the laws in existence new more severe laws were established to control the negative impacts developing from overriding or disregarding the present laws.

When these new mind-sets spread to the common masses, an underground, unrecognized attitude of 'anything goes' festered, and chaos grew. Since the unfair shift of wealth into fewer and fewer hands had worsened the economic plight of the common person, many desperate souls, fearing for their own families' survival, blindly adopted or believed this rhetoric and joined in supporting changes to undermine regulations and traditions that had been in place for centuries. After the old laws and customs were entirely eroded away, the safeguards in place to protect the common person were completely warped.

"By 2030, pollution was rampant. After 2050, it was discovered that pollution wasn't only taking a toll on the environment and the animals around us but also compromising the health of many humans. The common workers were affected the most, since they were doing physical labor and had the greatest exposure to pollutants.

"Finally, in 2065, in an effort to eliminate all restrictions on big business, the US government, which had been created for and by the people, was officially branded as a hindrance to the worldwide economy and mostly disbanded. Shortly after that, observable chaos erupted as martial law was declared to rid the government of those in power who were still resisting the mounting tsunami of the necessity in accepting any of the new technological changes propose by the 'new elite'. The industry was now in control of regulating itself, which only gave it more of an unfair advantage in the market place. This radical changeover spanned a thirty-five-year period, and during that time, random executions of existing officials who resisted this new mindset became commonplace.

"By the beginning of the twenty-second century, a new android peace-keeping force based on the roots of this technology, had been established worldwide to curb the fighting and unrest. Since these androids were impervious to almost all firearms developed before that time, the elite thought it wise to completely disarm the people, supposedly for their own safety.

"From 2104 to 2109, a mass effort was established to confiscate and destroy all personal weapons. Following that five-year period, laws were then instituted to make the possession of any firearm or weapon a crime punishable by immediate execution without the privilege of a hearing, never mind a trial. The skirmishes regarding the disarming of the common people lasted for the rest of that century.

"In the twenty-third century, the spreading strife in the common people's lives caused unrest, and whispers of a revolution finally surfaced. By 2210, this talk of revolution gnawed at the nerves of even the most callous and protected elite and created an insidious, overwhelming fear in most with wealth. To counteract this, upper society's new goal became to establish additional, allegedly better laws to exert more-restrictive controls over the masses once more.

"Ultimately, these new restrictions aimed at supposedly controlling the common person only enabled those in power to keep most of the wealth they had amassed to themselves. By then, the legal structure of their world had been compromised to such a degree that the supposedly better laws proposed by the wealthy slipped into place with little resistance. By the year 2213, things had gotten so bad that anyone who fought this established elitism was secretly killed or imprisoned, and ignorance and the absence of empathy in the elites' behavior were driving the health of the world economy to the brink of devastation.

"As in the previous centuries, the last decade of the twenty-first century was a time of rapid change. The unconscious fear that had been festering in the common people for their safety and survival became infectious and slowly spread to the ranks of the upper class. That infection didn't stop once it entered the ranks of the elite, and as I said before, once it reached a certain momentum, it spread like wildfire. To escape this growing dread and to minimize their own contact with pollution and overpopulation, most of the elite sequestered themselves into the most sparsely populated areas, constructing elaborate strongholds for themselves and their loved ones as far away from the people and pollution as possible. Many of those who had already escaped the cities because they felt unsafe relocated to several chains of large estates in the most remote areas of the world.

"In the cities, the few elite who remained developed and retreated to underground strongholds for their safety. These strongholds were located off the old abandoned subway tunnels that had been sealed off during the mid-twenty-first century. Back then, the new regime had deemed it no longer cost effective or necessary to provide public transportation for the masses. City life had become the norm almost half a century before because it provided the most conveniences for the escalating population, but as the people's numbers increased, for most those conveniences became too costly, so over several decades these conveniences also were slowly eroded away.

"This eradication of public transportation was only one of the lost services justified by those in charge at that time. 'The Controllers' soon became the adopted nickname of those elite as they conveniently assumed that all the common people's needs were available at the touch of their fingertips online and that they didn't need to go outside or travel around. Back then, most people in the cities became prisoners in their own neighborhoods, if not their own homes.

"After public transportation's demise, the elite seized the old subterranean system of tunnels for their own use and blocked all access to this underground network. Following that, they sealed all the above-ground entrances and constructed elaborate dens, thus creating a safe harbor only for themselves. Over time these dens were burrowed out beneath the old subway lines and reinforced like secret citadels under most of the larger cities.

"At the turn of the twenty-second century, with most of the privileged having been safely sequestered in below-ground fortresses or remote strongholds for a decade or two, the privileged and their families were buffered as much as possible from the negative impacts of their society's two most pressing problems: pollution and overcrowding. Since these things now had little effect on them or those they loved, the elite grew more insensitive and complacent to the common person's needs. During this time, they became even more unsympathetic to the plight of the common person, and finally, the problems that the rich's greed had fostered were no longer their problems and were only the plight of the commoners.

"Around 2175, to justify their indifferent behavior toward all others, the elite embraced the belief that humans were too abundant on their world and began searching for new ways to control population and isolate themselves from the masses.

"Shortly after completion of the elite's strongholds in the cities, rumors started cropping up and circulating among the masses about secret underground fortresses. However, the privileged had been crafty, for no one but the engineers and workers who had constructed these strongholds knew of their whereabouts, proposed uses, or designs.

"By this time, the elite's main workforce consisted only of androids, so they had little worry that the common person could confirm these rumors or gain access to their strongholds. At that time, a massive campaign to discredit the rumors was started. The city elite fought to hide and prevent the discovery of their underground fortresses at all costs. As a safeguard, upon completion of each fortress, the owner would dismantle or destroy all the androids that had been involved in the project. They had deluded themselves into believing that this would prevent their secrets from being discovered.

"The growing threats in the cities forced the elite there to reinforce and prepare to defend their underground fortresses somewhat earlier than their counterparts in the country found it necessary to do. It also forced them to institute more safeguards and more-rigorous defenses in response to the escalating threats. Thus, this group built and stockpiled an extensive series of androids to defend their fortresses. If a fight came, they would be prepared to win at all costs. They still didn't realize that their winning at all cost only meant that their world would eventually have to shoulder greater devastating losses in the future.

"Soon afterward, the elite who had set their strongholds in the remote, formally uninhabitable countryside also felt the need to reinforce and set up defenses for their estates. Since inaccessible areas were becoming more and more limited over time, the elite estates expanded and grouped together. Tight elite communities were formed as others in their ranks sequestered neighboring lands and established their own estates adjoining those already created. They feared that in the event of a mass uprising, these collections of estates would also need an impenetrable defense system.

"The first course of action was to establish detection fields at a one-hundred-and-fifty-mile radius surrounding the perimeter of each community of country fortresses. Upon completing final construction of their facilities, the elite converted their existing android workforces into soldiers, which they stockpiled in a semi-inactive state just inside the perimeter of their compounds. If any detection field was triggered, two androids were automatically activated to determine if the threat warranted further action. Once these scouts finished assessing the level of threat, the rest of their stockpiled army could be activated at a moment's notice.

After all the elite had isolated and protected themselves as best as they could, they grew more indifferent to the increasing problems of the outside world. When uncontrolled pollution started showing up in the water supplies after 2180, the upper class directed their scientists to develop new technology to filter water. However, this technology was too expensive and wasn't practical for common use, so they kept its knowledge for the use of their ranks only.

"Shortly after I was born, the flourishing pollution that had seeped into the groundwater over the past century, along with the drugs that had been intentionally added to our drinking water for decades to control our behavior and reproduction rate, took its final toll on many of the workers and their families, mostly those living in the cities.

"As a child, I personally witnessed many people in my city falling prey to a mysterious illness, as over a relatively few years, tens of thousands fell sick and died. The prevailing suspicion at that time was that the majority had perished from the man-made effects of the chemicals that then permeated our water. The medical professionals of that time tried every known drug to combat these illnesses, but nothing curbed the spreading outbreak. The drugs only seemed to exacerbate the problems related to the toxins, acting like additional polluting chemicals in the bloodstreams of the victims and causing many to die more quickly.

"I can remember speeches by those in power when I was a girl. They berated the workers for not being strong enough and for 'succumbing' to the effects of this man-made pollution. Once again, the victims were blamed, as if it was their fault that they were not strong enough to resist the effects of these mostly man-made toxins introduced into the environment, allegedly to help the people.

"The widespread mind-set of the elite then became 'It's their own fault for not being fit enough to be able to withstand the pollution or smart enough to avoid the fate this pollution inflicted on them.' The elite, who had been protected from many of the pollutants because of their status or wealth, assumed that the strongest would survive, multiply, and reproduce. Secretly, of course, in their opinion, this meant their ranks and their loved ones only.

"Over the centuries, they had been too busy making more money and increasing their wealth to be concerned about the masses. Their prevailing attitude was that any of the common people in the workforce who managed to survive and reproduce would provide them with an even hardier workforce, if they were ever needed.

"During my childhood, social Darwinism, at its best or worst, became the new creed. This twisted interpretation of natural selection was supported and reinforced by those in power, because they now had androids, which were considered a superior workforce anyway. Thinking they finally didn't need the common person any longer only reinforce and justified their belief in this new ruthless philosophy of 'Only the strong survive.' Of course, by 'strong,' they meant only the elite."

Resha pauses suddenly, realizing that her stomach is distracting her. "I think this may be a good place to stop. I need something to drink. Are you hungry?"

Swallow smiles. Getting to know this woman has been a treasure for her. "Yes. That was a pretty depressing part of the story, and I think a break is in order. Besides, I'm hungry, and it would be great to eat."

*'Be careful, for greed may bite back and
devour all in its path, including you.'*

15

THE BEFORE TIME (CONTINUED)

After eating, Resha briefly stands up and closes her eyes, stretching while focusing on the warm, satisfied sensation in her stomach. After this brief interlude, she reseats herself and leans against their tree, yawning. While looking at Swallow she leans back on their tree and nuzzles her back up against the rough bark of her second-favorite companion, silently thanking it for providing the welcome shade, before she continues the day's tale. "I'm ready to start in if you are."

Swallow, taking her customary position across from Resha and nearly worn out by the morning's tale, lies down in the dirt, closing her eyes to better imagine Resha's coming tale and thinks. *Hopefully this afternoon's tale will be a bit more uplifting.*

"Okay, where did I leave off? Oh, that's right. I wanted to talk a bit about the effects of the pollution and overcrowding at the turn of the twenty-second century.

Swallow sighs as she ponders. *Oh no not again.*

Resha sensing Swallow's dismay says. "I know it's depressing but you asked for it. Just let me finish this part and then we'll be done with it. OK"

"As I began saying this morning, the effects of overcrowding and rampant pollution were driving more and more people to doctors' offices. There were so many people requiring care back then that the cost of the standard government-provided medical services had been escalating out of control for some time.

"Over the last half century, those who had been sick and whose care had been paid for by their employers or the government's health care system, which had been previously subsidized by taxes, had grown out of control. Meanwhile, the numbers of people still getting sick and needing care exploded. To complicate matters, hand and hand with the cutbacks to the workforce came, the enviable reduction in employees' wages. The elite couldn't justify paying people top dollar when they had a much more efficient workforce in the form of androids at their disposal, free of charge. Along with the decrease in wages and spending, fewer and fewer people were paying taxes, and those few paying taxes were paying a smaller amount, so the services that had been previously paid by the government continued to suffer.

"Roads and other services that had, in the past centuries, been subsidized by the federal government became the responsibilities of the states and eventually filtered down to the cities and towns. At first, the cities had some monies for repairs, but the smaller municipalities didn't, so people were forced to move into the nearby cities to survive. As the population expanded, so did the cities, until the majority of people dwelled in these ever-expanding cities. As the federal subsidies began to worsen, the states' portions dwindled. The first victims of the inevitable cuts were the social services. All suffered but the elite, as the whole infrastructure that had been in place for centuries to protect all people crumbled.

"As I said earlier, since big business was now the norm and since, under its control over the past three centuries, new laws had been instituted requiring big business and the elite to pay little or no taxes, the tax basis that the government had depended upon to help pay for social programs, including health care, had been painfully eroded away.

"From early on in the twenty-first century, the few governmental subsidies still intact had been directed toward medical care. With government support paying for it, the medical industry had also developed into a big business. Over centuries, as medicine evolved into a large conglomerate, care and concern for the patient slowly eroded away, and was replaced by increasing concern for the bottom line. For the first time in history, a new callousness toward human life developed because of the rapid growth in population which had joined forces with the focus on money as the top concern in most industries. Society was becoming colder toward the concerns of human life, and the poorest of the people suffered the most.

"In the medical industry, this was a deadly combination, as the focus on making money replaced the desire to provide the best care. Then with the rise in population, competition heightened, and with this shift in focus came a shift to preventing disease instead of treating disease. However, much of the dis-ease now developing wasn't purely physical but stemmed from the fact that overcrowding carried with it its own problems that caused a new type of malady.

"Unfortunately, this fact was minimized by the predominant medicine at that time, and since the new spirituality was the spirituality of money, the need to treat this new disease in a manner other than physically went unrecognized for a long time. With physical medicine still being the focus and holding most of the power in the medical industry, new physical maladies were being developed to explain symptoms that were not physical at all. Ultimately turning a blind eye to the real problems of society and solely focusing on the physical, the medical industry then developed prescreening for physical problems.

"Over the next few decades, with the discovery of many 'supposedly' newly developing physical diseases to explain the new symptoms being displayed in the masses, the underlying problems that were the real cause for this dis-ease remained hidden. Since all disease was considered to be, by and large, solely caused by physical ailments, physical prescreening for diseases became the new norm. During that time, the number of newly discovered diseases blossomed, and as they were accepted and became established, their acceptance as diseases supported their existence.

In addition, the new technology was developing more complex ways to detect the underlying causes for these newly invented physical maladies by using new high tech machines to detect them. Since these high tech machines were being developed and supplied by the elite of course they only confirmed the diseases existence.

"Since up until that time the government had been subsidizing the care of the people, there was even less pressure to question the basic beliefs of the status quo that all diseases were exclusively caused by underlying physical problems. The government provided health care for all meant that the taxes of the people covered the bulk of the costs of all these newly discovered illness no matter how expensive the machines to detect them or testing became. With the government providing plenty of money to go around it was easy to ignore any discrepancies or faults in these basic premises that had allowed this status quo to follow their faulty assumptions in the first place. However now, with the government tax structure being undermined by the new tax laws, which allowed the elite to keep more and more of the money they earned for themselves, the government's coffers were slowly drying up. At the beginning of the twenty-second century, in response to a lack of funding by the federal administration and due to the supposed budget constraints of the medical multinational corporations, all preventative health measures were in time slated to be done away with.

"To compound the government's fiscal problems, over the last few decades of the twenty-first century, with more and more people's jobs being replaced by androids, the number of common folks paying taxes had dwindled away to almost nothing and there was a lack of money in the hands of the populace. With jobs being scarce and the average person having little to occupy his or her time for the last twenty years, the birth rate had been escalating out of control. There were many reasons the birth rate was on the rise but one of the underlying reasons no one wanted to admit to, was the peoples' fear for their own survival. With no hope of a comfortable life of their own many parents turned to their children to provide that hope. So they seized what little happiness they could from the joy and innocence of their babies.

"Since the government could no longer afford the ever-swelling costs that the medical corporations deemed necessary for adequate care, to save money, the governmental insurance programs were forced to cut the number of medical services they were covering. Given that by 2098, the human workforce was methodically being eroded away and many had little or no money after providing for their basic needs, the responsibility for the cost of medical care was steadily and gradually being shifted back onto the shoulders of medical big business, where because of the greediness of the profession in the past, it probably belonged.

"However, it was soon recognized by the business leaders in the medical field that these additional expenditures, if left unchecked, would eventually overwhelm the multinational medical corporations' budgets, so to prepare for this, maintain the status quo and to maximize their profits, those in charge of the medical facilities proposed a primary comprehensive measure to curb costs. Since the doctors were supposedly taking care of the people, they justified this cost-cutting measure by using the defense of an age old philosophy, 'survival of the fittest'. Recognizing that they were indeed the fittest they adopted this tenant in secret and instituted it carefully to avoid a revolution. Shortly after that, chaos erupted in the board room when some of these measures were proposed to the full board of directors who at that time included some well intentioned doctors. In order to remedy this problem and finally reach a consensus that would enable the board to expedite the urgent care that was 'needed', a few top board members arranged to meet behind closed doors. The outcome of this meeting determined that over time, all medical prescreening tests would eventually need to be eliminated.

"Because of its increasing costs and what the board considered a slim profit margin, prebirth screenings were targeted as the first to be eliminated. The elite knew that if they could do away with this particular prescreening, a test that had been widely used since it was established almost a century and a half earlier and one the people deemed most needed, elimination of the other prescreening tests would be easy. Besides simply because of the exponentially increasing population, this particular test had become the most costly due to the escalating expenditures of regularly improving the testing and the augmented demand. At that time, because of the inflated number of births, the prebirth screening budget of the medical conglomerate had climbed to new heights. With the government providing the money to pay for these services, the medical conglomerate had been able to amass a tidy profit so the cost of the test did not concern them, but now, with that governmental financial backing starting to wane, those profits started disappearing.

"In the long run, when the government was no longer able to pay for any medical services and their funding to the medical conglomerate was cut off, completely, medical big business would eventually be forced to pick up the slack, and the medical community's bottom line would be eroded away. Because of these projected fiscal problems, the elite in charge of the medical conglomerate decided that many tests that had been used and deemed necessary for scores of years were now found to be unnecessary.

"This made me wonder if medical big business had known all along what had been really going on and was only concerned about their profits."

"By 2102, those in charge swiftly axed prebirth screenings from their budget. In addition, something was discovered but kept from the masses. The scientists working under the control of the upper class recognized, based on a final comprehensive review of the results from previous prebirth screenings, that the widespread pollution was having devastating effects on the health of the people, particularly newly conceived fetuses.

"In 2105, a few scientists secretly speculated that one of the reasons prebirth screenings were the first to be targeted for elimination was to squelch faint rumors that this prescreening was detecting something wrong with many of the unborn infants.

"After medical big business got wind of these scientists' speculations, one by one, these scientists were singled out and ordered to keep their mouths shut. For some reason, the elite in charge at that time thought that to avoid widespread unrest, the knowledge regarding the effects of pollution needed to be kept hidden. If any of these scientists refused to comply with the first warning to stop talking about this problem, extreme measures were taken as many were jailed, and some disappeared.

"To complicate matters, since the human workforce was being replaced by an electronic one, few humans still were employed. This reduction in jobs meant less and less money was being contributed by individuals or their former employers for their related health care coverage. In addition to this loss, over a short span of time, large sums of money were being reallocated from the Medical Conglomerate's budgets to produce a new robotic workforce of their own. A funny aside here is that, because health care employed the most human workers it was leading the way. With more people demanding care and less money available, the expense of good, quality health care started to rise and soon became prohibitive for most.

"Unfortunately, the common people had gotten used to having their health care paid for, and because of this few had dreamed or prepared for having to assume the costs of their own care. Now with the cost of basic care rising again many were forced to go without adequate care.

"As a result of this, during the last few decades, health care costs rose out of control, as the quality of care suffered. Here again, the masses fear for their health and safety had become a self fulfilling prophecy. Even the medical conglomerate couldn't escape this fear, so they began instituting cost-saving measures in order to cut costs to protect themselves and their profits. By 2120, the head of the medical industry had decided that every possible tactic should be used to protect the health care industry's profits, and no form of care was protected from the looming future cuts deemed necessary.

"By January of 2122, the medical corporation had streamlined health care as much as they thought possible, but it was still not curbing enough of the rising costs to prevent them from eating into their profits. Those in charge then decided that additional measures were needed. In order to do that they then proposed that to reduce costs further, they needed to eliminate most of the human support staff working with the doctors. This final cost-cutting measure was swiftly implemented, even though the medical conglomerate had been one of the largest employers of people throughout the last century.

"Without even questioning the idea, those in charge accepted the belief that an android workforce would be more competent and efficient than humans. Then to justify replacing the supporting medical staff with androids they blamed the lack of quality healthcare on their own human workforce. Of course, the initial outlay to fund this workforce changeover was astronomical, but this staffing change allowed those in control to be able to pocket more and more of the profits over the long term. No one spoke of the fact that the elite were also monetarily benefiting from the production of these new android workers. I'm sure it was never considered that this provided another sustainable source of income for those in charge. Of course, when this plan was finally presented to the heads of the board of directors it was unanimously approved and carried out without hesitation.

"A secondary benefit after this change was implemented was that those in control of health care now had a mute, uncomplaining workforce of androids without consciences providing health care and never questioning the board's judgment or orders. However, most people didn't realize that the ultimate underlying reason for this upgrade to the androids workforce was to support the elite's developing android technology, which they had been working with and holding the market share and patents on for some time.

"Along with replacing the human staff, supposedly to update health care, many supplementary medical tests were again discontinued or eradicated. To appease the masses, the elite arranged to replace some of the old standard testing with new, more efficient, modern types of testing, or so they said. This new testing required the use of the elite's newest godsends: automated technology and advanced robotics.

"With this change all the proposed replacement tests were computerized, so they could be performed at a fraction of the time and cost of the older tests. Unfortunately, this new testing wasn't as rigorously scrutinized as the previous testing, because the changeover to these new tests had been rushed before their results were confirmed and the bugs were completely worked out. These two facts, plus the new android workforce, which had no previous experience and had been preprogrammed to accept the new testing without question, were the medical corporations' fatal mistakes. There were now no experienced human workers to make sure these tests truly reflected what was wrong with the patients. And so once again, the bottom line was the determining factor in the quality of health care provided by the medical conglomerate.

"After eighty percent of the human support staff in the medical field was replaced with the android workforce, the resulting added costs of upgrading the workforce to androids temporarily inflated the overhead costs of health care further. Expectedly, because of these initial increased costs, the quality of the medical care suffered once more, as the monetary outlay of upgrading the whole health care system into solely using the elites' robotics was deemed the first priority. This change also meant that humans, except for the doctors and the twenty percent of specialized caregivers, were no longer being paid and receiving an economic return from the growth of this industry.

"Over the next year, as the population grew, more and more people were falling ill 'supposedly' due to exposure to rampant pollution and poor nutrition. In response the android staff was stretched thin, and the standard of care deteriorated more rapidly.

Eventually, the people began demanding better care. To keep up with these demands, more androids were brought in, and during this changeover, the remaining twenty percent of specialized human caregivers, who had been promised long-term job security, were also laid off and replaced by androids. Predictably, because of the broken promises, many who lost their jobs protested. The months dragged on, and with more and more people out of work, with nothing to occupy their time, large masses of striking employees, ex-workers, and the homeless began to gather outside many of the large medical facilities. With tempers rising and the size of the crowds increasing, the protesters ended up blocking access to these facilities. Inevitably, over several months' time, riots broke out as more and more patients were denied care because the strikers were jamming the entrances, and patients were afraid to seek help.

"When law enforcement, which had undergone a similar change into using an android workforce a few years earlier, was finally called in, a bloodbath ensued, and a widespread slaughter began.

"Immediately after the skirmishes died down, the new android rescue and cleaning forces were called in to attend to the mass of dead and dying bodies surrounding the medical facilities. They needed to remove the bodies and clean up and disinfect the areas as soon as possible so that the patients who hadn't had access to the facilities during the riots and needed care could be attended to.

"Without a touch of human compassion, the bodies were taken to a collection center, sifted through to separate out the dead, identified, and processed for immediate cremation. The mass cremations were completed within a week. Since this was a new task for the androids and they were not properly programmed or trained some unforeseen problems arose. Also they were hurrying to complete this task because all the dead bodies were considered a health risk so they were not as careful as they could have been and some who were not quite dead also met a fiery end. By the time the crematory fires were cooling, the medical facilities were operating in full swing again and were already inundated with patients since many had been denied access to care during the riots. But because the ex- healthcare workers no longer had health care coverage, many of these maimed and dying ex-workers of the medical conglomerate who had survived the riots and escaped the mass cremations, were secreted away in a storage warehouse waiting for any relative to come claim them. Those former ex-healthcare workers ended up becoming the ironic victims of their former employers because they were now their past employers' last priority.

"This meant that the medical corporations were still not able to increase their profits to where they believed they should be. So in the year 2136, to combat rising costs once again and to delay addressing the underlying problems causing the people to fall ill, many types of the newly instituted automated testing were again eliminated or replaced. By 2162, the health care industry available for the use of common people had been decimated, and quality health care was only available if a person had the money to pay for it or had the privileged status of the elite. Of course, the elite, their families, and those bearing the children of the elite got whatever they needed, no matter how trivial or expensive.

"Up until 2125, the cost-cutting measures of care only aided in hiding the mounting problem of birth defects. Since the elite were in control and their offspring weren't affected, these mutations were of little concern to them. Besides, their world's increasing population had become the main problem decades earlier, so by then, the death of a few commoners' infants meant nothing to them. The privileged only cared about their families and the costs of the production of goods. Survival of big business and profits were still their main concerns. Therefore, since this problem wasn't widely recognized, the number of supposedly stillborn children grew unchecked over the next five years.

"In the spring of 2130, the hidden secret of the extent of the birth defects in the masses' unborn infants was discovered by an innocent records clerk. Unfortunately, the problem was already out of hand. At that time, this clerk, thinking that the problem had simply been overlooked innocently, reported this error to the elites in charge. Those in charge determined that for things to proceed in a systematic manner, the growing problem of these previously discovered mutations needed to be concealed for as long as possible, and with this the clerk needed to be eliminated.

"In an attempt to squelch the spread of the knowledge and cover-up of the escalating number of infant deformities, home births soon became outlawed. By 2132, in an attempt to smother any rumors at their source, the elite established birthing centers, and it became mandatory for all expecting parents to receive care and give birth at one of these centers.

"To keep the mounting problem of the deformities hidden, the elite directed the androids in charge of the birthing centers to falsify older records to reflect a low incidence of birth defects in the preceding twenty-five years. This also gave the medical conglomerate a valid excuse to justify their latest cost-cutting measure. It was then conveniently deemed with the swipe of a pen that all prebirth screenings were unneeded.

"In the early years, the misshapen children who managed to survive birth were speedily isolated to prevent so-called contamination and then humanely executed. Their bodies were then wrapped to prevent contamination, or so it was said, before they were cremated. Of course, the real reason for the wrapping was to keep them hidden from prying eyes until they could be burned to ash. Those in charge justified these procedures because of health concerns, and since cremation was the accepted practice of disposing of remains at that time, it was easy to hide the evidence of the first few generations of severely deformed living babies. So the massive cover-up that had begun in 2125 and spanned into the next century was again safe for a few more years.

"During those eighty years, the doctors kept the terrible secret of the severity of the birth defects, even from the parents of these children. The deaths of the unseen deformed infants were normally explained away as stillbirths or as the failure of the infants to thrive. Then the remains of the pitiful offspring were swiftly skirted away and easily cremated before their parents could even lay eyes on them.

"So things had moved along without major incident for about sixty years. Then, toward the end of the twenty-second century, a growing number of the children born with these horrible mutations began surviving birth. How to deal with the growing number of surviving deformed infants became the elite's next great concern. Keeping these children alive would be a threat to their secret. Besides, they thought it too costly. Only one viable solution seemed plausible to the elite: the deformed infants all needed to die as quickly and quietly as possible.

"Over the next few years, with the malformed children's survival rate continuing to increase, the remaining human doctors were forced by the elite to kill more and more living babies to keep their abnormalities secret. This brutal new directive forced the doctors to finally open their eyes, as they could no longer ignore the severity of the mutations they were witnessing during birthing. At last, driven by guilt, they reported this to the elite, but the prevailing attitude back then about survival of the fittest was so ingrained in the elite's belief system that at first, the elite only rationalized these reports away and didn't even attempt to bury them.

"By 2190, the problem could no longer be totally ignored or explained away. At that point, a widespread cover-up to hide or minimize the truth by any means became necessary and was instituted, as the problem once more escaped widespread detection.

"Inevitably, in 2195 a few of the doctors finally did some testing and discovered some of the underlying causes for these mutations. This had occurred only after the first extensive horrible human mutations were finally discovered in my parents' generation, almost a century after mandatory chemical birth control had been instated and placed in the drinking water of all the common people. It had been rationalized that up until that point, most of these mutations were naturally occurring and had been fatal, or so the people had been told. By that point in time it was then confirmed that these mutations were being caused, at least in part, by the mandatory prescribed birth control. This discovery, however was suppressed and was kept well hidden for another few years. When this secret was finally discovered around 2198, the formally undisclosed documentation revealed that many of the mutations were directly related to and potentially caused by the birth control that had been added to the water supply to help control the population numerous decades earlier. Up until that time, the common belief of the few people outside of the elite who knew about the infant mutations, mainly the supervising doctors, had been that it was a slowly developing issue directly caused by the overpopulation problem itself.

"Before that disclosure was made, the doctors in control of health care had truly felt they had no responsibility for the cause. In the minds of those working under the elite, overpopulation had always been to blame, and along with this rationalization came the belief that time and Mother Nature would take care of the problem. They had used that justification to explain away all the deaths of any malformed infants in the last eighty or so years. This past blindly accepted attitude by the doctors only enabled the elite to further minimize their responsibility, and it gave them another excuse for not recognizing the ultimate results and cruelty of their greedy past actions. But now the jig was up—or so they thought.

"The knowledge the treating physicians had discovered about the deformities became the elite's next major concern, and the potential threat of these doctors could no longer be overlooked. Those elite in control speculated that the information about the growing number of deformities was creating too much conflict among their staff of human physicians, and thus, these doctors were a danger to the elite's control and power. Continuing to stifle this knowledge would be the elite's next challenge to conquer.

"As the problem escalated out of control around the turn of the twenty-third century, the human doctors who recognized this problem and were increasingly bringing it to the attention of the elite, oddly, started meeting with mysterious deaths. Afterwards, they were mourned and then publicly honored for their noble contributions to the medical field that had employed them. The information that had caused their deaths was again buried and ignored, but by that time, the problem could no longer be totally concealed, and rumors began to fester.

"It was then 2204, and over the next five years, in order to provide more efficient care, new doctor androids were developed. After the first series of tests was completed on the prototypes—they allegedly exceeded all expectations, and of course—they were slated for mass production. These prototypes' first trial assignment was to immediately take charge of overseeing and attending to all births in the prebirthing centers. Being threatened with replacement the human doctors in these positions began causing a ruckus, but their disturbance didn't curtail the elite's plan to move ahead. Despite this, the elite in charge replaced all human doctors in control of the prebirthing centers with guillotine-like precision.

"In the next five months, the few doctors who had begun to speak out publicly against their android replacements simply vanished, and a number of other physicians and their families were threatened. With ill will between the physicians and the elite festering, the elite were becoming more and more suspicious of the human doctors and concerned they might leak critical, damning information to the public. In order to allay their fears, the elite in charge began secretly killing off the human physicians who demanded that the sacrificing of these poor mutilated infants stop.

"After being warned several times to keep their mouths shut, the doctors who refused to stop causing trouble disappeared or supposedly left the county. A few of these doctors had accidents, and they and their families were ultimately discovered dead in the wreckage of their fancy cars or private planes. Some also committed suicide, and the news stories about their deaths publicly stated that those found dead had cracked under the strain of being replaced and had taken their own lives.

"Rumors were intentionally spread about the others who disappeared. The most common of these rumors was that they had supposedly transferred out of the country in order to work elsewhere. The elite figured that after the androids were securely in place, the eradication of any other doctors who resisted would barely be noticed.

"Then they had android doctors immediately take over for the surrounding medical staff. The few human doctors who couldn't be bribed or convinced to retire in silence also met untimely ends. The elite in charge felt justified in what they were doing, because with overpopulation, human life had become nearly worthless, and preventing a leak of vital information had become the elite's only concern.

"However, one major problem still remained unresolved, though: the elites in charge had assumed that they had the total support of the upper class, so they figured it would be easy to accomplish replacing the human doctors. After all, by this time, didn't humankind believe that androids were better at any job than their human counterparts anyway? However, a small number of the elites in charge were still doctors themselves, and those in the medical profession held as much power as any other faction of the upper class. The proposal to replace all human doctors, including the elite doctors, with androids concerned the upper-echelon doctors. They felt that the substitution of androids was too threatening, and they resisted this substitution by publicly questioning if the quality of care might suffer.

"As a result, these elite doctors began to question the supremacy of the elite in charge, particularly with regard to these elite doctors being replaced. Some also began to question where all this would stop, as the ultimate control of the medical profession seemed to be being placed in fewer and fewer human hands.

"In order to prevent an insurrection of the elite doctors, the immediate planned android replacement of all doctors had to be slowed down. This gave the elites in charge time to deal with the dissenting elite doctors in whatever way they deemed necessary to maintain their silence and not attract too much attention. They determined that the substitution of the doctors had to be done more gradually in order to keep peace. When the replacement was finally complete, it had taken a little over seven years to swap out all the human physicians around the world with machines and had cost many of the human doctors concerned and their families their lives.

"Over that seven-year period, the cost in resources and lives of keeping the severe infant deformities a secret began to affect the elite's bottom line, as they had known it would. At last, they were forced to deal with something they couldn't ignore: the loss of their money. They were facing the devastation their greed had created, and they couldn't disregard the consequences any longer, as their past decisions had started to eat away at their own profits.

"In retrospect, I see that they were able to keep their secret for so long simply because things were changing so fast and because by 2167, most births were performed by cesarean section. The C-sections were deemed necessary mainly because by that time, the deformities of many newborn infants made natural childbirth almost impossible. With the rising number of deformities, one of the new changes instituted in the next few years required all expectant mothers, whether they were having surgery or not, to be heavily sedated before giving birth. This modification made it easier to hide the deformities of the newborns from their mothers, because they were knocked out during the delivery of their babies. Up until that time, the common people had always trusted those providing their medical care, so there was no reason to question or resist these new changes.

"However, by 2206, the elite were in complete control of the androids in charge of all the medical facilities. This fact further decimated human health care, and once more, the established procedures were altered. When, in order to streamline the birthing process and save money, the elite mandated that all mothers needed to be sedated and all births were to be done by C-section, there was almost no one left to resist so the change was barely noticed. The elite rationalized that by using a surgical procedure instead of attempting natural birth, there would be little chance of any information of the increasing number of infant deformities leaking to the public. They rationalized this switch by saying that C-sections were more cost effective because they took less time and were safer for the mothers. At that time, there was no reason to resist these new changes, so these mandates were easily authorized and put into practice by the newly instituted android medical staff.

"A century had passed with little change in attitude, and very few questioned the new, efficient medical machine. Then, near the end of the twenty-second century, when the people began to develop immunity to the widespread chemical birth control that had been secretly added to the water supplies for scores of decades, pregnancy became the new disease as the birthrates exploded. After they lost this final control over conception, overpopulation became society's greatest recognized challenge. In 2194, with the number of pregnancies escalating exponentially out of control, the elite fashioned a new secret doctrine regarding overpopulation: 'Anything that naturally reduces the population is considered a godsend.'

"Adopting the belief that the birth defects were just a natural solution to keep the population in check and not caused by the rampant pollution that they themselves were indirectly or directly responsible for, the elite again rationalized their past greed and mistakes. The new directive to screen out and kill all deformed fetuses became just the next step in the elite's so-called natural checks to control rampant overpopulation. Why waste their precious resources if the fetuses weren't viable in the first place?

"From 2100 to 2200, the android workforce expanded into all phases and sections of society, usurping more and more jobs from their human counterparts. Because of this, there was even less need for the common person to work. With overpopulation still uncontrolled and considered the focal problem, the elite had little concern for the common people or their offspring. After all, there were still plenty of workers who could easily take their places in the future if they were ever needed, which by that time, the elite considered doubtful.

"The androids took over all factions of the workforce in all industries, and few humans had jobs. Everything was done for the humans by their magnificent robot support network. Unfortunately, there were so many people without money and the masses were occupying so much space on the planet that there was little else to do. Overpopulation had obliterated most forms of outdoor activity and most of the available outdoor space itself. With this the outdoor activities to occupy one's time outside of family or individual dwelling chambers, all but disappeared.

"Over a century before this time, virtual games had started replacing all forms of entertainment and activities. Since now there was no place to go, nothing to do outside, and no way to travel around, virtual reality had become the people's sole source of entertainment, and thus the new norm.

"As the mounting psychological pressures of overpopulation made living in the real world difficult for many, they eventually retreated en masse to the virtual world to safeguard and maintain their sanity. Many humans spent all day every day existing solely in this escape, and some even created virtual worlds that allowed them to retreat back to a time when they could pretend they still had jobs and a purpose.

"Virtual reality had become the new drug, the new addiction, and it was an addiction most were not even aware of, never mind able to escape from.

"However, this obsession, unlike addictions in the past, wasn't considered bad and was left untreated, for it was the only thing the people had left to escape from the pressures and pain of their useless everyday lives. Given that this habit had little impact on the provided needed services or how things functioned for the elite, because they no longer needed a human workforce, they again justified their behavior of using any means to control birth and life of the masses.

"During the past century or so, the elite had gradually grown to consider the human workforce a less-than-useful commodity. Moreover in many of the elite's minds the human population was now their world's most critical problem. And this was a problem that needed to be dealt with in a swift and merciless manner. This attitude had become so widespread that the cost of their medical care was now considered extravagant and a waste of money. Of course, in the elites' minds, this just meant another cutback in medical services, including all prescreening provided to the common person. This cutback again aided in burying the knowledge of the growing problem of the fetus mutations.

"Unfortunately, all these changes took quite awhile to fully enforce, especially the mandates requiring all pregnant women to only use the birthing centers and always be sedated. Since prebirth screening had been done away with, many women weren't aware of their pregnancies till after they began to show. This delay in instituting the directive that all birthing would now be done by the androids, compounded by the lack of supervision that ensued from all of the constant changes, provided an opening for another threat to invade. With all the changes, no one was sure of the procedures that needed to be used at any one time, and the lack of communication from the elite while the androids were being reprogrammed after each change caused even more confusion.

"During the five preceding decades leading into the twenty-third century, many arranged medical accidents occurred that curtailed the lives of women who accidentally discovered too much. These deaths were considered acceptable losses because their deaths were necessary to seal any leak of vital information about the growing number of deformities and keep it from falling into the wrong hands.

"Of course, those wrong hands, or so the elite thought, were the hands of the common people. So once again, those in control managed to keep the severity of this mounting problem masked for awhile.

"After the android workforce was securely in place and supervising every pregnancy, a new procedure with a different purpose for the prescreening of all expectant mothers was reestablished. At that point, an imperfect test was developed to determine if a newly conceived fetus had even the slightest latent possibility of being defective.

"The accuracy rate of this new test was only fifty percent, but if the test was even assumed to be positive, the pregnancy was terminated a week after conception. If any problems were even suspected in a fetus, the mother would be quickly and quietly given a drug without her knowledge or consent to abort the developing child and sent home to have a miscarriage. Considering this test was developed to detect any malformations, even those not causing harm to the offspring, many potentially healthy pregnancies were intentionally or unintentionally terminated during this time.

"If for some reason a baby was suspected to be abnormal and the mother was too far along to be safely miscarried, a secret abortion was performed under the guise of some other pathology, and the mother was told that she was never pregnant in the first place but only had a benign tumor growing in her uterus.

"As long as the deformity rate didn't become common knowledge, the elite could again justify the mutation problem as a solution for a larger issue and pretend it wasn't caused by their callous ways. In addition, since pregnancies were now indiscriminately terminated, the elite considered themselves to be performing a public service by providing another population check. By that time, the elite's focus had shifted to overpopulation as the main problem. They rationalized that mutations were really only a symptom of the larger problem: overpopulation.

"In the end, the elites' actions only defended their belief that they were not the cause of the birth defects but were just providing a humane, viable solution for these unfortunate, pitiful creatures.

They claimed these tragic birth defects were only Mother Nature's way of dealing with overpopulation. Once again, the elite projected their responsibilities onto Mother Nature or the surrounding natural world. The elite figured they could kill two birds with one stone by withholding information and just letting Mother Nature take the blame and correct her own course, so to speak.

"During my grandparents' generation, the number of infant mortalities increased dramatically, and this went on for nearly forty years before one woman who was inadvertently not properly sedated during a clandestine late-term abortion accidentally secretly bore witness to her doomed fetus. Later, after the sedation finally took effect, her deformed child disappeared with little explanation. At first she questioned her own sanity about what she had witnessed but couldn't dismiss the nagging loss of her child. Fortunately for her, she was wise enough to keep her mouth shut. After being released and sent home, she secretly started a campaign to find out what was really going on.

"Had they discovered that Alicia Kramps, a reformed computer hacker turned programmer, had seen her infant, she would have been swiftly eliminated like many others before her who discovered the secret.

"After what Alicia accidentally witnessed, she spent the next year secretly interviewing others who had also lost their babies in her area. While she conducted these interviews, others also began to question what they had experienced during the stillbirths of their children. At that point, Alicia enlisted some of the more inquisitive women she had interviewed as helpers. This movement spread across their local region almost instantly. By 2206, Alicia had established a female spy network that was able to hack into many of the computerized systems of their country's tens of thousands of regional birthing centers. Because of the constant radical changes occurring in the medical industry, her hacker force went undetected for almost a year. This gave them ample time to amass a great wealth of information.

"They also managed to tap into the surveillance system that recorded and stored video footage of each pregnant woman's initial screening, its findings, and the birth. During this covert investigation, they happened to stumble onto a ghost of a lost file that contained all the prescreening data the system had collected for the previous fifty years. Those in charge had order that this file be deleted and destroyed a decade earlier, but for some reason, a ghost of it had been buried deep in the memory of their computer network. There it lay undetected until it was accidentally discovered by Alicia's second-in-command. Alicia spent the next two weeks tracking this ghost within the system, and she was finally able to retrieve it and access the information it contained. What they discovered after opening that file not only horrified them all but also caused Alicia great concern.

"They finally had proof that in the past five years, more than sixty-seven percent of their children had been aborted or miscarried in their region alone. Adding to that, another forty-seven percent of the women who were carrying children to term had 'stillborn' babies or lost their babies shortly after birth 'due to complications'. This left their potential next generation depleted by nearly eighty-five percent of the present population. The straw that finally broke the camel's back was when Alicia discovered that there was really no reliable information that many of these aborted infants had been deformed. She was horrified, so she leaked this information onto the net, and it went viral.

"Still, those in control of these procedures quickly attempted to suppress and discredit the leaked information by labeling it as a hoax or some type of scam. Over the last two centuries, there had been so much misinformation online that the elite almost succeeded with this cover-up. People from around the world outside of Alicia's country refused to believe something like this could be happening in their home regions, but there had been so few successful births in the last decade that they were finally forced to delve into the matter more deeply themselves. By 2210, each area had set up independent citizen task forces to address and investigate this suspected potential problem.

"Confirmation of this information was again postponed for another few months, as the preexisting Internet security was suspiciously increased just before Alicia was ready to release the documentation supporting her findings. Then the courts stepped in, and any new information release by groups of people researching the subject of medical malpractice related to birth defects, were delayed by court order. This delay prevented action against the regimented control for an additional year or so. The people just refused to believe such a horror story about those in medicine, and the elite were so good at suppressing and withholding information that when this information was finally confirmed to the populace, chaos erupted, and a deep-seated mistrust of those in control was finally cemented in place. After this massive cover-up became common knowledge, there wasn't anything the elite could do to regain the populace's trust.

"Before Alicia even went public, some of the elite's internal ranks must have also recognized the potential for trouble in withholding the birthing information. With this in mind they began to consider the repercussions of the rapid decrease in population on the planet. By that time, the level of fear was so high in the upper class that the elite's response was only to augment production of the androids in order to use them as additional workers or soldiers to protect themselves if the need arose.

"With an easy switch in programming, these newly developed androids could always be used as caretakers, overseers, or soldiers, if protection of the elite proved to be unnecessary.

"When this information about the birth defects was finally validated in 2211, violent revolts against those in power erupted, but by that time, most of the elite had gone into hiding, so they weren't at immediate risk. Still, even with the increased number of androids, the elite couldn't control the masses. So they determined that the number of androids they had originally produced was insufficient. To correct this error they simply increased production once more.

"With the masses threatening widespread vicious revolution and the eradication of the elite, things finally escalated out of the elite's control. Fear and self preservation now governed the elites' actions as most retreated deeper into hiding. The androids active at that time were then reprogrammed to act as ultimate soldiers and assign the task to protect the elite from any threat of a potential uprising at all costs.

"This was the world I grew up in. During my youth, many common people were executed by these ultimate soldiers. This allowed the elite the power to keep their illusion of being in control alive for an additional few years. After the leak regarding how they had mistreated the common folk for more than a century, the elite at last began to fear for their lives and were driven to take permanent shelter in the fortresses they had designed and built during the previous few decades.

"Swallow, this was only one part of the disaster that so radically changed my world. I know this doesn't address all that happened or the complicated reasons for what led up to this, but for now, this is all I have prepared about the end of the Before Time."

"Resha, the more you tell me, the more I wonder about our ancestors and how they survived. I cannot understand such greed. How could the elite have been so callous to the hardships of so many of those living around them?"

"It was a different type of world, Swallow, and because I was only a child and relatively innocent, I can only speculate on the reasons for the elite's behavior. There were a number of things in their world that led the elite to attempt to control the masses by manipulation, withholding information, and intimidation. Besides, the hoarding behavior in the elites' ranks had developed slowly and stemmed from their own suppressed and unadmitted fears. This vast disparity in the distribution of wealth also caused the common folk to live in fear for their survival.

"Those in control had learned centuries before that fear, if properly used, could be a great manipulator and motivator. It only took one culminating incident to finally set this fear deeply in the hearts of those alive at that time.

"In the mid-twenty-first century, the internalized fear that had been seeded very early in that century created a feeding frenzy among those who had knowledge and power. They were driven by a desire for greater and greater security, and their thirst for power rose. Fueled by their own unrecognized, repressed fear, they could easily justify using the new technology to take advantage of those who possessed less money, knowledge, and power.

"This technology made it easy for the first time in their world's history to manipulate and control the information around them. In the succeeding years, with this information, they found it easy to manipulate and control the economy of their world.

"Many who hadn't fit well in the pre-computer world before the technology became commonplace found either a new place with power or escape and solace by creating havens in their own custom-made virtual worlds. As they all explored the potential of this budding technology, it became apparent that there were new ways for many to become integrated into society and make a living solely by using the technology, even if it meant taking advantage of others.

"More and more people succumbed and became addicted to the ease of accumulating the great wealth promised by working with computers and online. With the focus shifting solely to depending upon online information, this information determined the fate of their society and, finally, their world.

"Another bonus in using this form of providing information was that it could be controlled and manipulated in any desired fashion much more easily and quickly than in the past. Thus, for the first time in history, the information could be chosen, filtered, and released worldwide in a timely manner in the way those in power wished it to be released. This control of the information enabled those in power to maneuver the economy in any way to illicit any desired effect.

"I must say here that I still believe most of the developers of this rising technology had good intentions during their time. They were only trying to help create a better world.

"Then a critical event, nicknamed 9/11, occurred in America, an important part of the free world in that time period. This event caused widespread fear in that nation's populace, which radically changed their people's focus. Before that fateful day, their nation had been a country filled with hope and innocence and had been a leader of the free world. Throughout their history, the people of the United States considered themselves champions of justice and freedom and a potential savior of their world. However, with this newly instilled fear, many of their people began to hoard wealth, and they didn't realize they were creating a potential economic imbalance not only for their country but also for their world. This imbalance grew as things went a lot further in the use and abuse of their new computer technology.

"At that time, many complicated factors added to great numbers of people earning a better-than-normal living by using this new technology, which bolstered a massive uprising in support for its widespread use. This is a common pattern in the evolution of any new life-changing skill or technology: people become addicted to new things without realizing their faults and shortcomings and the responsibility of using them.

"To sum it all up, when the people became afraid and money became the bottom line at the expense of all else, things really got off track."

'The ills of the world are solely the ills of the world
and shall not be projected onto any one individual.'

16

In Preparation

Resha's so engrossed in her studies that the next few days pass quickly. Upon waking on the third morning just before sunrise, she notices it is already promising to be a glorious day. Rolling over in bed and concentrating solely on the clean feel of the air blowing across her skin, she realizes that the effects of the drugs have finally begun to loosen their hold on her.

The day after tomorrow is her scheduled monthly trek to the bunker for the village's supplies. Sitting up on her bed, she grabs a piece of paper and begins to prepare a list of things that her fellow villagers have told her they desire, in addition to the normal food stores she always picks up.

Recalling her last trip to the bunker, she remembers that there is still one more journal she put aside that she needs to complete her studies of the Before Time. She does not want to forget it again, so she jots down a reminder on the bottom of the list.

Realizing that tomorrow's trip will also be a good opportunity to search for parts for her new torches, she idly sketches some possible designs for them. *From these makeshift designs, I can get an idea of what potential items might be useful in their construction.*

After reviewing her lists again, Resha decides she will probably need at least one cart just to bring back all the supplies requested by her fellow villagers. *Wow, since the drugs have started wearing off and I've started my teachings, the monthly supply requests have grown.*

After checking the lists one more time, she realizes it's probably a good idea for her to bring two carts, or she will need to make an additional trip. Shaking her head, she remembers the last time she took someone to help pick up the supplies. A few months back, because she had so many additional supply requests from her villagers, Resha realized she would need someone else's help. One afternoon three days before her trip, she offhandedly said so while sitting down at tea meal. Krey immediately jumped in and volunteered his help. After that trip with Krey, she didn't want to risk asking just anyone to come 'help' her again.

This day, she's engrossed in her preparations for the coming trip, and the hours quickly fade. The first time she's aware of anything outside herself again, it's nearly tea meal time. The time has passed with such little effort that it seems as if she has been napping, only awakened by the grumblings of her stomach just in time to eat. She heads out the door, walks the short distance to Swallow's hut, and knocks. After patiently waiting for Swallow's answer, she turns to leave and spots Swallow waving at her in the distance, heading in her direction. Resha realizes for the first time while admiring Swallow sprinting toward her just how striking Swallow is. As she watches her running, Resha's feelings about this young woman suddenly shift imperceptibly. At once, she senses her heart more deeply, and as she focuses more closely on how she feels, she notices that the ground beneath her feet feels a bit more solid yet forgiving.

As she's gotten to know Swallow better, the anticipation of her presence has taken on a new meaning for Resha, and this feeling catches her off guard. Mystified by her potent reaction to seeing Swallow, she briefly looks down to regain her composure. Upon raising her head once more, she sees that Swallow has slowed and is only a few paces away. As she nears, Resha notices a few beads of sweat glistening on Swallow's brow, and for a split second, her breath catches in her chest.

"Good day, Resha. Were you looking for me?"

"Yes, dear, I wanted to come get you so that we could help prepare tea meal together."

Vaguely unnerved by her compelling reaction to Swallow's presence now looming in front of her, Resha tries her best to mask her feelings. However, she's uncannily aware of Swallow's scent as Swallow brushes past her to enter her quarters. For an instant, Resha feels compelled to reach out and touch Swallow and has to restrain herself. Pausing to gain a semblance of composure, Resha hesitates slightly and then tentatively follows Swallow in stopping a short distance behind her, powerless to prevent a vision of their first encounter from invading her thoughts. Momentarily losing her focus in the present, Resha drowns in a past memory. *We met right after our clan arrived at our new village. Swallow's mother was her only family, and shortly before the move, she fell ill and died of an unknown cause. Her mother's death left Swallow alone, so she now has no kin with which to share quarters.*

Upon arriving in the new village and discovering that she and I were distantly related, Swallow first approached me to ask if she might move in with me. I found this young woman very engaging and was flattered by her request. I briefly considered the idea, but since Swallow was much younger and alone now, I thought that maybe it was time for her to have her own hut.

"I think it's time for you to choose and lay claim to your own place," I told her.

Being one of the few young ones to live alone, Swallow felt honored but was somewhat at a loss since she had lived primarily with her mother since birth and had never lived alone.

After all the families chose their new homes and started settling in, Swallow spent a few hours looking at all the remaining empty huts, including one neighboring my new dwelling. Feeling drawn to me and wanting to be near me, Swallow chose that hut as her first home.

A few days later, during my first visit to Swallow's new hut, I discovered it was almost a mirror image of mine. All it lacked was an extra chair in the bedroom, so my first reaction was to say, "Swallow, I can pick up an extra chair for you on my next trip to the bunker, if you'd like."

At that time, Swallow, not being accustomed to talking, held her tongue and simply nodded as she timidly began to rearrange the meager furnishings of her new home. I joined in to lend a hand and as Swallow moved into the bedroom, heading toward the bed I followed. Taking off Swallow's lead, I grabbed a bedpost, and we dragged the bed to the wall farthest from the window. Facing the bed this way, Swallow would have a clear view of the sunrise in the early morning and from this new vantage point, she could also see the path leading to my hut but back then, this subtle detail escaped my notice. At the time, I thought that watching the sunrise was her primary concern and a novel idea and told Swallow so.

After she finished arranging her new home, Swallow paused to sit on her bed. "Would you like my help in rearranging your hut now?"

The next memory that lazily drifts into Resha's mind is the first time she ever touched Swallow. At first, this memory seems like a dream, and then it sharpens and shortly becomes crystal clear to Resha. *Moving up behind her, I placed a hand on this gentle young woman's right shoulder, and feeling the tension in her, I absentmindedly began rubbing the base of her neck. "Yes, I think I'd like to do the same thing to my bedroom after we're done here."*

I still have a clear picture in my mind of how pleased Swallow was by my praise as she turned her head to smile up at me and nod her agreement.

A half hour later, Swallow and I were standing in my bedroom. After rearranging it, we both realized I would not have as splendid a view as Swallow's since her hut faced a slightly different direction. I thought the change would be good anyway. Swallow, somewhat embarrassed at having a better view then I eagerly offered to switch huts with me.

This simple act touched me deeply, and on that day, the first seedlings of fondness for this noble young woman settled in my chest, flourishing from that day forward.

"No, Swallow, that hut's yours. This view will be good enough and a distinct improvement over what I have been waking up to," I said.

Ricocheting back into the present at a half-sensed movement, Resha shakes her head to break this old memory's hold on her. Now fully engaged in the present, all she can see in front of her is Swallow's back as Swallow bends down to place her pack on the floor next to her fire pit. Resha's next action surprises her as she finds herself slowly tracing the curve of this precious young woman's face down to her shoulders with her eyes. Half unconsciously watching her open her pack, Resha sees her remove something and can't seem to escape noticing how lovely and strong Swallow is. After a moment's pause, Swallow rises and turns toward Resha, extending a closed hand in her direction. "I found this on my trek the other day and remembered your story about the crystals, so I thought you might like it. It might look good sitting on the wall surrounding your fire pit."

Opening her clenched fist, she reveals a small, odd-shaped forest-green crystal about a quarter of the size of her palm. As Resha reaches to take it from her, she's mildly stunned by the touch of Swallow's warm skin on her fingertips and pauses slightly, not wanting to break the connection. Confused and slightly taken aback by this sensual reaction, a moment later, Resha picks up the crystal, turns, and walks toward the window, pretending she needs more light to look at her gift. With her back toward Swallow, she tries to resist any reaction to these new feelings that are invading, but she's unable to block them completely and blushes slightly. "It's beautiful," Resha says as a tear comes to her eye with her back turned towards Swallow so she doesn't give her true feelings away.

Being deeply sensitive, Swallow feels Resha's awkwardness, and not wanting to embarrass her further, she picks up her pack and walks toward the door, where she pauses and quickly changes the subject. "Are you ready to go eat now?"

"Yes, if you're ready." Turning to follow her, Resha wipes the tear from her own face and pockets the crystal, still mildly bothered by her body's veiled response to Swallow when she had brushed past her earlier. Even though she thinks she hid her feelings well, she's unnerved by catching herself admiring this young woman. Swallow drops her pack next to the doorway before walking out, then stops and turns to look at Resha, waiting in silence for Resha to join her at the door.

After leaving her quarters, they head directly toward the dining area. As they walk together in silence, Swallow reaches over and touches Resha's hand. Once more, Resha's caught up in her gentle touch and left pondering her true feelings for this young woman. To break the contact and prevent herself from doing something foolish, Resha absentmindedly reaches up and scratches the side of her own face. Moments later, they arrive at the dining hut, and Resha follows Swallow inside, still overwhelmed by an emotion strange to her—an emotion she can only label at this point in their relationship, as a loss of control.

As usual, these two women are early, since Swallow likes to be early for everything. Inside, they find three others waiting to start preparing the community meal. One of them has already moved the vegetables and meats from their storage chambers onto the center table.

Swallow heads into the front room, where the knives are stored, and returns with two hatchet blades. Meanwhile, Resha gathers a handful of vegetables and moves them to one corner of the massive cutting block. Swallow places the knives in the center of the cutting table as Resha heads off to get the meat. Resha picks up a handful of dry synthetic meat, places it at the opposite corner of the table, and stands back, patiently waiting for Swallow to make her choice. Swallow hands one hatchet to Resha, moving toward the corner of the table where the meat is waiting, and then begins chopping. After moving to the opposite corner of the table, Resha starts dicing the vegetables.

While they are preparing the food, the others start the fire, and by the time they are done chopping, the kettle is almost boiling. At last finished with their task, they add their precious morsels into the mix. While waiting for the stew to finish cooking, they occupy themselves by cleaning up. This takes little time, so they gather the wood to start the fire under the griddle as Doris begins making the apancake mix.

Shortly after, the clan begins slowly filtering into the eating hall and forms a line along the front serving table as the steaming pot is placed for all to take their portions. Resha quickly leaves Doris to the task of finishing cooking the apancakes. She gets in line so that she can eat quickly and return to crafting her plan for her trip to the bunker. Swallow picks up the first tray of apancakes, placing it next to the stew pot, and joins Resha in line. Resha is usually one of the last to get in line, so by serving herself early, she has attracted the attention of all the people around her and they are now staring at her. Since they are not the usual crowd she eats with, her company seems to have disturbed them.

Attempting to ignore their odd stares, she smiles to herself and for the first time it dawns on her that the whole village is on a preset schedule, which most of them seem to be unaware of. As she looks around, she grasps that they are just repeating the same things in the same order day after day. This schedule leaves them always eating with the same people each meal. Until that day, she has not fully realized how repetitive their lives have become.

After getting her food, Resha sits down to eat in silence. Soon Swallow places her plate across from Resha and sits down. Still slightly embarrassed and bewildered by her earlier feelings about Swallow, Resha focuses on the plate in front of her, attempting to evade Swallow's gaze. She concentrates solely on eating as quickly as possible in order to finish and leave before the crowd she usually eats with arrives, hoping her change in schedule doesn't attract too much attention. Driven to distract herself from her unsettling feelings about Swallow, Resha focuses on her latest revelation and wonders how much she might be able to alter her present routine without upsetting the others around her. *Even with this small change in eating companions, I've already been getting reticent looks from those not used to me being here.*

Most of her fellow villagers seem to be in no hurry, so when Resha quickly gets up to leave, a few lift their heads with questioning stares. Swallow, not missing a beat, is right on Resha's heels. She grabs the uneaten apancake from her plate and stuffs it in her pocket before the two women head back toward their quarters. Resha is anxious to get back to work so that she can complete her planning as soon as possible. When they arrive, Resha pauses at the entrance of Swallow's hut, turning to her with a question.

"Have you ever been to the bunker before?"

Swallow's face lights up, but she has no hint of anticipation in her voice when she answers. "No, Resha. I have always been curious, but I have never had the occasion to be able to go."

"If you are available, I'd like your help gathering and bringing back our monthly supplies the day after tomorrow. For your trouble, you may also look around the bunker and see if there's anything you might wish to bring back for yourself. Maybe a second chair for your front room would be nice?"

"I don't know about that chair, but I would love to have the chance to look around the bunker. It would be an honor to help you, and I'm curious to see some of the things you've told me about from our past."

Once more sensing a tender feeling toward Swallow invading, Resha turns and departs to avoid another perplexing interaction. As she quickly retreats toward the shelter of her own hut she says to Swallow over her shoulder, "Okay, it is settled then. We will leave in two days' time, just before dawn. We'll probably be there all day, so if you wouldn't mind, could you pack some snacks for our tea meal?"

"It would be my pleasure to do so. I will get them after dinner tomorrow night." Entering her hut, Resha smiles to herself, absentmindedly fingering the crystal in her pocket. Upon sitting down on the edge of the fire pit, she removes it from her pocket and places it next to her on the ledge, as Swallow suggested earlier.

Her thoughts soon drift back to the preceding encounter with Swallow and the feelings of embarrassment that possessed her upon admiring her. Resha hopes for the second time that she hid the true cause of her embarrassment beneath the guise of receiving her gift. Looking down at the crystal again she reflects. *It truly is a beautiful gift. Just like the person who gave it to me.*

Shaking her head to chase away this distracting thought, she returns to her planning. But as she picks up the list of supplies she finds it difficult to focus on reading the paper, because her heart keeps drifting back to Swallow. In an effort to deflect her mind from envisioning Swallow once more, she forces her attention toward something else. *If all goes well, I'll have about a week or more between my trip to the bunker and my return trip to the cave. This will give me ample time to build at least a few of the new torches I need, so I can try them out. Fortunately, this coming trek to the cave will take less time since I've discovered a more direct route to the entrance of the cave.*

During this upcoming trip, she wants to spend as much time as possible exploring the cave, so she ponders how not to raise suspicions by missing tea meal again. At last realizing that no matter what she does, she will probably be gone for the whole day, she thinks that if she wants to avoid any bothersome questions, she might need to prepare those around her ahead of time for her absence.

Maybe I should just spend a night or two in the cavern and get them really used to missing me. If I do choose to stay out overnight, maybe the best course of action is for me to let a few carefully chosen souls in our village know that I'm going on a trek to explore the desert past the hills and will be away for a few days. Then, if any questions arise in my absence, hopefully those who know will spread the word so that I may avoid most of the disturbance my being away might otherwise cause. If all goes well, by the time I get back, most of the curiosity will have died down, and I won't have to answer too many questions about my whereabouts.

As her thoughts shift to planning her return to the cave, Resha decides that if she manages to leave a few hours before dawn and is gone for three days, she will have two full days to leisurely explore the entire cavern.

Pondering her trip to the cave, stirs thoughts of her pack with the light creatures in it, which she left on the outskirts of their village. She needs to retrieve it sometime and their upcoming trip to the bunker would be a good time to do this. Solving the dilemma of how to retrieve it is the next problem she needs to deal with. Since she is taking Swallow along to the bunker, Resha wonders how she can pick up her pack without raising Swallow's curiosity about it. *Swallow and I will pass right by it on the way to the bunker, but if I stop to retrieve it then, there will be no hiding its contents from her.*

Still hesitant about revealing too much information too soon, even to Swallow, Resha chides herself. Her lingering distrust of Swallow mildly annoys her, and this feeling, along with knowing she can't settle this matter now, causes a mild restlessness to grow inside her. In an attempt to chase away these unwanted feelings and thoughts, she looks around for something to distract herself.

First thing this morning, she finished all her chores and now she regrets having done so because she has nothing left to occupy her time. Motivated by her feelings of uneasiness, Resha thinks, *I must find something useful to do, but there's nothing left in here that needs my attention.* Her mounting unwarranted suspicions of Swallow only cause her to become more on edge and annoyed with herself. Eventually, these thoughts circle around and lead her back to the locked door of her intentionally ignored feelings about Swallow and burst it wide open.

What would be so wrong with sharing my secret with Swallow? And why was I in such a hurry to complete my chores this morning? Now I have nothing to do but wait for dinner.

Still not ready to deal with the self imposed censored on her feelings, Resha's willing to resort to almost anything as a distraction. To busy herself, she ends up going for a walk around the village to double-check her supply list.

Hopefully this will consume the rest of my day.

This turns out to be a wise move for Resha for she winds up talking to a few villagers she didn't see earlier and gets caught up in these conversations. Fortunately for her, this task takes longer than she thought it would, and before she knows it, she finds herself arriving late for dinner. *I'm glad this day is almost over.* In the nearly vacant dining hall, she absentmindedly collects her food and sits down to eat. Still attempting to avoid her befuddling feelings toward Swallow she is relieved to be eating alone. But they are trying desperately to surface, so she barely picks at her food. Finally giving up on eating, she cleans her plate and heads back to her hut as thoughts of her warm, cozy bed dance alluringly in her head.

> *'Distant cousins in life sometimes become not-so-distant bedfellows in our dreams.'*

17

RISING EARLY

Waking early the day after next, before any light has cracked the dawn, Swallow is filled with eagerness about her first trip to the bunker. Not wanting to disturb Resha this early, she lies in bed with her predawn half dreams of the coming day dancing in her imagination.

As she sees the first glow of dawn sneaking in through her bedroom window, she rises to dress in the half light and then heads into her living room to double-check the lunch pack she prepared the night before. She knows that she is just killing time, but she's filled with an excitement she can't seem to contain. She feels she must do something, or she might erupt and spill out of herself.

In the meantime, Resha has risen and dressed and is preparing herself for their journey by mentally reviewing all the supplies that she and Swallow need to bring back from the bunker. Last on the list are objects that might be useful in making new torches so that Resha can return to the cave. Remembering the cave brings back her dilemma about when it might be best to stealthily pick up her pack with the light creatures in it.

On her way home from her first visit to the cave, Resha carefully fashioned a small hiding place out of rocks ten paces off the trail a few kilanss beyond their village and stashed her pack there for safekeeping. She is not worried about whether or not it will still be there, for she hid it well, and she knows others could walk right by it and not see it. However, sometime during this trip to the bunker, she needs to retrieve it without Swallow noticing. Resha is torn about what to do in regard to picking up the pack. If she stops to get it on the way, she will have to reveal the creatures to Swallow, which will mean explaining what they are and where she found them. Still feeling unsettled about disclosing her discovery of the cavern, she shakes her head. *What am I going to do about this?* She remains hesitant to reveal her secret.

Thinking about the light creatures makes her wonder if it might be prudent to bring the jars she found in the dining hall.

If nothing else, they will be a secure place to store some of the creatures for safekeeping. If I pick them up on the way to the bunker, I might be able to transfer them into the jars there. Also, having them in a jar will allow me to safely bring some of them back to my hut if I wish. Kneeling on the floor, she pulls out a chest from under her bed and opens it. The large trunk contains the five jars she took from the kitchen, which are huddled in the right corner, and a journal she found under some boxes on an earlier trip to the bunker, which are located at the opposite end of the trunk.

Hmm, but I don't want to risk losing any of the creatures by leaving them in the bunker, where they might be discovered later on by someone else. I could fit the whole pack in this trunk, undisturbed, if I like. In fact, it might be prudent not to open the pack on the trip, for risk of losing some of the creatures. Bringing it back here unopened and secreting it away undisturbed until I'm ready to make the torches might be my best plan of action. Huh. That reminds me to check for another pack when we get to the bunker, so I'll have a spare.

After thinking about it, Resha finally decides that it will be best to pick up her hidden pack on the way back from their trip. If she leaves the creatures safely in the pack until she can get them home, she will eliminate any possibility of losing any of them or of someone else finding them, which might raise unwanted questions.

As she kneels next to the trunk on the soft earthen floor of her hut, a new idea emerges. *If I plan it right, I might be able to fall behind Swallow on the trip back home, and then I might be able to retrieve my pack without Swallow seeing.* Deciding that this is the best option, she leaves the jars behind and settles on bringing her pack back to her hut unopened. With the items in the trunk left untouched, she closes the lid and pushes the trunk back into its hiding place under the bed.

Looking out the window into the dark, Resha still feels it's a bit early to disturb Swallow, so she sits down on her bed and remembers her last trip to the bunker and what a disaster that turned out to be.

The only good thing about that trip was when I discovered this chest that I keep under my bed.

On that trip, Resha agreed to let Krey help. She had done this trek many times before, but most times, she'd traveled alone. For months, Krey had been bugging her to take him to see the bunker. Needing help, she had finally relented, allowing Krey to come along a few months ago. On that trip, as she and Krey left the village on their monthly supply run, she realized almost immediately that taking Krey was a mistake. From the beginning of that trip, Krey kept trying to engage Resha in conversation by telling her how to do everything. She didn't know if he was talking because he was nervous or if he was just trying to be bossy. She wanted to assume the best about him, so at first, she tried ignoring his insistent blabbering. Unfortunately for them both, that didn't work, and as the day went on, things became more and more uncomfortable for Resha.

The last straw for Resha was when she finished loading all of their village's supplies on her own as Krey attempted to supervise her. After finishing the loading, she stopped to look around in the bunker for a special treat for herself, as she usually did. She did this on occasion to reward herself for making the monthly supply runs for her villagers.

By that point in their trip, she was already wondering why she had even brought Krey, for he had been just standing around for most of the trip, not doing much except talking while Resha did most of the work. The last straw for her came after she located the trunk she wanted to bring back, when Krey scoffed at her and shook his head in impatience as he watched her attempt to load her newfound treasure chest alone. "What could you possibly use that for?" he said as she struggled by herself to get the strongbox into the cart. "You do know it's going to make our job of pulling the cart back that much harder. Don't you?"

Resha didn't understand why he was complaining, since she had been the one to pull the cart most of the way there. "Instead of criticizing me, maybe you could try helping," she said.

He'd chosen not to, so she ignored him as best as she could and made a mental note not to bring him along again on her trips to the bunker—or anywhere else, for that matter. If he was going to scrutinize her every move and not let her enjoy her trip, she didn't want or need his meager stabs at what he considered helping.

She decided soon after that trip that she would appreciate her solo treks even more. She is now certain that if she needs others to accompany her to help, they need to be ones who know how she values her silence. She treasures her independence and peace of mind and needs these treks as a way to maintain those two things.

Lately, it seems to be becoming more difficult to find companions who understand that. Since most of the villagers have learned to talk, there are fewer and fewer people she feels she can choose if she wants to maintain these treks as silent meditations to keep her peace. Thoughts like these sometimes make her regret her decision to teach the others to talk.

Emerging from her thoughts just as the crimson moon falls beneath the horizon and the initial rays of the first blue sun peek through her window, she knows she will soon need to go get Swallow to start today's expedition. She smiles as she finds herself actually looking forward to the trip with Swallow. She hopes that with

Swallow as her companion, this chore will also be an enjoyable adventure and something fun to treasure.

Resha leaves her hut and walks directly toward Swallow's doorway. She finds her waiting just inside, as eager as she is for the journey ahead.

> *'The right company can make all the*
> *difference, even in a dreary world.'*

18

THE BUNKER

As they approach the bunker, Swallow suddenly grabs Resha's hand and whispers, "Thank you, Resha, for taking me here with you." This new emotion bursting from Swallow catches Resha slightly off guard. It's almost as if Swallow fears that if she speaks too loudly, the image of the bunker will disappear like a mirage of water in the desert before a thirsty traveler.

Resha sighs, thankful that their trek to the bunker has been pleasantly silent so she simply nods in response to Swallow's gratitude. While walking toward the main food storage bunker Resha smiles to herself, she knew talking Swallow along would make the trip pleasant. As they approach the building, the heat rising off the hot desert sands creates an eerie scene, playing tricks on their eyes by generating wavy lines that make the image of the bunker look surreal. *It does look a bit like a mirage, doesn't it?* In addition over the years, the desert sands have covered half the main storage bunker and its surrounding metal buildings have rusted to a ruddy color, enhancing this surreal impression. This disconcerting feeling is only enhanced by the parts of the walls of the bunker that are not covered for they are almost the same color as the desert, so they blend with the neighboring background and make one doubt his or her own senses. What's left of the surrounding two and a half dozen or so smaller buildings, if one can still call them buildings, are mostly wooden sheds with a few other ones made of metal scraps that look as if they were piled together by some unknown giant with a ghoulish sense of humor.

Swallow places her hand on top of Resha's as Resha begins to unlock the door to the main bunker. Hesitating, Resha looks at Swallow, smiles, then removes her hand and steps away to allow Swallow the honor of opening the door.

As they enter inside, the front room is illuminated by the light pouring in through the open door and surrounding windows partially covered by sand.

"I'll leave you out here to load our carts, if you don't mind. Here is a list of the supplies we need for the village," Resha says, pointing toward a series of labeled shelves lining the whole left side of the bunker. "Most of the sundries we need can be found over there on those shelves. Load each of our carts equally. I'm used to pulling a fully loaded cart back." She smiles. "So please don't try to spare me. I need to explore the back room for some additional things, so I'll be in there if you need me or have questions." Walking toward a formidable metal door at the back, Resha adds over her shoulder, "After you are done loading the supplies, feel free to look around and pick out some things you might want for yourself."

Leaving Swallow to the front room, Resha travels about three-quarters of the length of the bunker and stops at the entrance of the back room. The door is large and solid, made of reinforced metal. As she attempts to push it open, its hinges groan in protest, their sound assaulting her ears. After pushing with all her might, the door only opens a few inches and then it momentarily freezes in resistance. *It seems this door has been sealed for some time.* Finally, she resorts to putting her full weight against it, and she is able to force its hinges to give way. *In fact, it might be that it's never been opened by anyone from the village before.*

As the door gives way, it opens into pitch black, and Resha realizes there are no windows in this room, or if there are, sand has long since masked them over. Leaving the door open just a crack so that she can see, she sighs as she momentarily stands there to allow her eyes time to adjust, wondering how to proceed. Finally, shaking her head, she prays for at least enough light to see around her, wishing to find some type of torch to light her way.

If I had only picked up my light creatures on the way here, as I first planned. Feeling around in the dark, she looks for something to light her way. *Maybe like in the cavern, there will be a torch somewhere.* However, unlike the cavern, there is very little light to guide her way. While inching along the wall next to door, feeling for a torch, her fingers instead find a button, so she presses it. A radiant greenish light bursts from the ceiling, illuminating one corner in the back of the room. In the dim light she notices three adjacent buttons so she turns her attention toward the ceiling and can barely see three additional lights nearly cloaked in the remaining three darkened corners.

It would be nice to have these in the cave.

Turning to close the door before pressing the other buttons, she wonders why the lights even work, since their electricity was long ago lost. After the door's completely shut, she presses the remaining three buttons, and the whole room is bathed in a radiant greenish glow. Confused by how the lights are powered and not having the time or desire to delve into that mystery, she finds herself being grateful for the light that is now available.

Resha immediately starts looking for parts that she can use to construct her new torches. Following a narrow path that snakes toward the back of the room, she finds herself lost among head-high stacks of boxes. Many of the cartons sitting on top have no covers, and sticking out of them is an abundance of bits and pieces of unused, abused, and discarded items. Some appear to be high tech, and some very simple, but they all have found their way into this same graveyard of long-forgotten and discarded bones.

It seems to Resha that the androids kept everything for fear that these things might be needed in the future. In a flash, it occurs to her that this might've been a carryover from the hoarding instilled in the androids by their masters and the original controllers, the elite. Toward the end, when the elite were finally forced to flee their homes for their lives, they took into hiding with them everything that they perceived might be of any value.

Many of their isolated compounds and underground fortresses must have looked somewhat like this place. Ah, at last, my mind finally seems to be waking up. It's a good thing I'm limiting this search to the one corner of this room where the odds and ends are kept, because if I had to sort through everything in here, it would take me several weeks, if not longer.

Resha begins her sorting as far back as she can get in the right corner, where she spots a rack of shelves filled with transparent man-made objects similar to the jars she found in the kitchen. She opens a few boxes resting on the floor surrounding the shelves and finds that several are filled with odd shapes and different-colored glass cylinders.

Some of these can easily contain my light creatures and still allow light to shine freely. The different colors might be pretty.

Resha figures that after more trips to the cave, she will eventually need more containers than just the jars she took from the kitchen, so she puts two boxes full of cylinders beside the door leading into the front room.

For now, this should be enough. When she finally returns to the corner and looks around, all she can see around her are dozens of boxes overflowing with an assortment of strange objects of different sizes, colors, and shapes.

I have no clue if there is an order to how these things are stored or if they were sorted at all. As she looks around, it seems to her that bits and pieces of similar looking parts are located all over the place.

A few boxes, one of them labeled "Wires," hold things she assumes are called wires, which stick out of the boxes at odd angles. They look useful for fastening, so Resha moves the smallest box containing some of these next to the two packages of glass cylinders by the exit.

While putting that box down, she notices a list hanging on the wall to her left. Thinking that it might aid her in locating what she is looking for, she clears a path to get to the list. After all that work, while staring at the list, she discovers that her task of sorting the boxes will not be easy.

Since I don't know what I'm looking for and the names of most things on this list bring no images to mind, it's probably best just to continue with what I've been doing. As I identify items of boxes that might be useful, I can stack them at the front of the room for later sorting.

Resha soon knows that finding what she needs is going to be a far bigger job than she imagined and its going to take her much longer than she originally planned. Somewhat overwhelmed and disheartened by this realization, she shakes her head and then digs in. Wanting to take her time but not wanting to take too long, she randomly opens the first sealed box next to her right foot. It's another box of glass cylinders.

It seems I'll have all the containers I could possibly use for a long time. This process would be more efficient if I organized this room, but that could take forever. Mildly concerned about being discovered, she reminds herself that exploring beyond the front room is prohibited, and she's now in forbidden territory. However, Resha is one of the few who visits the bunker regularly, and remembering this dampens her fears and allows her to relax a bit. After this she decides she needn't be overly concerned about being caught investigating where she shouldn't be.

But there is still a chance one of the androids might come and discover I've been back here. I know Swallow won't tell anyone, but what if someone else finds out? How will I explain?

Since Resha has seen fewer and fewer androids lately, she calms herself once more and wonders if she might be able to convince the others in her village that it's time to start exploring the things that formerly were considered forbidden and off limits.

After all, if the clan agrees, there will be no one to stop me except the androids, and if they attempt to intervene, at least some in my village might support me.

Scrutinizing the room more closely, Resha spies three partly concealed doors near the back of the room. The two on the side walls look like closets of some sort. The double door located on the back wall, however, is a big finan metalloid one that looks as if each side can slide into the adjacent wall. This door particularly catches her attention because it reminds her of something she recently saw in a book she was studying about the Before Time.

She struggles to remember its name. *It looks like the doors to an elevator, but that doesn't make sense, for they were used in tall buildings to swiftly move up and down many floors at one time.*

Glancing at the ceiling, Resha slowly shakes her head, still struggling to fight off the effects of the drugs, which intermittently throw her into a lingering confusion that still has a weak hold on her. *This building is only one floor. There are no others on top of me.* Momentarily baffled, she questions if it is an elevator or not. Then it finally dawns on her why an elevator might be needed in the bunker. *If it is an elevator, maybe there are other levels below us, below ground. Maybe this is an old entrance to a storage area underground disguised as a bunker. If it is, who knows how many floors there might be down there? Since the lights are still working, maybe I can get the elevator to work. If so, I might be able to access the floors below, and who knows what I'll find there? Now, that would be fun. I still think I should keep this all hidden from the rest of the village for the time being, at least until I know what's behind those doors.*

Looking around once more, she realizes that there are boxes stacked up everywhere between her and that door. *I'll have to clear a path to even get near the door to see what it is, never mind opening it.*

Intrigued, she starts moving boxes aside one by one, struggling to make her way toward the massive doors. Finally, after a few hours of backbreaking work, only three rows of boxes are left standing between her and her target. Now all she needs is to move the three rows leaning up against the door itself.

After all this work, she's tired and sore and has lost track of time while clearing a path to the double doors. She knows this task has taken her quite awhile, but hasn't realized yet, that it's nearing time to eat lunch. Then just as she's about to start in on the last three rows, she hears a knock coming through the door to the front room, from where Swallow's working.

"Resha, are you hungry? Would you like to break and join me for tea meal?"

I can barely make out Swallow's voice scratching through the heavy steel door, and I was so engrossed in what I was doing that I didn't notice how hungry I was getting.

Resha shouts back an answer, hoping Swallow will hear her. "Yes, Swallow, that would be great! I'll be right out!"

Apparently not understanding her, Swallow starts to push the door open. In a flash, Resha finds herself sprinting across the room, half tripping, trying desperately to reach the door before it opens too far. Stretching out her arm to catch it, she arrives just in time to almost bump heads with Swallow as she sticks her head in to peek around the door. Amazed by what she glimpses, Swallow says, "Wow, what is all this junk—I mean stuff? There are an amazing number of boxes in here." Then she notices that there are no windows. "Huh. Where's the light coming from?"

Resha shakes her head in response, trying to explain. "I have no idea what this is all for but I think the androids kept everything for fear of throwing away something of value." Still almost nose to nose with Swallow and fighting back the confusion that always arises by being too close to her, Resha looks up and finds herself staring into Swallow's blue eyes. In order not to lose her focus, Resha quickly averts her eyes looking down without a sound, but the sight of Swallow's striking blue eyes have forced her to question why she would want to keep Swallow out of there—and her life—in the first place. This thought helps her relax a bit, as it's necessary for her to finally admit to herself that it is too late to keep Swallow out anyway.

"I don't know how the light works, but do you want to come in here to eat?" Resha says.

Shaking her head no, Swallow responds. "I think it's a bit crowded, don't you? Besides, this place is so closed in that I'm dying to get some fresh air. Can we eat outside?"

"That's a great idea. Wait a moment." Resha moves behind the half-open door and shuts the lights off. Startled, Swallow backs out of the doorway, tripping over a chair, falling backward. Reaching forward, trying to grab Swallow's arm, Resha just misses as it slips through her grasp. Swallow lands on her backside on the floor, next to a chair she knocked over during her tumble backwards. Shaking her head and blushing slightly, she looks up and asks, "Did you do that? What just happened?"

"You fell."

Glaring at Resha, Swallow shakes her head as her mouth spreads into a full grin. "I know I fell. I mean what happened to the light?"

Embarrassed and stifling a giggle, Resha responds, "I just shut off the lights by pressing the buttons behind the door." She moves back behind the door and into the room pressing the button, to turn on the lights once more. After shutting them off again she returns to the front room and closes the door behind her. Talking a few steps, she stops in front of Swallow, offering her hand to help Swallow get to her feet. "This was how we used to light indoor spaces when I was young, when we had electricity. I don't understand how this one is being powered, since I thought all the electricity was gone." Steadying herself, she reaches forward to grasp Swallow's hand. "Are you all right?"

After clasping Resha's hand, Swallow jumps to her feet. "Thank you. Yes, I think I'm fine." Once she's up, she avoids looking at Resha but refuses to let go of her hand. Using her free hand to pick up her pack, Swallow leads Resha outside.

I guess she was more shaken by all this than I thought. She doesn't seem to want to let go. As they leave the bunker, Resha is again mildly disturbed by Swallow's touch. Drawn in by Swallow's casual approach, Resha loses her stubborn resolve to keep her out and says, "Maybe you can help me move a few of the larger boxes in the back room after lunch, if you're done and don't mind."

Wordlessly, Swallow takes Resha to a spot of shade in a cluster of large rocks a short distance away. They stop there, and Swallow turns abruptly and silently stares into Resha's eyes. At that moment, all of Resha's senses are heightened as Swallow is forced to be uncomfortably close to her in this tight space. All Resha can do is half smile as she looks around, trying to avoid Swallow's gaze, and awkwardly says, "This looks like a great spot to eat." Swallow hesitates for a moment, as if waiting for something more to happen. Smiling, Resha finds a good place to sit down, and picks a spot that allows her to lean back and recline against a slightly slanted large, flat rock behind her. Swallow's finally forced to release Resha's hand as she sits down across from her and places her pack in the middle.

Resha closes her eyes and leans back to test the comfort of the rock. "Yes, this will do just fine."

Swallow's tempted by the comfortable pose Resha has adopted so she scoots over next to Resha's side, leaning back against the rock. "Yes this is nice." She says opening her pack to take out their food.

Taking the apancake Swallow's handing her, Resha feels as if something has shifted between them and she's inadvertently missed it.

Unexpectedly, a few moments later, Swallow leans over and brushes a strand of hair out of Resha's eyes.

Thanking her, Resha smiles, but it's as if she's afraid to say too much, for fear her words might betray her feelings.

Sitting side by side with their backs against the warm rock, the two women eat in silence. After they've satisfied their bellies, relaxed and full, Resha briefly closes her eyes as she leans back to rest, and soon she drifts off to sleep. What seems like only moments later, she's jolted awake, horrified to find her head resting on Swallow's right shoulder.

Concerned Swallow might be mildly upset by this transgression, Resha looks up at her only to notice Swallow's smiling and gazing down at her. "How long have I been asleep?" Resha asks. Looking down to mask the color rising in her face, she immediately sits up and moves a few inches away from Swallow. "I'm sorry. I—"

Slightly amused by Resha's flustering, Swallow takes her hand and says, "It's all right, Resha. We were both comfortable, and we just dozed off. It touched me that you felt at ease enough to sleep on my shoulder." She lifts Resha's chin, forcing Resha's eyes to meet hers.

Resha avoids raising her gaze, for fear those aqua-blue eyes will discover the secret she's desperately trying to keep hidden even from her own thoughts and heart.

Eventually, Swallow's forced to bend down so that her eyes are able to capture Resha's, and she says, "Resha, why does this embarrass you so?"

Standing up, as if to leave, Resha responds, "I don't know. For some reason, as of late, I have begun to feel awkward when I'm too close to you. It's as if I'm unable to compel myself to stay away, and that makes me feel on edge."

'Attraction is attraction is attraction.
It sure baffles one's heart and mind.'

19

AWAKENING

Although Swallow slightly forced this last interaction, she's now not sure what to do next. Standing up in front of Resha, not wanting to be seen as the aggressor, Swallow shifts her focus onto Resha's lips as she's speaking. Now all Swallow can hear is the sound of her beating heart rising in her ears, slowly whitewashing Resha's words into some mysterious abyss. Using Resha's lips as a focal point so that she doesn't act hastily, Swallow zooms in on her mouth, and it brings to mind a picture Swallow discovered earlier that morning in a box near the front door of the bunker. The photograph portrays two thin blush-colored petals floating in a small portion of what appeared to be a green algae-covered pond. After discovering this photo, she wondered what kind of flower had lost those seemingly aimlessly drifting petals. In the snapshot, the petals appeared to be barely touching, but somehow, she knew they were tied together for all time. For some unknown reason, the image affected her deeply and captured her imagination, so she put the picture aside to bring home, planning to hang it on one of the walls of her bedroom.

Now clearly recalling this image while looking at Resha, she realizes that the petals must have just fallen, because in the picture, there are still traces of faint ripples in the surrounding water. Drifting into present time, Swallow is so drawn in by the movement of

Resha's mouth and captured by the overlying image in her mind that the faint sounds of the outside world gray and, for just a second, fade to silence. A few minutes later, as her present world invades, she's stunned by what she finds herself in the midst of doing.

Emerging from her blurred memories, Swallow discovers herself reaching up and tracing Resha's lips with her index finger, as she did with the petals in the picture earlier that day.

Pulling away slightly, Resha says, "Maybe we had better get back to work." Abruptly Resha pushes around Swallow, almost knocking her aside. Momentarily stunned by Resha's unexpected roughness, Swallow pauses for a moment before she gathers the leftover contents of their meal puts it into her pack and follows. A sulky silence pursues the two women as they one by one reenter the bunker.

Walking through the front door, Swallow catches Resha hesitantly standing before the door to the back room so she rushes ahead to stop her before she disappears into the room. Touching Resha's arm to get her attention Swallow whispers, "Do you still need my help?"

Resha keeps her back to Swallow as she reaches out to put her hand on the doorknob and hesitates for a brief moment, refusing to turn to face Swallow "Maybe in just a bit. I've got a few smaller boxes to move first. I'll call you when I'm ready."

The frosty tone in Resha's voice cuts Swallow deeply. To defend herself, Swallow looks down, turns her back on Resha, and walks away. A pile of things she collected earlier that day, with the picture of the blushed petals still sitting on top, catches Swallow's eye. Knowing there is no way to explain or excuse her actions, she whispers, mostly to herself, "I'll be here if and when you need me."

Shaking her head, Resha drops her hand from the knob, turns, and takes three steps toward Swallow's back, closing almost half the distance between them. "I'm sorry, Swallow. I didn't mean to be so harsh." Wanting to reach out, she's held back by some unseen force and finds she's only able to stare at Swallow's unflinching shoulders. "Swallow, I—"

"It's okay, Resha. I think I understand."

Frustrated by her own behavior, Resha attempts to explain, but the words are trapped in her throat. She stands there, dumbfounded, in silence. The minutes tick by as the air grows thicker between these two women until Resha, shaking her head, is able to murmur, "No, you don't. I don't even understand, so how can you?"

Swallow turns toward Resha slowly, feeling as if the air is almost freezing her in place.

"I don't know what to do with these feelings I have for you," Resha blurts out. "You're so much younger than I, and I'm not used to feeling this way. It's been a long time for me."

After pausing to consider Resha's statement, Swallow thinks she might now understand. "I'm confused too. In fact, I'm not used to feeling this way at all. Besides the things I felt when my mother died, this is the first time in my life that I have ever felt anything toward another. Imagine how baffled I'm."

Stepping toward Swallow, Resha falters but still extends her hand. After walking forward silently to close the distance between them, Swallow tenderly laces her finger into Resha's right hand.

The two women's hands are drawn together like dampened leaves blown in concert by a fall breeze. When their fingers are firmly interlocked, Resha turns and pulls Swallow after her in the direction of the back room. "Come on. I'm being silly." *You'd think that after all this time, I would be happy to feel anything again.* Resha puts an arm around Swallow's shoulders as the two women head toward the back room. "Maybe we should both just relax and slow down."

Opening the door leading into the back room, Resha shifts her focus to the task at hand. "Okay, let's start here. I've already cleared a path to those large doors over there. If you wouldn't mind moving out everything in front of them that would be great."

After letting go of Resha's hand, Swallow starts picking up the boxes between her and the double doors and placing them against the left wall. Meanwhile, Resha finishes gathering the things she has put aside to take back with her. After Resha carries these boxes to the door exiting the bunker, she pauses to look at them. In the intervening time, Swallow has nearly completed her task of clearing away the boxes in front of the massive doors. Turning toward Resha with the second-to-last box in hand, she says, "Okay, after these two boxes, we'll be able to get to the doors. What's next?"

"If you can load those five boxes I've stacked by the entrance over there into my cart, I would appreciate it."

Swallow picks up the last box in front of the two massive metal doors moving it against the far wall. On her way to the front of the room, as she and Resha pass each other, she puts her arm around Resha to playfully spin her around.

Resisting and slightly annoyed at first, Resha can't help herself; she catches herself smiling at this lighthearted gesture. Inevitably captured by Swallow's overflowing joy, Resha relinquishes and returns Swallow's embrace. The world seems to stop for a moment as the two women gently hug.

Slightly letting go of the embrace to allow herself a look at Resha's face, Swallow says, "See? Isn't this more fun than being by yourself?"

Resha, totally lost in their merriment, stands on her toes and kisses Swallow on the tip of her nose. It is just a peck, but Swallow turns scarlet in response, yet she does not let go. Pulling Resha closer to her, she hugs her even tighter. The two women quietly stand near the center of the room, locked in an embrace, for what seems like forever. Still smarting from Resha's earlier abruptness and not sure if she should go further, Swallow finally breaks the encounter and continues toward the entrance into the front room. "I'll be done with this in no time. Remember where we were. I'll be right back." She picks up the first of the boxes she needs to load in Resha's cart and heads out the door as Resha walks over to the two massive silver doors to get a closer look.

Returning to get the fourth box, Swallow glances at Resha and sees her standing facing the two metal doors in the back of the room. Resha's just standing there, appearing to assess the situation.

Swallow decides not to disturb her and turns to head out the door with the fourth box in hand. As she's leaving, out of the corner of her eye, she sees Resha running her hands around the outer edge of the doorframe.

After loading that box, Swallow hurries back one last time and picks up the final box. Before heading out to load it, she turns with the box in hand toward Resha, briefly pausing in the doorway, hoping to be noticed, and her curiosity inevitably gets the best of her. "What are you looking for?" Unable to resist any longer, she places the box back on the floor walking toward Resha.

Resha doesn't respond till Swallow's by her side. Then, turning her full attention to Swallow, she says, "I'm trying to find some way to open this thing. There's got to be a hidden button or a latch here somewhere."

Swallow backs up to get a better look and pauses about five paces in front of the huge double doors, and on the sly, she takes a moment to admire Resha from behind. Resha then backing away from the doors, joins Swallow on her left side. For a moment, the two women stand side by side, both staring at the doors as if to open them by sheer willpower.

As if by magic, a few seconds later, the doors start to slide open. "Good! You did it. What did you do?" Swallow says.

Resha turns toward Swallow, laughing. "I didn't do anything." Before Swallow can respond, Resha's kneeling next to Swallow and inspecting the floor. "Would you take a step forward?"

As Swallow treads one step ahead, the doors begin to slide shut. "Wow!" Swallow raises her left eyebrow. "It must be me!"

Still kneeling but now running her hands across the stone floor where Swallow had been standing, Resha looks up and says, "There must be some kind of trigger or sensor here somewhere." Crawling around the spot, Resha inspects every inch but can find nothing, and the doors remain shut. "Well, that doesn't make sense."

Finally getting to her feet, Resha raises her arms above her head, waving them around, hoping she might trigger a sensor above her.

Still, the doors don't move. "I don't get this. Swallow, what did you do?"

Swallow shrugs, and Resha grabs her arm, pulling her back to the spot where she was standing when the doors first opened. For a moment, the two women stand flanking each other and stare at their images reflected in the metal doors. Viewing themselves standing side by side, Resha notices for the first time that Swallow is only a few inches taller than she, although all this time, she has pictured Swallow as being much taller.

At last, the doors shudder and move, opening once again. Swallow shakes her head. "That doesn't make sense. If I move forward, they'll only close." Testing her words, she takes one step toward the doors and stops, waiting. Sure enough, they begin to close. Immediately, Swallow quickly steps back, and the doors reopen once more. "How can we enter that thing if we can't get to it without the doors closing?"

"Let me try something." Resha heads toward the door. She's only able to take two quick steps forward before the doors start to close once more. She swiftly runs toward the closing doors but isn't quite fast enough to get there before they slam shut. Then turning to look back at Swallow, Resha laughs. "Humph."

In response to Resha's unuttered question: *What do we do now?* Swallow shrugs and shakes her head.

Looking around, Resha spots something on the other side of the room and a few seconds later, a slow smile wanders across her face.

Swallow, bemused at Resha's almost devious expression, laughs questioning. "What is it?"

After quickly retrieving the item, Resha returns to Swallow's side holding a thin metal rod a few meters in length out in front of her. A few seconds later, the door begins to reopen.

Looking at Resha, Swallow smiles and shakes her head. "Not yet. Stay put."

With the doors now fully open, holding the rod like a sword in front of her, Resha rushes forward and manages to get the rod in between the doors just before they close on it. Letting go, Resha leaves the rod hanging in midair jammed between the doors, sticking straight out toward her.

Swallow claps. "Great!" She runs to Resha's side. "Now what?"

"I don't know." The doors are open barely wide enough to slide in a hand. Raising her right eyebrow, Resha looks at Swallow. In near unison, the two women say, "There must be a trigger somewhere."

Swallow slips her hand into the opening just above the rod and moves it up as far as she can, but nothing happens.

"Feel around for a trigger, maybe a lever of some sort along the edge of the door," Resha says, while she slides her hand in just below the rod. About halfway between the bottom of the rod and the floor, Resha feels a small metal latch, which she flips downward. They hear a a clicking and whirring sound off to the right of the doors as a panel about half the size of Resha's hand opens in the wall next to them, revealing a series of three buttons. Resha and Swallow stand and pull their hands out from between the doors, looking at each other.

Swiftly, Swallow grabs Resha's arm and pulls her over so that they are standing directly in front of the newly opened panel. The three buttons, sitting in a line from the top of the panel down, stare blankly back at them. Standing there and smiling at each other, Swallow then hastily grabs Resha and kisses her directly on the mouth. It is only a wisp of a kiss, but it is still their first kiss. Their lips leave the kiss too speedily for either woman's liking, but their bodies linger close together for a few moments more as they gaze into each other's eyes. This time, Swallow doesn't let go of Resha's hand.

Glancing sideways at Resha, Swallow says, "Well, what do you think? Should we push them?"

Nodding uncertainly, Resha shrugs at Swallow.

In response, Swallow places her free thumb on the first button in the panel and presses it. It lights up, but nothing else happens. She tries the same thing with the other two buttons, but there is still no movement from the doors. Swallow silently wonders if Resha should try.

The two women look at each other again. "Now what?" Resha is clearly baffled.

"Maybe you have the magic touch," Swallow says, pulling Resha in front of the buttons.

Resha reaches out with her left hand and places a finger on the top button. When she presses it, it lights up again, but the doors don't move, and nothing else happens. Repeating the movement with the other two buttons, as Swallow did, she's not surprised when she also gets no response. "I'm stumped." Moments later, the panel begins to close, so she withdraws her hand, and the two women are left stewing in their own confusion.

Swallow faces Resha, and at last, their hands part. Covering her eyes, Resha again shakes her head with disappointment.

With a hand now on Resha's shoulder, Swallow says, "Looks like someone was a bit mistrustful and wanted to keep others out, huh?"

"Well, they at least wanted to make it a challenge. But we've gotten this far, so there must be a way to get in." Resha backs away toward the original spot on the floor that first triggered the doors to open.

"That doesn't seem to work without me," Swallow says, moving to a place by Resha's left side. This time, the doors don't move. "Now I'm really confused. Clearly, whoever designed these controls didn't want just anyone to be able to get in."

For a long time, the two women stand side by side, staring at the unmoving doors. Then Resha's face lights up. "Let's try this." She moves to the other side of Swallow, putting them in the original places they were in when the doors first opened, and they wait, but again, nothing happens.

After a few minutes of frustration, Resha tenderly slides her hand into Swallow's once more. "Well, I'm all out of ideas." No sooner have the words left her mouth than the sound of the rod clanging to the floor captures her attention, and she looks up just in time to see the doors slowly slide open. Resha looks at the rod now lying on the floor in the middle of the open doorway, shaking her head. "I'll be damned. Now, what did that?"

Laughing, Swallow shakes her head. "It looks like the doors want us to be holding hands, but we're still no better off. If we move, I know they'll close again."

"Let's try anyway." Resha drops Swallow's hand and makes a mad dash for the open doors. Before she's able to take two steps, they snap shut around the rod, leaving a clanging sound mocking her and echoing in her ears. Turning back to Swallow, she scratches her head. "Now they're closing even faster." Once more moving back into her original place next to Swallow, Resha sighs and waits for any movement.

Swallow chuckles and puts her arm around Resha. "Maybe it'll just take a little extra time for them to open now." The two women stand there in silence, waiting for something to happen. Several minutes drift by as the silence becomes almost deafening.

Finally, Resha can't stand it any longer. "Well, at least we've gotten this far. I hate to give up now, but we can't do this all day. Besides it's time for us to start our trek back home."

Swallow sighs. "I think you're right, and I must admit I'm getting a bit flustered by all this. Anyhow, even if we were able to open the doors and get in today, we don't have time to explore what we may find. Also, we need to get the supplies back to the village tonight, or they'll come looking for us and discover what we have been doing." Tenderly patting Resha on the arm, she says, "And that would really mean trouble. I can just hear Krey now."

Both women snicker as Resha nods in agreement. "And if that happens, we will never have the peace to be able to do what we want. Let's wrap this up and finish loading the carts so we can leave."

On her way out of the room, Swallow picks up the last box she needs to load, and exits the bunker with it in hand. Following close on Swallow's heels, Resha shuts the light off in the back room, and closes the door after her. She turns just in time to see Swallow bound down the stairs off the porch and sprint, box in hand, to the cart. Pausing at the front door while watching Swallow, she sighs. *She really is beautiful.*

Resha then leaves the bunker, heading toward her cart.

> *'Admiration can be a wondrous thing*
> *or a never-ending, brutal curse.'*

— 20 —

SWALLOW'S NEW CALLING

It's early, and as Swallow opens her eyes to the new day, she can see her first glimpse of the three suns rising outside her window. Lying in bed, she can barely hear Resha in her hut, going through her early morning ritual of greeting the first sun as it comes up.

Remembering back a year ago to the day after they first moved into their new homes, Swallow recalls one of her first glimpses of getting to know this woman.

As the first sun came up the morning after we finished rearranging Resha's bedroom, I woke to her talking to herself. Even now, I clearly remember the first time I heard Resha performing her ritual.

I was standing in the front room of my hut, getting ready to go on an early morning hike, and I heard her voice. At first, I thought she was talking to me, so I walked out into my front room and spied her through her bedroom window. I waved to her but she didn't respond and I soon realized she was looking past me at the rising suns. Smiling to myself at her odd behavior, I continued on my way out the door.

That morning, now almost a year ago, I thought it peculiar to hear her go to the window and say good morning to no one but the suns. But after living alone next to her this past year, I have become accustomed to her ways. As each day passes, more and more, I look forward to her voice waking me from sleep on the chance mornings when she rises before me. *During this past year, I have come to know what it's like to live alone, and with each passing day, Resha becomes more and more of a tantalizing curiosity to me. I must admit that I still find some of her ways a bit strange', but now they have become endearing to me. Today, while lying here, I think that after all, especially at her age, with the trauma and drastic changes she has seen in her long life, she's entitled to be a bit strange at times.*

This particular day, Swallow watches the dawn's blues and crimsons swirl into a spectacular early morning display of color. Lying there hypnotized, she witnesses the other two suns rise to escort their moon, and for some reason, she's reluctant to move. Hearing Resha's voice in the distance, she loses focus and drifts back to sleep as a vision of yesterday's trip to the bunker drifts to mind.

With the final word of Resha's morning ritual echoing in her ears, she closes her eyes and lets yesterday's trip to the bunker flood her mind. The last clear thought she has before sleep invades a second time is wondering if this might be a good day to plant the seeds she discovered by chance on her way back from their trip for supplies.

Suddenly in her mind, it's yesterday again. *We stopped, standing on the edge of the outskirts of the bunker's compound with our carts full. "Can I come back with you on your next trip here?" I said.*

A grin travels across Resha's face as she answers. Her smile makes her look more youthful and attractive. "Of course. It would be my pleasure to have your company anytime you'd like."

As Swallow lies there, drifting in and out of sleep, she wonders about her feelings for this woman and where they are headed. Hovering in between yesterday and this morning, she half remembers and half dreams the details of their trip home yesterday.

Picking up their overly filled carts, the two women started their trek back to the village. About halfway there, Resha said she had left something behind and needed to go back for it. Smiling to herself, Swallow watched as Resha headed off to retrieve her forgotten item. She told Swallow to continue on with her cargo and said she would catch up or, if Swallow was too far ahead, would meet her back at the village.

Swallow waited a short while and then decided to follow, figuring she could explore the shed that had caught her eye as they were leaving the compound. Since Resha had gone back, that might just give her enough time to take a quick peek inside it. This shed was small and stood on the outer edge of an assortment of buildings that surrounded the main bunker complex. For some reason, that small wooden building haunted Swallow when she first saw it, and she couldn't draw her attention away from it. It looked to her like a humble, wooden, lonely outcast surrounded by mostly haphazardly reinforced, stark metal buildings.

Right then, she had wanted to stop to explore it, but not wanting to hold Resha up, she'd continued walking in silence. Since Resha had said Swallow could come back with her on her next trip, she'd made a mental note to explore it then.

Resha's forgotten item now gave Swallow time to do what she needed. If she was quick, she could get there and return without Resha ever knowing. Just in case Resha returned while she was gone, Swallow left a short note pinned to Resha's cart before heading out.

With her pack slung over her right shoulder, she hurried off in the direction of that alluring little shed. Sprinting as fast as she could, she soon had the bunker complex in sight. However, she was mildly surprised that she hadn't seen Resha on her travels back. She looked around for Resha once more, but she was nowhere to be found, so Swallow focused on what she had gone back to do.

After entering the shed, she discovered that it was filled with shelves upon shelves of clear containers labeled with strange names. Each bottle was filled to the brim with unfamiliar-looking items. Most of these were small, roundish in shape and had a hard outer covering. They varied in size and color: green, tan, brown, gray, and black. However, their appearance was too similar for them not to be somehow related.

Moving the jars around on the shelves, she could see that some of these strange, unknown things were very large, while others were very small. After pulling a few jars off the shelf and opening them, she found that each specimen seemed to be covered by some type of hardened shell. Then, on one of the bottom shelves, tucked away behind the jars, she discovered a book. It listed the items by name and contained pictures and brief explanations of what they were and what they could grow to be.

As she skimmed the first few pages, the book revealed that these jars contained things called seeds, which were used to grow different types of plants, such as their story tree. The pictures in the book showed not only what the seeds would grow into but also what the book called their potential flowers and fruits. It said people ate some of these fruits. It also contained planting, growing, and care instructions for each type of seed. Suddenly aware of the passing time, Swallow became concerned that Resha might return to the carts and find her gone, so she quickly took the book and randomly grabbed three jars filled with seeds. After putting them into her pack, she started her journey back to where they had left the carts, planning to read about the seeds before going to bed that night. She was hoping to discover some plants that might survive in their new climate.

Heading up the path to where they had left their carts, Swallow could see Resha coming toward them from the opposite direction in the distance. For some reason, she stopped and ducked behind a bush so that Resha would not see her as she came toward the carts. She stayed hidden there, watching Resha place the pack on top of her cart and carefully cover it with the stack of brightly colored blankets she had taken earlier from the back room of the bunker. While she was focused on placing the blankets just so, Swallow came out of hiding and resumed walking toward the carts.

As she got nearer, Swallow waved to her, but Resha hesitated, looking slightly puzzled, before returning her greeting.

After she arrived at the carts, Resha asked her, "Where did you go? I was worried that something might've happened when I discovered both carts here and you were not around."

Smiling, tickled at Resha's concern, Swallow said, "Didn't you see my note?"

Resha shook her head.

"It must have gotten covered by a blanket. Anyway earlier, on our way out, a shed caught my eye. Since you went back to get what you forgot, I decided to return there and take a quick look inside. It was interesting, and I found a book that I would like to study and show you. Since I didn't know when you would be coming back, I figured I would be faster than you, so I decided to chance a quick look. I hope you're not mad."

"No, no, I was just a bit worried, although I know you can take care of yourself. And don't be concerned; I welcome your company on any future expeditions I might take. Besides, you seem to have more freedom than I do to move about unnoticed. In fact, barring any protest, I think you can come here on your own if you'd like. What the others don't know won't hurt them." At last, heading around her cart to pick up its handles, she said, "Are you ready?"

After placing her pack on the top of her cart, Swallow paused to unstrap her waterskin. Since she had run most of the way to the shed and back and they hadn't had much to drink, she figured a quick sip would be nice. "It's nice to have some water on these long treks, especially on hot days, isn't it? Would you like a drink? It's been especially hot today, and I collected some water over this past week from the orange crystal. I particularly like the taste of its water."

Resha, watching Swallow take a mouthful, became keenly aware of the few drops of water that ran down Swallow's chin and neck then landing on the front of her shirt.

After drinking, Swallow silently pushed the waterskin in Resha's direction and Resha feeling thirsty herself, took it from Swallow saying, "Thanks. Yes. It is hot." She wasn't sure if Swallow was serious or just teasing her about the tastes of the water collected from the different colored crystals, so she said, "You can really taste a difference between the water gathered at each colored crystal?"

"Well, I have only gathered water from the three closest crystals, but to me, the water collected from each color tastes slightly different."

Resha raises her left eyebrow. "I've never noticed. In the future I'll have to pay closer attention."

Intrigued by her ability to instruct Resha on something, Swallow explained further. "Colors seem to affect the taste for me, but maybe it's just my imagination. I will have to start collecting from other crystals to see if this still holds true."

Handing the skin back to Swallow, Resha said, "I would love to try a comparison of the tastes of the water from the different-colored crystals with you if you'd like. It would be fun. Maybe one night, we could collect from five or six different ones and compare them the next morning. If I can't discern any differences, then you might explain how their tastes vary, and I could drink again and pay closer attention."

"That sounds like fun. I would appreciate your input." After taking back the skin and refastening it to her pack on the front of her cart, Swallow picked up the cart's handles and waited for Resha to signal that she was ready.

Soon Resha had the handles of her cart in hand. "Are you ready now?"

Swallow nodded, and they headed back toward the village with their carts in tow. On their trek home, Resha kept expecting Swallow to question her about her approaching the carts from a direction that was opposite the bunker, but their journey back was silent, and Resha was thankful Swallow didn't ask what she had gone back to get.

After they entered their village, the two women's first stops were their own huts. Each of them took their pack, a chosen blanket, and a few personal items into their hut. Swallow then helped Resha bring the five boxes of materials she collected for herself from the back room into her hut.

As Swallow emerged from Resha's home, she was eager to unload the carts so that she might have some time to herself before dinner to look at her new book. A few moments afterward, Resha shut her door, stretched, and nodded to Swallow. They pulled the carts toward the dining area and parked them at the back door to the kitchen. Swallow was still keen to get back to her hut, so she swiftly started unloading the carts.

Resha, sensing Swallow's impatience, said, "You can leave the rest to me if you have something else you'd like to do."

"No, it's okay. I will at least help to unload, but if you wouldn't mind putting away the supplies so I can leave after that, that would be great. I would like to read a bit of my new book before dinner if there's time."

"It's a deal."

The two women worked in silence as they stacked the boxes of provisions on one of the tables nearest the shelves and pantry.

When the carts were completely unloaded, Resha smiled and said, "Go on. I can handle it from here." Walking Swallow out the back door, but not wishing to part from her so soon, Resha pauses in the doorway to watch her go. Their day together had been one of the most pleasant days she'd had in a long time.

As she headed off, Swallow turned and waived calling out after her, "I will see you at dinner!" She then turned and hurried in the direction of her home.

Resha silently lingered, watching Swallow leave, until she could no longer see her, as she went around a corner and disappeared between some huts. Resha then went back inside and started to put away their provisions. After finishing, she stacked the dozen or so extra blankets they had brought back on the table in the main eating area and put a sign on top that said Free.

By the time Resha was done, it was nearing meal time, so she removed the supplies needed for tonight's meal and placed them on the table for those preparing dinner. She walked out back; stowed the two carts up against the back wall of the dining hall, where they were usually kept; and headed back to her hut.

Upon arriving, she sighed. "It's been a long day, and I'm tired. Since I'm not preparing dinner tonight, I might just have time for a quick nap."

'To sleep, perchance to dream or not to …
dream—whatever you may choose.'

21

NEW LIGHT

Suddenly sitting up in bed, Resha notices the bloodred eye of the moon shining in through her skylight. *It's hanging too far above the horizon. I may have missed dinner.* The second thing she observes is the silence echoing in her village. Shaking her head, then realizing. *Everyone else must be asleep. So maybe I did sleep though dinner. Oh well.* By the moon's current location, she can tell it must be the middle of the night.

She lies back down, sighing to herself, desperately trying to recapture her elusive companion, sleep. Yet she suspects that it's left not only her bed but also her hut for this night. The minutes tick by, but her eyes refuse to close. Rolling over on her side she tries to go back to sleep but she's finally forced to admit to herself that she might be up all night, so she decides to get out of bed.

Rising then throwing her legs over the edge of the bed, Resha sits there wondering what she should do next. She looks down at herself and realizes she fell asleep in her clothes, and they and now her linens are covered in dust. Noting that she will need to shake her clothes and bed linens out in the morning, she undresses getting into clean bed clothes. Stripping her bed, she places her dirty laundry on the chair in the corner and pulls out fresh linens to remake her bed. *I will attend to the dirty items in the morning.*

Recognizing that she will be up for a while, she kneels and pulls the chest from under her bed. As she opens the trunk in the darkness, she can see a faint light in the right corner, filtering out from the seams of her overfull pack. The dim light is also faintly reflecting off the glass jars she brought home from the kitchen earlier and had tucked away at the other end of the trunk. She takes out her pack, carefully placing it upright on the floor leaning against the end of the trunk, and unfastens its straps to open it.

Knowing the two boxes of empty glass containers they brought back from the bunker earlier are still laying neatly stacked by the door in the front room, she sighs. Not wanting to stumble around in the dark in order to get them, she removes the five jars she packed in the trunk for safekeeping. The first two open easily, but the third jar's lid sticks, so she bangs it against a slate stepping-stone on the floor next to her to try to loosen it. The jar breaks with the second strike and the glass shatters in her hand. Even before she feels it, she can see in the shadowy light that a sliver of glass is sticking out of the webbing between her thumb and forefinger. Alarmed that the sound of breaking glass might've disturbed Swallow, she briefly pauses to listen to see if she can hear any response from Swallow's hut next door.

Nothing but silence echoes in response from the night, so she turns her attention to her injured hand. Worrying that if she pulls out the glass, blood might flow all over everything, she goes over to her nightstand and removes an old, worn shirt from the top draw. In order to avoid a mess, she uses her mouth and her uninjured hand to rip off a few long strips of bandage and drops the rest of the shirt back into the draw. After carefully sitting back down next to the trunk, she pulls the glass from her hand, quickly pressing a strip of cloth against the wound.

In the eerie light escaping from her pack, Resha can see her iridescent blood flowing onto the bandage, forming a rainbow spot about the size of her big toe. Next, she counts to a hundred to make sure the bleeding has stopped, silently hoping the cut is not too bad. Letting the cloth drop to the ground, she sits there for a few moments and waits to see if the bleeding will start again. *Good. It's stopped. That means it's not too deep.* After wrapping a clean bandage around her hand, she goes back to work. *I need more light to clean up this mess and the broken glass before I continue.*

She dips the two open jars into her pack and fills them halfway with the flakes, careful not to spill any. Then she loosely screws on the top of one of the jars and shakes it. The jar brightens considerably as the creatures respond to her shaking. After gently placing her new lantern on the floor in the area of the broken glass, she opens a third jar, carefully picking up the shattered glass, and places it inside the empty jar to keep the jagged pieces out of the way. When she has finished, she closes the jar and puts it aside.

The light from the creatures in the jar with the lid begins to fade, so she picks the jar up and shakes it once more, but for some reason, the creatures don't respond. Shaking it a few more times, doesn't seem to work either as she watches their light continues to grow weaker. No matter what she does, the light keeps dimming, to the point of almost going out. Concerned, she looks over at the other open jar filled with the creatures; they are still glowing brightly. Swiftly, she takes off the top of the closed jar and stirs the creatures with her fingers. They slowly start to brighten, so she stirs them again, and as in the cave after she burned them, she can almost feel their sense of relief as they come back to life. *Well, that may be a problem. Apparently, they need air, but I need the tops on to keep them safely contained in the jars.*

Knowing now that she has to modify the tops of the jars so that the creatures can breathe, she gets up looking for something to use to put holes in the lids. The tools she has collected from the bunker are located in the bottom drawer of her nightstand, so she carries one of the lighted jars over and sets it down next to the drawer so that she can see. *Having this light really comes in handy.* After first taking out a hammer from drawer, she continues to sift through the remaining tools for something suitable to use to punch holes.

She is mesmerized by the sheer number of tools she's collected; she didn't realize she had picked up such an odd assortment of them over this past year. Settling upon a few small, straight metal rods with points, she pulls two out and takes them back with her to the trunk and the awaiting lids. These tools do the trick, and she soon has all the tops speckled with holes about a tenth of the size of the tip of her smallest finger.

After ripping the leftover bandages into thirds, she lines the lids with cloth and screws them back onto the two filled jars. She shakes them both once more and watches them for a few minutes to check if the creatures are happy. After she's sure they're content, she places the two half-completed torches aside and goes back to what she was doing.

With the two full boxes of jars in the front room, she knows she will have plenty containers for what she needs. After opening and filling the remaining two empty jars in the trunk she then recloses her half-empty pack and places it in the chest, along with the four glowing jars. By then, she's starting to feel tired, so after closing the trunk, she slides it back under her bed. *Maybe I should try to go back to sleep now.* She picks up the jar filled with glass fragments and puts it on her nightstand before getting into bed.

Lying there for several minutes, yawning, she waits but sleep does not come easily. She patiently lingers in the darkness, longing for the sweet relief of slumber, and eventually, she focuses her attention on the night sky filtering in through her skylight. Silently wishing her eyes might close by themselves and finally let her drift away, she gazes out into the night. Now peering into the sky through her roof's window, she can see the emerald stars surrounding the moon. Still, sleep is elusive, so she forces her eyes closed and imagines that most of the bright green stars are chasing the moon and attempting to caress it. In her mind, the moon manages to elude its potential captors for a long time. At one point in the chase, the moon resorts to using her crimson color as a shield. Then one lone star that appears brighter than the rest and has not taken part in the previous chase drifts into the crimson moon's orbit. Now dreaming, Resha watches as the celestial bodies are gradually drawn together by some unknown energy, finally kissing. She can see the moon's choice has been made as she lazily drifts off into the shadows of sleep.

'Sometimes in the darkness, Angels enter our rooms and bring sorely needed lullabies into our lives.'

22

RESHA'S PLANS TAKE AN UNEXPECTED TURN

Early the next morning, still restless, Resha rises before dawn, wanting to complete the torches so that she can make her return trip to the cave sooner, rather than later. Kneeling to remove the trunk from under her bed, she reaches in but stops as she hears a knock followed a few seconds later by Swallow's voice and the audible creaking of her front door.

"Resha, are you here?"

"I'm back here, Swallow. Come on in."

Swallow quickly passes through the front room, pausing at the entrance to Resha's bedroom peeking in. All Swallow can see is Resha's head buried under her bed and her rear end sticking up in the air. Swallow can't help herself as a grin breaks out on her face. "I was wondering if you might want to take a trek to the ruins I spotted when I was exploring the hills last month. They're located a couple days walk to the east of our village and I was thinking of going sometime later this week, if you're available. They appear to be the remains of a city, and they don't seem too far from here, but we'll probably have to stay out overnight a few days."

"You mean Rhipame City?" Resha says, as her head emerges from under the bed. Still kneeling next to it, she imagines herself as a little girl and a fleeting image of a praying youngster dances in her head.

She turns, looking up at Swallow. "The city toward the southeast?" The sight of Swallow standing in her bedroom doorway looking so striking unnerves and delights Resha but she purposely keeps any sign of her feelings from being visible. "That sounds like a great idea. I've wanted to go to that city for some time now." Getting to her feet Resha's emotions invade and take control as a smile crosses her face. Slowly walking toward Swallow, she momentarily pauses half way there. In an attempt to regain her composure after stopping, she looks down. Then after a few seconds her gaze is drawn back towards Swallow as she slowly steps forward. Her demeanor has suddenly changed becoming deadly serious as she closes the distance between herself and Swallow. "We'll need to pack some food." Miscalculating the distance, she stops a bit too close to Swallow for either of their comfort, asking, "Do you have a bedroll?"

A puzzled expression crosses Swallow's face. Then, meeting Resha's gaze, she smiles and asks, "What's a bedroll?" The blush rising to her face is scarcely noticeable as Swallow's arm accidentally brushes against Resha's side. The two women's eyes lock and the feeling of losing all control overtakes Swallow as she instinctively reaches over to sweep away a strand of Resha's cosa hair that has fallen across her face. Her hand pauses in midair a few inches from her intended target and Swallow raises her left eyebrow in a silent question. It seems as if she's seeking permission or clemency for some transgression that has not occurred yet. Frozen and standing there, a curious grin slowly spreads across her face.

Resha can't help herself returning the smile. She feels as if she's falling out of herself as an urge to get closer to Swallow invades. Instead of moving, she leans into Swallow's hand gently nuzzling it with her cheek. Not believing what she's doing Resha feels almost as if she's standing beside herself, viewing a scene in the distance of some other two women. A faint pink flush rises to color both her and Swallow's face, as they both look away focusing anywhere but on each other. It's as if they aren't certain how to proceed next.

Then Resha looks up at Swallow, but it's Swallow who is withholding this time. Her gaze is still fixed on the floor, refusing to meet Resha's eyes. The older woman's mounting edginess finally forces her to break their encounter by brushing past Swallow and entering her living room. *Why does she keep doing that? By now, she must have some idea of how it affects me.*

Irritated by her own lack of control she's straining to break free so a few paces away Resha turns, facing Swallow's back. She feels raw and rebuffed by Swallow's staunch refusal to meet her gaze. "A bedroll is a blanket and pillow we can carry with us to sleep on." Her voice shows little trace of her true feelings but she's unsure of how to proceed so she adds, "I can go get two of the blankets left in the dining hall from our trip to the bunker, if you'd like, or we can get them together, and I'll make us each a bedroll." *Now I sound as if I think she can't do anything for herself.*

Clearly still flustered and not able to regain her balance, Resha sighs, doing everything to distract herself from what she really wants to do. Closing her eyes, she runs one hand down her face, stopping with it clasps over her mouth. *Why does she do this to me? Why does she affect me this way?* When Resha opens her eyes again, Swallow's standing directly in front of her. She finds herself staring back into Swallow's eyes which are now impossible to avoid. *What? What do you want from me?* Blinking several times, to break the hold that Swallow's aqua-blue eyes have on her Resha still refuses to react as the sensation of falling starts to overtake her once more. To combat this feeling, Resha's finally forced to look away.

Swallow takes a deep breath and exhales. "Before we do anything I think we need to talk," she says, and then she waits.

Resha looks up and immediately mentally trips, falling even more deeply into Swallow's eyes. Trapped by their blueness, she notices that today they look even deeper and more inviting than usual. Resha imagines them beckoning her, inviting her to swim and drown in them. Taking Swallow by the hand she leads her over to the bench by the fire pit and they sit down. For several seconds the women sit side by side not facing each other. They are now uncomfortably close and are still holding hands but refuse to look at each other. To break the awkward silence Resha remarks, "I don't want to assume anything here, so what are we doing?"

Placing her free hand on top of their two clasped hands, Swallow responds. "To tell the truth, I'm not quite sure."

Resha stares at Swallow trying to gather a clue from Swallow's expression and is struck by the fact that all traces of Swallow's previous smile have faded from her face. *She's serious.* Then a thought finally occurs to Resha. *She's not playing here she doesn't have a clue. She's never felt this way before.* "We really can't do this. I'm much too old for you."

Swallow continues to stare into Resha's eyes until Resha's forced once more to look away. *I'm also too old for this, and I'm especially not experience with courting a younger woman.* It's clear to Resha that Swallow's waiting for her to make the first move. Dropping Swallow's hand, Resha gets up and walks to the other side of the room, stopping in front of the window to stare outside. She hopes that putting some distance between her and Swallow will allow them both time to regain some composure. She's fighting not to bend and break to her own desires and so she concentrates on the dry breeze blowing in from the window. In that moment, Resha feels parched and older than her many years. For a second, an awkward silence hangs heavily in the air, and this feeling reminds Resha of her old world's long-gone and forgotten rain clouds laden and weighty with moisture.

To break the silence, still staring out the window, Resha says, "If we're going to go to the ruins, we'll need to gather our supplies." She hopes a change in topic will break the tense emotional, glass wall rapidly forming between her and Swallow.

"Oh, that's a good idea," Swallow says with no hint of emotion to betray her feelings. In a split second, it's as if they've never even spoke about how they feel.

Resha follows Swallow's verbal lead and is finally able to calm herself. "Were you thinking about leaving today?" she asks, turning to look at Swallow.

"Well, no, not really. How about we gather our supplies today and plan to leave early tomorrow?" Swallow stands heading toward the door. Finally stopping in front of the door she turns to briefly look back at Resha and waits.

Suddenly Resha gets up walking toward Swallow. When she's within reach she puts her hand on Swallow's shoulder. "How about you pack us some food, and I'll get the bedrolls ready? We can walk over to the dining hall together to get our supplies and pick up the blankets we left there yesterday. They'll make great bedrolls. Oh, I almost forgot—I have some straps in my nightstand that I can use to bind them." Resha runs back into her bedroom, grabs four straps from the middle drawer of her nightstand, and tosses them onto the bed. Then she rejoins Swallow at the front door, as they hastily leave, heading toward the dining hall.

The stillness of the early morning village makes the two women feel as if they're the only two up, and they relax enjoying their walk to the dining hall. Until halfway there, they pass Krey heading in the other direction.

"You ladies are headed out early this morning," he says.

Resha looks at him and sighs. She doesn't want to deal with him this morning. Krey starts to say something else, but Swallow, sensing Resha's discomfort, cuts him off.

"Good morning, Krey. Sorry, but we're busy, and we don't have time to chat right now." Stepping in between the two women and turning his back to Swallow, Krey ignores her remark addressing Resha directly. "So, Resha, what are you two up to?"

Resha pauses, not wanting to answer. When Krey doesn't get her silent message and refuses to budge, she responds softly, "It's really none of your business, Krey. I'm sorry, but as Swallow said, we're—"

He moves in closer than Resha likes and touches her arm, deliberately cutting Resha off. "Come on, Resha. Don't be difficult."

At times like these, she regrets ever teaching him to talk. Stepping back to force Krey to let her go, Resha stares at him, daring him to try that again. She has had enough of his taking liberties with her.

He attempts to move in closer once more, but Swallow steps in between them. "We're busy, Krey, and I'm sorry, but we really don't have time for—"

Discounting Swallow once again and looking past her, Krey speaks directly to Resha, attempting to force the issue. "Resha, I asked you a question."

Moving next to Swallow, Resha puts her arm around her to keep it out of Krey's reach and clearly display her feelings. "I know, and I gave you all the answer I'm going to give."

The silence among the three is deafening. Swallow finally breaks it, turning her back to Krey and looking directly at Resha. "Resha, are you ready?"

The two women stare at each other, then Resha turns her back on Krey, and they leave. "Good-bye, Krey," they say nearly in unison.

He tries to call after them, but they ignore him scurrying off.

As they enter the dining hall in the half light of the early morning, the quietness caresses Swallow and Resha, dulling Resha's smoldering anger about what just occurred. It's still too early for morning meal, so the place is deserted. Heading directly toward the back room, Swallow departs to get their food, but Resha grabs her arm, stopping her. "I'm sorry, Swallow."

"For what?" Swallow asks, hoping this will break the ice between them.

"He was rude to you," Resha says.

Swallow was expecting a different answer, but she doesn't let it show. "He was rude to you too. And you don't need to apologize for him, Resha. You did nothing wrong." Swallow looks down to Resha's hand, taking it and smiles. In the following seconds she lifts her eyes to meet Resha's gaze. "It's Krey who needs to apologize to us both."

"I know, but I don't like the way some of the older ones treat the young ones, and sometimes I feel responsible. They can be so snippy at times, especially Krey."

"It's okay. I'm used to it," Swallow says, placing her other hand on Resha's arm.

"That doesn't make it right." The two women stand there calmly for a brief moment. Then they part as Swallow heads into the back room.

Resha looks around, spotting the pile of blankets tucked under a table out of sight in the far corner of the room. Apparently, someone moved them there before dinner last night and forgot about them. Counting nine left, she realizes that only one has been taken so she shakes her head smiling to herself. *I guess it may be awhile for the others to feel comfortable enough to take them. Perhaps they don't know what to use them for. Oh well. I do.* Resha grabs the top four as Swallow emerges from the back room with an armful of food.

After placing the food on a table in between her and Resha, Swallow grabs a box off a shelf on the far wall and starts to pack it.

Looking up to see what Swallow is doing Resha says "The food looks good food, but I think we'll need something else to carry the supplies in besides that box, though."

Swallow grins and then runs into the back room, saying, "I think I spied the perfect thing." A few moments later, she returns carrying a multicolored net. It looks as if it was made from many different pieces of leftover string. "We can tie the food up in here."

Swallow begins packing the net and after she's finished, the two women leave the dining hut with their bounties in hand. They arrive back at Resha's hut before most of their fellow villagers have even ventured out for morning meal.

After placing the blankets on her bed, Resha picks out a green and a blue one, putting the two others in the corner of her room. She then takes two small pillows from the half dozen or so on her bed, rolls one pillow in each blanket, secures each roll with two straps, and then hands Swallow the green one.

"What if I want the blue one?" Swallow asks.

Resha looks up at Swallow and can see she is toying with her, so she responds. "Then I'll give you the blue one. No worries"

Swallow's grin broadens. "It's OK. The green one will do just fine."

They part, agreeing to meet early the next morning and Swallow heads to her hut.

After Swallow leaves, Resha places her bedroll next to her bed and goes back to assembling the torches. She starts by removing the trunk from under the bed and lining up her supplies on the floor. Experimenting with the best way of constructing the torches she weaves the wires together into a net she uses to secure the jars to the rods. It is late into the afternoon before she is done. Looking down to admire her handiwork she's crafted ten empty torches and four filled ones. *I won't be able to fit them all in the trunk. Good thing I didn't fill any more of the jars with my creatures. It would be hard to hide glowing torches at night if they weren't securely closed up and hidden under my bed in the trunk.*

After cramming nine torches into the chest next to her half empty back pack she notices how cozily the four lit one glow at her from their new nest. Closing the trunk, she places the remaining five empty torches on top, sliding the chest under her bed. *I will need to collect more of my glowing friends to fill them all, but that can be done in the cave.* Preparing her hut for her three-day absence is easy and she finishes just before heading off to dinner. She has purposely taken her time and waited till late into the meal to arrive, hoping to avoid running into Krey. To her relief, the hall is more or less empty. After fixing herself a meager plate, Resha sits alone in the moonlight, picking at her food, her mind occupied only with bed and tomorrow's adventure.

*'Avoiding some people sometimes is
the only way to keep peace.'*

23

THE TREK TO THE RUINS

The next morning, Resha leaves her hut before sunrise. While walking to Swallow's door, she's almost deafened by the stillness of the early morning air encircling her. It feels particularly parched this day, so she breathes in deeply, and as she does, she senses a faint crackling in her chest, reminding her of the feeling of crumpling paper.

This must be how the dry air is affecting my lungs.

Arriving at Swallow's door, she hesitates for a moment before she knocks, and wonders if Swallow might still be asleep. Knocking anyway she waits, but no answer comes. *She must still be in bed.*

Looking down at the dusky red dirt beneath her feet, she turns and walks back to her hut, casually thinking about Swallow and the trek ahead.

About half an hour later, as the day's first light peeks above the horizon, Resha returns once more to Swallow's door and knocks. There's still no answer, so she opens the door and sticks her head in. The hut is deadly silent and there is no visible sign of Swallow.

"Swallow, are you in here?" The air is still and quiet. Against her better judgment, with her curiosity increasing, Resha questions if it might be best to go in and wait. As she debates what to do, a tempting thought breezes through her: *Just go in.* It's so unlike her to enter uninvited that it's almost as if the thought is foreign and not of her own making. After finding Swallow's hut empty this second time, she begins to worry. Driven by an escalating concern about Swallow's absence and not having a clue where to begin looking for her, Resha finally decides to go in. *It'll be okay to wait in here.*

In the past, she has not spent much time in Swallow's hut. It seems that whenever they're together indoors, it's at her place. She wanders from the front room to Swallow's bedroom, assessing Swallow's meager belongings. The place seems stark compared to her hut. The only touch of color is the new orange blanket they recently brought back from their trip to the bunker, which is now resting comfortably on Swallow's bed. Pausing at the bed's foot, her hand drops to the soft orange surface, which reminds her of peeling a similar-colored fruit as a child. Memories of sharing this fruit with her mother flutter into her head. This recollection is a rare, cherished image, because by that time in her childhood, all fruit had been marked as contraband and its consumption was forbidden.

As her hand sinks into the soft blanket, her mind automatically compares its texture to the peel of the orange fruit in her childhood fingers. *It doesn't even look as if she slept here last night.* Sitting down on the bed, she again absentmindedly runs her hand across the vivid-colored blanket, half wondering what it's made of.

A few minutes later, the sound of an opening door pulls Resha into the present. Caught in her childhood recollections of forbidden fruit, she's now struck by the size of her hand as its present image merges with her fading childhood memories. Feeling trapped, her first response is that of a young child who has done something wrong as panic rises in her throat. Instinctually, she looks for a place to hide. Then, coming fully into the present, she fights this impulse off, realizing there's no place to hide except under Swallow's bed. *I'd look pretty silly if Swallow came in and found me trying to crawl under her bed.*

"Is someone in here?" Swallow says, slowly walking toward her bedroom.

Resha's still seated on Swallow's bed. Her words catch in her throat as she opens her mouth to respond. After clearing her throat, she says, "It's just me, Swallow. I came earlier to get you, but when you didn't answer, I thought you were asleep, so I just left. When I came back this second time and found you were still gone, I decided to wait here for you." *I don't have to mention that I was worried. Besides, what I just said is true.* "I hope you are not mad that I let myself in."

Finding Resha sitting on her bed as she enters her bedroom, Swallow smirks with amusement dancing on her lips. To her recollection, this is the first time Resha has been in her bedroom since they rearranged it. "You look pretty comfy," she says, sitting down next to Resha, putting her hand on Resha's knee, and gently shaking it.

Clearly embarrassed, Resha looks at Swallow and shrugs. "What can I say? I do like the blanket. It adds a touch of color to your drab surroundings." She arches her left eyebrow as she says this, hoping Swallow will catch her sarcasm.

"Now I'm drab, am I?" Swallow asks teasingly, as she laughs. "In return, I must say that you look pretty awkward just sitting here."

"Well, what was I supposed to do—hide under your bed? I'd look even sillier if I was caught with my head under your bed and my bum in the air again as I tried crawling in to hide. Besides, you would have sensed I was here anyhow."

Sharing a mutual delight of that comical image, the two women grasp hands. When their laughter has subsided into giggling, Swallow says, "Yes, I can picture you trying to crawl under the bed with your behind in the air. It really does look silly."

Standing, to help gain her composure, Resha says, "Where were you? I was worried." *There. I've admitted it.*

Still snickering, Swallow shakes her head. "I decided to sleep out under the stars last night to try out the bedroll. It's not as comfy as my bed, but it's really nice to sleep in."

Resha raises her hand, feigning a fake smack to Swallow's head, but her hand falls feebly to her side before she completes her swing. "You had me worried."

Letting go of Resha's right hand, Swallow sits pulling her back onto the bed and then pushes her down, pinning Resha underneath her with both hands over her head.

They both laugh some more. "No fair—you are bigger than me," Resha says. "And younger."

Swallow stops laughing, and smiles down at Resha.

Wriggling one hand free, Resha says, "Come on. We have to get going, especially if we don't want Krey meddling in our business this morning. You know, if he catches us leaving, he may just follow us all the way to the city."

This thought greatly unnerves Swallow. "He'd better not try it." After standing up with Resha's hand still grasped firmly in her own, Swallow, in one movement, drags Resha to her feet, hauling her into the front room.

Pointing to her gear next to the front entrance Swallow says. "See? I have everything ready. I even found a way to attach my bedroll to my pack, so I don't have to carry it."

On her way out the door, Resha stops and takes a closer look at Swallow's pack. "Nice idea," she says as she leaves the door open behind her and heads toward her hut. "I'll be just a minute picking up my stuff."

"I'll wait for you out front," Swallow says, watching her go. She swings her pack onto her back and leaves her hut with the net full of their food, in her right hand. A few moments later, Resha emerges from her place with her pack already on her back and joins her.

The second sun is rising as they leave their village, heading south in the direction of the ruins. Swallow has already raced a few paces ahead of Resha. "It's going to be hot today," she remarks, as she slows to let Resha catch up. "If we're lucky, we'll get out of here before Krey sees us."

Right on cue, Krey's voice booms from the center of the village. "What are you doing there? Letta, put that down!"

Whispering to Swallow, Resha says, "You wouldn't think such a small man would have such a big mouth."

The two women look at each other and chuckle as they head out of the village in the direction of the ruins.

Resha turns to Swallow. "Poor Letta. She'll have to deal with Krey alone today."

"I know she can handle him," Swallow says.

The last sound they hear before they're out of earshot is Letta yelling at Krey to leave her alone.

"Mind your own business, or I'll break your arm!" Letta's voice rings out, fading in the distance.

"Stop that! You're hurting me," Krey says.

"Well, are you finally going to leave me alone then?" Letta asks.

Endearingly, Resha smiles at Swallow. "They've already come to blows. Thank you, Letta, for keeping Krey busy and away from us," she jokes, folding her hands as if to mimic praying.

Swallow laughs. "I told you she'd set him straight. Most of the younger women are much less tolerant of the men's shenanigans than you, Resha."

Resha hurries forward to catch up to Swallow. As Swallow turns, she smiles at Resha and links arms with her.

Returning the smile, Resha says, "This is going to be fun." She's looking forward to being away from the village for a few days.

They travel in silence for the rest of the morning. As they cross the open desert under the noon suns, it's hotter than Resha ever remembers it being since the new clouds appeared. To fight the heat, the two women have fashioned water-soaked rags to cover their noses and mouths to ease their breathing. Two hours into their afternoon trek, when they see a small stand of about a half dozen crystal towers to the east, Resha diverts their route slightly, heading toward the towers.

"You know that not following the direct route will add more time to our trek, don't you?" Swallow says. "Heading this way may add another day's journey."

Only silence echoes back. It's well past midday, and they haven't taken a break yet. The heat and dust are taking a toll on them, and Resha knows they need a cooler place to rest and eat. It's deceptive how far away the grouping of crystal towers is, so by the time they reach the first crystals, it's nearing dinner, and they're too tired to be anything but thankful for the shade and a place to stop.

"This place is farther away than it looked," Resha says. The two women sigh as they take their packs off and sit down in the shadow of a red crystal at the edge of the grouping. "I think this is a good place to rest and eat," Resha murmurs. "It's getting late; maybe we should stay here for the night."

"I may have underestimated the time it'll take to travel the distance to the ruins. At this rate, we may be gone for a week or more," Swallow says. "I hope we have enough food."

Shifting her position Resha leans back against the crystal. Only seconds later, she rebounds from it in discomfort. "This thing's still hot." Resha is craning her neck, trying to look over her shoulder in an unrealistic effort to see her own back. "Well, depending upon how long we want to stay in the city, we may have to ration our food. At least staying here, we can collect a bit more water tonight. Even if we can't carry more, it will feel good to wash up a bit in the morning." Wincing slightly, Resha places her pack as a buffer between her and the hot crystal and gingerly leans back against it again.

"Staying here for the night sounds like a good idea to me," Swallow says. "We can get up early and leave before sunrise. Hopefully we'll reach the city before it gets too hot tomorrow." Noticing Resha's continued pained expression, Swallow asks, "Did you burn your back on the crystal?" She moves toward Resha. "Here—let me take a look."

As Swallow approaches, Resha leans forward moving her pack out of the way to aid Swallow in peering down the back of her shirt to inspect the damage the hot crystal has inflicted.

"Well, it looks okay. A little deeper in color but no blistering," Swallow says as she gently touches the darkest section. "How does that feel?"

Cringing a little, Resha replies, "Careful. It's a bit tender, but I'll be okay. I think I may have some cream in my pack, if you wouldn't mind putting it on for me." She grabs her pack, reaches in, and withdraws a small brown jar. "I found this when we were exploring the bunker the other day. I took it even though I didn't think I would ever use it."

Swallow opens the jar dabbing at it with her finger. "It feels funny, smooth but cooling. Okay, we'll try it." Holding the jar to her nose, she raises an eyebrow and licks her lips, saying, "It smells delicious but it's for your back, of course."

Leaning forward, Resha lifts up the back of her shirt to allow Swallow to apply the cream. As Swallow gently rubs it in, Resha says, "Oh, that feels good." Letting her shirt down again, she asks, "Are you hungry?"

Swallow hands the jar back to Resha so that she can return it to her pack and then reseats herself before answering. "More tired than hungry." Lying down in the cool, shaded sand, Swallow closes her eyes.

"The shade feels good," Resha says as she lies down on her side across from Swallow, and shortly, both women are sound asleep. Neither woman stirs again till well after sunset

The feeling of the strap of her pack slipping from her hand wakes Resha. A moment later, she opens her eyes and sees a set of smaller yellowish eyes at her feet, staring back through the evening dusk. She's quick enough to slip her foot into the strap to prevent her pack from being skirted away. Peering into the half light, she can barely make out the shape of a small animal tugging at her pack's free strap, with its snout. It is only about half an arm's length from her left foot.

"Who are you?" Resha whispers.

The familiar sound of Resha's voice rouses Swallow from her sound sleep. Yawning and stretching with her eyes still closed, Swallow sits up and in response to Swallow's stirring, Resha murmurs, "Shhh, quiet. Don't spook it."

Opening her eyes Swallow smiles and turns to get a better look at their surprise visitor. "What is it?"

"I have no idea, but don't move. It's an animal of some sort, I think. Some type of rodent—maybe a ground squirrel? It woke me up trying to steal my pack."

The animal is just out of Swallow's reach, but in the dim light, she can see that it is small and doesn't seem particularly spooked by the two women's presence. Pulling the netting with their food closer to her she picks it up, puts it on her other side and out of the little creatures reach.

The rodent's so intent on freeing its prize from Resha's foot that it mostly ignores Swallow. Swallow opens the netting, takes out a small piece of apancake, and tosses it between her and the creature. Immediately, the creature drops the strap, takes two steps toward the morsel, and then pauses, sniffing the air, waiting.

"What's it waiting for?" Swallow asks in a hushed tone.

"I don't know. Maybe it doesn't like the smell of the apancake. That clearly makes a statement about our food, doesn't it?" Resha jokes. "Something attracted it to our camp, though." Slowly sliding back in the dust, Resha reaches her hand behind her trying to accesses the temperature of the crystal which had earlier seared her back. Finding it lukewarm, she then leans back to relax, and slowly pulls her pack back to her side with her foot. Picking it up she places it on her lap and reaches in. Following her first instinct she removes the cream and opens the jar placing it on the ground an arm's length from her side. The animal quickly turns, raises its nose in the air, and perks up its ears. "That got its attention."

The rodent carefully creeps forward in the dust toward the open jar. Upon reaching it, the creature hesitates for a moment sniffing at the jar. Then plunges its whole head in and, just as quickly, comes out sneezing and licking, with its snout full of cream.

"It obviously likes that," Resha says. "I wonder what's in it." As Resha reaches over to pick up the jar, the creature backs off and Resha brings the jar to her nose. "It smells sweet like honey." Then she replaces the top and puts the closed jar on a crystal shelf above her head so that it's out of the animal's reach.

"What's honey?" Swallow asks.

"That's a complicated story, and I'm not sure I know how to answer that," Resha responds. "I remember it from when I was a small child, but I was never quite sure where it came from. It was this thick, gooey treat we used to sweeten things."

"What do you mean by sweeten?" Swallow's clearly lost.

"I don't really know how to explain that either. It made things—I don't know—taste better. Sort of like water tastes when you're really thirsty." Grabbing the jar from the shelf Resha opens it again and dips the tip of her littlest finger inside. Still licking its chops, the animal tentatively takes two steps forward, expecting another treat. Resha then closes the jar and puts it back on the shelf, out of the reach of their little friend. Sitting down by her feet, the animal appears content to wait. After Resha brings her finger to her tongue, she says, "Mmm, it tastes sweet all right. Here." She offers her finger with the cream to Swallow.

As Swallow scoots closer, the animal skips out of the way and finally, after a few moments' wait, moves off into the brush, seemingly satisfied for the time being. When Swallow is close enough to Resha, she sticks out her tongue.

Putting her finger on Swallow's tongue, Resha says, "Lick it."

"Hmm, that does taste good. It would go well with the apancakes."

Wiping the rest of the cream onto her skin, Resha looks at Swallow as Swallow shakes her head in puzzlement. In response to Swallow's confused look, Resha says, "Since we don't know what's in it, I don't think we should be eating too much of it."

For a moment, the two women sit in the shadowy stillness. Swallow then tilts her head wordlessly, directing their attention toward their food.

Resha sighs and says, "I'm really not that hungry. Are you?"

"No, not really. Besides, if we have to ration our food, we may as well start with not eating unless we're really hungry." Swallow reties the netting around the food and gets up to place it on the shelf next to Resha's tightly closed jar of cream, out of any small animal's easy reach. "Just in case," she says.

"That's smart," Resha replies.

Swallow unfastens her bedroll from her pack and lays it out next to Resha.

"Good idea. We may as well get comfy," Resha says, following suit. Soon the two women are laying side by side, waiting for sleep to drift in. A few minutes pass as the moon glides behind the clouds, and darkness falls.

As the two women settle in, Swallow touches Resha's arm and asks, "Do you think the animal will come back?"

Resha rolls over, lying on her back. "It may, but I don't think it will harm us," Before she has even finished the statement, she hears Swallow's measured breathing, suggesting sleep. "Swallow, are you awake?" Resha whispers. Her answer comes in the form of one snort followed by further measured breathing and then silence. From that response, Resha knows Swallow's soundly sleeping. Turning away and onto her other side, Resha soon follows Swallow plummeting into sleep. They both sleep soundly, not stirring till they wake in the early morning hours. Given that they haven't eaten anything since the morning of the day before, they both awake famished.

As Swallow rises to get the food off the shelf, she notices that some water has pooled in a depression next to the netting holding their food. "I forgot to set up to collect the water last night," Swallow mumbles, half to herself, shaking her head. "But some has collected in a hole here on the shelf." She fills two cups from it, handing one to Resha.

Still concerned about their food, Swallow prepares a meager breakfast for them: an apancake and some dried fruit with their water. "There's enough water left on the shelf to freshen up after we've eaten, if you'd like."

The hungry women quickly devour their meager meal and immediately start packing up their sparsely laid-out camp.

Rolling up her bed, Resha watches Swallow attaching her bedroll to her pack. "Do you happen to have an extra set of straps so I can do the same thing?"

"I thought you'd never ask." Swallow chuckles as she removes two extra straps from a pocket on the side of her pack and hands them to Resha. "Would you like me to do that for you?"

Resha smiles to herself, touched by Swallow's offer of help. "I think I can handle it myself, Swallow, but if I can't, believe me—you'll be the first to know."

They split another cup of water between them and then quietly, in the half dark, wash up to wait for first light. Shortly before sunrise, the two women have already gathered the remaining odds and ends of their camp and put their packs on. Soon they are leaving the shade of the crystals behind as they head toward the open desert.

"Good. We're getting an early start," Resha says. "Maybe if we're lucky, it won't be so hot today."

About a kilanss into their trek, Swallow asks, "Is your pack all right on your back?"

"My back's still a bit tender, but I think I'll be okay," Resha says, shifting the pack slightly to get more comfortable.

A gentle breeze intermittently blows in from the north as they leave the crystal behind and head directly toward the city. Upon entering the open desert, a flash of the first sun's light reflects off the rosy crystalline sand shedding an indigo cast on the morning's vista as the suns rise on the horizon behind the ruins. This has a mellowing affect on the entire scene. As the morning passes, every so often, dust devils that look somewhat like petite sunburned cherubs dance on the desert floor surrounding the two women. The wind gusts around them in time with the cherubs' ballet. "It's a good thing that breeze is blowing. I think the suns' rays are even hotter today," Swallow says.

About an hour later, they stop. The wind's still blowing wildly around them, so they remoisten the cloths and retie them around their faces. This time it's more to keep out the sand than the sun. There's no sign of life in the surrounding wicked desert as not even another set of empty footsteps can be found.

By midmorning, they have traveled far from the crystal towers, but the ruins still loom farther away in the distance ahead. By this time, Resha has fallen ten paces behind, so Swallow decides to stop and wait for her. Swallow's a bit concerned, for in the past, Resha has never had trouble keeping up with her, but in this heat, Resha seems to be lagging behind.

Stopping and turning around to face Resha, Swallow asks, "Are you all right?" Resha only nods in response. When she catches up to Swallow she continues on, walking past her. Swallow follows, but this time, she slows her pace to keep time with Resha's steps. At this point, exposed in the open desert, there is nothing either woman can do but continue their trek.

By late afternoon, the image of the ruins has grown considerably larger as the two women draw closer. Stopping a little in front of her Swallow turns to face Resha and the image of the ruins loom behind her. At that moment the sand swirling all around her is so thick that it almost blocks out Resha's view of the city.

"I need to moisten my lips," Swallow says, pulling at her waterskin, which is loosely fixed to her pack by a cord. She brings it to her lips, drawing the cloth on her face aside. On sip is enough to wet her moth and lips so she then offers the skin to Resha. As Resha shakes her head Swallow asks. "Are you sure?"

Wordlessly Resha closes her eyes, nods, and keeps walking. By now, sand and dust cover every visible part of her face. The sand has drawn three pink lines on Resha's forehead, reminding Swallow of the first day they met for their talks. Swallow then pulls the cord securely, refastening the waterskin to her pack, and follows slowly in Resha's footsteps.

A few hours later, they arrive at the edge of the first set of ruins. As they draw nearer to this section of the city, Swallow says, "There's much more left of the city than I had thought." They can see now that the main part to their left consists of a dozen or so blocks made up of many larger buildings that sporadically sprout up amidst the rest of the ruins. Many of the smaller surrounding building have crumbled and decayed into less than half their undamaged glory. In this area of town the lower floors of half dozen or so main buildings are somewhat intact surrounded by a number of smaller structures that are barely recognizable as such. There are about three dozen or so additional groups of smaller buildings on the outskirts of this main group of structures.

They are now standing on the outskirts of what appears to be the remains of a series of smaller, barely identifiable three to four- story shops. Most of the crumbling remnants are maybe a story or two tall. This area appears to be near the original entrance of the city. Over time, the city's nameplate, pieces of debris, and parts of other buildings have filled in much of the space between and around these still partially standing shops.

"It's going to be like an obstacle course just to get to those three largest buildings over there," Swallow says as she puts her arm around Resha. "The city's much larger than I thought it would be."

Even though Swallow can't see Resha's mouth, a smile echoes in Resha's eyes as she nods her agreement. Nearing sunset, the two women enter the city, gingerly walking around and in between piles of debris that dwarf them.

A half hour later, they have arrived at the block leading to the nearest larger buildings they spotted earlier. Resha stops and puts her pack down in order to remove the cloth from her face, which she then uses to wipe her face and eyes. "That feels good." This is the first she has spoken all day, and she's surprised and mildly relieved that the voice coming from her parched throat is still so clear.

Joining her, Swallow drops her pack, takes the facecloth from Resha to remoisten both hers and Resha's, and hands one back to Resha. Swallow then uses the other to clean her face, arms, and hands as Resha does the same. "We had better find some shelter before it gets too dark."

"How about over there?" Resha asks, pointing down the block as she walks in the direction of the largest building. They are soon standing out front so Resha peeks inside. There's still enough light filtering in through the openings where the windows used to be to see most of the front room. "It looks relatively sturdy. At least I think it won't fall in on us."

Swallow walks in and, pushing on the nearest wall, says, "This'll do just fine for tonight."

Resha joins Swallow inside. Piles of rubble are everywhere. The spot that looks the least congested is located in the far right corner of the room. There are no windows on that wall, so the floor in that area is relatively free of broken glass. The two women place their packs next to the entrance out of their way and begin to scoot the remainder of the junk on the floor in the corner, against the far wall. They are attempting to clean out the larger debris from one corner. After they have finished they retrieve their packs and drop them in the recently cleared corner so that they can better clean up the spot they've chosen to sleep in for the night. Completing this chore, they unroll their bedrolls and pick up the food bag in order to prepare something to eat.

Their trek this day has been unmercifully hot and windy, and as they sit down on the stone floor, they welcome the feel of the floor beneath them which is cool and inviting. Swallow places the food bag between them, opening the net. She then spreads out their rations. This night, they will fill their bellies and put off worrying about rationing their food till morning.

> *'Sometimes a full belly is all one gets*
> *to ease their pains and suffering."*

24

A MIDNIGHT JOURNEY

Being in an unfamiliar place, Resha wakes in the middle of the night and after opening her eyes, she's unable to return to sleep. She rolls over, facing Swallow. It's too dark to see her clearly, but in the pitch black, Resha can hear Swallow's steady breathing so she whispers. "Swallow, are you awake?" The sound of Swallow's unfaltering breath tells Resha that she's sleeping deeply. *She's exhausted.* For nearly an hour, Resha lies there tossing and turning with an energy growing inside her, preventing her from drifting back into sleep.

I'd hate to disturb Swallow's rest, so I'd better get up. She rises as quietly as possible and goes outside. In the darkness, Resha looks to the moon, hoping to glean an idea of how long she must wait till morning arrives. *It's going to be a long time before sunrise, and I'm really not that tired.* The moon is shedding enough light for her to do a little exploring. *Now I wish I had brought along one of my torches or at least a lantern.*

The shadows of the broken city dance in the moonlight, haunting her, and soon her imagination morphs them into eerie suitors whom she rebuffs one after another. As she roams the streets in search of a way to expend the energy still growing inside her, Resha's imagination fashions monsters out of the rubble at every turn, which only incites her already heightened emotions, driving her into a near frenzy. *I must find something physical to do to tire myself out and get rid of this energy.* Turning down one deserted street after another, she begins to feel closed in by the seemingly haunted ruins of the city. She's not used to being surrounded so closely by anything, especially not by wrecked buildings. A chill creeps up her spine as she searches for a comforting sign of some sort—something that feels more familiar, that feels like home. Turning another corner, she hopes to shake this feeling of fear mixed with anger that has gripped her soul. *There's no reason to be afraid; we're the only ones here. You're just uncomfortable being so far from home.* Staring down the street into the dark night, she steels herself as she spots a glint of reflected moonlight nearly at the end. Moving toward it, following its shining beacon, she wanders alone in the night. About halfway down the street, another gleam off to the right, buried under a pile of large chunks of unrecognizable pieces of scrap, catches her eye.

There's something down there reflecting the light. Heading toward the closest reflection first, Resha climbs up a pile of debris covering the object and removes the smaller pieces of the rubble sitting on top. About a quarter of the way down, she runs into a much larger piece. Straining to move it, she knows immediately that she alone won't be able to budge it. *Well, I guess I'll have to wait for Swallow's help.*

Climbing off the remaining wreckage, she directs her attention to the bottom of the pile, and lies down on the ground next to it. She's trying to catch a glimpse of what's down there through the rubble. After moving a few smaller pieces at the base out of her way, she's able to clear a hole large enough to reach into, but the gleaming object at the bottom is still too deep and out of her reach. After working awhile longer, she's finally able to dig out the entrance so that it's large enough for her to shove her whole arm and shoulder into. Struggling to put her hand on the elusive object, she soon realizes there are other pieces of rubble she won't be able to clear away that are still blocking her way and preventing her from seeing what's down there.

Momentarily turning her attention away from the hole, Resha rolls over, spotting a collection of scraps with a couple of metal rods sticking out lying up against a neighboring building. *Those might be useful.* They are out of her grasp, so she gets up and walks over to retrieve the rods. She brings them back to the side of the pile where she's been working. After laying one down next to her, she takes the second and pushes it down the hole she's just finished digging, in the direction of the reflected light. About three quarters of the rod's length is buried before it hits bottom and makes a clanking sound. *Hmm, the sound of metal hitting metal. I wonder what's down there. I need Swallow's help. I can't handle the larger pieces alone, but together we might be able to move them out of the way. Maybe in the morning.*

Getting to her feet, she picks up the remaining rod, and she heads down the street to explore the initial glint that caught her eye before this one had distracted her. The wreckage pile covering this other object is even larger than the one she has been working on, but it looks as if most of the fragments are at least a size she can manage. She puts the rod down next to the pile and begins clearing away the ruins piece by piece. After she's cleared away about half the pile, the toll of this night's heightened emotions and the physical labor Resha has been doing over the past few days finally hits her. Realizing just how tired she is, she stops as her weariness sinks into her bones and finally invades. *I'm too tired to finish this tonight. It'll wait.*

Concerned that in the morning light, she might not be able to find this spot again, Resha picks up the second rod and plunges it halfway into the mound, marking the exact spot where she first saw the glint. *There. That should be easy to see from up the block.* With exhaustion finally setting in, she retraces her steps back to the shelter of their camp, occasionally looking over her shoulder to memorize the path leading back to the pile, so she will be able to find her way back there tomorrow.

Standing before the entrance to their camp's shelter, she pauses briefly, realizing how sore this night's escapade has left her. As she enters the building, the welcoming sound of Swallow's familiar breathing greets her. As quietly as she can, Resha climbs inside her bedroll, hoping she will now be able to sleep. She's not sure if it's her imagination or reality, but the last thing she hears as she floats off into sleep is Swallow, sweetly whispering her name.

> *'Come into my dreams, my love, and hold*
> *me tight till morning's light invades'.*

25

VISITORS

Early the next morning, a strange commotion jolts the two women awake. Resha immediately realizes that it's a sound she's never heard before in her life, a noise she can't recall even from childhood memories.

It doesn't sound threatening to her, but Swallow, surprised by any noise in their silent world, is the first to react. "What's that?" Swallow swiftly gets up and goes to the door to look outside. Just as she reaches the door, a small creature glides in over her head. It's brilliant blue with a green back and a red chest. Holding something in its mouth, it still manages to make a twittering sound as it flies across the room. It seems to her that this creature is the source of the mysterious sound.

The creature lands at the entrance of a small hole about three gliers (meters) above where the two women have been sleeping and disappears into the shadows. Strange scratching and rustling sounds drift out from its hole; it seems to be busily working on something. A few minutes later, it flies out of the hole with an empty beak, heading out the door once again.

"What's that?" Swallow says, walking over to a spot beneath the hole. Shading her eyes, she peers up at the hole.

"I have no idea," Resha responds. "I've been searching my mind to see if I have ever encountered one before, but I can't recall such a creature, even from my early childhood." Just then, the little animal returns, flying in about a foot over Resha's head. She can see that it's carrying some leaves and moss in its pointed mouth. A few seconds later, another almost identical creature silently follows, also with its mouth stuffed to the brim. They enter their tiny cave and stay for a while, busily chattering, before they fly out once again.

"Well, I'll be," Swallow says. "I wonder what they're doing."

Getting up, Resha moves to Swallow's side. The two women stand there for some time in silence, staring up at the hole. Finally turning to Swallow, Resha says, "Well, what do you think they're up to?"

Swallow shrugs, leaving Resha's side and heading toward the largest pile of rubble closest to the hole, leaning against a wall in the center of the room. She hopes that by standing on the top, she will gain a clear view into the open hole. After reaching the crest of the pile, she stands up on her toes trying to peek inside the hole and speculates. *I'm still not quite high enough. It's too far away to actually see anything clearly, because the hole is shaded, and where they are working is in the shadows.* Challenged by her blocked line of site, she moves closer to the opening to get a better look by climbing onto the remains of a neighboring, slightly higher window ledge. Then scooting from one window ledge to the next, she continues on until she's next to the hole and close enough to get a good look inside. "They appear to be building something," Swallow says.

"What does it look like?" Resha asks.

"There are two little stacks of leaves, moss, and twigs about a hand's length apart from each other, and in the center is a bowl like structure made of twigs, leaves, a strange fur and hair. The twigs and moss appear to be woven together by different colors of hair and an unusual fur of some sort. At least I think it's fur. There's a loose piece in the corner. I'll grab it and bring it down for you."

Swallow reaches in, removing a small, flattish blue object about the length and width of her finger. She then places it between her lips for safekeeping on her climb down. Retracing her path down she's finally able to jump back onto the pile that is leading to the floor.

As her foot lands on the pile, both creatures simultaneously fly in close over her head, making such a racket that Swallow loses her footing and tumbles the remaining way down the pile. She lands on her side near the ground. The fall has twisted her sideways, leaving her lying partly on her belly and partly on her right shoulder. Taking stock of her body for potential injuries, she lies still for a few moments. Then she awkwardly shifts position onto one side while dragging herself off the rubble and onto the floor. Now looking back over her shoulder at the hole, she can see the two small creatures standing guard at its mouth, still seemingly verbally accosting her for trespassing into their home.

Running over to Swallow, Resha says, "Are you all right?" She squats down next to Swallow's body lying askew on the floor and touches her arm.

After a second or two, Swallow stirs and rolls onto her back. She's still holding the piece of fur between her lips as she sits up. Needing to remove the object from her mouth before she can speak, she nods while her face turns crimson. After taking the fur from her mouth, she says, "I'm fine. Just slightly banged up and a bit shaken is all." In order to assess the scrape on her knee, she hands her prize to Resha asking, "Ever see anything like this before?"

Resha stands up, examining it by running it through her fingertips several times. She then offers a hand to Swallow, helping her to her feet. After doing this she turns her full attention back to the object in her hand and notes that it's soft and blue. It's also arranged in a distinctly odd pattern. It doesn't look like any fur Resha has ever seen. It looks more like a mini–tree branch, only different—much more elaborate and organized.

Swallow moves in closer behind and looks over Resha's shoulder at the so-called fur. "There were others like this woven into and sticking out of the central structure," Swallow says. "They were a variety of different-colors—some green, some red, and some orange, all of different sizes. The little thing they're crafting is just beautiful. This fur, or whatever it is, is woven into whatever they're making with a variety of different-colored hair. The hairs look almost human. In fact, some of them are the color of your hair. These unusual colors make whatever they're building look just spectacular. There are browns and greens accented with the brightly colored fur, hair, and small stones." Swallow gently lifts the fur like object from Resha's grasp in order to get a better look at it. By that point in time, both little creatures have quieted and retreated into their hole once more, but soon afterward, they fly out again, presumably on another gathering mission.

After the creatures have left and things have quieted down, Resha and Swallow go back to their makeshift beds and sit down. Swallow places the piece of fur on the ground and puts a small rock on it to hold it down so that it doesn't get lost.

A wisp of a smile crosses Resha's face as she watches Swallow's tenderness with the fur, and she asks, "How big is the structure they're building?"

Swallow, rubbing her eyes to try to remove the last grains of sand from yesterday's trek is momentarily silent. When she's finished, she turns her attention back to her discussion with Resha. "It's about the size of both my hands cupped together. Like this." Swallow places her hands side by side to show Resha what she means. "Sort of shaped that way too." As their suns' cerulean light streams in through the glassless window panes and onto Swallow's hands, their yellowish-green hue magically turns aqua before Resha's eyes.

Moments later her excitement waning, Resha says "Hmm," as she stretches and lays back down. "If you don't mind, I think I'm going to go back to sleep for a while. I was up exploring for most of last night, and I'm still a bit tired."

"That's fine by me, but I'm going to get up and do some looking around on my own. I'll try not to disturb you when I get back."

As she drifts off to sleep, the last thing Resha sees is Swallow's back as she is heading out the door. Half awake, she watches Swallow disappear down the road and turn onto a side street. Then Resha's eyes wearily close. *I hope you enjoy.* Resha drifts off, as the soft blanket of sleep rewraps itself around her, comforting her and gliding her back to her long-forgotten dreams.

> *'Circling down into a rabbit hole, I lose myself as reality becomes twisted with my dreams, and my senses fall away.'*

26

THEIR FIRST MORNING IN THE CITY

Upon waking, Resha opens her eyes to discover Swallow sitting by her side. Swallow seems lost in thought, gazing away from her and down at the floor. Still half asleep, Resha smiles and absentmindedly reaches over to stroke Swallow's hand lying next to her bedroll. At the first contact of Resha's fingertips on her skin, Swallow smiles and turns her attention to her dear companion.

Gently laying her hand on top of Swallow's, Resha stretches and closes her eyes once more, asking. "Have you been there long?"

"No, just got back a few minutes ago, but I didn't want to wake you. I was just waiting here, daydreaming. I figured when you woke, we could eat."

"What if I didn't wake up?" Resha lifts her head, briefly opening one eye to look at Swallow. Moments later, she lays her head back down, closing both eyes, and chuckles. Still half asleep, she lazily runs her hand up her friend's forearm, and absentmindedly starts circling her thumb around the inside of the crook of Swallow's elbow.

"I would've just waited," Swallow answers with a smile dancing in her eyes.

Leisurely sitting up, Resha rubs the sleep from her eyes with her free hand and yawns. She's always surprised by the ease she now feels when she's alone with this woman. Even though she's still a bit alarmed by the depth of her feelings for Swallow, she can no longer deny that when she's with Swallow, these feelings are beginning to delight and amuse her. Looking down, she's startled to discover her thumb of her right hand gently massaging the inside of Swallow's elbow. Now totally awake, she slightly shocked by this over familiar action and finds herself somewhat embarrassed by the intimacy of caressing this young woman's arm in this manner, so she hastily removes her hand. Silence hangs in the air between the two women as Swallow reaches over, trying to recapture Resha's retreating fingers. "Why did you stop?" Swallow asks as the two women's hands come together, scarcely touching.

"I don't know; it somehow felt inappropriate. After all, I'm so much older than you." Sighing, Resha attempts to distract them from their current topic as she feigns a leisurely stretch, in the guise of shaking away the last remnants of sleep.

"And why does that matter so much to you?" Letting go of Resha's hand, Swallow stands, and slowly walks a few paces away, trying to occupy herself with anything but Resha and the jumbled feelings inside her at that moment.

Hesitating and having no sensible answer to the question Swallow has just posed, Resha remains silent.

After a few moments of stillness, Swallow turns toward Resha and repeats her query. "Why does our age difference matter so much to you?"

"I don't know," Resha says, looking down and turning her full attention to fidgeting with the sleeve of her shirt. She's flabbergasted at not having a sensible answer, so she finally blurts out, "How do you come up with such questions?"

"Quit stalling, and please answer me." Swallow turns, walking in Resha's direction and halting only when she's standing immediately above her. Resha's silence hangs in the cool morning air, forming symbolic icicles in the now seemingly frosty fog occupying the space between these two women. For a long while, Swallow stands there, before sitting down next to Resha. *She almost looks like a small child who's been caught doing something wrong.* In response to her own thoughts, Swallow touches the side of Resha's face, casually sliding her hand to Resha's chin, then lifting it, and forcing Resha to look up at her. "Why does it matter to you?"

"I really don't know. Maybe I feel it's not fair to you. You have so much of your life ahead, and I—"

"And you're old, huh?" Swallow smiles, holding Resha's eyes captive with her grin.

"Well, I'm older than you," Resha retorts.

"Uh-huh, you're ancient." Swallow chuckles.

"Well, as a matter of fact, I—"

"No, you're not, Resha. You have more life in you than most of us half your age. Look at all you've done this past year."

"I know, but that's not really me, Swallow. It's just that someone had to do something, and I did what I could. That's all."

"So who are you really, Resha? Tell me who you are. Better yet, let me see who you are." Taking Resha's face in both hands, Swallow says, "Do you even know how beautiful you are? And I'm not only talking physical beauty here. You've done so much for me." Swallow drops her hands to the small patch of ground looming between her and Resha.

The distance between their hands is small, but at that moment, it feels almost impassable to Swallow. Although she has turned her gaze so that she's now looking away from Resha, the fingertips of her right hand are still pointing towards and nearly touching Resha's. Their two hands are but a wisp apart. In a short span of time, their fingers have covertly crept so close that they are separated only by a hair's breadth. Then turning toward Resha once more, Swallow notices their hands proximity and is drawn to point it out to Resha. Unfortunately, while staring down at the deceptively small space between their hands, she cannot make herself utter a single word. *The secret our hands can't conceal is exactly what Resha's trying so hard to deny.* Struggling to find the right words while lifting her eyes toward Resha's face, she simply smiles.

"It's not fair to you," Resha says, searching Swallow's features. Still blindly caught merely in their conversation, she has not yet noticed their hands.

After a few moments, Swallow meets Resha's gaze and says, "I'll decide what's fair to me, because that's not your decision or anyone else's to make. That's my choice. Please tell me what's really bothering you."

Silence hangs in the air between these two women for what seems like a long time. Finally Resha whispers "I'm scared," At the same time she deliberately directs her gaze back down at the floor.

"And I'm terrified," Swallow says, shaking her head, returning her attention back to their hands. Despite Resha's resistance, Swallow is relieved that their feelings are finally out in the open. She fleetingly looks at Resha's face in an effort to recapture her eyes and then, being unsuccessful, returns her attention to their hands once more. "So what do we do now?"

Resha raises her eyes and says, half jokingly, "I don't know. How about we go out and explore the city? We both know we haven't sorted this all out yet and are not ready to do anything about our feeling." She sits there, searching Swallow's face, trying to recapture the attention from Swallow's icy blue eyes.

Swallow smirks finally looking up at her. "Just like you to change the focus when we're finally getting somewhere." After making a halfhearted attempt to get up, Resha's held prisoner by Swallow's unrelenting grasp.

"Come on. Resha then says. We know we have a limited amount of time here, and you know I'm right." Finally looking down at their hands, Resha lets her fingertips slowly inch forward till they're touching Swallow's. "This isn't going to go away anytime soon if it's real—both you and I know that. And besides, we have things to do."

"Are you pulling rank on me again?" Swallow asks.

Smiling, Resha says, "No, just feeling like it's time to get up and get going." Still looking down at their hands, Resha adds, "What do you think? Should we get going?" As she says this, she slides her hand up Swallow's arm and once again absentmindedly rests her thumb in the crook of Swallow's elbow. With the simple touch of Swallow's skin, she's at last able to still her inner fears.

Reluctantly, Swallow rises to her feet. "Sure, Resha, but I want to say just one more thing before we're done here. I love you," she says, extending a hand to help Resha get up.

Resha quietly blushes. This day the touch of Resha's hand and the color in her face are the only replies Swallow will receive.

> *'The touch of the warm skin of a beloved has a way of melting even the most ice-bound heart.'*

27

RUMMAGING THROUGH THE RUINS

Bending down, Resha opens the netting holding their food. *If we ration it right, we should have enough to last three, maybe four more days.*

This means that at most, the two women have two full days left to explore the city before they need to start back. Walking over to stand above Resha, Swallow asks, "Do you want me to get that?"

"No, it's okay, Swallow. You've been taking care of the food up till now. Let me handle breakfast." She pulls out a medium bundle of synthetic dried fruits and a similar-sized wrapped package, which contains bits of dried synthetic meat. Two other packages still remain in the net.

"The biggest one is the apancakes," Swallow says, removing her waterskin from her pack. "The other's a special treat I brought along to surprise you. Let's wait till we've finished all the others, to open that one. Okay?"

Resha smiles and nods at Swallow, honoring her wish. She knows that they've a busy day ahead, and these two packages are quite full, so she doesn't skimp on the portions. The two women eat their meal in silence, and then Resha rewraps the leftover portions, replacing them in Swallow's net.

Afterward, Resha reaches into her pack and takes out two clean bandanas she's been saving. She dampens both and tosses one to Swallow. "Don't you think we should save these for later?" Swallow asks opening hers and laying it on her pack.

Resha smiles, considering Swallow's question, and nods in agreement. "That's a good idea; we have a busy day ahead," she says as she casually hangs hers on her pack to dry. "While you were outside, did you happen to see the little project I started last night?"

"No. I really can't say I did. It all looks like rubble to me. What did you do?"

Nodding toward the door, Resha says, "Come on. I'll show you." Resha heads outside with Swallow following close on her heels and retraces her steps back to last night's project. After navigating through the narrow streets, she turns a corner, heads down a long passageway, and stops about midway down the block. She walks to the first marker that she left sticking out of a large pile of rubble last night and pauses, touching the biggest piece of wreckage on the top. Pulling out the rod and casting it aside, Resha says, "We're going to move this pile off of whatever it's sitting on."

Raising an eyebrow while assessing the task, Swallow notes that the pile is chest high, and she spies right away that there's one huge chunk sitting on the top.

Resha says, "Last night, I couldn't move that top piece, and there's something underneath here that's, well, let's just say, is interesting."

Standing in front of the pile, Swallow slowly examines the chunk on the top. *Fortunately, the top piece is somewhat round.* "Okay," she says. "The piece directly on the top looks like the largest, so if we're able to move that, I think we'll be okay."

"Maybe it would be best to slide that one piece partway down the pile and try to get it onto its side," Resha says. "Then we can hopefully roll it down the rest of the way and keep it rolling till it clears the pile and is out of our way."

The two women get on either side of the slab, sliding it off the top and down the steepest side of the pile. It ends up resting about halfway down the pile, almost upright and standing on one end. Resha holds it in place while Swallow climbs up on the pile behind it.

After getting a secure footing on the pile, Swallow asks, "Are you ready?"

"As ready as I'm going to get," Resha responds. Together they maneuver the piece so that it's heading mostly downhill toward the ground. Pushing it as hard as she can, Swallow signals Resha to get out of the way. The weight of the piece causes it to tumble down the pile and roll about ten paces beyond, where it finally stops when it collides with the remains of what appears to be an old lamppost. Swallow immediately starts throwing the smaller pieces that were underneath it as far off the pile as possible. Resha starts work on the other side, doing the same and in no time, they've reduced the pile to half its former size.

"I hope this is worth it," Swallow says. They spend most of the rest of the morning clearing away the debris in their way. About an hour later, dusty and tired, they've reached the bottom. When they finally finish moving the last piece off, a silver plate about a glier which equals a meter square is staring back at them. It's located flush with street level, embedded in concrete, and has a latch with a lock with two conjoining arms on one side.

Swallow grabs a large piece of concrete and begins pounding at the lock. The hammering doesn't even put a dent in it, so she gets up and goes looking for something to wedge in between its arms, while Resha turns her attention to examining the lock closer.

About a block away, Swallow enters the nearest large building to check it out for something to use to break the lock. Letting her instincts guide her, she ends up standing in the center of the room, looking around where she first spots a floor-to-ceiling panel leaning against the far wall. A few minutes later, she is sifting through some wreckage in front of it to clear it away. After unblocking the panel, she easily slides it aside, discovering a closet behind it. The door is jammed, so she pulls on it as hard as she can. It takes her a couple of tries for her to get it open. Peering into the closet, she sees a number of odd-looking objects. *I'll have to come back and explore the rest of this stuff later.* Focusing on finding something to open the lock, she spies a couple of long metal pry bars in the back corner.

After she pushes a few things aside, she grabs the largest bar, feeling its weight and its potential power in her hands. *This will do just fine.* The bar is about an inch thick and is nearly her shoulder height.

With the tool in hand, she jogs back to Resha, who is still standing above the lock, and wedges the bar between the lock's arms. Resha moves aside to give her room as she pushes down on the bar with all her weight, trying to pry the lock open. Almost immediately, the bar slips free, falling to the street. She almost falls with it. A loud clanging sound echoes in the streets as the bar bounces off the concrete collar surrounding the silver hatch and rolls onto the sand-covered ground. After recovering it, Swallow shoves the bar deeper into the lock's arms and twists, pushing downward, but the bar again slips free. Fortunately, this time, she manages to hold on to it. On the third try, she repositions the lock and shoves the bar against the metal door beneath. With all her strength, she pulls up on the rod, and the lock's arms at first give ever so slightly and then spring open. "They sure didn't make these locks hard to get into," Swallow says in jest.

Moving next to Swallow, Resha focuses only on the plate in front of her as a scene from her childhood suddenly flashes through her mind—an image of when she was but a tiny tot holding on to her mother's hand and walking down a street.

In this memory, she can't be more than three years old, and she is holding on to her mother for dear life. It's one of the first times she has been taken out for a walk in their city.

The city is noisy, with people bustling by her on all sides. Resha feels threatened and almost overwhelmed as she looks up at her smiling mother by her side. Her feeling of fear disappears as her mother takes her hand.

Apparently, her mother has to run some type of urgent errand, and Resha is getting to be too heavy for her to carry all the way there and back. Her rickety stroller broke the week before, so Resha's mother's forced to make the trip by intermittently putting Resha down and letting her walk in short spurts throughout the trip.

Halfway through this first outing, Resha remembers a lot of shouting as an emaciated young man running by her nearly knocks her over. He is carrying a burlap bag over his right shoulder, and he pauses to look back at something, just behind Resha and her mother. A frantic energy overcomes him, as he starts running once more. In his panic, he doesn't see little Resha and nearly runs into her. He falls down in the process of trying to avoid her, and now, at eye level, she can see the fear in the eyes of his dirty, tear-stained face.

Resha's mother looks down at him, offering him a hand to get up, but he refuses. Then looking up at the toddler Resha, he briefly smiles before the panic overtakes his features once more, and seconds later, he's up on his feet and running past them. They hear the sound of breaking glass behind them, and several men's voices shout some profanities from a short half block behind.

Resha's mother, fearing for her child's safety, sweeps Resha into her arms, and Resha can now clearly see the small mob starting to engulf them. After they pass by, they begin peppering the young man with the sticks and rocks in their hands. There are about a dozen or so of them, and they appear as bedraggled and ragged, as the young man who passed did. At first glance, they seem to all be young men approximately the same age as the man carrying the burlap sack. They are shouting and trying to stop him, and as they pass, Resha can feel her mother's fear rise through her body as she tries to protect her baby.

From her mother's arms, Resha can see the mob stop a short distance ahead. Despite her fear for the safety of her child, Resha's mother pushes through the crowds ahead with Resha in her arms and stops just at the edge of the mob. By now, the shouting has stopped, and the men are looking down at something. Their hands still full of sticks and rocks now lie at their sides.

One man moves aside, and Resha and her mother can see that they are staring down at the crumpled remains of a burned body lying on a shiny plate. What remains of the burlap bag is lying underneath the figure.

Alarms sound. In response, sirens echo through the distant streets behind, and the mob starts to disperse. One lone figure remains: a boy several years younger than the rest. He's kneeling at the edge of the smoldering body afraid to touch it. Resha's mother places her on the ground, takes her hand and moves to the side of the youngster, placing her free hand on his shoulder.

He is crying and beside himself. Resha's mother picks her up and takes his hand as the rest of the gathered crowd begins to scatter to escape the looming sirens closing in on them all. Her mother leads him about halfway down the street to a shop, removes a key from her pocket, opening the door, and quickly enters the shop. There's enough sunlight streaming in through the front plate-glass window to dimly light the entire place.

After placing Resha in a playpen in the corner, she pulls a chair out and puts it next to the playpen, instructing the boy to sit. "Please watch her while I go get some things."

The boy with the haunted, dirty face briefly looks around. As Resha watches him, she can see a look of fear grip him. For a split second, as his panic begins to rise, she can see the features of the young man with the burlap bag in the boy's face. Resha smiles at him and touches his hand, and the panic disappears as tears begin to stream down his face once more.

Moments later, Resha's mother is standing by his side with a washcloth and a morsel of food in her hands. After he's eaten, he tells his story, and they learn that the dead man was his older brother. Jacob was his name, and he had been trying to rescue a pregnant cat from the mob of young men, who were proposing to cook and eat her.

Leaving her memories and returning her attention to Swallow Resha says, "I remember these doors now. As a precaution, they were also wired with lethal electrical shocks and alarms to deter break-ins. Those unaware of the danger they held were usually killed trying to gain access, and then the controllers would swoop in and disperse the remaining alleged would-be thieves."

"Why didn't you tell me of that before? I could've been killed!" Swallow says, looking at Resha in horror.

"I didn't remember that fact till just now. Besides, if I'm right, usually the whole top plate was electrified. Since we both touched that while clearing away the rubble and nothing happened, I think we'll be all right." Putting her hand on Swallow's arm to dispel her fears, Resha moves her aside and reaches for the plate. "I think I know how this thing opens," she says, tossing the latch open, bending down, sliding the door inward and then up and out, removing it completely from the square concrete hole. With the door gone, the open hole reveals a hatch beneath. The hatch appears to be marginally larger than the width of Swallow's shoulders. "Great," Resha says, half laughing. "Another daunting task."

"After all this, I'm realizing they didn't make anything easy, did they?" Swallow says, bending down and getting on her hands and knees. While brushing away the remaining crumbling dust, she looks for another latch. "Let's open it."

"You didn't even ask if this hatch was electrified," Resha says, shaking her head.

Swallow looks up at her and smiles. "Well, by this point, I hope you would've stopped me if it was. I can't find a latch, though."

Resha, shaking her head, smirks. "If we can't break in, it's okay. We have another pile down the block to clear away that we can take care of first."

Rising to her feet, Swallow looks at Resha with a questioning gaze. "Are you kidding?"

Shaking her head, without a word, Resha heads down the street in the direction of the second pile. *At least we tackled the larger one first.*

The second pile is the one Resha spent hours on last night, slashing it nearly in half. One side of the heap is leaning up against what is left of a building. This pile is less than half the size of the pile they just flattened to the ground. Shortly, Swallow joins Resha and says, "Well, at least this one's not as big."

"That's only because I worked on it most of last night." Resha raises an eyebrow, turning toward the pile to begin their task.

After two hours of work, they can just make out a set of stainless-steel double doors underneath the remaining wreckage. The two doors slant, rising from the street up to about a foot's height and ending nearly resting against the side of the building. "This looks promising. They might lead to somewhere under the building," Resha says.

"Do I need to be concerned about being electrocuted here?" Swallow says, half in jest.

Resha shrugs and raises her left eyebrow.

Looking at Resha, Swallow briefly hesitates, and then she begins to cart away the lingering chunks of debris. In front of her stands a set of silver doors much like the ones she and Resha found in the bunker. However, unlike the elevator in the bunker, these doors clearly have a visible latch in the center, and there are no side walls for the doors to disappear into.

After clearing off the left door, Swallow notices the remnants of a rusted lock lying broken and crumbling just below the latch. Glancing at Resha, Swallow then sweeps away its remains to allow her to open the latch. When done she grabs the door's handle and tries to pull it open. The hinges are made of the same substance as the door and easily give way.

As Resha suspected, a stairwell descends under the building into darkness. "Must be a cellar of some sort," Resha mumbles reaching in, and feeling the left wall for a button or a switch of some sort. She finds none.

Swallow has no idea what a cellar is but decides that this is not the time or place to ask. "What are you looking for?"

"I was hoping to find a light switch like in the back room of the bunker. Maybe we should get this other side open and check there." Resha says gesturing toward the right door.

Swallow and Resha immediately go to work clearing off the other side, and soon that door is also open. Reaching inside, Swallow feels the right wall for a switch but finds none. In the fading light, the two women can see that the stairs are open, not bound by walls on either side. Fortunately, the remnants of a handrail lead down one side. After the twentieth stair, the handrail disappears as the stairway sharply turns to the right, and their vision careens into total darkness. "Looks pretty dark down there. I think we may need some sort of light to explore this place," Swallow says, pointing down the stairs. "Maybe we can find something to use as light in one of the larger buildings or possibly if we can get it open, in the hatch."

Leaving the doors open, the two women retreat back to the first project of their day: the hatch.

'A unknown entrance below is still an entrance below and cannot lead to the doors of heaven.'

28

THE HATCH

Swallow stops at the hatch first returning to her search for a way to open it as Resha heads off down the street looking for a something to light their way. She ends up stopping in front of the building that they used as shelter last night. *I knew I should have brought one of my torches along.* Resha goes inside, and feverously starts searching for something to use to light their way into the underground vaults. When she can't find anything that looks promising, she decides to return to Swallow. Heading back towards the hatch she sees Swallow still kneeling over it searching for some type of release trigger to open it. Resha walks up behind her briefly stopping to watch over Swallow's shoulder.

Swallow looks up and points down the street. "I got the bar I used to open the lock from a closet in that building over there. Maybe you should check it out for something to use to light our way, while I work on this," Swallow says, before turning back to the hatch. *Opening the double doors earlier was simple compared to this, but maybe if I'm lucky, this hatch won't be as hard as it looks. I just have to discover its trick.*

"When you picked up the bar, did you see anything to use as a light?" Resha asks. Swallow shakes her head, no. "Then let's get this open first. We can always go look in the closet later."

Searching her memories for anything that might give them a clue, Resha recalls that when she was a little girl, she had seen a similar hatch that had required a key to open it.

Swallow still kneeling over the hatch, again runs both hands around the outer edge and under its lip, feeling for anything that might release it but nothing feels out of the ordinary.

Resha moves into a position across from Swallow and kneels down, looking for anything that might resemble a keyhole. No keyhole is visible on top, so she bends down and closely examines the rim. After carefully inspecting the outside rim, she finds no place to insert a key. *Well, I guess it doesn't really matter since we don't have the key anyhow.* Trying to remember if she's ever seen anyone open one of these in her childhood, she can't and her mind's a blank.

Looking at their surroundings, Resha wonders if this hatch had previously been indoors. *It's out in the open now, but it could have been inside before the city crumbled.* She knows that if it was, the release mechanism could be hidden anywhere in the adjacent rubble. Looking at her surroundings she realizes that this might be especially true if the hatch was located in a secure building of some sort. *Maybe this effort will turn out to be futile. After all, if the hatch was inside, the release mechanism could've even been destroyed when the surrounding structure crumbled.* Although it is hard to tell for sure, after perusing her surroundings, Resha doesn't think the hatch had previously been located indoors.

In the meantime, frustrated by not finding a way to open the hatch, Swallow puts her hands on either side of the hatch cover, trying to lift it, but it won't budge, so she grabs the bar she used earlier and tries to pry the hatch free. After a few failed attempts, she wedges the bar under the hatch rim and secures it in a corner of the square concrete encasement surrounding it. In a desperate effort to pry the hatch open, she sits on the bar, but it won't move. *Nothing.* Next, she tries jumping on the end of the bar, but the bar only slips from under the rim, and as Swallow tumbles to the ground, it clangs onto the street, rolling a short distance away. Lying in the rubble, Swallow closes her eyes in exasperation and shakes her head.

Concerned that Swallow might've hurt herself, Resha jumps to her side and offers her a hand. "Are you okay?"

Smiling up at Resha, Swallow's slightly amused by her own antics and nods that she's okay. Getting up on all fours, she turns crawling toward the hatch. Immediately she goes back to work, looking for a way to open it. "Maybe if I twist it, I can loosen the seal." Grabbing the hatch with both hands, Swallow twists it to the right, but it will not budge.

"Maybe if we try together," Resha says as she kneels back down opposite of Swallow and grabs the two free sides. "Try turning it left this time." After several minutes of working together and struggling with the hatch, they are finally able to get the top to move about an inch to the left.

"Let's try one more time," Swallow says. "Now that we have been able to move it, it might be easier. One, Two, Three!"

They put everything they have into it, and at last, it twists free. After turning it one complete turn, Swallow tries once more to lift it, but she's thwarted; the hatch is still firmly in place, refusing to yield.

"I think I may have seen something similar in a book somewhere. Just keep turning it in the same direction," Resha says. Both women keep twisting the cap till it's completely free. Swallow then slides the cap off the entrance and over onto one side of the surrounding concrete.

Looking down into the hole together, all they can clearly see are a dozen or so rungs of a ladder beneath them secured to one side of a wall. These rungs descend into the dark, open mouth of the chamber below. As their eyes follow the ladder's descent downward, the women's vision grays and soon disappears into a velvety darkness. A faint odor rising from below, hints that something not quite palatable has taken up residence down there. From up here, the smell only teases their noses and tempts their eyes to water.

"Well, this looks like another dead end, at least until we can find something to light our way. But let me check it out anyway," Resha says.

Swallow puts her arm in front of Resha, stopping her. "Maybe we should wait for the smell to clear for a while before you head down there."

"Nonsense, I've smelled worse and it's only a smell," Resha says, mounting the ladder and starting her descent. As she heads downward, the metal rungs feel cold and dusty in her hands. After climbing down a few feet, she searches every wall for a light switch of some sort. Upon entering the darkness, a cornucopia of smells and tastes rises from below, assaulting her nose and taste buds. Some of the smells are tolerable, and others, like the first whiff that hit them, are distinctly unpleasant.

One brings to mind a familiar smell from her childhood. It's the smell of old papers that have been stored for centuries. In the darkness, a fond memory of watching her mother open a sealed box full of her great-great-great-grandmother's collected papers drifts through her mind. As she slides down farther into darkness, the smells grow stronger, till she feels her last meal threatening to rise into her throat. A sensation of uncertainty invades, followed by fear. As it heightens, she pauses. *It's so strange in here, and I can't see a thing. I don't know if I'll be able to stand it much longer.* Stopping once more, Resha reaches out into the darkness, and her hand touches nothing but a cool stone wall and air. A slightly sticky, sickening sensation again rises in her throat, as she believes she's almost had enough.

Meanwhile, Swallow is topside, lying next to the hole and peering inside. She watches while the darkness consumes Resha. A few minutes after Resha's disappearance, Swallow becomes concerned and yells out, "Find anything?"

"Too dark to tell down here, but no switch as of yet!" Resha shouts back from the blackness.

"Come on back up then," Swallow says, feeling a chill crawl up her spine. "It's getting late, and we should probably quit soon anyhow. Besides, we haven't eaten anything since breakfast today, and I'm getting hungry."

Looking up, Resha starts climbing the ladder toward daylight and says, "I know, but we've gotten a lot done today." Before emerging from the darkness, she stops one more time to feel around the neighboring wall, still hoping beyond all hope that she might find a switch.

Looking up toward Swallow, with her eyes now fully adjusted to the dim light, she spots something hanging from the ceiling just on the edge of daylight. It dawns on her that she might've missed something on the way down. As she rises out of the gloom, she senses an object hanging from the ceiling located about five feet below the hatch, a few feet away. It's still virtually concealed by the shadows so she hurries her ascent, trying to get a better look. When she's about a foot below it, she can make out something hanging from the ceiling about three arm's lengths to the right of the edge of the entrance hole. From where she's standing she can't quite tell what it is.

After climbing up a few more rungs, she stops even with the object hanging about five meters below the street. On her way down with her eyes unaccustomed to the dim light, it had been concealed by the edge of darkness hanging there in the shadows. She still can't quite make out what it is so she leans out as far as she dares while holding on to the ladder with one hand. Reaching over in the direction of the object with her free hand she swings her arm to the right, and her fingers graze the half-hidden thing, which until now, she thought might only be a mirage of some sort.

After touching it, she's sure it's real, and she can tell it's cloth. She takes two more steps upward and hooks her lower legs into the ladder. With one hand still firmly grasping the ladder by her right knee, she leans backward, using the other hand to try to capture the elusive object. At first reaching blindly into the shadows, she only grazes it, and it swings farther out of her reach. A jangling sound echoes as the object moves. On the second try, as the cloth swings nearest her, she can see that it is a medium size duffle bag. On the next swing she manages to grab it, but it's still hooked onto a chain of some sort, and she can't free it using only one hand, so she lets go.

Watching this all from above, Swallow says, "What are you doing? Do you need my help?"

"Not yet. There's something down here, but I can't quite reach it. I almost had it this last try," Resha says, straining to grab it once more.

"Why don't you let me try?" Swallow says. "I'm taller than you."

"I can do it," Resha responds as she braces her feet around the lower rung and leans back letting go of the ladder with both hands this time. Reaching as far back as she can, she struggles grasping out into the darkness, and catches the object in one hand again. Using her free hand, she's finally able to unhook it from its bondage. After letting the chain go it swings wildly in the air nearly crashing into her. Bringing the bag with her into the light, she says, "Wow."

"What is it?" Swallow's now leaning down into the hole to get a better look and blocking Resha's light.

"I don't know yet. It's a bag of some sort," Resha replies. "I'm coming up with it, so we can open it together. I'm not sure, but if it's what I think it is, we're in for a real treat."

The bag reminds Resha of the food sacks she saw the controllers carrying when she was a small child. These bags were stocked with all sorts of treats used to appease the starving. She recalls that in her youth, whenever a large skirmish broke out, the controllers would dump hundreds of these sacks onto the mob to stop the fighting and help disperse the mobs. This technique worked surprisingly well. Dumping food was much easier than physically going in to break up the fighting. As long as they had enough treats to drop into the crowd, the tactic minimized the number of people who got hurt and decreased the chance of damage to one of their own. After climbing up the remaining few rungs, Resha hands the bag to Swallow, who's now kneeling at the edge of the hole, peering down at her. After taking the bag, Swallow offers a hand to Resha helping her out of the hatch. "What did you find down there?"

"It's really too dark to see much," Resha says, sitting on the edge of the hole and dangling her legs as if to test the hungry mouth of the darkness. "We'll have to find something to make a torch if we want to explore further down there." Then, in one swift motion, Resha swings her legs onto the ground next to her and quickly lays the hatch cover over the opening. She then scoots closer to Swallow and her prize discovery.

Swallow's sitting a few feet away with the bag next to her. *At least I know what a torch is.* "Maybe we can jury-rig some type of lighting. We can work on that for the rest of the day and spend all day tomorrow exploring our two finds after we find a source of light."

Resha and Swallow are now sitting on the ground a few feet from the hatch with the bag between them. "Do you want to open it, or should I?" Resha asks.

Swallow shrugs uncommittingly, so Resha smiles and pushes the bag toward her. "Let's take it inside, and then you can do the honors," Resha says getting up and heading toward their shelter.

After the two women enter the building harboring their camp, they head for their bedrolls to sit down. One of their early morning visitors is now perched on the edge of its home, singing. Thinking to herself, Swallow notes that she's grateful for its sweet melody. "Would you like to eat first?" she asks, leaning back against her pack.

"Maybe we should open the bag up before that," Resha says.

"Okay." Swallow quickly grabs the bag, unties the drawstring and then, without looking inside, dumps its contents onto the floor. This way, both she and Resha can share in the surprise together. On the ground is a medium-sized pile of strange objects. Buried in a heap among these objects are about a dozen sealed foil packages. Resha shrugs, raising her left eyebrow.

"Not quite what you expected, huh?" Swallow says.

"No, it's not, although the foil packages look promising." While separating out the foil-wrapped packages from the rest, Resha counts eleven in all. She randomly grabs one and puts it to her nose, sniffing it. Surprisingly, the packaging has remained intact all these years, so she's unable to detect any odor. *Good thing. If they'd gone bad, it would have smelled terrible.* After Resha breaks the seal on the first package, a new, enchanting aroma quickly overcomes their noses and makes the two women's mouths water.

Immediately, Swallow asks, "What's that?"

"I'm not quite sure," Resha says as she speedily finishes unwrapping the package. She then places the package on the floor between her and Swallow with a couple of its contents sitting on top. "It looks like candied nuts of some sort, and please don't ask what candied nuts are. I'll explain later if you really need to know. For now, just try one." After putting a morsel in her mouth, Resha picks up another piece, lifts it in the direction of Swallow's mouth, and tells Swallow to open up. Obediently, Swallow opens her mouth, and Resha eagerly pops a nut inside.

"Oh, these are good," Swallow says, chewing and reaching for another.

"Well, it looks like at least we won't be starving on the way home," Resha says, taking a few more nuts for herself and offering some to Swallow. Soon she begins opening up the other ten packages. Each is filled with a different type of treat. After sorting the packages by contents, Resha explains to Swallow, "These three are candy, and these four are filled with dried fruit. The remaining four contain dried meat of some sort. The meat and fruit look real. I mean, they don't look like they've been synthesized," Resha says.

Hungry, they both sample a couple of small pieces from each of the open packages. The last two bits Swallow picks up are the meat. She takes one piece and scrutinizing it to examine it more closely. It appears similar to the synthetic meat she's used to, only richer and more textured. "So you think this is real, huh? It does look somewhat different from what we're used to."

"Taste it, and tell me what you think." Resha closes all the packages putting them away in Swallow's food net with their other rations to save for later. Then she removes a leftover apancake and offers half to Swallow. "Would you like some?"

Shaking her head no, Swallow places the piece of meat in her mouth and closes her eyes. Beginning to chew, she immediately realizes she's never tasted anything quite like this before. At first, the texture is a bit unpleasant, too tough for her liking, but the flavor more than makes up for that. Chewing it slowly, she eventually appreciates the consistency and she's ultimately thankful for it. *It just makes it last a little longer.* Upon finishing the second piece, she says, "This is wonderful, but I think you're spoiling me." Grinning, she teases, "I don't know if I'll be able to go back to our other food after this. It's so good."

"Well, what we have here isn't going to last forever, so you'll eventually have to. Sooner rather than later, I'm afraid," Resha says, smiling. "I'm glad you like it."

Having finished their meal, the two women turn their attention to the heap of remaining odd objects in front of them. After removing the food packages the size of pile has been cut in half. Nothing looks familiar to the two women but three similar-looking shiny metal cylinders are the first thing to catch their eye. Pulling one of the cylinders from the pile, Swallow says. "What do you suppose this is?" As she hands the object to Resha she puts its two comrades off to her side for safekeeping.

Resha takes it, exploring it as if she is blind, and eventually says, "I'm not sure, but there's a button on the side." After pressing it, a beam of light is shinning out of one end. "I remember hearing about something like this in my youth. I think they're called flashlights. Although I had never seen one, some of these were still around and were collector's items when I was a child. They were very rare. I can't believe it still works." Just as the words leave Resha's mouth, the light dims, sputters, and goes out.

"Just our luck. We could have used that to explore the chambers below," Swallow says. "Can you get it to work again?"

"I don't know; it just went out." Perturbed, Resha presses the button on the side in and out a few times, but nothing happens. "Well, there are two others here, so don't panic yet." As Resha picks up the second flashlight she says. "In fact, this one's a bit different, and if I'm right, it might be rechargeable. See here I think that's a solar charger on the side. We might be able to recharge it, that's if the batteries are still good.

Swallow looks at Resha shaking her head totally baffled by Resha's last comment.

Although I don't know if it will be able to be recharged since the suns' light spectrum have changed and I don't know if solar charging, with our new suns will even work." Opening the top, she sees that it has never been used, as the paper breaking the contact to the batteries has not been removed. She pulls the paper to free the contact and takes the flashlight to the window sill, laying it in the suns. "It will need to be recharged, but if it charges and the batteries hold, this may be our answer."

Swallow doesn't even know where to begin asking Resha to explain what she just said so she's silent. After a few moments pause she finally gets up and says. "Maybe we should leave this all for later and use the daylight while we still have it to go check out the closet in the other building that I found earlier," Swallow suggests.

"Actually, that sounds like a great idea," Resha says, putting down the flashlight and getting to her feet. Offering a hand to Swallow she pulls her up, and the two women leave the building, heading down the block toward the structure where Swallow discovered the closet earlier.

"The suns' light is waning, but it might still be good enough to get a decent look inside," Swallow says, entering the building.

They head directly toward the far wall opening the closet door. Two big packs hang just inside the door, one on each side across from each other. They are fully loaded and larger than any packs Resha and Swallow have ever seen before.

"You didn't mention these earlier," Resha says, pulling them down off the wall. "These may really be useful." One by one she takes them both down and places them against the wall by the building's exit. "We'll pick these up on our way out. We can explore what's inside later," she says while walking back toward Swallow and the closet.

Meanwhile, Swallow's rummaging through the odds and ends in the closet. Most of the remaining objects are unfamiliar to her and she doesn't have a clue what they might be used for.

Resha walks up behind her and peeks around Swallow into the closet to see what's left. About half a dozen different brooms and some tools are visible in one corner. "In the future those may be useful. We'll have to remember them for later. With all these things we're finding, I already know that we'll be making another trip back here to the city." Looking around again she notes a dustpan hanging on the back wall. Resha thinks that the things in the closet don't seem particularly useful for their task ahead. "Let's leave these other things here for now. We can always come back for them if we need them." Resha then spots a shelf above their heads, and points to it saying. "Did you check up there yet?"

Shaking her head, Swallow offers Resha a boost up to take a look.

"There's another small bag up here. Can you boost me up a little higher?" Resha says. She snatches the bag, flings it over her shoulder onto the ground. Then grabbing the shelf with both hands, lowers herself down. "It feels almost empty, though."

"Maybe the bag may come in handy," Swallow responds, picking it up, as she and Resha walk toward the door.

On their way out of the building, each woman picks up one of the larger packs and puts it on their back. Then they proceed down the street to their shelter for the night. Entering, the building that harbors their camp they place their new packs against the wall nearest their bedrolls, before sitting down. Remembering the treat they had earlier, Swallow feels her mouth begin to water, so she grabs the net with their food and opens it. "Are you ready for dinner?"

Distracted, Resha's looking toward the front window, where their world's first sun is now setting. Peering through this window, she sees that a solitary sun is now poised on a piece of pointed broken glass located at the bottom of the window frame. Silently, Resha grabs Swallow's arm pointing towards the window. With the two women looking on, for a second, it seems as if the sun is being stabbed by a knife of glass, and then the illusion is broken as the sun slowly moves toward the bottom windowsill in its unyielding descent toward the horizon.

"How beautiful," Swallow says. "I never noticed such things before I met you."

"Yes, it is, isn't it? Then the meaning of Swallow's earlier words finally dawn on Resha. What do you mean? Am I hungry? We just ate an hour ago, so no, I'm not really that hungry, but you can eat something if you like," Resha answers.

Grabbing two pieces of real meat and putting the food pack aside, Swallow says, "On second thought, I'm not really that hungry either. This will do just fine."

Resha laughs, raising an eyebrow, as Swallow hands one of the pieces to her and places the other in her own mouth.

"Maybe while we still have light, we should see what's in the two new packs we brought back," Swallow says, getting up and dragging them back to where Resha's sitting. She plops down next to her.

"I'm tired. Can you wait till morning for us to check these out?" Resha says, yawning.

'Sometimes life provides just what we need just when we need it the most.'

29

EXPLORING THEIR NEW PACKS

At first light, the women wake, prepare a small meal, and eat. After finishing, they turn their attention to the unopened packs they had discovered yesterday, which are now lying by their sides.

Resha unlaces the top of hers opening it. Even at first glance, she knows there're things in this pack she has never seen before. She almost can't believe the first thing that catches her eye. Right on top are several identical blue boxes with red-and-white design covering them about the size of her hand. She pulls out a single box, not fully believing what she's found.

"These can't possibly still be good," she mutters to herself, and in response to her statement, a little voice in her head says. *That's what you said about the flashlights too.*

As Resha takes out one box to show Swallow what she's found, Swallow looks up from her pack, and asks, "What have you got there? There are about a dozen of those boxes in my pack also," Swallow says. Most of the objects in her pack are intriguing to her, but they don't look all that useful.

"You won't believe this," Resha says, sliding the box open. She takes out a thin stick about the length of her littlest finger and holds it up, scrutinizing it closer. The stick has a little blue-and-white tip at one end. "Watch this." Resha says rubbing it along one side of the box, as it makes a snapping sound, but nothing else remarkable happens.

"What am I supposed to watch?" Swallow asks.

"Wait. Hold on a second. Let me try again." Resha once more rubs the stick along the side of the box. Suddenly, a light bursts from its tip. Swallow, fascinated, immediately reaches for it, but Resha quickly pulls it away, and the flame dies. "Careful. You'll burn yourself."

"What's that?" Swallow asks.

"Something I thought I'd never see again. It's called a match. They were so cheap that they were still being made right up until the disaster happened," Resha responds.

"Good thing you knew what they're for. I would've thought them worthless."

"These may just be the solution we've been looking for." Rummaging deeper through her pack, Resha removes all the matchboxes and stacks them beside her. Swallow then hands Resha the ones from her pack to add to her collection. When they're finished, almost two dozen boxes are sitting by Resha's side. "These packs look like they might've been survival packs. They became popular when everything started to crash. Most commoners couldn't afford them but they were for sale or trade everywhere back then."

With renewed interest, Swallow reaches into her pack and pulls out a box standing on its end along one side of the pack. It's about the length of one and a half of her feet. She places it on the ground ripping off the tape sealing it. "What are these?" she asks, lifting one from the box. She hands Resha a thin, tubular white object that tapers at the top and has a string sticking out.

"I think you've just found the other half of the solution to our problem," Resha says. She lights a match and holds it to the tip of the string on one of the newfound objects. As the flame steadies on top, she holds it up for Swallows inspection. "Well…what do you think?"

"I like the flashlights better, but these might be more dependable."

> 'One single light in the dark can, if used
> correctly, illuminate the whole world'

30

TRESPASSING INTO THE UNDERWORLD

Resha, staring down into the black hole, holds a flashlight in one hand, and as a backup, she has a candle and a box of matches securely tucked in her shirt's front pocket. She mounts the ladder and heads downward, periodically stopping to turn on the flashlight to check her surroundings. About thirty feet down, she pauses and shines the light into the darkness encircling her. Up until this point, she has seen no sign of a light switch or a button of any sort. Directing the beam downward into the blackness, she catches a glint of light reflecting off something below.

"It looks like the floor is about another fifty feet down!" she yells up to Swallow. "You can start down now if you like."

"I think I'll wait for you to get to the bottom first, just in case!" Swallow yells down in response.

Heading down once more, Resha continues to pause about every twenty feet along the way to look for the elusive switch that might turn on the light. About ten feet above the floor, she stops one last time to look around. While pointing the flashlight beam downward, she sees, captured in its light, something that looks promising. It's located about four feet above floor level and to the right of the ladder just a bit. After switching off the flashlight to preserve the batteries, she continues down once again. As she reaches the bottom step just above the floor, a question from above shatters the eerie silence around Resha.

"Are you almost to the bottom?"

The disembodied voice from above catches Resha off guard, and she nearly loses her balance as pieces of Swallow's words bounce off the walls and echo around in the darkness surrounding her.

"I have one step to go, Swallow, and I think I may have found a switch. Wait a bit, and I'll see if it works!" Resha yells upward. Relief flows through her as she places her first foot on the concrete floor. She can feel Swallow's concern and anticipation tumbling through the darkness and colliding into her. "Just a sec."

The switch is similar to the one she found in her village's bunker. *Let's hope this works. It'll take us ages to explore this place if it doesn't.* She presses it, and a solitary light located on a wall in the far left corner of the room winks and then steadies, barely illuminating the darkness with its dim glow.

Swallow seeing the light from above, mounts the ladder. Peering down below into the hole, she can barely distinguish Resha with her hand on the wall, looking off to the right. As Swallow takes her first step downward, she feels a sense of relief in knowing that Resha is safely on the floor.

Resha looks around, surveying the room. It's more like a wide hallway than an actual room, and to her far right stands a closed door. The door looks formidable, but it's held shut only by a simple slip latch, and from what she can make out, it doesn't appear to be locked. Wondering about Swallow's progress, Resha directs the flashlight beam upward and discovers that Swallow's about a third of the way down the ladder already. "You're making good progress."

"I'll be down there in no time. It's much easier with that light on."

Resha walks towards to the closed door to the right, scrutinizing the room on the way. There's nothing remarkable about the room or the door except that it's here in the first place. *It feels like a concrete vault of some sort.* After reaching the door she starts to examine its latch, and she can see that as she suspected, it's not locked. *I was right. It doesn't have a lock.* Confirming her suspicions that this must be one of the underground vaults of the elite, she wonders. *They must've figured the hatch and their android guards stationed above would be enough to stop anyone who discovered their hideout.*

As she flips the latch open and pulls the door toward her, its old, neglected hinges moan an easily audible protest that echoes in the darkness. *This hasn't been used for a very long time.* Resha then turns, almost bumping into Swallow, who is coming up behind her. "Welcome. You made it."

A broad smile crosses Swallow's face as she places her hand on Resha's shoulder. She shrugs, implying that the trip down was easy. Now standing by Resha's side in front of the door, Swallow grabs its handle swinging the door completely open.

As Resha reaches into the dark room, she searches for a switch to the left of the entrance. After feeling around for a few moments, her fingers encounter a button similar to the one that turned on the lights in the front vault. Then turning to Swallow, she says, "Keep your fingers crossed."

Swallow, having no idea what Resha means, merely shrugs her shoulders in response. *I hate to say it but I think I'm getting use to being clueless.*

When Resha presses the button a row of lights running the length of the ceiling, dance to life. The two women stand in the doorway, purveying their newfound territory. It's an immense, narrow, empty concrete hallway with a set of stainless-steel double doors at the far end. Off to the left of this pair of doors is another single door with a padlock on it.

Looking at Resha, Swallow raises an eyebrow, and in seconds, she's disappeared back in the direction they just came.

Standing in the doorway, as if waiting for permission to enter this newfound room, Resha laughs at herself and shakes her head. She then enters, thinking. *Not this again.* Immediately, she heads toward the double doors to inspect them. About halfway to her target, she stops, driven by some unknown force to look upward. The lonesome dark lens of a small camera returns her gaze. It's located directly above her head, about nineteen feet above the floor, a foot below the ceiling.

Returning about five minutes later, Swallow enters the room to find Resha kneeling on the floor in front of the two gleaming, massive doors. "Do you really think praying to them is going to work?" Swallow asks jokingly while walking up behind Resha.

Without turning, Resha laughs, saying, "I'm not praying but at this point I'm willing to try anything." In the silence following this exchange, a previously elusive idea clears in her mind. *It's funny that the concept of prayer was never forgotten during these past two centuries. I would've thought that with everything else we lost, faith and hope would have also died with the disaster or in time's passing afterwards.*

"Find anything?" Swallow asks.

Resha shakes her head, concentrating on running her hands along the floor at the bottom of the doors, feeling for a trigger.

"Do you think it's another elevator?"

Turning in response to Swallow's last question, Resha looks directly into her eyes, and once again, the beguiling aqua-blue of Swallow's eyes makes her momentarily lose her breath. Mesmerized, and unable to speak for a few seconds, she raises her eyebrows and shrugs before she answers. "I sure hope not but I'm not certain. They sure look like the other one." She notices the pry bar in Swallow's left hand. "So you went back up to get that. I was wondering where you'd gone."

"Figured it might come in handy," Swallow responds, pointing the bar off to the side toward the padlocked door.

Not finding an immediate way to trigger the double doors to open, Resha gets up off her knees, dusts herself off, and follows Swallow in the direction of the other door. Swallow has the lock sprung in no time, and after sliding the dead bolt back, she begins opening the door. There is a growling sound as the door's hinges scream in protest, at first refusing to fully give way. Resha steps in behind Swallow to lend a hand. A few minutes later, with both women tugging on the door, the hinges finally relent with one last rusty snarl.

Swallow, leaning on the pry bar, reaches in to the side of the door, checking for a switch. She finds one and flips it, and the lights flicker on. What lies in front of them surprises both women. The light rains down upon a descending staircase.

Swallow and Resha move to the railing and look over. Four flights slither down below. They can easily see a door exiting off each of the landings.

Resha looks at Swallow and shrugs. "Should we go down?"

Nodding, Swallow leads the way. A few minutes later, standing in front of the door on the bottom landing, the two women look at each other, nodding their consent to forgive their coming trespasses. Swallow immediately starts working on that door's lock. This one is a bit trickier, but after five or so minutes, it finally gives way. After placing her gigantic lock pick against the wall next to the entrance, she grabs the door handle pushing the door open. These particular hinges must have been kept well oiled, for they offer little resistance as the door smoothly and silently glides inward. Pausing at the entrance, the lights in this new room come on automatically.

Entering they're engulfed by how enormous this room is. It looks like a warehouse, with various types of furniture and other items packed into every square foot. It's so vast and methodically packed that exploring it carefully would take several days. A canvas like protective cloth covers many of the items. Leading away from the entrance is a singular wide path that meanders into the center of the room. Off this path, narrow trails snake throughout islands of lost and forgotten objects organized and piled together as if seeking each other's refuge and comfort to ward off fear and loneliness.

"We're going to need much more time than we have this trip to go through the stuff in here." Resha shakes her head, looking at Swallow. "I wonder what's behind the doors off the other landings." Leaving the room Resha heads up the three flights of stairs to the top landing, one floor below where first entered.

As Swallow exits, she closes the door to the lowest room and grabs her pry bar. In no time, she is on Resha's heels.

When she reaches the first-floor landing, the two women discover a lockless door, so Swallow again lays her bar against the wall, as Resha's sliding the door inward. They stare into unrelenting darkness, and since after a few seconds nothing happens, Resha reaches inside, trying to locate a switch. She accidentally presses it, and a few faint lights dangling from the high ceiling above sputter to life. A dimly lit shoddy reproduction of the room they just left stares back at them from the other side of the doorway.

"There's not even enough light to see what's in here," Swallow says.

Not bothering to enter and puzzled by what they've discovered so far, Resha shuts off the light, closes the door, and immediately heads down to the second-floor landing.

Swallow once again is right behind her.

The next door appears to be identical to the one above and also opens into darkness. After turning on the lights in this room, they can see it's almost an exact copy of the one they just left. They leave not even bothering to shut this door, and at once head down the stairs to the third-floor landing. Arriving there, they find themselves standing in front of a replica of the door above, except this one has a lock.

Without delay, Swallow, using her handy pry bar, springs the lock, and in seconds, she has the door open. A solitary light comes on, revealing another locked door about five feet in front of the two women. Baffled, Swallow shakes her head, turning around to face Resha.

Shrugging at Swallow, Resha remains silent, not knowing how else to respond.

A few minutes later, Swallow has broken the lock on the interior door, and they enter a hallway lit by a lone dim bulb. Yet another door looms about thirty feet ahead. As the two women walk toward this door, they can see that in place of a padlock, there is a keyhole.

The minutes tick by as the two women stand silently before the door, seemingly worshipping the impenetrable locked entryway, wondering what they should do next.

In frustration, Swallow begins hitting the door with the bar in her hands. She stops when she realizes her efforts are only damaging her own hands.

Resha and Swallow, frustrated by the formidable door blocking their progress, stand in the sparsely lit one-and-a-half-meter-wide hallway, quietly staring at it. The room is bound on all four sides by concrete. Suddenly, a scene Resha read in a mystery book, months earlier sweeps into her head and she looks around the room for anything that might conceal a key.

There's nothing here but four concrete walls and this locked door. Again turning away from her foe, Resha retraces her steps back the way she and Swallow entered, scrutinizing every inch of space. *There's no place to hide a key in here.* Pausing briefly before leaving this hallway, Resha looks back over her shoulder at the two women's latest nemesis. *It looks very much like the other doors we've opened today, except for the keyhole.*

In one last effort before leaving the thirty-foot hallway, Resha pivots back toward Swallow, who is still standing in front of the keyless, locked door. She peers back at the difficult door, looking everywhere for a hidden key. Suddenly she realizes that if sheer will could open it, the door would swing agape on its hinges just from Swallow's intentions. Re-examining the walls of the long hallway, she knows there's no place to hide a key, so she turns and directs her attention to the entryway back into the shorter first hallway.

Leaving the thirty foot hallway, she walks back into the smaller preceding hall, Then Resha turns to look back at their foe. Comparing the two doors, she searches for any slight difference between the doorway now directly in front of her and the one in the distance with the locked door blocking their progress. She's looking for any place that might conceal a key. Realizing that there's something imperceptibly different about the entrance now directly in front of her, she closes her eyes and reaches out with her mind, trying to recall the other doors they've come through this day.

As she clearly recalls each doorway, she compares it to this entry. A subtle but distinct difference pops into the silky darkness of her mind. Its then that she realizes that this door has an outer frame around it, which the others didn't.

Standing on her tiptoes, she reaches up placing her fingers on top of the doorframe. Trying to hold on for support, she gingerly moves her fingertips along the top of the outer frame. About a third of the way, her fingers brush something off and it falls to the floor with a clanking sound which in the silence, assault both women's ears. As the object bounces off the concrete floor, through the open doorway, and into a dark corner of the thirty-foot-long hallway Resha swiftly follows.

Swallow, moving towards the sound walks to Resha, and says. "What have you got there?"

Resha's shines her flashlight into the corner, and a key is winking back at her. "I think I've found it." Resha says, picking up the key.

> *'Seemingly fruitful trespasses into the netherworld have only so far led us on a merry chase to more mysteries.'*

31

Discovering a Key to the Past

Standing in front of the locked door, Resha slips the key in place and tries turning it, but the key is frozen in the lock and won't budge. She pulls it out again, not wanting to force it, for fear that it will break off in the lock, and then all will be lost.

"Do you want me to try?" Swallow asks from behind her.

"No. If we force it, we may snap the key. Then we'll never get in." Resha removes the key from the lock, and turns it over and over in her hand, trying to discern some type of subtle problem with it. *It might not be the right key, although it goes into the lock easily enough.* "Maybe over all these years, it's lost its electronic release? If it ever had one. I just can't believe that they would be so cruel or foolish to plant a fake key."

Swallow is silent, not knowing what to say.

Pulling the key through her thumb and forefinger, Resha closes her eyes, attempting to feel for any flaws. Then she vigorously rubs each side of the key against her shirt.

Time fades into the past as an image of her father standing before the door of her childhood home and doing this exact same thing pops into her head. *So that's where I got it from.* Smiling as a flood of fond memories momentarily block out the horror of the last one hundred fifty years, and Resha's a kid again, smiling up at her dad, hearing him say, "Sometimes even things just need a little extra help."

Rubbing her right hand down her face to transports herself back to the present she opens her eyes, to the key resting in the palm of her left hand and watches as it slowly drifts into focus.

"Let's try this once more," Resha says, inserting the key into the lock. She mimics the memory of her father's actions, as she taps the key once to make sure it is in place. Turning to glance at Swallow, Resha says, "Just for luck." She then focuses her attention back on the key as she slowly tries to turn it, while feeling for any sign of release in the lock. As the key twists, the dead bolt struggles to let go and finally gives way.

After Resha pushes the door open, the lights come on, and for a second, she's a child again, standing at the entrance to her family's home. However, unlike the entrance to her old home, this present door leads into a passageway full of books. With one foot in the past, she pauses as the room's odd arrangement, momentarily confuses her. Then the old illusion in her head slowly begins to meld into the present, as she now find herself peering into a room beyond this book filled entrance way. The far room is a large, luxurious living space with several doors leaving it, very unlike her childhood home.

The instant after she sees this new space, the pieces of her former childhood home fade as the image in her mind is replaced by this new living room. The fixtures in front of her are impeccably arranged to give it a welcoming, warm, and cozy feeling, despite its large size and the apparent luxuriousness of its trappings. The first thing that catches her eye is a cream-colored baby grand piano in its far corner.

"Wow!" Swallow says. "I've never seen anything like this before." Brushing past Resha, she stops in the hallway and places her hand on the bookshelf to her right. Running one finger along each of the books, as she slowly passes by them. Swallow stops about halfway through the room upon seeing a book that has a familiar image on its binding. Pulling the book from the shelf she turns, showing Resha her discovery. "Here's a picture that looks very much like our little visitors." After flipping through several pages, she hands the book to Resha, saying, "There are many different types, and they're called birds."

Inspecting the first few pages slowly, Resha gazes at a few pictures in the book. "Wow, look at the colors. I faintly remember my mother and father talking about birds, but I never saw one, so I didn't know what they looked like. My parents had said that because they were indicator animals, they were one of the first groups of the natural world to completely die out. Their class and something called amphibians, which I've also never seen, died out very early on. Apparently, those two groups were much more sensitive and couldn't adjust to the increasing toxic wastes the humans were producing."

Flipping through another few pages, Resha stops on a picture similar to the birds above their bedrolls. "Look. This one looks almost exactly like our birds." Running her hand across the page as if to pet the picture, Resha says, "I wonder what they feel like." She silently thinks to herself, *How did they survive and where did they come from?*

Meanwhile, Swallow, entering the living room, is drawn to touch all the things she passes by. Running her hands along each item in the room, she glides through and lets her fingertips drink in the different textures, stopping to fondle each thing she passes. In all her life, she has never felt such a variety of sensations. One after another, these feelings engulf her senses, making her slightly dizzy, and almost giddy.

Having finished with looking at the book for the time being, Resha lays it back on the shelf, making a mental note to pick it up on their way out. *I want to take this back with us.* Pausing at the entrance to the living room, she closes her eyes to take in the feel of this place before entering.

The room smells like my grandma shortly before she died. I was only about three, but I remember sitting on her bed next to her and holding her motionless hand. It smells like a combination of bread dough, baby powder, and dust in here.

p.roscoe

Recalling her grandmother, she again mentally drifts into her past. This time, she's in a scene with her mother telling her to be careful with her grandmother, because by that time, she was very frail.

> _Now looking at her grandma through her childhood eyes, even at such a tender age, she knows her grandma is already gone. However, her mother doesn't seem to want to face this fact, quite yet._ Then a crystal-clear image of the past solidifies in her mind. _Turning toward her mom, she briefly thinks of telling her about her grandma being already gone. Looking closely, she can see tears forming in her mother's eyes and recognizes that it's already too late. On some level, her mother knows; she just doesn't want to accept it yet._

Still with eyes half closed, Resha flashes forward a few years, realizing this room also feels like the old cathedral she and her mother visited when she was five. Every week for almost two years, they went there to light candles in memory of her grandma after she had passed. Although her mother wasn't religious during her life, she sensed something dreadful coming a year and a half before the disaster, so shortly after the death of her mother, she began frequenting that place for comfort—and maybe forgiveness.

Now at 168 years old, Resha remembers only two things clearly from their visits to that place: the silence and the smell of burning candles.

> _The idea of making any noise in this cathedral feels like a grave sin, as the stillness here seems to engulf and suppress all anticipation of sound and emotion._

Opening her eyes to the present, Resha finds herself in the living room. Here she finds Swallow drifting through the furniture, and like an infant ghost who has recently lost its body, she's become engulfed in the surrounding sensations. *We are both so out of place in here,* Resha thinks, heading in Swallow's direction. As Resha passes a red velvet couch, she pauses, attempting to get Swallow's attention by waving. When she fails with this silent effort, a sound inadvertently escapes her throat. "Swallow?" It's barely audible, but the room is so silent that it feels as if thunder has exploded next to her.

Jumping, Swallow turns with a jolt. "Sorry. You scared me. This place is so quiet. It feels like what I imagine death to be."

"No worries," Resha says, approaching Swallow. "It is deadly quiet in here." Pointing to one of the four closed doors in the room, Resha says, "Maybe we should see what's behind the other doors here before we get too caught up in our explorations of the furnishings we've seen so far."

Nodding, Swallow randomly picks the nearest door, heads toward it, and opens it.

Resha, standing behind Swallow, can see that the door leads into a bathroom. She hasn't seen one of these since her family's exodus from the city as a little girl. With her curiosity getting the best of her, she brushes past Swallow and enters. Pausing in front of the sink, she turns on the faucet. To her surprise, water flows from the tap, so she quickly shuts it off again. Swallow who's still standing in the doorway behind her, asks, "What was that?"

"It's water, and it looks like the plumbing still works." Looking down at the faucet, Resha runs her hand along its brushed-silver finish. "These fixtures look almost brand new."

Swallow's flabbergasted. "Water? Down here?"

Turning to face her friend, Resha says, "The storage tanks must be located somewhere on one of the levels above and must still have water in them. It flows by gravity down to here."

"Like the water I gather from the crystals, right?" Swallow's still standing outside the entrance to the bathroom, as if afraid to intrude.

"Very similar," Resha says, nodding.

"What's that over there?" Swallow asks, pointing to a funny-looking thing resting in the back corner of the bathroom. It appears to be an odd-looking chair.

Resha's smile broadens almost to the point of laughter. "It's called a toilet. It's where a person goes to the bathroom."

"Oh, so that's where that term came from. I always wondered why we said we had to 'go to the bathroom,'" Swallow says, shaking her head. "So this is a bathroom."

Resha nods, stifling a laugh as she heads back into the main room, closing the door behind her. *I'll save the explanation of the treat of taking a shower till we've finished exploring.* "Let's check another door. Okay?"

Resha follows Swallow as she takes the path to her right, passing by the baby grand piano. As Resha goes by it, she stops to toy with the keyboard, playing a few notes.

"What was that?" Swallow spins around looking at Resha standing over the keyboard.

"Is that all you know how to say?" Resha asks, amused at Swallow's innocence.

Shaking her head, Swallow snaps back. "Don't make fun of me. I haven't ever seen most of the things we've encountered since we got here. I think I've been pretty good about not asking too many questions."

Resha, trying not to laugh, shakes her head instead. "Yes, you have. You've been very good. It's called a piano, and it's a musical instrument. I think we've talked about these before, haven't we?"

"Yes, you told me they were used like the drum we recently made, but this doesn't look like a drum. It looks more like a fancy piece of furniture," Swallow says, pressing down one of the keys.

"I have a book I can lend you when we get home. It shows many of the old types of instruments. I think it'll help." Moving past Swallow, Resha then heads off in the direction of the nearest set of doors.

'As old things are brought back to life,
a new, amazing world opens up.'

32

OUR HISTORY

Stopping in front of a pair of brown metal doors reinforced with heavy metal strapping, Resha turns to Swallow and says. "These two look sort of interesting. They're not like any we've seen before," Resha says, stepping aside. "Would you care to do the honors?"

As Resha steps back, Swallow moves forward grabbing the lever handle. Not sure how to open the doors but determined to hide this fact from Resha, she accidentally pushes the handle downward, and both doors start to open. Automatically, the lights come on inside. At first glance, Swallow can see this room is going to be mostly Resha's territory, so she moves aside, letting Resha lead the way. Resha hesitates as she peers into a small room about ten gliers (meters) square. It is mostly empty, but she recognizes its arrangement from a childhood memory.

Entering, Resha says, "Wow, I think we've hit the jackpot here. These things can't possibly still be working." She gazes around, not believing her own eyes. A bunch of foreign-looking high-tech objects fill the room. "This looks like a computerized control room of some sort." *Over there could be a media center with touch-screen controls.*

She walks over to the only piece of recognizable furniture in the room and stops at a single white table and chair, where a series of five crystal balls sit perched on small silver stands. "These must be the master controls, although I've never seen anything quite like this setup before." Resha pauses, looking for a switch to turn on the system. Laughingly she pulls out the chair, steps up to the table, and says, "I don't even know where to start or how to turn it on."

Coming up behind Resha, Swallow says, "Can I help?"

"I don't know. Can you? Have you ever seen anything like this before?"

Swallow looks down at Resha and then the table. Mystified, she stands there dumbfounded, shaking her head.

"Then I think I'm on my own," Resha says, sitting down and placing her hand on the table in front of the crystals.

"What do these do?" Swallow asks removing the smallest of the crystal balls from the pedestal it's sitting on.

Resha shrugs. "I have no idea. I don't think they're just decorations, but who knows? Since they're displayed so prominently, they must be important. I can't even find a switch to turn this thing on."

Swallow turns the small crystal ball over and over in her hands, hoping to discover some hidden switch. "I didn't find anything here," she says, replacing it on its stand. Still toying with it, she absentmindedly turns it a quarter turn to the right. The crystal emits a strange, dim greenish flash and then quiets again. Swallow looking at Resha, shrugs as she reaches over and similarly rotates each of the four remaining crystals in order of size. They each flash a different color, but after their flashes dim, nothing else happens.

Looking at Resha, Swallow shakes her head and says, "This reminds me of the elevator." Next, she places her hand on top of the largest crystal and tries turning it again, but nothing happens, so she turns it back to its original position removing her hand. Swallow again looks to Resha for guidance, but Resha only tilts her head to the side, shrugs her shoulders and raises her eyebrows.

"Well, I don't know what to do next," Swallow says after a few minutes have passed. "They sure liked to make it a challenge to figure out how things work, don't they?"

After a minute or so, by chance and intuition, Resha passes her hand repeatedly a hair's breadth above the top of the largest ball. After the third pass, all five of the crystals start to emit a soft yellowish glow. "Well, that's something," Resha says, turning to Swallow. "What next?"

Swallow shrugs. "Let's try this." Swallow copies Resha's movement with the other four crystal balls, and the glow in each crystal changes to the color of the flash it emitted earlier.

"Now we're getting somewhere," Resha says.

Swallow looks at Resha and laughs. "Yeah, but where? I'm still lost. How about you? All we've done so far is make five crystal balls each glow a different color."

Both women start laughing hysterically. Resha's laughing so hard that she almost falls off her chair. "I guess you're right. After all the time we've spent, this really isn't much of an accomplishment, is it?"

With tears streaming down her face, Swallow shakes her head. "No, I think anyone with any sense probably would have given up by now."

Resha, stifling a laugh, looks up at Swallow. "Not Krey?"

As both women start laughing uncontrollably once more, Swallow puts her hands on Resha's shoulders and then sighs. "No, I suspect you're right. He would be here pushing you to go faster or, worse yet, pushing you out of the seat and taking over himself."

Suddenly, all five crystals start to glow brighter, and a low-pitched humming noise is audible in the background.

Unbeknownst to the two women, a virtual control panel appears, floating in the air behind them in the far right corner of the small room. After a few moments of staring at the five balls and seeing nothing else happen, Resha turns toward Swallow. "Now, what do you suppose that's all about?" Then, spotting the control panel behind Swallow, she says, "Wait—what's that?"

Swallow turns to see a few colored objects floating in midair behind her. "You're asking me?"

"No," Resha says, laughing. "I really don't expect you to know." She gets up, takes Swallow's hand, and leads her toward the lights. Stopping directly in front of the panel, Resha says, "This looks like a virtual control panel for some type of video game." Silently studying the formation for a few minuets before she speaks. "When I was a child, I once went with my father to visit a wealthy client. His two children were playing video games in the next room, so my father's client took me to join them in hopes that his meeting with my father would not be disturbed. I learned a lot in those few hours of playing," Resha says, turning to face Swallow. "I might be able to operate this."

Swallow smiles, wrapped up in Resha's excitement. "Okay, show me."

Resha places her hands on the two glowing objects located in each lower corner of the screen. To Swallow, the two objects look like a red cogwheel in the right corner and a simple blue button in the left. After pressing the button, Resha looks around. All four walls of the room are now starting to glow, and six more objects that make no sense to Swallow, appear on the screen.

Directing her attention back to the screen, Resha tries to understand the function of the new objects as she takes the cog in hand and turns it fully to the right. A list of about twenty items appears in yellow, covering the right side of the screen in front of her. Turning to look at Swallow, Resha says, "Well, what do you make of that?"

"I don't know. I'm still lost." Reading the list, Swallow scratches her head in confusion. She has never heard of most of the things on the list, but one stands out to her. The fourth item on the list is the word *video*. Pointing to it, Swallow says, "Let's try this one."

Resha touches it, and the list disappears replaced by another list, this one in green with only eight items. Second on the list is "Our History." Resha turns to look at Swallow once again, and Swallow nods her approval. Touching that item, Resha watches as the four walls of the room dance to life with an assortment of images. Next another list, this one in blue, appears on the main screen. This list is in chronological order, accounting their world's history, starting from the mid-twentieth century and ending after the year 2350. The final item on the list is "The Present."

"Looks like I might not have to do that research after all," Resha says, smiling.

Resha presses "1945–1960," and the images surrounding the women change, placing them in an ancient, unfamiliar world. Looming behind them is the projection of a mushroom cloud, as the two women become encased in their world's multidimensional past.

"Maybe we should start from the beginning," Swallow says, pressing "Introduction."

> *'The meek may inherit the earth but in this case only ...*
> *after the aggressive have nearly destroyed it.'*

Edwards Brothers Malloy
Thorofare, NJ USA
December 14, 2016